Poland Interrupted

A Journey

A Novel

by

Gordon Snider

For Paul & Julie
Best Wishes

MERRIAM PRESS

HOOSICK FALLS, NEW YORK

2019

First published in 2018 by the Merriam Press

Second Edition

Copyright © 2018 by Gordon Snider
Book design by Ray Merriam
Additional material copyright of named contributors.

ISBN 978-0-359-56874-1
Library of Congress Control Number: 2018960040

This work was designed, produced, and published in
the United States of America by the

Merriam Press
489 South Street
Hoosick Falls NY 12090

E-mail: ray@merriam-press.com
Web site: merriam-press.com

The Merriam Press publishes new manuscripts on historical subjects, especially
military history and with an emphasis on World War II, as well as reprinting
previously published works, including reports, documents, manuals, articles and other
materials on historical topics.

Author's Notes

*P*oland Interrupted: A Journey never would have been written if Kit, a friend and reader of my novels, had not brought an old manuscript to me and asked if it was publishable. It had been written years ago by her father, John Truax, based on a series of interviews he had conducted with a man named Kaz Kowinsky. Kaz grew up in Poland and led a rather colorful life.

After reading the first hundred pages of the manuscript, I told Kit that I did not think it was publishable in its current format, but I found the story compelling and read on. I was between projects at the time and not certain if I would even write another novel. But thanks to Kit's query and John's literary efforts, fate intervened. When I finished the manuscript, I told Kit that it had the potential to become a darn good novel, and I would like to write it.

It developed into a most unusual project. John Truax and Kaz Kowinsky passed away many years ago, but I could feel them both looking over my shoulder as I progressed with the novel. I wrote it as fiction, but I was determined to follow John's manuscript as closely as possible, and the result was a collaborative effort between the two of us that echoed through time.

I suspect that the phrase "based on a true story" is a bit abused at times, but in this instance, it is truly the case. Fact and fiction have been woven into story lines so intermingled, there are times I have trouble distinguishing the two myself. The result is a journey filled with hope, disappointment, abandonment, love, determination and heroism.

In the end, Kaz's journey is continually interrupted, just like Poland's.

Part I

Poland Reunited

Chapter 1

KAZ Kowinsky arrived in Poland with his parents in the spring of 1920, less than three months before Russia attacked Warsaw. According to his father, it was a tumultuous time. Poland had not existed for over a hundred years, but it was once more a nation and he wanted to be part of it. "We are Polish, after all," he exclaimed. "Always have been, even without our country." The concept was a bit confusing to an eight year old, and Kaz screwed up his face in consternation at the idea of belonging to something that had not existed. How was that possible, he wondered?

"Our country wasn't just occupied," his father continued with a wave of his spidery hands. "It evaporated ... disappeared ... like a puff of smoke, devoured by the ravenous empires of Austria, Prussia and Russia." He blew a stream of cigarette smoke from his mouth to emphasize his point. "Poland was thrown into the black pit of history, but war has resurrected it."

Kaz knew he was talking about the Great War that had nearly devoured Europe. He was also aware that Poland was currently entangled in a war with Russia, but that didn't seem to diminish his father's enthusiasm. So, they packed trunks with clothes, linen, plates and books, and boarded a train from Czechoslovakia destined for Krakow. Kaz had said goodbye to his friend, who lived down the narrow street from his apartment, and joined his father and mother on what he saw as a great adventure.

It was Kaz's second great adventure. The first had taken place three years earlier when he traveled by train with his mother to visit his father at a military hospital in Debrecen, Hungary, a bewildering city filled with horse-drawn carts, trolleys, bicycles and throngs of people. It was one of his earliest memories of his father, who had disappeared when Kaz was three to fight in the Great War in Europe. Now, he was recovering from his injuries in a poorly lighted building that reeked of antiseptics and festering wounds. They found him, pale and reedy, resting on a cot in a corridor lined with fellow soldiers bound in bandages and casts, and covered by frayed, gray blankets that looked as thin as his father. One leg was hoisted in the air and held suspended by ropes and pulleys. Kaz kissed his unshaven cheek at the request of his mother, all the while wondering how this stranger would change his life.

When his father was able to walk, the family moved to Widchovice, Czechoslovakia, where, despite his heavy limp, he was offered work as a locomotive engineer in a steel mill. On several occasions, Kaz joined his father at the mill, where he experienced the thrill of riding in the giant engine as it hauled forged steel from the factory to nearby rail yards. Kaz studied the levers his father used to shift gears, stop, start and move the train back and forth, until he knew them by heart. It was one of the few times when Kaz felt close to his father, and he vowed one day to take control of the levers himself and to drive one of those wondrous machines.

Kaz found the man who had so unceremoniously entered his life formidable, even though he lacked the size of most of the men Kaz saw on the streets of Widchovice. What his father lacked in height, he overcame in stature. Even with his limp, he walked taller than he stood, and his voice echoed with authority. He was a hard, belligerent man, given to fits of temper. At home, his words commanded attention and were obeyed without question. There were times when he engaged in drinking bouts with his fellow workers. These lasted a day or two, during which time he took out his frustrations by shouting at Kaz and his mother. Kaz didn't understand the reason for his anger, but he knew better than to get in his way. Most evenings, his father sat in his overstuffed chair, smoked an endless chain of cigarettes and read the newspaper from beginning to end, all the while muttering about Europe's economic and political troubles. Kaz understood little of what he said, and if he tried to interrupt, Mother shushed him away. His father never hit Kaz, but there was little joy in their relationship. Other than an occasional hand on his shoulder, there was no physical contact between them. If Kaz tried to hug his father, he sensed a stiffening of muscles and a straightening of spine, and after a few seconds, his arms were gently pushed away. Kaz looked up to the man, but in a somewhat fearful way. To make matters worse, the commanding voice was accompanied by a penetrating gaze that made it difficult for Kaz to face him without looking away.

Father's stern manner was compensated by his mother's warmth. Where he scowled, she smiled. While he sat, she busied herself with the household chores of cooking, cleaning and keeping order in the tiny rooms. Kaz associated her with the odor of baking bread and cheerful words. Her rounded face and plump figure gave her a matronly air that

POLAND INTERRUPTED

Kaz found comforting. Best of all, her hands always found time to caress his cheeks and to tousle his hair.

While his father drove his train back and forth between the steel mill and the rail yards, Kaz toiled at school, a task that required him to sit for endless hours on a hard, wooden seat while he listened to the droning utterances of his teachers. Time crawled; his fingers fidgeted; his mind wandered. The sound of shuffling feet told him many of his classmates felt the same. His only salvation was the brief periods of freedom when everyone fled to the school yard for exercise and games. Kaz had never interacted with so many children, and he soon realized that he lacked the size and physical development of many of the other boys, just like his father. He stood half a head shorter, and his arms were as thin as broom handles. What he lacked in size, he overcame with grit and speed. He never shied away from the rough play of the bigger boys, and he excelled at foot races across the grassy, weed-infested yard. He was always chosen when teams were formed for contests favoring courage and quick feet.

School brought him new friends, but also a mystery that hung like a dark cloud on the horizon. The mystery developed when Kaz's mother took him to register for classes. His mother had his papers in order, but his last name was wrong. He knew how to spell it, Kowinsky, but the form on the clerk's desk read Kowalski. He pointed to the error, but his mother shushed him and pulled his hand away. "It's a bureaucratic mix up," she told him as they left the building. "At home, you are still Kowinsky, but at school you are Kowalski." Her explanation only confused him further, but he sensed it was best not to pursue the matter.

No sooner had Kaz adapted to his new surroundings than his world tipped upside down. Father's leg had not healed as hoped, which made it difficult for him to operate the locomotives at work. Twice, he failed to brake in a timely manner, causing near collisions. The company had no choice but to put him on medical leave without pay. He looked for another job but found none. Meat soon disappeared from the dinner table, and bread was baked every other day. Kaz had always understood that they were not as wealthy as the finely dressed folks he saw on the streets, but he'd never imagined himself to be poor. His small allowance disappeared with the meat, and his clothes had to be mended more frequently, rather than replaced.

It didn't take long for the apartment to fill with talk of Poland. Father limped through the rooms in an agitated state of excitement. A resettlement program was under way in eastern Europe, he explained.

Poles were being encouraged to return to their newly minted homeland. Poland had risen from the ashes of war, and the country needed workers. It had been badly damaged and lay close to economic ruin. Industries had been destroyed; rail tracks lacked integration between the previously partitioned sections controlled by Austria, Germany and Russia; trade was meager; and three fourths of the country consisted of farmland tilled by peasants. Able-bodied families were needed to help raise Poland by its bootstraps. Kaz's father was assured that he would find work there.

It was time to pack their trunks.

A busy web of gleaming rails told Kaz that they were approaching Krakow, and he eagerly pressed his nose to the window as the train slowed to avoid careening into cars on nearby tracks. Rows of tree-lined streets with multiple-storied buildings marked the suburbs of the ancient city. Weathered facings and peeling shutters revealed signs of disrepair, but all were intact, indicating that they had been spared major destruction during the war. Finally, the train creaked its way around a bend and hissed to a stop inside the railway terminal.

Father immediately made his way to the baggage car to reclaim their belongings. The trunks were stacked on the platform, and Kaz was put in charge of guarding them from eager porters' hands while he went in search of a horse and wagon to carry them to the address he had written on a piece of torn paper. He returned shortly with a brawny, older man who sported a mustache that reminded Kaz of an overgrown bush. It took two trips to haul everything to the man's waiting wagon outside the terminal. Mother joined Father and the driver on the wagon's seat, and Kaz clambered aboard the flat bed with the trunks. His heart pumped faster at the sight of the Fifteenth century Gothic churches, office buildings, apartments and synagogues sailing past him as they clattered through the busy streets. The synagogues were new to him. He couldn't remember seeing one before. They were driving along the edge of the Jewish quarter where new visions awaited him in the form of black top-hats on men's heads and beards half-an-arm's length in size.

They turned into a side street off the Miodowa thoroughfare and stopped in front of a time-worn building with a pitted stone facing. The wooden door looked like termites had nibbled at it, and the steps leading to it were chipped to the point of crumbling. Kaz's excitement waned as he looked at the place. The air was warm, and the street had no trees to shade the buildings from the afternoon sun. Two annoying flies buzzed his face. No birds sang. Some older boys shouted as they played stick ball half-a-block away, and a trolley dinged its way around a corner behind him. Otherwise, the place looked deserted and smelled of decay.

Father climbed the steps, opened the door and limped into the building. Mother hesitated, then followed. Kaz sat on one of the trunks in the wagon and waited. He studied the other apartment buildings along the street. They all looked as colorless as the one before him. By the time his parents emerged again, the air had turned uncomfortably hot under the glare of the sun, and Kaz was sweating.

"We're on the top floor," Father announced as if this was a good thing. Kaz knew better. The building was five stories tall, which meant four flights of stairs and rooms that would trap the summer heat. Kaz tried to help his father drag the trunks up the steep stairs, but the wagon driver ended up doing most of the lifting. When the work was done, Father reluctantly pulled a wad of wrinkled Polish zlotys from his pocket and peeled off over half of them for the driver. Kaz sensed that what remained was far less than needed to meet expenses and saw his allowance flying away along with his hopes of eating meat.

"Well, we made it, didn't we? Here we are in Poland!"

Father's encouraging words lifted Kaz's spirits, and he looked to his mother for reassurance. She smiled but said nothing. Kaz inspected the rooms --- two bedrooms, a sitting room and a kitchen with a small eating area attached --- and was pleased to find them larger than the rooms of their previous apartment. Windows facing the street and overlooking a small courtyard in back yielded sufficient light to make the main rooms cheery, but the bedrooms lacked sunlight and were somber.

Everyone was hungry after the long journey, so mother fixed sandwiches with boiled eggs and day-old bread she had brought in her bag. A badly scuffed kettle sat on the cooking stove. Mother found matches in a drawer and soon had water boiling for tea. The familiar bubbling sound gave Kaz comfort. Life was slowly returning to normal.

"I must find the union office," Father announced when they were finished. "I'm told they have job listings and will help me find employment."

"Can I come?" Kaz asked anxiously. He was eager to see more of the city.

"You stay here and help your mother by unpacking your belongings." His father's stern voice told Kaz that he would brook no argument.

After he was gone, Mother ruffled Kaz's hair. "Don't fret," she said softly. "There will be time to look around once you have your things put away." Kaz smiled at the prospect and tore into his trunk of clothes.

After Widchovice, Kaz was no longer intimidated by a large city. He found the bustle in the streets familiar, and the language was no problem. School had been taught in Czech, but his father preferred Polish at home, and there had been a large Polish population where they lived.

He'd gone less than a dozen blocks when he stumbled upon an amazing sight: a vast cemetery shadowed by large tree branches that allowed only streaks of light to touch the endless rows of granite tombs and headstones. Several women wearing head scarves and men in long coats and top hats prayed at grave sites while others wandered along narrow, dusty pathways. Kaz had seen cemeteries before but none like this one. The people were dressed strangely, and there were no crosses.

"What do you think of our cemetery?"

Kaz jumped at the unexpected voice behind him. He turned to find a towering man with a tangled, gray beard staring down at him. He wore the same long coat Kaz had noticed on the other men, but also some sort of cloth underneath with strings tied in topknots dangling down his chest.

"I ... I don't know," he admitted. "It looks spooky."

The man laughed gently. "Your first time in a Jewish cemetery, no doubt."

"It looks old."

"It *is* old. Nearly 400 years. It's one of the greatest Jewish cemeteries in Europe, or the world, for that matter."

"Where are the crosses?"

Another laugh. "In the Catholic cemetery. Here, you will find the Star of David." The man gestured to a headstone near Kaz's feet. "See the six-pointed star? It is called a hexagram." The man enunciated each word as though it were a treasure. "And that is our synagogue, much like your church. There are several here in Krakow and many throughout Poland. Your country has welcomed us, and many Jews have settled here."

Kaz marveled at the words 'your country.' He'd been in Poland less than a day, yet it was already his country. The idea swelled his chest.

"I must go now, but please visit again. You will always be welcome here." The man gave him a broad smile and walked with a rapid gait toward the synagogue.

The next few weeks sparkled with adventures and surprises. Summer was in full bloom, and Kaz was free to explore Krakow at his leisure. No droning teachers stood in his way. Best of all, his father found work as a machinist in a factory that had survived the war unscathed. Meat reappeared on their dinner plates, and Kaz's allowance was restored. He did return to the Jewish cemetery, but he never saw the bearded man again. He quickly expanded his horizons to include the historic city center, featuring Rynek Glowny, the main market square. The giant market place swarmed with cafés, shops, and merchant stalls where Kaz's allowance was exchanged for sweets and ice creams. People gossiped, conducted business and shopped. Aromas of baked bread and rich spices mingled with cooked veal on skewers and mouth watering hams. Freshly picked fruits and vegetables added a rainbow of reds, greens and yellows to the scenes. In the middle of the square stood Cloth Hall, an elongated Renaissance building made famous for its textile trade. A Gothic City Hall Tower sprang from the ground at one end of the hall, and the imposing Church of St. Mary with its famed Hejnal Tower rose majestically into the sky at the other. A trumpet call, known as the Hejnal, resonated from the tower every hour in memory of a trumpeter from medieval times who was killed while sounding an alarm. Ringing the square were large complexes of townhouses and commercial buildings with small streets dividing them.

The market square may have been an enchanting beehive of activity, but it paled in comparison to the Wawel Royal Castle which commanded a small hill several blocks away. Medieval walls, fortifications and towers protected the castle's Gothic cathedral, royal burial chapels, royal apartments, treasury and armory. Everywhere Kaz looked, he saw a history filled with courtly monarchs and bold knights. Naturally, it was the armory that captured his full attention. Gleaming swords, shields and body armor beckoned to him with tales of chivalry and courage. Kaz could feel the ground rising and falling beneath his feet as he imagined riding a powerful horse into battle. He returned so many times, the guards soon knew him by name and greeted him with small treats.

Summer galloped along without incident, until the clouds on Kaz's horizon reasserted themselves. It happened without warning when his mother took him by the hand to the public school where she registered him for fall classes. Once again, she presented his records, and, once again, he saw the name Kowalski printed in bold type on the forms. The letters leered at him with malice. He stared at them and caught his breath.

"My name is Kowinsky," he declared with a tremor in his voice.

The clerk peered over his glasses at them.

Mother shifted her feet and looked down at the purse she held in her trembling hands. "We'll talk about it at home," she replied in her usual soft voice. A hand reached out to caress his cheek, but he twisted away. The warmth of her touch couldn't calm the tensions churning inside him. He sensed something menacing hidden in those papers, something lurking in the shadows that threatened his idyllic life.

Kaz spent a tormented afternoon waiting for his father to come home from work. Mother had refused to answer his questions. When he heard the uneven staccato of Father's footsteps clomping up the stairs to the apartment, he opened the door and ran to him. "Why must I be Kowalski at school," he cried in a pleading voice. "Why can't I be Kowinsky?"

This time, Father didn't push Kaz's arms away, but led him to the sitting room and sat him down on a stool next to his chair. He heaved himself into the chair and closed his eyes for what seemed an eternity.

"I suppose you're old enough to know the story," he replied at last. He picked at his jacket's sleeve and avoided Kaz's eyes. It was one of the few times Kaz didn't feel the withering heat of his father's gaze. "I've been in contact with someone you shall meet. Let's call her Aunt Katarzyna for now. She lives in Warsaw. The Russian army is nearby, but I'm told it's still safe to travel there. We shall go this weekend. She can answer your questions."

The train creaked its way along the wobbly tracks toward Warsaw. Father had deflected Kaz's questions about his name and added little regarding his mysterious aunt, other than to say that she had lived in Poland for many years. To distract him, Father told Kaz about the war being waged between his new country and Russia. It had started in February of the previous year when Poland's desire to reclaim land lost to tsarist Russia clashed with Lenin's goal to spread his revolution throughout western Europe. Pilsudski, Poland's great military commandant, had taken the initiative and pressed his advantage as far as Minsk in Belarus, but Stalin's great red army had quickly massed into a formidable strike force that pushed the Polish army back on itself. Now, Russia was advancing toward Warsaw, and there seemed to be little that Pilsudski's forces could do about it.

Father's distraction worked. Kaz nearly forgot about his trip's purpose as he pondered the idea of clashing armies so near to his doorstep. His imagination returned to the armaments he'd seen in Wawel Castle. Swords had now been replaced by rifles and canon, but his father told him that horses were still used. In fact, it was the First Calvary Army of Russia that broke through the Polish defenses and turned the tide of battle.

"Our government has asked the western powers for military assistance, but none has been sent." Kaz's father grimaced as he spoke. "We're all that stands between the Bolsheviks and Europe, but no one will lift a finger to help us. It's always been so for us Poles. We absorb the blows of history while our allies forsake us."

As Kaz walked with his father from the train station into the heart of the city, he expected to see signs of chaos: people scurrying about, throwing up barriers, fleeing their homes. Instead, he was greeted by a great calm. Trenches had been dug and entanglements of barbed wire stretched across several thoroughfares, but there was no panic. It was obvious that many families had already left, the streets were half empty, but those who remained went about their business as if it was a normal summer day. Most walked or rode bicycles among a smattering of oversized cars driven by those with wealth.

Kaz followed his father along a wide boulevard described by gated entrances, columned buildings, baroque churches and noble palaces. It quickly became clear to him that Warsaw was more than a gathering of homes and businesses. It was a magnificent city, one filled at every turn with imposing buildings. Everything was built on a grand scale. They crossed a vast square surrounded by townhouses standing shoulder-to-shoulder, then plunged into narrower streets protected by ancient city walls. They passed through a much smaller square graced by an ornate church, then moved through a busy neighborhood of shops and cafés. The aromas of fresh bread and fried fish reminded Kaz that he hadn't eaten since morning, but his father's determined pace told him there was no time to dally. Twice, Father asked a passerby for directions, then strode purposely down another colorful avenue.

At last, they entered a narrower side street with small, carefully groomed trees. They proceeded slowly while Father checked the numbers on the doors. Kaz heard two voices, man and woman, bickering by an open window above him. A gray cat scooted past with a wary eye. Kaz found his mind wandering as he inspected his surroundings. The street was not as grand as the ones with churches and palaces, but it showed the promise of a place where one could live a comfortable life.

"Down here." The first words uttered by his father in some minutes snapped Kaz back to the present, and he followed him through an archway into a pleasant courtyard framed by potted plants and four, blue doors. Father knocked on the second door and stepped back. Seconds clicked past while they waited. A car's tires whined along the trolley's rails imbedded in the street behind them. Birds chirped in a nearby tree. A slight breeze chilled Kaz's cheek. Despite the cool air, tiny rivulets of sweat had formed on his forehead from the long walk.

The door opened without warning, causing Kaz to jump. A round face, heavy with makeup and framed in coal black hair, appeared in the doorway. The face belonged to a plump woman wearing a dark brown skirt and a beige blouse. She looked at Kaz with the same wary eye as the cat he'd noted before.

"Hello Katarzyna." Father nodded in recognition. "This is Kaz."

"Come in." The woman opened the door wider and stepped aside.

Kaz followed his father into an expansive living room with a couch and two cushioned chairs facing each other over a glass coffee table cluttered with typed letters and what appeared to be bills. A bronze clock ticked merrily on a nearby mantle above a small fireplace. Glass figures danced in a cabinet along the far wall. A single floor lamp, lighted despite the sun swooping in the window, stood like a beacon by the couch. Kaz saw a roomy kitchen and a polished wooden dining table in the next room. A hallway led to what he supposed was a bedroom and bathroom.

Kaz sat on the couch opposite the woman and wiggled his feet, uncertain what to say or do. His father remained standing.

"You can call me Aunt Katarzyna," she announced without preamble. "I'm your father's sister." Her posture was stiff with unease. She sat on the edge of her chair, her legs to one side, as if she were unsure about her guests. Father still stood behind Kaz. Tension pulsated through the sunlit room.

"Aren't you worried about the Russians?" Kaz blurted. He blushed at his awkward question.

A thin smile crossed the woman's face. It almost looked like a frown. "I've lived in Poland most of my life. Why should I be afraid? Warsaw has been occupied before, after all. The prospect of foreign troops isn't so daunting."

Slowly, the three were drawn into a stilted conversation. The aunt asked his father about work and Kaz about school. After a few more questions, the words drifted to subjects that didn't concern Kaz. His mind dulled and his eyes wandered to the papers on the table. He didn't mean to pry, but he couldn't help reading the name addressed on the envelopes and statements: Katarzyna Kowalski. It took a moment for the name to register. When it did, his vision blurred, and his head filled with a buzzing noise that made him feel as though he was trapped inside a beehive. He wiped his eyes with the backs of his hands and looked again. Kowalski. The same name as the one on his school documents. How was that possible? What could it mean, other than the fact that this stiff, unfriendly woman seated across from him was not an aunt but his mother, and the man who had ruled his life these past few years was not his father. Kaz's mind spun as he worked through the implications. The dark cloud that had lurked just beyond his grasp of understanding swept across the sun, making the day as bleak as the tombstones in the Jewish cemetery. If Katarzyna was his mother, who was his father, and why had he and this woman abandoned him?

Silence settled over the room. The conversations had ended. Kaz's questions hung in the air, unanswered. When they rose, he mumbled a goodbye without making eye contact. No one attempted to touch the other. No hands were shaken or arms circled in hugs. No kisses were planted on cheeks. They could have just as easily been tenants dropping by to pay the rent.

Kaz slouched along behind the man he'd always thought was his father while they made their way back to the train station. It was hard to know what to think of him, now. If he was truly the woman's brother, that would make him an uncle. Uncle. The word sounded foreign on his tongue. And what about the warm, smiling woman who caressed his cheeks? No longer a mother, but an aunt. Another foul sounding word. The concept of living with someone other than his parents baffled him.

He waited in silence for their train and sat opposite his uncle when they boarded it. Others piled in next to them, making it difficult to talk. The swaying train car calmed Kaz, and the silence gave him time to think. His discovery explained why the man seated across from him had displayed so little affection since entering his life. Kaz had been foisted on him, not because Kaz was an orphan, but because nobody wanted him. Certainly not his mother. That was evident from today's encounter. And what about his real father? He seemed to be missing entirely, which meant that he wasn't interested in Kaz, either. He'd been abandoned, and his uncle had rescued him, not out of love but because of duty. It was the wrong role. An uncle was supposed to make appearances at Christmas gatherings and birthday parties, not be a father to his sister's son. No wonder he was so unhappy most of the time.

I'm like my country, Kaz thought. *I'm like Poland. Abandoned and partitioned. No one wants me. I'm a blank spot on a map, there to be occupied and shunted into the shadows of history. And if I disappear, no one will care.*

Chapter Two

KAZ stood in the dust of his schoolyard and listened to the taunts of classmates being hurled down upon him. Tears stung his eyes. He tried his best to hide them, but he couldn't. His lower lip trembled. At any moment, he feared he would bawl like a new born calf. Somehow, word about his uncle and his real mother had leaked out and swiftly spread among the children. He'd seen the girls talking behind his back as he slunk red faced through the school corridors. He'd imagined the words they were whispering: orphaned, unwanted, abandoned. He needn't imagine them any longer. Today, they were being thrown in his face with the wallop of rocks.

Weeks had passed since Kaz's visit to Warsaw. Russia had reached the outskirts of the city as predicted, and newspaper headlines foretold the impending doom. It was hopeless to try stopping the great red army marching toward the capitol, they said, but Commander Pilsudski refused to surrender. Then, a miracle occurred. They were calling it the Miracle of Warsaw. At the very moment when the enemy was poised to enter the city, the Polish army undertook a desperate gambit that involved marching exhausted troops hundreds of miles to Warsaw to reinforce the front lines. Russia should have attacked at once, but overconfidence betrayed them. Victory assured, they took too long preparing the final blow, which gave Poland's fragile defenses time to reform. When the attack came, the Poles refused to yield to the superior forces arrayed against them. They held their ground. A frontal attack on the Vistula Bridge was repulsed. It proved to be a pivotal battle, because it gave the Polish cavalry and foot soldiers time to encircle the enemy in a stunning reversal of positions. Before the Russians knew what had happened, the Poles carved through their rear guard and fell upon the invaders. The rout was complete. Over one hundred thousand Russian troops were captured as the red army retreated, broke ranks and ran. In the end, Lenin had to abandon his dream of conquests in western Europe and sue for peace.

Now, Kaz faced his own Armageddon in the dirt filled schoolyard where he stood. The mockers were too numerous to count, and they seemed just as certain to defeat him as the Russians. They were led by a tall boy named Charlie whose broad shoulders gave him the appearance of a young boxer. He stood in front of the others, feet spread apart, hands on hips, and dared Kaz to challenge him.

Kaz considered his options. The school was Catholic, run by priests and nuns. It was not the sort of place to put up with fist fights and mayhem. His uncle (he no longer thought of him as his father) would have preferred a secular school, but there were now more Polish children in the country than seats for instruction. He'd been lucky, his uncle proclaimed, to get Kaz admitted, and he made it clear that he expected Kaz to behave.

"Otherwise, you'll find yourself on the street," he thundered.

Kaz wanted to behave. He didn't relish facing his uncle's temper, but he couldn't control the rage boiling inside his chest, or the way his face burned with shame. His vision clouded until the taunting faces melded into a seething cauldron of torment. He knew he had to do something, or the tears welling in his eyes would soon be tumbling down his face. A spurt of anger propelled his feet forward. He heard his voice screaming as he advanced toward the laughing faces. There was no thought to his actions, no plan. All he wanted to do was stop the voices, and that meant confronting the boy in front of him. All he saw was Charlie.

The two boys collided in a scrum of flailing arms and pummeling fists. Soon, they were rolling on the ground in each other's arms, two wrestlers caught in the heady excitement of battle. Kaz felt his fists landing blows, felt his adversary's biting blows of retaliation. Dust raised by their scrambling bodies stung his eyes and filled his lungs. Jeers from the onlookers danced in the air, but they didn't matter. The cries faded. His world was reduced to sweaty head holds, straining muscles and hot breaths.

A louder voice boomed above the others. Rough hands pulled the wrestlers apart. Kaz found himself being lifted to his feet. Pain streaked down his nose. He swiped the back of his hand across it and saw blood, realized he was bleeding. He was pleased to note that a bright crimson smear covered Charlie's face, as well. The two boys looked at each other with a sense of triumph, as if they had somehow defeated a common foe.

They were quickly marched to the principal's office. Kaz was still breathing harder than normal, more from excitement than exertion. Charlie hardly glanced at his surroundings, and Kaz wondered if he'd been there before. The bespectacled priest seated behind the desk confirmed as much when he greeted them.

"You know where to sit, Charlie." He gestured to two chairs facing the desk. Charlie sat down with the air of someone invited to dinner. He didn't slump or let his gaze wander. He sat up straight and looked directly at the priest. Kaz admired the boy's manner and tried to emulate it. He assumed the other chair was for him and took it.

"You two boys are off to a bad start," the priest intoned. He picked up a ruler as he spoke, and Kaz wondered if he intended to use it on them. To his relief, the ruler was returned to its place on the desk. "The school year has hardly begun," the man continued, "and we cannot condone such behavior. This is a place of learning and worship. If you wish to remain here, you'd better change your ways. Let's begin by shaking hands. Whatever the disagreement, I'm sure we can put it behind us."

The boys stood in unison.

"You're a good fighter." Charlie grasped Kaz's hand.

"Not bad yourself," Kaz acknowledged. "But if you make fun of me, we'll just have to do this all over again."

"I know. That's why I think we should be friends." He gave Kaz an uneven smile that broke the tension between them.

A sense of comradeship swept over Kaz, a sense of well-being. He knew that they *would* be friends, good friends.

That gave Kaz two new friends. He'd already met Woz, a classmate with curly black hair and an easy laugh. Woz endeared himself to Charlie and Kaz when he showed them where to crawl under a fence that guarded a stretch of railroad track known as "blood alley." It was a favorite spot for reckless souls who raced across the tracks in front of oncoming trains. The challenge was to wait until an engine appeared around the bend less than a hundred meters away. The train had to slow for the curve, but it was still traveling plenty fast. A man's bravery was tested by how long he waited before making his leap across the tracks. This had resulted in many injuries and a few deaths. The fence was erected to save such fools from themselves, but it hadn't helped. The daredevils had simply dug a depression and snaked their way under the barrier. The three boys did the same, then looked uncertainly toward the bend and waited for a hurtling ton of steel to appear. None did, and they departed without being tested.

Charlie and Woz joked about what they would have done if a train had appeared, but not Kaz. His mind whirled at the prospect of tempting fate. It was a new feeling for him. He'd never deliberately put himself in the path of danger, but given the chance, he would have done so. His outlook on life had changed. He no longer had an anchor to steady him. No one wanted him.

Kaz reached this conclusion when he returned home from Warsaw and learned the truth about his family. His real parents had been married in a Catholic church, but after Kaz was born, his mother discovered that her husband was already married and had another family tucked away in Wroclaw. Once his duplicity was uncovered, the father fled and was never seen again. His mother had the marriage annulled but kept the name Kowalski to maintain the image of a married woman. That did not change Kaz's circumstances, however. In the eyes of the church, he was a bastard, and his mother refused to accept him as her son. She left him to be raised by her brother. He tried to convince her to take Kaz back, but she refused. She wanted nothing to do with a child spawned by such an evil man.

So, there he was, a piece of flotsam floating through the rapids of life. It was better to die, he concluded, than to continue an existence filled with such despair. The idea of escaping his dilemma by taking his life appealed to him, but he didn't think he had the stomach for suicide. That was a coward's way out. It was better to put his life on the line, to show courage in the face of death, which was why he was so drawn to blood alley.

His new resolve soon revealed itself back in the schoolyard where a set of four swings offered a chance for fun and adventure. The swings were guarded from behind by a metal railing meant to keep children from standing too close. The front opened onto a pit of sand. The girls squealed as they swung back and forth in dresses that fluttered in the breeze. The boys hopped on the seats, raised their feet and pulled mightily on the swings until they were soaring through the air. Then, they slid off their seats and flew as far as possible before landing in the sand. A contest developed to see who could fly the farthest. Charlie was the winner, followed closely by Kaz. It didn't take long for Kaz to tire of the game, however, and to turn his attention to the rail barrier behind him.

"Who wants to bet I can clear that railing?" he demanded one chilly afternoon.

All eyes swung to him. A shock wave of fear and expectation stirred the air. Several of the boys had looked at that dangerous barrier, but none had shown the courage to challenge it. Even Charlie had shied away. Kaz felt his own pulse rising at the idea. An inner voice deep inside him prodded him forward. He stepped toward the swings.

"I bet you can, but don't try."

Woz's voice shattered the quiet that had blanketed the crowd. Kids coughed and snuffled their runny noses, but no one else spoke. Kaz spotted Charlie as he walked to the swings. A look of concern was scrawled across his friend's face, but he didn't speak. Kaz sat down backwards, pushed off with his feet and violently pumped his arms and legs until he reached all the height and speed that his frail body would allow. He looked at the rail rising and falling before him with satisfaction. Here was the challenge he'd been seeking. The pain from his distorted life vanished. He felt purified and blessed by God.

Kaz made one more valiant push with his legs, rose toward the rounded bar and flung himself into the sky. At first, he thought we would clear the rail with ease, but as gravity tugged at him, his momentum faltered. He was falling short of the trajectory he'd envisioned, and the rail was looming larger and larger beneath him. One minute he was immortal; the next he was plunging to earth. He saw with chagrin that he wasn't going to make it. His feet clipped the hard, metal surface with a jarring reality that tossed him head first over the rail and slammed him into the unyielding ground. His world went black.

He slowly became aware of light and opened his eyes to a sea of worried faces. A girl in pigtails loomed into view, frowned, then floated away. His whole body ached. It took him a moment to recall where he was and what had just happened. He was lying on his back, but when he tried to lift his head, the faces looking down at him spun wildly. He decided not to move. Then, Charlie's face appeared, and he felt himself being lifted off the ground. His classmates crowded around to congratulate him. He stood on wobbly legs and stared in amazement at the railing that now stood between him and the swings. A lightheaded feeling of victory surged through him. He'd looked death in the eye, and he hadn't blinked. The desire to kill himself had retreated. This realization gave him peace, but he sensed it was only a battle he'd won, not a war. The beast still lurked within him.

School settled into a daily routine that combined long classes with field trips and afternoon visits to church for prayers and talks about God. Kaz shared some classes with Charlie and Woz, but found himself separated from them in the afternoons. One of the field trips took him to Wawel Castle, where he rediscovered his fascination with Polish history. His favorite guard warmed him with a smile of recognition. The visit was much too short, and he promised himself to return again. The two-hour church sessions were the most boring part of the day. Kaz had been baptized a Catholic, but his uncle and aunt rarely took him to church. He found the prayers and religious lectures stupefying. He began to plan his escape.

His class left the school every afternoon at precisely two o'clock and marched in columns of three for eight blocks to the church. There, they remained until exactly four o'clock when they marched back to school. Attendance was always taken when they returned but never at the church. There was often only one teacher at the head of the lines to monitor the children. Kaz calculated that his best opportunity to escape came after three blocks when the formation turned a corner. For a brief period, the students at the backs of the columns were out of sight. Kaz lingered near the rear, and when the front of the class turned the corner, he slipped into a doorway, pressed himself against the door and waited until everybody was gone.

The first time he did this, he held his breath and waited for an angry voice to call him out, but nothing happened. He was greeted by street traffic, bicycles, sunshine and freedom! For two hours, he could explore the city on his own. He skipped down the street in a state of ecstasy, but he knew he had to be careful. He couldn't just wander anywhere he liked. There was the constant danger of a policeman spotting him and returning him to the school. So, he avoided the main boulevards and slipped down side streets until he reached the formidable walls of Wawel Castle. He spent magical afternoons there immersed in the stories of brave warriors, bishops and kings, and enjoyed the tasty treats offered by the guards. Time was his only enemy. He had to leave the castle in time to retrace his route and slip into line as his classmates turned the corner on their way back to their classroom. He also knew better than to perform his disappearing act too often. The teacher was no fool. Kaz limited his unauthorized visits to once or twice a week.

Time passed pleasantly enough. The turmoil Kaz had experienced when he returned from Warsaw gradually faded, along with thoughts about the stiff woman who seemed to be his mother, and the shadowy figure he envisioned as his father. His aunt was as kindhearted as ever, and even his uncle warmed a bit. Despite Kaz's inattentiveness at school, he managed to get passing grades, and weekends were shared with his two best friends. One of their favorite haunts was the muddy banks and fast-moving currents of the Vistula River, where they fished beneath the protective walls of Wawel Castle for the red finned suckers and great, sluggish carp that hugged the sandy river bottom. The boys used cane poles with baited hooks to nudge the fish and coax them into biting. As the warm sun arced toward the horizon, Kaz would triumphantly march home with the day's trophies, knowing that his aunt would fry them that night for dinner.

When they weren't fishing, they swam out to one of the side-wheeler river boats that churned up and down the river, where they grabbed onto handholds at the back just above the waterline. They held on as long as they could while the wheel's paddle blades cascaded them with foaming water and the boat pulled them upstream. Exhausted, they would finally let go and float back to the river bank, where they flopped on the shore and watched pole men on barges dredging sand from the river bottom The muscular men worked from early morning until dusk hauling buckets of sand to the surface and piling their loads onto the barge's deck. When the barge was full, they maneuvered it to shore and transferred the sand onto wagons to be taken to a local cement company.

On rainy days, the boys liked to hang around the candy factory in hopes of snaring the occasional piece of chocolate that tumbled onto the floor under the assembly line where ladies sorted and packed the confections into baskets. In exchange, the boys would run errands for the foreman, a man with a fat stomach and heavy jowls named Optima. However, Optima was moody, and there were days when he called the boys scoundrels and shooed them away. When that happened, they would retaliate by tipping over empty sugar barrels or singing raunchy refrains through the open factory windows. The foreman would angrily shake his fist as they ran away laughing, but when they returned a few days later, Optima would be in a good mood and all was forgotten.

It was an idyllic life for a boy growing up in Poland, but as much as Kaz enjoyed these outings with his friends, he couldn't quell the demon that lurked in the fringes of his consciousness. It whispered a steady stream of taunts about the mother who'd rejected him and the father who'd disappeared. It reminded him of his empty life and encouraged him to defy the odds of danger, just as he had on that playground swing. His need to take risks was never far from the surface of his mind. He was always the last to let go of the paddle boats, making it harder to return to shore before losing the last of his strength, and he often swam into the faster currents near mid-river where larger boats plied the rougher waters. More than once, he was nearly caught in the undertow of a passing ship's propeller.

"You take too many chances," Charlie scolded him. Woz nodded his head in agreement. "Why do you do that?"

Kaz waved them off with a laugh. "Because it's thrilling. Because it helps me forget."

"Forget what?" Charlie demanded.

Kaz nearly said 'my worthless life,' but he fell silent. There was no need to burden his friends with his troubles. It was his problem, not theirs. He would deal with it in his own way.

Chapter Three

THE bullet that zinged past Kaz's head, a ricochet off a nearby lamppost, reminded him that he was only days away from his tenth birthday, and he wanted to live to see it. He hastily crouched down at the corner of a building, but he couldn't take his eyes off the scene unfolding before him. Despite his fear of being shot, the danger drew him closer.

Kaz had been following his usual route through the back alleys to Wawel Castle when he heard a crescendo of loud voices coming from nearby Stradomska Street. Curiosity overcame caution, and he hurried up a side street until he discovered the source of the racket, a mob of protesters angrily shouting demands as they marched down the middle of the boulevard, bringing traffic to a standstill.

He halted at the corner and held his breath as he watched police with fixed bayonets and loaded rifles arriving to confront the demonstrators. At first, the workers were content to hurl curses at the nervous officers, but before long rocks were thrown. Pitched battles broke out between the demonstrators and uniformed men. Throngs of bodies seethed along the sidewalks in tightly knit clusters of raised clubs and menacing guns. They made Kaz think of wild animals turned loose in the street. Shots rang out. Puffs of white smoke billowed forth in exploding patterns that reminded Kaz of his uncle's cigarettes. Terrified voices echoed among the buildings. An odor of burnt ashes permeated the air. And that wayward bullet zinged past Kaz's ear.

When it was over, several men lay dead; blood ran in the gutters. Kaz stared at the scene in disbelief, then turned and ran home to tell his aunt and uncle.

"It's the same all over Poland," his uncle declared when he returned home from work that evening. He was so visibly upset, he didn't bother to question Kaz about why he'd skipped school that day. "Workers and peasants are unhappy."

Political instability was making it impossible to govern, his uncle explained. It was causing frustration and unrest. The country's presidents were changing faster than a baby's diapers. One, President Narutowicz, was assassinated after only five days in office. Vast agricultural estates were still owned by a small number of wealthy families. Peasants had been promised land reforms, but less than twenty percent of farmland had been redistributed to the impoverished masses. Factory workers faced inhumane conditions. They were expected to work like machines for long hours with little rest. Men toiled in twelve-hour shifts for a pay voucher that barely covered the food, clothing and rent needed to keep a family together. There was little extra and no safety net in case of injury or illness. Workers called strikes, and there were riots.

"I see it where I work," Uncle finished with a heavy sigh. "I'm expected to work more hours, but there's little extra pay to show for it. If I complain, somebody is waiting to take my job."

While Kaz and his friends were enjoying unauthorized trips to Wawel Castle, wild rides behind paddle boats and rollicking adventures at the candy factory, Poland was unraveling.

There was one man who possessed the stature and prestige to put an end to the chaos gripping Poland. However, he had remained on the sidelines where he observed the anarchy with increasing alarm. He'd hesitated to become directly involved in the political turmoil that was bubbling out of control, but when another government coalition failed, and another coup was threatened, he knew it was time to act. On March 12, 1926, Marshall Pilsudski, the hero of the Miracle of Warsaw, stepped out of the shadows. With the backing of several of his old regiments, he marched on the district of Praga in Warsaw and seized the bridges spanning the Vistula River. He was confronted by the President of Poland, Stanislaw Wojciechowski, who told him to stand down, but there was no turning back. Pilsudski signaled his troops to attack the brigades arrayed against them. The ensuing battle raged for three days. At one critical juncture, government reinforcements might have decided the issue, but they were prevented from joining the battle when the socialist railway union ordered a strike and prevented the fresh troops from reaching Warsaw. The President of Poland was given no alternative and admitted defeat. He resigned, and Pilsudski became the de facto ruler of the country. He retained the parliament and had others installed as Premier and President, but he took firm control. Opponents were arrested, and soldiers with revolvers at the ready welcomed the Chamber of Deputies when it reconvened.

Kaz's uncle applauded the news. His own circumstances had deteriorated, and he hoped the Marshall would improve job opportunities and working conditions for people like himself.

Kaz returned to school the day after the riot, but his weekly visits to Wawel Castle ended. His absence had been noted, and an extra teacher was assigned to watch over the students as they marched like silent demonstrators to the church each afternoon. It was no longer possible to hide in doorways and to slip away. He sat trapped in the church and sang hymns, although he hardly heard the organ music or the words. His mind fled the church walls that confined him; his imagination wandered the streets and alleyways leading to his favorite castle.

One afternoon, he came home to discover that a new set of walls was about to close around his life. His uncle and aunt were seated at the kitchen table blowing the heat off fresh cups of tea. They looked up expectantly when Kaz entered, their expressions hooded by detached smiles. It was too early for Uncle to be home. Something was amiss.

"Come in here, boy. Sit down." Uncle waved him to the table with a great sweep of his arm. Kaz settled on the hard, wooden chair offered by his uncle and waited.

Uncle turned the cup in his hands around and around on the uneven surface of the table. "We have news." The cup made a scraping sound as it continued its circles. "Your aunt is with child."

Aunt leaned forward with a more joyful smile. "We've tried for so long, we'd nearly given up. It's a miracle." She reached out and touched Kaz's arm with moist, warm fingers in an effort to reassure him that his world would remain as it was.

"Things will change around here, of course," Uncle remarked in contradiction. "We'll all have to pull our weight." He didn't explain what he meant by pulling weight, but Kaz suspected that it didn't bode well for him. The dark clouds were gathering on his horizon, once more.

Kaz had six months to adjust to the idea of sharing his life with another child before a baby boy was born. He was named Jozef in honor of Jozef Pilsudski, and the apartment instantly became smaller and noisier. A second-hand high chair was added to the kitchen table; a tiny, unpainted crib was hauled up the four flights of stairs and squeezed into the main bedroom; and a pair of lusty lungs howled day and night. Despite the disruptions to their quiet life, Uncle and Aunt fussed endlessly over their new son. Uncle's voice softened, and he stopped smoking in the apartment. Even his evening newspaper was often ignored. Kaz had never experienced such affection. He wanted to share in the joy he sensed around him, but he felt excluded. Disappointment filled his heart; he eyed the newcomer with envy.

His thoughts turned to the cold woman who'd refused to accept him as her son. Even though he felt no affection for her, he still longed for some sign of kindness, something to tell him he counted. There were his friends, of course, but they had their own families. The world was clamping down on his head with the grip of a large vise. He grew lethargic, unable to cope with the family scenes unfolding before him. His aunt still greeted him warmly each day when he pulled himself up the stairs after school, but she no longer tousled his hair. He sensed a hint of restraint in her manner. The affection he'd enjoyed from her lost its glow. His uncle showed even less interest in Kaz than he had before. Evening discussions about the news ceased. His attention was consumed by the wriggling figure wrapped in his arms. Kaz retreated to his bedroom, his only sanctuary in the apartment, and stared for hours at the ceiling. It took all his strength to present himself at the dinner table, and his appetite waned. The apartment no longer felt like home.

Disturbing thoughts skittered through his mind, thoughts about metal railings and the undertow of river boats. Life, he decided, was nothing more than a deck of cards, only his deck held too many deuces and not enough aces. Every time he shuffled the cards, he drew a losing hand. One thing was certain. He didn't fit into the family puzzle anymore. He would be better off somewhere else, but where? Not with his mother. She didn't want him anymore than his uncle. Kaz was still orphaned, still abandoned, and now he'd been pushed aside by a crying baby who demanded everyone's attention. He had an overwhelming desire to run away, but there was nowhere to go, no place to hide.

The disturbing thoughts grew more insistent. The inner voice he tried so hard to suppress pushed itself to the surface. It cantered forth with fresh promises of danger and adventure. It told him it was the only way to relieve his pain. His blood stirred. He knew what he must do.

"I'm going back to blood alley," he announced to Charlie and Woz during lunch at school. "I want to take on that train."

Charlie scratched his head. Woz scuffed the floor with his shoe. Neither looked at Kaz or said a word. They hadn't returned to blood alley since their first visit. They'd talked about it, about the men that went there to test their courage, but something had held them back. Charlie had finally admitted that the idea of a train bearing down on him was more excitement than he needed. Kaz hadn't agreed, but he'd kept quiet, until now.

"Are you coming?" Kaz demanded.

"The last time you did something like this you damn near killed yourself." Everyone knew Charlie was talking about the swings in the school yard. "Why should we be part of another one of your crazy stunts?"

"Because you're my friends, and I don't want to jump alone. But if you're too scared, then I guess I will." Kaz gave Charlie a fierce look that dared him to say no.

Charlie stared back, his body stiff with resentment. He and Kaz had always been competitive with one another, but not like this. This was more than a dare. Kaz was asking Charlie if he had backbone. This was a challenge that couldn't be ignored. He met Kaz's glare and nodded.

Woz let out the breath he'd been holding and did the same. "If you go, we all go."

"That settles it then," Kaz said with satisfaction. "There's a freight train every afternoon about half-past four, but we should get there early, in case there's other jumpers. Make sure we get a good spot. Let's go tomorrow."

They met at four the next day and slithered under the wire fence protecting the tracks. Two men already stood by the rails looking at the curve where the train would appear. Soon, two more arrived. They glanced at the three boys with surprise.

"This is no place for youngsters," one of them warned.

"Just as right for us as you," Kaz responded with defiance. "All you need is the will to jump."

The two men shrugged and moved on. Kaz surveyed the area. The men were all standing by the tracks near where they entered. They smoked and chatted while passing the time. Kaz estimated by their casual demeanor that they had been there before. They'd chosen prime spots, but there was still room for two or three more. Charlie and Woz stepped forward and picked an area where the ground looked firm. They nervously turned their attention to the tracks. The fence where they'd entered was about ten feet away at that point, leaving enough room for half-a-dozen steps before making the jump. A black coating of cinders from the trains' smokestacks blanketed the area. To Kaz's left, the fence sloped away from the tracks to avoid an outcropping of rocks, which left more room for a running start. Here, the black cinders mingled with loose gravel, and the footing was less certain. He wandered over and inspected the ground. The problem was simple. If he could run faster, he could jump when the train got closer, but if he slipped, all would be lost. It was a matter of timing and luck. All he had to do was time his jump properly. The voice in his head laughed; it liked his thinking.

Kaz tested the ground where he would plant his feet for the jump and tried a few quick starts. The gravel shifted under his weight, but the soil underneath remained firm. His heart thrummed in his chest as he calculated the distance he would need to travel and the time it would take. He wiped his clammy hands on his trousers and counted the steps. He was momentarily distracted by the sound of trucks clamoring along a nearby thoroughfare. He glanced toward the sound, but the trees and bushes outside the fence blocked his view. Kaz returned his attention to the tracks, set his feet and sprinted forward. He hit his takeoff spot and leaped across the rails in a graceful motion. He was ready.

No sooner had he finished his practice run than a great shriek split the silence. It resonated in the chilled air and swept over the waiting men with the force of an ocean wave. All eyes swiveled to the place where the tracks disappeared. Anxious moments passed without any sign of the monster approaching them. A flicker of hope pulsed through the group. Perhaps, it wasn't the train after all. That hope was quickly dashed when a geyser of angry, gray smoke burst through the foliage, and a fiendish face in the shape of a blackened, full moon rounded the bend, accompanied by the heaves and sighs of a laboring engine and the squeals of metal wheels grinding on iron rails.

Kaz knew instantly that this was a far greater challenge than anything he'd faced before. The train charging down the tracks both frightened and mesmerized him. He wanted to defy its power and embrace it at the same time. Would it be so bad to jump into its arms? His life would be over, but his pain would be gone. He recalled the bullet that had zinged past his ear. It had nearly ended his life, but he'd been glad to escape it. He realized that he had no desire to die now, either. Not by his own hand. Only a hunger to test the limits of his courage.

There was no more time to think. His friends were already in position next to the four men. Kaz hurried to his spot. The sounds of the engine straining against the limits of its power roared at him as the train hurtled forward. Events began moving too quickly for him to do more than react to what he saw. The first two men ran and jumped across the rails well ahead of the engine. The next two waited longer, poised in a contest to see who was the braver. One leaped and cleared the train with feet to spare. The other followed, but too late. The engine's great, blackened face seemed to snarl as it struck the man's leg and sent him spinning off the tracks. He disappeared from sight behind the charging train. Charlie and Woz froze when they saw the body flipping away from them and didn't move. Kaz ignored them. All his thoughts were focused on that cunning blackened face rushing toward him. Instincts took over and he was off, sprinting across the gravel into the mouth of hell. A rush of air pushed at him as his feet left the ground and his body soared into the air. The noise of the roaring engine enveloped him. His mouth, dry as sand, opened in a scream that joined the squeals of the tortured track beneath the train's wheels. The engine's face was so close, Kaz thought it would surely devour him. He braced for the impact of steel against flesh, but nothing happened. The face was gone, and the train whooshed past him. Hot air blasted him as he tumbled to earth beyond the rails. The train had had him in its grasp and let him go. Kaz rolled over in the cinders and watched in wonder as a parade of boxcars groaned past him. His right arm stung where he'd landed on it. His head ached from the noise. His lungs chafed from the choking smoke and coal dust. But he was alive! Slowly, the train retreated down the tracks with a steady *click-clack, click-clack, click-clack* that grew fainter and fainter.

Kaz's chest heaved with heavy breaths as he rose to his feet. The air tasted cool; he gulped it in. Charlie and Woz raced toward him with shrieks of laughter, but his attention was drawn to the man who'd been struck by the train, afraid of what he might see. To his amazement, he found him standing on his feet and leaning against his friend while he tested his right leg. He'd defied death just as Kaz had done and survived the challenge. The man caught his gaze and tipped his cap with two fingers in a salute of respect. Kaz nodded in return. He knew they had both beaten life's odds that day. It was unlikely either would return to blood alley to do so again.

Chapter Four

Kaz's battle with the train had been a triumph, and for a time he strode through the days with his shoulders back and his spine straight, a reflection of his new found confidence. His classmates whispered and gave him respectful glances, thanks to Charlie, who'd spread the word about Kaz's daring dance with death in blood alley. Kaz had already earned a reputation for audacious exploits when he challenged the railing behind the school swings, but taking on the train raised his stature to a whole new level. He was 'the man' as Charlie put it, and he reveled in everybody's admiration. Not even the squalling cries of Jozef could upset his good mood. The next few months were the best of his life.

Until the storm clouds gathered on his horizon, once more.

Kaz sauntered up the stairs to his apartment expecting to find his aunt playing with Jozef. Instead, he saw his uncle seated at the kitchen table turning a cup of tea around in his calloused hands. There was no sign of his aunt or the baby.

"Shouldn't you be at work?" Kaz asked with a sense of foreboding. The last time he'd found his father seated this way, he'd learned about the expected arrival of Jozef.

Uncle stood up, limped over to Kaz and placed his hands on the boy's shoulders. The touch of intimacy surprised Kaz. His muscles tightened.

"We've had a bit of a setback. The doctor says I have to rest my hip and leg. The bones aren't mending as they're supposed to. My work hours have been cut back. Which means we no longer have the money to feed everybody." His eyes bore into Kaz's with greater intensity than usual. Kaz looked down with a deep sense of misgiving. He understood that 'everybody' meant him. Questions tumbled through his mind. Would he have to work? What about school? Where would he live?

Uncle returned to the table and sat down to his cup of tea. "Come here," he said in a gentle tone that made the words sound more like a request than a command. Kaz joined him at the table.

"I've sent word to your mother," Uncle continued. "She's making good money in her job. In fact, I've asked her before to contribute to your lodgings here, but she's always refused. Now, it's time she took responsibility for you. Given the circumstances, there's no choice."

His uncle's words swirled around him like leaves scattered in a fall wind. He tried to focus on them, to understand their meaning. Slowly, they sunk in, and his lips pursed in a silent cry of alarm. Kaz was expected to go live with his mother! Memories of an unsmiling, powdered face with cold eyes rose before him. *He wasn't wanted there.* He thought he'd shouted the words, but the room was quiet. He was shouting in his mind.

"But, there's only one bedroom," he blurted foolishly. "Where will I sleep?"

His uncle shook his head. He didn't know the answer.

A flurry of letters over the next two weeks settled things. Kaz's worst nightmare was to be realized. He would go to live with the woman who didn't want him in an apartment without a spare room. Uncle and Aunt took him to the station and put him on the train to Warsaw. As the train departed, Kaz thought about blood alley and his triumph there. He'd never been so happy, but his happiness had been a dream. Reality was once more shoving him into a chasm of despair, and there was nothing he could do but make the best of it. His only hope was that the woman waiting for him would give him a proper home.

That fragile hope was quickly dashed. The woman he was supposed to call mother *was* waiting for him when he arrived in Warsaw, but not to take him home.

"There's no room," she informed him matter-of-factly, "and I keep odd hours. It's best you stay where you can be looked after properly."

With that, she whisked Kaz off to a three-story, crumbling, brick building in a manufacturing district of the city. The surrounding buildings housed offices, small businesses and production facilities. An ammunition plant sat next door, but it's gates were padlocked and tall grass and weeds pushed through cracks in the pavement. Dozens of children gathered out front to stare at Kaz and his mother as they made their way up a gravel path to the building's main entrance. The children scattered like geese when a nun appeared and shooed them away. Kaz stared at the old building in a state of shock. The faded lettering above the door told him all he needed to know. He was being dumped at an orphanage, much like a sack of garbage flung out the door! He'd heard about such places from the chatter of his schoolmates in Krakow. The Great War had orphaned many children, and the Catholic church had established a foster care system to look after them. Places like this, as much an asylum as a home, had been established all over Poland.

Kaz shook his head in disbelief. He wasn't an orphan. He had an uncle and an aunt, and a hateful mother who refused to take him in. He didn't belong there, yet there he was. He would learn, later, that not all of the children were without parents. A special name was given to them: social orphans. They were children who'd been abused or sent away by their families due to economic circumstances or health issues. A social orphan had at least one living parent but was raised outside the home in an institution with little family contact or sense of belonging.

"Come inside." The nun's voice from the doorway broke through Kaz's miserable thoughts. When he looked at her, he was reminded of chalk dust smudged on one's face after clapping blackboard erasers. Her forehead and cheeks were nearly as white as the garments she wore. Tiny wrinkles ran in rivulets down her face. Wide eyes peered at him expectantly. His mother nudged him forward. He followed the nun into the building and down a short hallway to an office commanded by a grand, mahogany desk covered with rows of neatly stacked papers and folders. Carefully arranged books lined a shelf on the wall to his right. The nun settled into a chair behind the desk and motioned for her guests to take the two chairs facing her. Her hand betrayed a slight tremor while she picked up one of the folders and read the paper inside.

"Mrs. Kowalski, we have agreed to care for Kaz, but since you are not paying for his room and board, we shall do so in exchange for his labor." The nun turned her wide eyes to Kaz. "You will attend school in the morning and do chores in the afternoon. Is that understood?"

Kaz nodded in numbed silence. There was nothing else to say. His fate was sealed.

The next few months trudged by in a procession of mindless days and nights. Classes on history, geography, language and mathematics were taught each morning by the nuns in two classrooms filled with rows of tables and stiff, wooden chairs. Poor ventilation made the rooms overly warm and stuffy, which made it nearly impossible to pay attention. Heads drooped and eyelids fluttered, until one of the nuns cracked a few backsides with a cane. Most of the students attended bible studies in the afternoons. Not Kaz. He and two other boys washed dishes, scrubbed floors and cleaned toilets to earn their keep. It was better than being stuck in religious classes, he consoled himself, but he still felt trapped. He longed to escape and to explore the city. Twice, he did manage to slip away, but he was caught both times while sneaking back into the building and punished with five cane lashings across the backs of his hands. He was sent to bed without supper.

His prospects brightened when he demonstrated a penchant for fixing things. It began with a leaking water pipe that needed tightening with a wrench, then a faulty light switch that had a loose wire, followed by a stopped-up bathtub. Next, he found some putty and patched a hole in the wall where a boy had kicked it in anger. When he wasn't certain what to do, he got permission to visit a supply store for advice and materials. He was soon relieved of his cleaning duties in favor of performing handyman chores and running errands.

Life at the orphanage settled into a routine. There were nearly fifty children, half girls, ranging in age from four to eighteen. The younger ones were mostly true orphans. No one came to see them. The older ones were often social orphans, like Kaz, and some of them received sporadic visits on Sundays from a family member, usually a mother. Not Kaz. His mother never came. Nor his uncle and aunt. At first, he watched these family encounters with a jealous eye and wished there was someone who cared enough to visit him, but when he saw how anguished many of the children were after the parent left, he decided it was better to be left alone.

Children were separated by age at two long dining tables for meals, younger at one, older at the other, and in the two classrooms. They were separated by gender for sleeping, four to a room, and bathroom facilities. Kaz was nearly fourteen, now, and shared his room with two boys about his age, along with a bigger boy named Edmund who was a year or two older. Kaz saw at once that Edmund was a bully who enjoyed bossing the younger boys around. They laughed at his antics and did their best to keep him in a good mood. Kaz ignored him. He just wanted to be left alone. But before long, Edmund turned his attention to Kaz, and he knew that he had to do something. He'd dealt with bullies before at school and found them to have more bluster than fight in them. So, when Edmund shoved him aside one morning on the way to the bathroom, Kaz spun him around and hit him on the nose. Edmund barked in surprise as blood trickled down his chin and ran to the nuns. Kaz accepted his five lashings without uttering a word. Edmund didn't try to bully him again.

The day Kaz's world changed, the day his heart leaped and his eyes lit up, began like any other, filled with dreary classes in a stuffy room.

He was staring out the window, ignoring the teacher's lesson on Polish grammar and longing for something to break the monotony, when the wide-eyed nun walked through the door followed by a girl with a hesitant smile. Brown, shoulder-length hair framed an oval face with a slightly flared nose. A pair of alert, green eyes peeked out from under dark eyebrows and quickly surveyed the room. The nun introduced her as Christina Nowak. Her expression was shy but curious. She wore a black skirt and white blouse buttoned to her slender neck. When she walked between the rows of desks, she reminded Kaz of a sapling swaying ever so slightly in a summer breeze.

The boy who usually sat beside Kaz was in the infirmary with a fever, and Kaz looked at the empty chair with a mixture of panic and hope. He was old enough to have an interest in girls, but he had yet to pair off with one. He teased and bantered with them, but that was all. There had not been any hand holding or exploratory kisses. He had not yet figured out how such a relationship worked, or what to do. So, when Christina stopped and slipped into the vacant seat next to him, Kaz became as flustered as a newborn calf. He avoided looking at her, and she ignored him. The teacher droned on about adverbs and adjectives, while he sat bewildered, not listening to a word being spoken. He suddenly wished he was back in blood alley challenging a train. At least there, he knew what to do. Here, he was all at sea.

"I'm Kaz," he blurted when the lesson was finished. Chairs were scraping around him as students rose to leave. "Kaz Kowinsky. Well, Kowalski, now. Used to be Kowinsky." He blushed and shut his mouth.

She faced him with a lively look that Kaz hoped showed interest. "I'm Christina, but you heard that already. Why are you no longer Kowinsky?"

Kaz explained about his uncle and aunt, then lowered he eyes and told her about his mother.

"That's awful," she responded with a pinched face. "My father died in the war, and my mother has taken a job in Krakow, but I can't go with her just yet. I do have a grandmother, but she's too sick to take care of me." Her tone grew wistful. "So, I'm here until my mother comes for me, although I don't know how long that will be."

The room was almost empty. Kaz stood to leave. "I have to do chores, but maybe I'll see you later," he said, hopefully.

"That would be nice." Christina smiled and walked away.

During the next few months, Kaz basked in their growing friendship. He didn't think they were a couple, exactly, although he did take her hand sometimes when they were alone. The touch of her flesh always sent sparks flying up his arm. It was enough that they sought each other's company. They soon discovered an attic above the third floor where they could hide away from the other children and from the watchful eyes of the nuns, and talk about everything from disappointments in the past to hopes for the future. When Kaz told her about his escapade in blood alley, she sucked in her breath.

"Why would you take such a chance? Are you crazy?"

"Sometimes, I guess. I don't know." He shifted uncomfortably.

"Well, don't do it again," she scolded him.

"I don't want to. Once was enough."

"I should hope so. I'd hate to lose you." She leaned over and kissed him on the cheek, causing more sparks to fly across his surprised face.

The kiss and the words spread over Kaz with the warmth of hot chocolate on a wintry day. The room tilted. He feared that if he stood up, he would fall over. His face reddened, and he smiled. It was the first time he'd been kissed by a girl, even on the cheek, and it made his heart flutter. Somehow, the word 'friend' didn't apply any more. Charlie was his best friend, and he missed him, but this was different. He missed Christina in a more indefinable way when she wasn't with him. He wanted to be close to her, to stay with her. That raised a new problem. Staying close to Christina might not be an option. They lived in an orphanage where children left without warning, some back to parents, others to strangers' homes. What would he do if she left? He would run away, he decided, back to Krakow where he could find Christina. That would take money, however, something he didn't have. Without it, he was trapped. Dark clouds were forming on his horizon, once more. He needed a plan.

"Do you have any money?" he asked Christina a few days later when they were alone in the attic.

"Some." She looked surprised by the question. "My mother sends me a little when she can."

"Can I borrow it, just for a week or two?"

"Why?" Suspicion crept into her voice.

"I've been thinking about what's going to happen. One of these days, your mother will come for you. When that happens, I want to leave, too, but I can't without money. I've got an idea how to make some, but I need a little to get started."

Christina sat in silence. Children's voices could be heard squealing in the back yard. Kaz tensed and waited for her answer.

"Where will you go?" she asked, ignoring his question.

He scratched the back of his head in thought. "Not my mother's. She'd just send me back here. Besides, you'll be in Krakow. Maybe I can hop a freight there. Beg my uncle for a place to stay. He might take me back if I pay for my keep."

Christina frowned and took his hand. "Krakow's a big city. Give me your uncle's address. I could give him a message."

Kaz's skin tingled from the warmth of her touch. He shook his head. "I've already thought about that. I'm not sure how much I can trust him. It's better if you contact my friend, Charlie. I'll give you his address. You can tell him where you're staying. "

"Okay," she agreed. "I'll loan you my money. Tell me your idea."

It was a simple plan. The older boys liked to smoke cigarettes and to drink beer, but there was little opportunity. Visits in the city were strictly supervised by the nuns, and even when one or two did manage to slip away and buy such contraband, there was little time to enjoy it and no way to sneak it into the orphanage. Pockets and bags were carefully examined when they returned from such outings. Kaz, on the other hand, was free to come and go with little oversight. During the afternoons, he often ran errands and bought materials to fix things. He'd already made contact with street vendors who could get him bottles of beer and Chesterfields, an American cigarette brand that was particularly popular with the boys. He hid his booty in an air shaft behind the abandoned factory next door and sold the merchandise to his classmates at premium prices. It only took two weeks to pay back Christina's loan. Soon, he was stashing a growing wad of zlotys in the air shaft along with his booty.

Things went so smoothly over the next few months, Kaz began to dream about making enough money to finance both of their escapes. His dream vanished in a puff of smoke one Sunday when he discovered that Christina had disappeared. The nuns never discussed such things, but the wide-eyed nun took pity on him and confirmed what Kaz already suspected. The mother had come and taken Christina early that morning. She couldn't say where they'd gone, but Kaz was pretty sure it was Krakow.

Chapter Five

Kaz spent the next few months hoarding his money and planning his escape. One afternoon, he visited the train yards to check the schedules of freight trains headed for Krakow. He was disheartened to find two guards patrolling the area. He was even more discouraged to see several men in rough clothes skulking about. Two of them quickly jumped into an empty boxcar when the guards were gone. It was possible to outwit the guards, he saw, but he didn't like the looks of the men. They didn't seem like the kind of people he'd want to run into with a pocket full of zlotys. It would be safer to save a bit more money and buy a ticket. He checked the passenger schedule and found a train leaving every afternoon for Krakow at two. Satisfied, he finished his errands and hurried back to the orphanage.

Three weeks later, he was ready. He hid a bag of clothes in the abandoned building next door and waited for his chance. The first two days, he was sent on quick errands. Neither offered sufficient time for him to reach the station and to catch the two o'clock train before being missed. On the third day, he broke the plunger used to clear stopped-up toilets and was sent to buy a new one. The plumbing supply store was farther away. It would be an hour or two before he was missed. He grabbed his clothes and ran for the train station.

Wawel Castle rose in the distance to greet Kaz as he trudged along the streets of Krakow. Confusing emotions churned inside his stomach. Apprehension at facing his uncle jangled his nerves, but nostalgia at seeing his aunt tugged at him, as well. When he reached the familiar, crumbling apartment building, he halted long enough to overcome his anxiousness before climbing the four flights of stairs.

Kaz smelled cooked cabbage and potatoes when he rapped his knuckles on the door. His knock stirred the patter of small feet beyond the door. A tiny voice squealed and a chair scraped the floor. A male voice mumbled something Kaz couldn't hear, then the door swung open. Kaz was greeted by a look of astonishment on his uncle's face and a small child holding a teddy bear and sucking his thumb.

"What are you doing here?" Uncle asked in a surprised voice that was mixed with a hint of irritation. There was no welcoming smile or embrace.

His aunt rose from the kitchen table where remnants of dinner lay scattered about and hurried to the door.

"I left the orphanage. I'm not going back," Kaz declared with as much bravado as he could muster.

"Orphanage?" His aunt looked confused. "What orphanage?"

"The one mother put me in."

"She never said anything about an orphanage," Uncle responded. "She told me you were living with her and going to school."

Kaz shook his head. "I got some schooling, but I haven't seen her since the day you sent me to Warsaw." Reproach tinged his voice.

His aunt rushed forward and gave him the hug he'd been missing for the past year. His body shook. Try as he might, he couldn't hide his emotions. Little Jozef watched them and ran forward crying 'mommy' in a fit of jealousy. She swept him into her arms and stepped aside for Kaz to enter.

They sat around the table while Kaz told them about the orphanage, Christina and his money making scheme. "I've got enough zlotys to pay for food for awhile," he announced. "And I've had enough of school. I want to work, pay my way."

"You can stay here awhile, I guess." Uncle rubbed his chin. "As long as you work. I'm still only part-time with this darned leg." He smacked his thigh in disgust. "I'll inform your mother. Don't think she'll care from the sounds of it. See what kind of job I can find you. I still know some people at the train yard."

Kaz pulled a handful of zlotys from his pocket and handed them to his uncle with a smile. It was as close as he ever got to feeling he'd come home.

The next day, Kaz hunted down Charlie and discovered a dashing young man in place of the rangy boy he'd last seen. His body had filled out with muscle, his bright eyes flashed with mischief and his smile charmed the world. They laughed, embraced and slapped each other's back.

"Woz is gone," Charlie announced sadly. "His folks moved to Gdansk. But Christina's here. She'll join us later by the river."

Kaz brightened at the good news. He couldn't wait to see her again.

A side-wheeler boat churned its way upriver while Kaz and Charlie waited for Christina. He'd thought about her a lot the past few months, wondered what sort of relationship they might have away from the orphanage. He knew they had not declared themselves to be more than just friends, but he hoped they might do so now.

In the end, the reunion was as bitter as it was sweet. Christina arrived with a shriek of joy and threw her arms around him. She planted a kiss on his cheek that warmed his soul, but when she withdrew, she stood next to Charlie. It was a subtle gesture, but for Kaz it spoke volumes. They didn't hold hands or touch; they didn't need to. He could interpret the body language between them. A burst of jealousy sparked Kaz's anger. His eyes blinked in disbelief. Denial swept over him. He was imagining things, he thought. His mind was playing tricks. It wasn't, though, and he knew it. Charlie's handsome face sported a sheepish grin, and Christina looked at him awkwardly. In a final declaration, she took Charlie's hand. Kaz wanted to scream in frustration at what he saw. Instead, he smiled. His anger faded, replaced by sadness.

It was always the same, he realized. Loving relationships remained just beyond his grasp. His mother. Uncle. Christina. They all tantalized him, but he always found himself on the outside looking in.

Under the iron fist of Pilsudski, Poland was slowly progressing. The economy was growing, and despite ongoing tensions with peasants and laborers, many men were able to find jobs. Pride and optimism were on the rise, although the working class remained restless. Unemployment still threatened many livelihoods.

None of this affected Kaz. His uncle found him an apprentice position in the rail yards working for a company that made metal parts for the trains. His boss was a gruff old man sporting a large belly named Filas. Filas didn't care what his workers thought of him. He pushed everybody to work hard, long hours. Kaz started on the forge, a hot, miserable job that taxed all his strength. He'd been promised a promotion after six months to an apprentice position as a machinist, but a year later, he was still struggling in the forge. Filas was in no hurry to let him go, and he delighted in criticizing his work. One of the machinists took pity on him, and when Filas wasn't around, he called Kaz over and taught him how to use a lathe and another machine that stamped parts from metal sheets. Kaz enjoyed working the machines and looked forward to his time with the machinist, but as soon as Filas was spotted, he had to drop what he was doing and move back to the forge. Filas would inevitably yell at him for being lazy and working too slowly. Kaz kept his head down and focused on his task.

Home life was equally difficult. He came home too late to eat with the family, so Aunt left a warm plate of potatoes and meat for him. While he ate, Jozef buzzed around the apartment with the energy of a bumblebee. Kaz had to share the second bedroom with him, which proved a challenge, because Jozef screamed and threw temper tantrums when Kaz wouldn't let him have his way. Kaz tried to be friends, but it was obvious Jozef resented sharing his tiny room with an intruder.

In desperation, he joined his fellow workers for beers after work at a local bar. By the time he got home, his plate of food was cold, but at least Jozef was in bed and the apartment was quiet. His prospects looked bleak, until one night when a worker named Dominik from the rail yard remarked that they needed more men to drive the trains. Kaz thought about the times he'd joined his uncle at the steel mill and learned how to work the train's levers.

"I can do that," he exclaimed. "I can drive a train."

The men chuckled. "You're a kid," one answered derisively. "What do you know about trains?"

"My uncle used to drive the train at the steel mill. He taught me."

Dominik gave him a hard stare. "You look mighty young, but we need people. Show up tomorrow at eight. We'll see what you can do."

"I have to be at the forge at eight. I'll be there at seven."

The man laughed and nodded. "Seven, then."

Kaz's heart thumped in his chest when he arrived at the rail yard early the next morning. He knew he was sticking his neck out with his claim, and if Filas found out what he was doing, he would catch hell. He *had* driven trains on several occasions, but only from the mill to the storage yards, and always under the watchful guidance of his uncle. He was pretty sure he remembered what to do, but he hadn't a clue how to drive a train outside the rail yard. He clamped his teeth with determination. He had to get the job, or it was back to the forge and the contemptuous remarks of Filas.

Dominik arrived with one of the engineers who drove the trains and took Kaz to an engine standing on a sidetrack.

"Take her up to the wheel house," the engineer commanded.

Kaz hitched up his pants and pulled himself into the engine's cab, followed by the engineer. He smiled with relief when he saw the controls. They were the same as those on the train driven by his uncle. The engineer settled into the rider's seat and waited for Kaz to get underway. Kaz started the engine, set the controls to forward, took a deep breath and released the brake. The engine churned to life and moved slowly down the track. When he reached the wheelhouse, he applied the brake and brought the locomotive to a halt. Relieved, he smiled at the engineer as he hopped down from the cab. Dominik arrived on foot moments later. He stood aside to confer with the engineer while Kaz watched them expectantly.

"Not bad," Dominik said when they were finished. "Have you driven trains outside the rail yard?"

Kaz cringed. It was the question he feared. A lie flew to his lips, but he realized it would do him no good. The truth would be exposed soon enough, and he would be out of a job. He looked Dominik in the eye and shook his head no.

"I thought as much," the engineer remarked, "but you have some experience. That counts for something."

"And I like your spirit," Dominik added. "Tell you what. We'll start you off as a stoker, shoveling coal to the engine's furnace. The engineer will show you what to do."

Kaz returned to the forge in triumph. It would be his last day under the harsh thumb of Filas. Tomorrow, he would become a stoker, someday soon an engineer. Filas flew into a rage when he heard the news. He stormed at Kaz, even threatened him with his tongs. Kaz stood his ground. Nobody in the yard liked Filas. Kaz wasn't the only one he berated, but Kaz had taken the worst of his insults for the past year. It was time to plot a little revenge.

Filas followed the same routine everyday. At twelve, he left for lunch, and he returned precisely at one o'clock. Once he was gone, Kaz heated the handles of Filas's tongs until they were red hot, then rubbed wet ashes on them with a thick cloth to make them appear normal. He laid them on the workbench and hid in the yard. Everybody saw what was about to happen. Tension zigzagged through the air as they all waited. Filas tramped into the forge right on schedule. The first tool he grabbed was his beloved tongs. At first, the thick calluses on his hands protected him from the heat, but as he gripped the handles tighter, he got the full treatment. A bellow split the air as he jerked his hands away and dropped the tongs. Furiously, he looked around for Kaz. The men in the yard began to laugh. No one came to his aid. Kaz watched as Filas stormed around the forge, then he strolled away. He didn't dare try to collect his last pay voucher, but it was worth it. The next day he reported to his new job.

A year slid by in a blur. Kaz saw Charlie when he could, but they no longer had leisure weekends to enjoy at the river. He was often gone for a week at a time, which was just as well. He still suffered bouts of jealousy when he saw his best friend with Christina, and the walls of the bedroom he shared with Jozef were closing ever more tightly around him.

Kaz worked hard as a stoker, but he didn't mind. He delighted in watching the towns, fields and mountains rushing past as he rode the trains across Poland. He enjoyed the air whooshing though his hair when he stuck his head out the cab's window. Best of all, he savored the hours he spent with the engineer learning about signals, schedules, safe speeds and routes. He was soon driving the trains with confidence. He knew it wouldn't be long before someone else was shoveling the coal.

The first time he drove a train into blood alley, Kaz watched in amazement as two men jumped the tracks in front of him. Neither came close to hitting the train, but their effort sent hot blood rushing to his brain. It amazed him to think that he had once stood by those tracks ready to defy the odds.

Kaz's dreams about taking the engineer's seat were unceremoniously interrupted by an economic depression that began rolling across Europe. Poland's fragile economy crumpled under the weight of lost trade and jobs. Kaz had never paid much attention to America, but when he was told about a stock market crash that was unleashing chaos in the country, he worried that Poland would somehow be affected. The impact on Europe was soon evident. Exports dropped, banks stopped lending and workers were laid off. Beggars took to the streets. His uncle lost his part-time job almost at once, which made Kaz the only source of money in the family. Meat quickly disappeared from the table. More potatoes were served. As people cut back on the amount of food they could afford, farmers overproduced and food prices tumbled. Peasants could not afford to harvest and sell their crops. They had to let their food rot in the fields while the cities went hungry.

At first, Kaz's job seemed secure. Trains kept rolling and the rail yard remained busy. But as businesses lost customers and demand for goods and services fell, orders for products and raw materials plummeted. Trains stopped running as frequently. Fewer stokers were needed. Kaz reported to work one morning to discover that the forge had closed. A week later, his job was gone. As one of the newest employees, he was among the first to be let go. He counted the zlotys in his pocket. Enough for a few weeks, but that was all.

Chaos continued to rain down. Christina's mother lost her job, and they returned to Warsaw to live with her ailing grandmother. Charlie was crestfallen. Even Kaz felt the loss despite his resentment about her and Charlie. He spent a night consoling his friend, all the while trying to suppress a twinge of satisfaction that came from knowing that she was lost to both of them. Then, Charlie's family left, as well, and Kaz felt abandoned, again.

The only bright spot was the Polish military, which was bolstering its forces in the face of possible threats from Germany and Russia. The army was only taking men twenty-one and older, but the navy would consider younger recruits with written consent from a parent. Kaz visited the recruiting office and brought home the required documents for his uncle to sign.

"I'm not your legal guardian," his uncle informed him as he studied the papers. "They won't accept my signature unless I can show legal custody, which I can't."

"What about my mother?"

Uncle shook his head. "She's still furious with you for leaving the orphanage and exposing her lie."

Kaz sat in frustrated silence. It seemed that every avenue he tried was blocked. His opportunities were slipping away.

"There is another option," his uncle continued hesitantly. "You've never asked and I've never said, but there might be a way to find your father."

Kaz straightened in his chair and looked at his uncle. "What do you mean? You said you didn't know anything about him."

"I don't, but I know someone who might. A Mrs. Ragowska. She's some sort of distant cousin of his. Your mother mentioned her one time. Never met her, but I know she lives here in Krakow."

Kaz's heart was suddenly beating intensely. Could the man who'd remained hidden in the shadows all those years be real? Could he find him? It seemed too much for him to hope. It wasn't just a signature on the navy's papers that excited him. It was the prospect of finally meeting the missing link from his past.

City records showed that Mrs. Ragowska lived on Janowa Wola Street, but there was no address. Fortunately, the street was only a few blocks long, so Kaz started at one end and began knocking on doors. It didn't take long to find an old woman who knew her.

"Children think she's a witch," she gossiped. "Stays secluded. Won't talk much to neighbors. The young ones used to sneak into her yard to look at chickens she keeps in back, but she chased them with a broom. Warned them to stay away. Not very friendly, but doesn't bother nobody."

Kaz found the rundown house described by the neighbor and knocked on a door with a tiny window covered by a lace curtain. He was greeted by silence. Kaz knocked, again, and this time heard a board creek beyond the door. The lace curtain moved to reveal an angry, wrinkled face with black eyes that gave him a piercing glare. Kaz retreated a step. She did look like a witch, he thought.

"What do you want?" a gravelly voice demanded.

"My name is Kaz Kowalski. You know my father."

The eyes continued to stare. Then, the lace curtain closed, and the door rattled open to disclose a stocky, gray-haired woman wrapped in a shawl.

"You're Kaz Kowalski?" Disbelief displaced the anger in her voice. "Yes, I can see the resemblance. You have your father's jaw, very strong and firm. Come in. Come in." Her mouth broadened into a welcoming smile. The witch's fierce gaze was gone. "I had no idea you were in Krakow. Last I heard, you were in Czechoslovakia."

Kaz looked at her in amazement. "We've lived here for years," he informed her as she led him into a sitting room filled with shelves of dusty books. An overfed, brown cat mewed from a chair in the corner.

"The families haven't stayed in touch. I lost track of you a long time ago."

Mrs. Ragowska made tea while Kaz talked about relatives and explained the purpose of his visit.

"Joseph was always a strange man," she commented after they were both seated with cups in their hands. "His world was inside his head. I haven't spoken to him in several years."

"But you know where he is?" Kaz asked hopefully.

The old lady studied his face as if she was deciding on her next words. She tipped her cup to drain the last drops of tea, rose from her chair and walked to the window.

With her back to Kaz, she said softly, "Last I knew, he lived in Czestochowa. That's the shrine of St. Mary of Czestochowa, the place of miracles. You might find him there. Check the city records. I imagine that's how you found me."

She turned and looked at Kaz with a tired smile. Kaz wanted to ask more questions, but she pressed her hand to her lips. Like an oracle, she had made her revelation and had nothing more to say.

Kaz boarded a train to Czestochowa the next day and went straight to the city records department. Sure enough, he found an address for a Joseph Kowalski, but when he went there, he learned that his father had moved three years ago without leaving a forwarding address. In a city the size of Czestochowa, he knew it would, indeed, take a miracle to find him, but he couldn't give up. He needed a signature on the papers in his pocket, and he wanted to take the measure of the man who had abandoned him all those years ago. He wanted to put that chapter of his life behind him. So, he spent the next day bouncing from city office to city office in search of someone who might give him a lead. His persistence paid off when he stumbled into the department of city tax records. At first, the man in charge didn't want to help, but when Kaz explained his dilemma and pleaded with him, he relented. After shuffling through several boxes in a large room filled with shelves of boxes, he pulled down the one he wanted. His fingers rifled through a stack of papers so quickly, Kaz could hardly follow them. The hands stopped and pulled a page from the files with the flair of a magician. Kaz could see his father's name, Joseph Kowalski, and a new address.

Kaz followed the directions offered by the clerk and arrived at the house, a rundown duplex in the outskirts of the city. He stood at the bottom of six stairs and eyed the building. It looked bruised and foreboding. A brisk wind chilled his neck. Nerves caused his hands to shake. It took several deep breaths and all his courage to overcome his inertia and to mount the stairs to the front door. After years of wondering, he was about to confront the man responsible for giving him life. He knew he should be filled with expectation and excitement, but the man had shown no interest in him over the years, had made no effort to contact him. Still, he *was* his father. Surely, that meant something. He sighed as he reached the door.

A haggard, middle-aged woman with a slack jaw and an ashen colored face answered his knock by holding the door ajar and staring at him with suspicion.

"I'm looking for Joseph Kowalski," Kaz announced. "Is he here?"

"Who wants to know?"

"Kaz Kowalski. I'm his son." The words rang hollow in his ears, as if they were spoken in a foreign tongue.

The door inched open a bit wider, enough for Kaz to see a man standing behind the woman. The man's hands quivered as he studied Kaz. "Don't have a son. Just two daughters. They're grown and gone, now." He raised a trembling hand to his face and rubbed his cheek. He appeared lost in thought.

Kaz looked at the man in disbelief. There was no mistaking the similarity in their facial features, especially the jaw and mouth. The anger that had risen to his tongue dissipated. The man standing before him was his father, no doubt, but he wasn't the vigorous man Kaz had envisioned. This man was frail, his body too thin and his hands unsteady. Pity wormed its way into his thoughts. How could this crumpled figure be his father?

"Your daughters were by a different woman. You had me with Katarzyna." A note of defiance crept into Kaz's voice. He'd come too far to be turned away by simple denial. "Look at me. You can see yourself in me."

Joseph leaned against the door. A look of bewilderment crossed his face. "I see it," he said at last. "Katarzyna claimed she had a boy after I left, but I didn't believe it was mine. She whored around. It could've been anybody's."

The door opened wider. "Come in."

The place was shabby, littered with newspapers, empty glasses and casually tossed clothes. Joseph's clothing was wrinkled and frayed at the cuffs. He didn't bother to introduce the woman who hovered in the doorway. He poured cheap vodka into two dirty glasses and handed one to Kaz, who ignored the lipstick on the rim and drank down the fiery liquid in a single gulp. Kaz hoped it would ease the depression that suddenly engulfed him. The pity he'd felt was gone, along with the need to know his father. All he wanted to do was finish his business and escape the place. He pulled the navy's papers from his pocket and explained what he needed. Joseph shrugged his shoulders and signed where Kaz indicated in a perfunctory manner.

Kaz fled the house as soon as they were done, relieved to be back among the noises of the city and the throngs of people going about their business. He didn't look back or feel a pang of regret at leaving so quickly. There was nothing there for him. He'd finally met the man who hid in the shadows of his life, but it made little difference. He knew he would never see him again.

Chapter Six

In late September, Kaz boarded a train for Tczew, the rail station for the military outpost thirty miles south of Gdansk. He joined some two thousand other naval candidates from all over Poland who arrived for a rigorous three months of screening and training. Men in navy uniforms waited for them at the station and divided them into groups of twenty. Each group was loaded into a lorry and transported to the reception center, where they were marched into a cavernous meeting hall and told to disrobe. For the next hour, everyone milled about, naked and shivering in the unheated building, while clerks checked off names against a master list of recruits. Once they were satisfied that everybody was registered, three doctors in white coats entered and called for the groups to line up in rows. Kaz rubbed his arms as he took his place in line, conscious of his short stature and young age. Now that he saw all the older, taller men around him, he feared he wouldn't be considered.

The doctors each took a third of the room and began inspecting the recruits, who stood at attention and tried not to look as cold as they felt. As the doctors moved down the lines, they stopped in front of each man. They tapped some on the shoulder and asked them to step back. Others, they ignored and moved on. It didn't take long for Kaz to realize that the ones moved out of the lines appeared less fit than the others, demonstrated by such physical traits as bulging bellies, sagging arms or weak posture. The recruits were being judged like cattle at a county fair. When the doctor reached him, Kaz stood as tall as he could and looked the man squarely in the eyes. He was pleased that he'd filled out in his arms, shoulders and legs, but he still worried about his height. The doctor looked at him skeptically and moved on. He hadn't touched Kaz's shoulder or told him to step back. He'd survived the first round of selection! Sure enough, when the inspection was finished, those singled out were told to retrieve their clothes and to go home. Kaz estimated that about one-third of the recruits had been dismissed.

Those who remained were told to gather their clothes and to march down a long, drafty corridor to a series of examination rooms where more doctors checked teeth, eyes, hearing, lungs, heart, coordination and feet. After each step in the examination was completed, Kaz received a different colored mark on his right arm. By the time he was finished, his arm looked like an Easter egg and more men were missing. Some of the Easter eggs had been sent home.

The process concluded at a supply station where long lines of men with arms decorated with red, orange, blue, yellow and purple marks waited impatiently while clerks doled out uniforms that never seemed to quite fit. Finally, they were marched to their barracks and told to stand in front of their assigned bunks. The squad of twenty had been reduced to twelve. The empty bunks were quickly assigned to eight men from other units. Each man announced his name and hometown. Kaz was the only one from Krakow.

The three months of boot camp training seemed more like three years. Every day, the recruits rose at dawn, ate a quick breakfast and began the day's drills, which included rifle assembly and care, target practice, digging trenches, marching, horsemanship and more. None of the drills had anything to do with water or boats. All of the drills were accompanied by orders delivered in loud voices and push-ups when things were not done to the drill sergeant's satisfaction. Kaz understood that they were pushing the men to their limits so they could weed out the weakest recruits, but it didn't make the days any easier or shorter.

The last few weeks were sandwiched around Christmas, and most of the men were given a four-day furlough to see their families. However, a skeleton crew was needed at the base, and extra pay was offered to those who remained. Kaz thought about his options. Christina and Charlie were gone, and he had little interest in seeing his uncle or sharing Jozef's room again. It was better to stay at the base. Those who remained spent Christmas day playing horseshoes or lounging around in their tents. Everyone was bored by the time they trooped into the mess hall for dinner.

Kaz was in the middle of his meal when a low ranking officer entered and called out his name for latrine duty. He wasn't thrilled to be singled out on Christmas night for such an assignment, but he knew better than to complain. It was another test, and he had to face it, but not until after he'd finished his dinner. He lowered his head and took another bite of his food.

"What are you waiting for?" the officer demanded. "Drop your knife and fork and report to the detail leader immediately."

Anger crept up the back of Kaz's neck. It was bad enough that some low ranking officer demanded that he do latrine duty on

Christmas night, but not being allowed to finish his dinner was more than he could tolerate. "I'll report as soon as I've finished eating, sir," he replied through clenched teeth.

"You go now," the officer barked. "You've dawdled all day. It's time to do some work."

Kaz felt like he was back in the school yard facing Charlie for the first time. He wanted to avoid trouble, but he couldn't back down. His temper flared beyond his control. "Either let me finish my dinner or throw me in the brig."

"Are you disobeying an order?" the officer shouted. Tendons stood out in his neck.

"No sir. I just want to finish my Christmas dinner. I'll report when I'm done."

The officer's face turned a blotchy red. Kaz tensed in anticipation of another tirade, but to his surprise, the officer turned and stomped out of the mess hall without saying another word. Ten minutes later, Kaz reported as ordered, gathered his mop, soap and bucket of water, and started cleaning the floors of the latrines. He was nearly finished when the door opened and the glowering officer thundered in with muddy slush on his feet. He crossed the room, stopped in front of Kaz and pointed to the muddy footprints he'd just made on the wet floor.

"You call that floor clean?" he bellowed.

"Not any more, sir."

"Then wash it again." The officer took up a position five feet away, feet spread and hands on hips. His glittering eyes followed Kaz's every move. Kaz tried his best to ignore the man, who reminded him of a snarling dachshund yapping at his heels. No sooner had Kaz wiped the floor clean, than the officer strode back across the offending area.

"You missed some spots. Do it again."

Kaz glared at the officer, but held his temper. He quickly re-mopped the area. Again, the officer tracked muddy footprints across the clean floor. "You'll keep doing it until you get it right," he yelled.

Kaz's anger grew hotter, not so much at the officer as at himself for staying on the base for Christmas. Why hadn't he taken the four-day pass and gone to Krakow? He would have been enjoying his aunt's cooking right now, or watching Jozef play, instead of standing in the latrine matching wits with a dachshund.

The ritual was repeated.

"I'll show you country boys how to clean a toilet, or I'll soak your scurvy head in it." The officer's shrill voice bounced off the tile walls and echoed around the room.

Kaz had had enough. Without a word, he withdrew his mop from the bucket of soapy water and slapped it across the officer's scowling face. His timing was spot on. The man opened his mouth to shout another command just as the mop smacked into it with a soggy 'plop.' The officer reeled backwards from the unexpected blow and sat down on the floor. Spitting and sputtering, he jumped back up, but instead of attacking Kaz, he ran from the room, wiping soapy water from his mouth as he fled.

Kaz wanted to laugh, but he knew better. He was in enough trouble already. In a matter of minutes, the officer barreled back through the door, followed by the company commander. The commander snapped Kaz to attention and berated him for striking an officer, all the while shaking a riding crop under Kaz's nose. Kaz stood in rigid silence and held the mop at his side as if it were a rifle. He did his best to look contrite, but every time he saw the remnants of soapy water still decorating the officer's face, it was all he could do to suppress a smile.

Kaz learned his lesson the hard way. He spent the next two weeks sleeping on a hard cot in a drafty cell and pulling latrine duty every day. He figured it was worth it. The officer who'd made his life so miserable never interrupted his meal again.

At the end of January, Kaz finished boot camp and received a duty assignment for advanced training aboard one of the navy's ships. Kaz soon learned that 'ship' was a loose term used to describe anything that could float. Most of the rusted ships he saw in the harbor at Gdynia were so antiquated he feared they might not sail at all. Many of the crew were in no better shape. The boat he'd drawn was called the Haller, a gunboat that had been built in Germany before the war. When he boarded with his duffel bag draped over his shoulder, he stumbled over a drunken sailor who was sitting on the deck. A boatswain greeted him and showed him to his quarters, which consisted of a cramped space with unmade bunk beds stacked three high and refuse strewn about the floor. Kaz chose the top bunk on the theory that it would be cleaner and less cluttered up there. He was told that the captain and most of the crew had gone ashore and would return later that day. Kaz decided to explore the vessel on his own. The briny air invigorated him as he wandered across the decks. The holds were a different matter. Fresh air failed to reach most of those musty places. They smelled of mold and overripe bodies. Nothing had been cleaned or repaired for months, including the engine room where grime covered the engines and the main boiler leaked.

The ship made short trips during the next few weeks along the coast while Kaz and the other new members of the crew drilled on procedures and gunnery. Ammunition was dear, so they didn't get to fire the guns. However, Kaz was soon adept at swiveling the big cannon into position and raising it to the specified height. All seemed to be going well until they encountered their first storm. The seas turned black and began to heave the small ship through great swells whose peaks rose higher than the forecastle. Several of the sailors promptly got sick and spent most of their time hanging over the rails, where they were soaked by the pounding waves. Dark skies and heavy spray made it difficult to see.

Suddenly, the ship jolted to a halt. Kaz was thrown to the deck, where he desperately sought a handhold to save him from sliding across the slick surface and splitting his head open on some metal casing. Word quickly spread that they had run aground on a rocky promontory. The ship was listing thirty degree to starboard, and it seemed to Kaz only a matter of time until it slipped beneath the unforgiving waves that were pounding the hull. It dawned on him that during all his training, no one had asked him if he could swim. He thought about those lazy afternoons swimming in the Vistula River and smiled. His smile quickly faded when he looked at the seas surrounding him. He doubted that he could survive in those waters for very long.

The captain sent out a frantic SOS and everyone cheered when a sister ship, the Pilsudski, hove into view. The ship maneuvered closely enough for lines to be cast between the two ships, and backed away before the heavy seas caused it to crash into the Haller. The lines were quickly secured, and the Pilsudski began to tug the Haller from its stony perch. The crew held its breath as the hull screeched against the rocks. Kaz was certain the rocks were tearing holes in the side of the ship, but after several agonizing minutes, the Haller was pulled to safety with its hull intact. No sooner had the Haller been set free then a new problem emerged. The Pilsudski had somehow fouled its rudder while performing the rescue and was now wallowing in the water with no directional control. It wouldn't be long before the incessant waves pushed the Pilsudski onto the very rocks that had embraced the Haller. To make matters worse, the two ships lost radio contact.

A frantic flag-waving conference produced a risky but necessary solution. The Haller became the rescuer and maneuvered itself alongside the Pilsudski. The two ships banged against one another in the rising and falling swells, but managed to stay close enough for new ropes to be exchanged. Frantic hands grasped the ropes and lashed the ships together. Once that was accomplished, the Haller took directional control for both vessels while the Pilsudski provided power. In this manner, the ships staggered back to port like two drunken sailors, swerving from side-to-side as the Pilsudski engines pushed them too far to port, and the Haller's rudder over corrected.

Kas soon discovered that similar stories abounded throughout the Polish navy. Antiquated ships were outfitted with hand-me-down equipment and were operated by crews that spoke half-a-dozen languages. Somehow, the little navy floundered along.

Kaz was reassigned to an old French cruiser, the Baltic, which never left the pier. Her hull plates were steel, but her underwater surfaces had been covered with thick, wood planking to protect her from floating mines. The additional armor made the ship too unstable to risk in a storm at sea. A long, underwater snout protruded from the bow. It had once been used to ram other ships. Now, it had the look of an aging dragon that couldn't even ram the pier.

Captain Hermann, a relic of the windjammer era, was the Baltic's commander. His sailing experience reached back into the 1800s. He was a heavy-handed, old school sailor who judged a man 'by the cut of his jib' and spent much of his time lamenting the fact that his sailing days were gone forever. He liked to stand at parade rest on the bridge and observe the ship's activities. At the slightest shortcoming of a crewman, his gray mustache would bristle like the quills of an angry porcupine, and he would bellow, "This is a Hell of a navy. In my time, we had wooden ships manned by men of iron. Now, they give me iron ships manned by wooden sailors."

Since the aged Baltic was no longer seaworthy, it had been towed into the port of Gdynia and converted into a floating training school for sailors, with everything from cutaway schematics of the ship's systems to mock-up engines. There was no power on the ship. In fact, the entire ship was blacked out except for a few power lines that had been strung from the shore to operate the machine shop. A sailor took his life in his hands after dark just walking from one end of the ship to the other. The upper decks were alive with rats searching for food and an army of cats searching for the rats. They didn't discourage the captain. He still commanded the ship as if it was being outfitted for a return to the high seas in search of Kaiser U-boats.

Kaz appreciated the discipline Captain Hermann brought to the Baltic, but he yearned for an opportunity to sail on a real ship at sea. One day, the captain announced that he was looking for men who could run lathes and other equipment in the machine shop. Kaz thought about this and decided to take a chance. He went to the captain's quarters and presented himself.

"Sir, I have some training on machines, but I don't want to be permanently assigned here. I want to go to sea. If I volunteer for the machine shop, I fear I'll lose my chance."

The old man studied him. "Can't say as I blame you, son. I wish I could do that myself, but those days are over for me. Tell you what. You take over the lathe, and if you do a good job, I'll keep an eye out for an assignment that will get you off this boat."

"You've got a deal," Kaz exclaimed with a smile.

During the next few months, Kaz demonstrated his skills on the lathe, but he saw no progress toward his goal. He began to wonder if the captain would be true to his word. The old man had always been forthright and done what he promised, so Kaz held his tongue and kept working. Surely, something would break his way. When his opportunity finally came, it was from an unexpected direction.

Kaz was finishing his work for the day when the suntanned face of Commander Stiyer appeared in the doorway. He brushed strands of gray hair underneath his cap as he strode into the room.

"Kowalski?" he inquired.

Kaz snapped to attention. "Yes, sir."

"Captain Hermann tells me if there's anybody aboard this ship who can help me, you're the man." The commander fished a handful of keys on a large brass ring from his pocket and tossed them on the workbench with a resounding thud. "It's these damned keys." He frowned and gestured toward the pile of metal. "I'm responsible for the security of over two dozen locations, and they all require a key to lock and unlock doors. I'm tired of carrying all this weight around, and the keys are ruining my pockets. Is there anything you can do to consolidate them?"

Kaz picked up the ring and fingered through the keys. "They are heavy," he agreed. "They all seem to be cut from the same stock. It might be possible to combine some of them. Give me a little time."

"Good. Bring them to me when you're done."

Kaz had planned on going ashore that night with his mates to drink in a local bar and to chase women, but he sensed this was his opportunity. The captain had recommended him. He was fulfilling his promise. Kaz hunkered down at his lathe and started measuring and comparing the keys. As he suspected, most of them were similar in their cuts. The more he studied them, the more they looked nearly alike. He moved them back and forth on the workbench until he established a pattern. Then, he went to work on the lathe.

Kaz reported to the commander's headquarters the next morning and was shown into an impressive office filled with cabinets, a conference table, and an over-sized desk. He stepped forward, plunked down the ring of keys and dramatically laid a single key next to them.

"As you requested, sir. You can now replace the entire set of keys with this." He pointed to the single key lying on the desk.

The commander raised his eyebrows with astonishment. "I must say, I'm impressed. It appears Captain Hermann is right about you. I understand you would like a new assignment." He rubbed his chin while he thought a moment. "How would you like to join our new submarine division?"

Now, Kaz raised his eyebrows. Submarines spent most of their time under the water, not sailing on top of it. He'd never considered such a possibility, and he wasn't sure how well it suited his interests. A chance was a chance, however. He knew that if he declined this opportunity, it was unlikely that he would get another.

He snapped to attention. "I'd like that very much, sir."

"Good. I'll make the arrangements." The commander picked up the key and stared at it with admiration. "And thank you for my new key."

Three days later, Kaz took his duffel bag and reported to a dock on the far side of the port where a battered German U-boat lay anchored to the wood pilings. He looked at it with misgivings. Compared to his two previous ships, it didn't look much bigger than a bathtub, and its scarred, dented hull suggested that it had seen quite a lot of action. Kaz worried that it might not be any more fit for duty than the Haller.

The inside was every bit as cramped as it appeared. Large tanks on both sides took up much of the space. He learned that they were filled with seawater while diving; the water was expelled for buoyancy when surfacing. More tanks held tons of fuel for the sub's twin diesel engines. Batteries lined the walls, and, of course, there were the torpedo tubes, two each in the bow and the stern. That left only one narrow corridor down the middle for the men, who were expected to eat, work and sleep in less space than his uncle's apartment.

Despite his misgivings, he thrilled at the sound of the great diesels the first time they roared to life, and his heart pounded to the rhythm

POLAND INTERRUPTED

of the propeller blade as the submarine got underway. He tried to maintain his composure, but the first time they dived he couldn't prevent himself from taking a mouthful of air into his lungs and ducking his head. This brought a round of knowing chuckles from the more experienced members of the crew. Kaz noticed that almost half the crew did the same. They were trainees, just like him, and none of them had been underwater before.

They spent the next few weeks learning the controls, filling and emptying the seawater tanks, loading the torpedo tubes and firing duds at stationary targets. Kaz quickly realized that life aboard a submarine was akin to living in a Finnish sauna. Heat built up from the engines and from the crew, and moisture could not be expelled easily. Body odors and the smell of diesel fuel flourished along with the humidity. There were no showers or facilities to bathe. They were down less than a hundred feet, but to Kaz it felt as though each intake of breath would be his last. Every time the craft surfaced, the men gathered by the conning tower and waited for the hatch to open so they could gulp in fresh air.

None of Kaz's training prepared him for one of the most basic functions of the crew: providing human ballast for the submarine. For all its controls and equipment, the tiny craft was quite fragile and subject to even subtle shifts in water currents. The crew had to constantly change their positions to balance the submarine or to facilitate its maneuvers. It was critical, for example, to dive as quickly as possible in order to evade an enemy gunship, but the craft had a tendency to flounder. The crew had to race to the bow to add ballast for the descent. When the ship wanted to surface, everybody moved to the stern to force the bow upward. Even the firing of a torpedo required the crew to re-position themselves.

There were other challenges. The submarine traveled underwater at a maximum speed of five knots and chewed up battery life at an alarming rate. If the batteries failed, the sub would sink to the bottom and everyone would die. Naturally, the crew preferred to travel on the surface where speeds were greater, the batteries could be recharged and the air was fresher. The only problem in wartime was enemy gunboats. The submarine could not outrun or outgun them. Its only advantage was stealth beneath the waves. Kaz concluded that life on a U-boat was part comedy, part bravado and part a juggling act of dives and ascents.

Kaz's training paid off in an unexpected way when Poland contracted in 1932 with the French government to purchase three new submarines. Kaz was assigned along with 150 other men to travel to Cherbourg for training and to bring the new vessels home. They were quartered in the French naval barracks near the harbor while workers finished detailing the subs. The crew spent their mornings familiarizing themselves with the controls, engines and torpedo procedures and the afternoons in classes. Kaz was relieved to find the French submarines superior in most ways to the old U-boat. They were larger, faster and more responsive. Quarters on board were still cramped, but roomier.

Kaz was assigned to the Rys, the first of the three subs to be commissioned, and he was anxious to see how his new home behaved in action during a series of shallow practice dives. Two French engineers came aboard to supervise the process, but amid all the excitement, someone failed to properly secure several wooden chairs on deck. Once the Rys lowered its nose and slipped beneath the waves, most of the decking was washed overboard amid a series of screeching sounds that reminded Kaz of seagulls squabbling over bits of food. All except for one chair that became tangled in a rope. The chair sailed along behind the sub like an aquatic kite, darting about on its long tether until the line snagged the propeller. The engines were stopped, and the sub drifted for several minutes while a diver went out to untangle the line. As soon as the propeller was freed, the nervous captain ordered the craft to the surface, leaving the poor diver to fend for himself. Luckily, the incident occurred in shallow enough water that the diver was able to surface without experiencing the bends. It was an inauspicious start to Poland's new submarine fleet. The diver received a commendation for his bravery, the captain a reprimand.

By the time Kaz returned to Gdynia, he was having second thoughts about his naval career. If it was this dangerous going to sea in peacetime, what would it be like in times of war? He decided it would be safer to stay on solid ground, but he didn't think he could leave before his three-year tour of duty was finished.

The Rys's first assignment was target practice. This involved firing torpedoes at a moving barge towed by a ship that looked even older than the Baltic. Once again, duds were used to save ammunition, and 'chasers' in rubber dinghies were employed to retrieve the torpedoes so they could be fired again. A friendly contest developed between the ship, which kept changing course, and the Rys, which focused on striking the target. All went well the first day, but on the next morning, the crew was confronted with large swells and heavy seas. The captain wondered if they should proceed with the torpedo drills, but the commander saw no reason to wait. He pointed out that such conditions were realistic in combat. The crew needed to be prepared. The Rys submerged and prepared for an attack. The first torpedo was pushed off course due to the rough sea, and the platform on which the tube was mounted came loose. The seaman responsible for loading the tube tried to secure the platform, but failed to do so properly. When the next torpedo was fired, a combination of recoil and rough weather deflected the tube and sent the torpedo spinning to the left, where it made a beeline for the old towing boat and struck it mid-ship. Everyone watched in amazement as water rushed through a gaping hole just below the water line. The ship began to list to the starboard side. Officers ran on deck shouting orders to plug the hole and to proceed under full steam toward the harbor, but the hole was too big. The engines quickly flooded. All the men could do was rush to the top deck and jump into the sea. In the end, everyone was rescued. Kaz and his fellow members of the crew couldn't help laughing at the spectacle. The Rys had sunk its first ship!

Kaz's tour of duty ended in January, 1933, a time when economic depression was rolling across the world. Given the circumstances, he thought he might sign on for another tour, but the Polish government was just as pressed for funds as other countries. It could no longer support the kind of military it had envisioned. Pay rates were reduced and personnel cut. That included sailors in the navy. Kaz was mustered out; his career as a wooden sailor was over.

In the same month, an ex-house painter named Adolph Hitler was named Chancellor of a resurgent Germany.

Chapter Seven

I told you not to worry. I told you I had connections. What more could an ex-sailor want than his own apartment in a whore house?"

Kaz had joined Charlie and Woz in Gdynia to search for work on the docks. Woz hadn't changed much. He was still the curly-haired, smooth-skinned boy he remembered. Time seemed to have stood still in his features. He remained slight of build, guileless, quick to smile and willing to undertake any adventure. However, Charlie bore little resemblance to the friend Kaz had last seen in Krakow. The man who stood before him was a newly minted version that he hardly recognized. A narrow waist and hips accentuated broad, hardened shoulders that reflected the long hours Charlie had spent loading trucks and stacking crates in warehouses before the depression cost him his job. His hair was casually parted, as though combed by hand, his skin tanned, his handsome face framed by a square jaw that made Kaz think of a prize fighter. As always, his dark eyes sparkled with mischief, and when he smiled, dimples magically appeared in his cheeks. There was a self-assurance about him that told the world not to take him lightly. The best word Kaz could find to describe his friend was 'debonair.'

The only one missing was Christina. She remained in Warsaw, out of touch and out of reach. Kaz still shivered when he thought about her. Had she been his first love ... his first heartbreak? It seemed so. How else could he explain the empty ache he still felt when he recalled their time together?

Kaz's new surroundings were a far cry from the orphanage. Charlie had promised to find them cheap living quarters, and he'd delivered. Five young women gave him coy smiles as he followed Charlie and Woz into the brothel. Charlie acknowledged them with a breezy "hi girls," which Kaz thought was an apt description. None of them looked older than sixteen. He stamped snow from his feet as he climbed a flight of rickety stairs and joined his mates in a sitting room with pink walls and cushioned chairs. In better times, the suite had been used to entertain customers. Two bedrooms with straw mattresses beckoned at either end of the room.

The brothel was a large, meandering place with similar arrangements of sitting rooms and bedrooms on three floors. However, the struggling economy had slowed business to the point that several of the rooms were closed off. The toilet was down the hall, and a communal kitchen and dining area sent cooking aromas wafting upstairs from the first floor.

Kaz dropped his duffel bag on the bare floor. A puff of dust billowed in all directions. He walked to the room's only window and tugged at the shade that dangled limply over the sill. It snapped out of his cold fingers and shot up with a clatter. Thick frost at the corners of the pane partially obscured the view of a similar building just a dozen steps away. Dead flies littered the dusty sill. It wasn't a palace, but it was a place they could call home while they looked for work.

"We can crash here for a few weeks," Charlie advised. "The girls will even share some of their food. But the madam has one rule that can't be broken. Fool around with any of the girls without paying, and we'll all be out in the street."

Woz groaned and rolled his eyes. It had been hard to resist the girls' flirtatious stares when they arrived. It wasn't going to be easy to keep their hands to themselves.

"I mean it," Charlie continued. "We get out of line, we're gone, and it's too damn cold to live on the streets."

So began life in a little apartment on the second floor of a weather-beaten building whose rump nestled back into the bank of a broad channel leading to the sea, and whose front turned toward the harbor. The building had once been painted light gray, but years of harsh weather had taken their toll. Most of the paint had peeled away, revealing pine siding underneath. Whenever the wind blew, the windows in their rooms rattled, and when the snow melted, they leaked.

Kaz and Charlie shared the front bedroom with one small window overlooking the water. Woz took the back room facing the channel bank. The men hoped to find work as merchant seamen, but the spindly fingers of the depression had wrapped themselves around ships and ports alike. There was little work, and with more navy men being mustered out every day, competition for seamen's jobs was fierce. Woz had a few zlotys saved and Charlie demonstrated an uncanny skill at cards, which he used to good advantage in the local bars. Kaz's ability to fix things landed him several days of work repairing an old freighter. They threw their meager savings and earnings into a common pot. Most was given to the girls to cover the cost of food.

POLAND INTERRUPTED

That left just enough for a few beers and a bottle of vodka. There was nothing left for rent, but the madam hadn't said anything. She seemed pleased that they were so well behaved. When there was still no sign of steady work by the end of the second week, however, they knew that their time was running out.

The five girls continued to flirt with them, but Kaz had the feeling it was more business than friendship. It hardly mattered. They couldn't afford to pay the girls. Nor did they want to test the madam's edict and end up on the street. As Kaz got to know the girls better, he found one, Alicja, more interesting than the others. She had red hair that bounced in ringlets when she tossed her head and translucent skin dotted with freckles. Her most outstanding feature, from Kaz's point of view, was her slightly flared nose. She was quick to smile, and often pursed her lips in a pout that was quite provocative.

"I had to get away from home," was the answer Alicja gave when Kaz worked up the courage to ask why she worked in her profession. "My father was a drunk, and when he lost his job, he started hiring me out to men for money. It made me feel dirty, but I decided if that was my life, it was better to be on my own. So, I ran away and started working the streets. That was okay, I mean I made good money, but it was dangerous. I never knew what was going to happen to me. I got robbed and beat up. Here, it's great. I'm protected, and I still make good money. Not as much as on the street, but I get to keep what's mine, and nobody hassles me."

Alicja's fingers twitched and fussed with the buttons on her blouse as she spoke. Her eyes darted across Kaz's face. She reminded him of a small bird hopping along the ground in search of worms while watching for cats. Kaz had been with a few prostitutes but had never known their stories. Alicja's open manner drew him closer. She made him think of Christina. They were nothing alike, of course, but when he talked to Alicja, he couldn't help but remember his first love ... and the orphanage. Living there had seemed like a prison sentence, but in retrospect it hadn't been so bad. Others lived in far worse circumstances.

Alicja gave him a sly look. "I know we aren't supposed to fool around with you, but maybe I can make an exception." She fingered her blouse again. "I mean, sometimes it's nice to do it because it feels good. I don't get that chance often, but I kinda think it'd feel good with you."

Kaz couldn't prevent a smile from slipping across his face. He had to admit that there was some mutual attraction. Whether it was

Alicja's flared nose or simply her sexual charm, the reason didn't matter. He'd had too little comfort in his life, too little human warmth. Christina and Charlie had each other. He was the odd man out, and he needed something. When Alicja rose from her chair and walked seductively toward one of the unoccupied rooms, he followed.

"Kaz, we're a bunch of free-loading bums, and I don't like it," Charlie declared a few nights later as they prepared for bed. "Maybe, we should throw in the towel and hop a freight back to Krakow. At least we know people there. We might stand a better chance."

Shrill laughter drifted into the room from the first floor where the girls were drinking with customers. Kaz thought of Alicja's restless fingers playing with another man's shirt. His time with her had been special. It made him want to stay, but he knew Charlie was right. It was time to move on. He thought about the rough men he'd watched sneaking aboard boxcars in the rail yard. That was a long time ago. It didn't seem likely anyone would bother them, now. They had nothing worth stealing, and they looked just as rough as those wayward men. His thoughts turned to practical matters. Returning to Krakow without money or a place to stay seemed foolhardy, and he didn't want to throw himself on the mercy of his uncle.

"We could bunk at my grandfather's place, at least until we get something steady," Charlie offered as if reading his mind.

"What about Woz?"

"Spoke to him earlier. He's going back to his parent's, which is just as well. There's not enough room for three at my grandfather's."

"Okay," Kaz agreed. "I'm in."

They said their goodbyes the next morning. The girls gave them quick hugs, except for Alicja. She held Kaz a little too tightly for a little too long and brushed her lips across his cheek. The other girls watched knowingly but said nothing.

"Visit us when you come this way," she demanded. Kaz nodded with a sheepish grin.

The rail yards were not as busy as before, but there were still guards patrolling the area. Kaz and Charlie hefted their duffel bags over their shoulders and followed the set of tracks headed for Krakow until they rounded a bend and were out of sight. A heavy freight train would still be moving slowly at that juncture. There would be little trouble opening a boxcar and boarding. They had barely settled themselves to wait for a train when two men appeared from a hiding place in the nearby bushes. The men were at least ten years older and looked a lot tougher than the men Kaz had seen before. Tensions flared as the men stared at them with stony eyes. Kaz felt his heart increase with unease. Silence built a wall of uncertainty around them.

"You stand out here in the open, you'll give us all away. The guards walk this line, you know." The man who spoke slid his right foot back as though preparing to launch himself and balled his fists. "Best you move on."

Kaz shifted his own feet, ready to fight. His back muscles tightened.

Charlie broke the spell when he stepped forward with a smile. "Ever hear of blood alley?"

The men continued their hard stares. "Seen it a few times," one responded. "Why?"

Charlie flicked his thumb toward Kaz. "He jumped the tracks in front of a freight there. Darn near got himself killed."

The strangers looked at each other and relaxed. "Well, damn, that takes nerve. You headed for Krakow?" The tension eased.

Charlie nodded. "Hope you don't mind if we ride along."

"There's room for us all, I guess. Just keep your head down."

It wasn't long before a freight train chugged into view. They all hid in the bushes until the cab was well down the tracks, then ran to a boxcar and slid the door open far enough to climb inside, where they found themselves surrounded by crates of apples. They were soon munching on the juicy fruit and sharing familiar stories. The two men had lost their jobs two years ago, and were traveling the country in search of new ones. They lived on church-sponsored soup kitchens and handouts and slept in boarded-up buildings. Kaz wondered what had happened to their families but didn't ask. He prayed he wouldn't end up living such a life.

Twelve hours later, the train pulled into a familiar siding in Krakow near Kopernick Street. Everyone tossed their duffel bags onto the cinders and jumped down before the train entered the rail yard. They were greeted by a cold, gray March morning. Kaz and Charlie waved goodbye to their new friends and headed into the city. Snow squeaked beneath their feet as they trudged down familiar streets. A forest of chimneys rose before them. Thin spires of steam and smoke spiraled upward from the slumbering furnaces of a metropolis not yet fully awake. A train's whistle shrilled in the distance.

"Things haven't changed much." Charlie surveyed their surroundings, his white teeth gleaming against his smudged face. "I can even smell old Optima's chocolate factory!"

Kaz sniffed the air. Sure enough, the faint smell of warm chocolate wafted past him on a chilly breeze. The familiar odor gave him hope. If the chocolate factory was still operating, all was not lost. They passed a deserted barracks. There was no sign of life in the old buildings, nor on the vacant football field next door. Smoke from a refinery beyond the Wisla Commuter Station billowed skyward. Men lucky enough to still hold jobs would be reporting about this time for the morning shift.

At the next corner, Kaz and Charlie went their separate ways after agreeing to meet later. Kaz passed a familiar delicatessen and turned at Dabrowski Avenue. It was a short walk from there to his uncle's apartment. He looked up expectantly at the windows of the old building as he approached. They were all dark. His uncle should be drinking his tea by now, he thought, yet there was no sign of life. Kaz entered the building and worked his way up the dark, wooden stairway. He still remembered where to place each foot so the boards wouldn't creak. He paused at the door to the apartment and listened intently. All was quiet. Kaz pulled off a mitten and rapped his knuckles on the door. The sound echoed through the hallway with the force of gunshots.

"Just a minute," his uncle's voice called out with the same annoying tone that Kaz had endured as a boy. "I'm coming."

Kaz heard his uncle's feet stop at the kitchen table to light a lamp. A yellow beam of light darted under the space at the bottom of the door. A key turned in the lock, and the door swung open.

A disheveled figure with thinning, tousled hair that sprouted in all directions stood before Kaz and squinted at him. He appeared much older and smaller than the intimidating man Kaz recalled. He licked his lips and worked his mouth in the manner of someone trying to dispel the foul taste of waking up. His feet rested in tattered slippers, and he was clad in a long-sleeve shirt and pajamas that had been faded by a thousand washings. A frown tried to mask the confusion on his face as he stared at Kaz. Then, a wan smile of recognition appeared.

"Kaz, is it really you? Come in. Come in. Cold as hell this morning, isn't it?" Kaz was surprised at the warmth of his uncle's greeting. He seemed genuinely glad to see him. Uncle gestured to the old chair at the kitchen table where Kaz had sat before. "Sit down. I'll make coffee."

The table was cluttered with dirty dishes, empty glasses and an overturned vodka bottle. Jackets and scarves lay in disorganized mounds in the sitting area. A worn broom leaned against the wall in the hallway leading to the bedrooms. Wooden toys had been shoved into a corner. A musty smell permeated the place, the kind of smell that said it'd been some time since a window had been opened. Furniture remained where Kaz remembered it, but the place didn't look the same. It no longer felt like home, if it ever had. More to the point, it was too quiet. Jozef should be running through the room by now, and his aunt should be making the coffee. Where was everybody?

A bedroom door closed in the hallway with a faint thump, followed by muffled footsteps. An ill-kept woman in a flannel nightgown appeared in the hallway. She stared at Kaz with watery, unblinking eyes.

"Who's this?" she asked in a voice still drowsy from sleep.

"This is Kaz," Uncle answered in a gruff tone. "Katarzyna's boy. I told you about him. Been in the navy."

The woman started to say something, but Uncle interrupted her. "Go back to bed, Mag. I have to talk to Kaz alone." She clutched her nightgown more tightly around her and turned back down the hallway.

Kaz watched the scene unfold in a state of disbelief. A hot wave of anger rose in his chest. His mind spun with questions and accusations. The world into which he'd been tossed had never been particularly kind, but this was too bizarre for words. It was as though someone had kidnapped his aunt and replaced her with a stranger. Nothing made sense.

"Where's my aunt?" he finally managed to ask in a feeble voice.

"Dead from influenza," his uncle responded flatly. "She was gone in less than a week. Happened last year. I sent word to you but never heard back. Figured you didn't want to know too much, so I didn't pursue it."

"I never got the message."

Uncle lit the stove to heat water and scooped coffee into a press. He spoke with his back turned. "I wondered. Didn't seem right not to hear from you."

Tears stung Kaz's eyes. Aunt had been the only adult to show him any warmth, and now she was gone, replaced by a worn-out woman who didn't belong there. And where was Jozef? Toys were visible, but there was no sign of him.

Uncle anticipated his questions. "I haven't worked for two years. Mag had a little savings, but that's mostly gone. We barely get by. I had to put Jozef in the orphanage so he could eat regular." He poured hot water into the coffee press and let it stand while he pulled two cracked mugs from the shelf above the stove. He filled the cups and handed one to Kaz.

Kaz eyed the empty vodka bottle and two dirty glasses on the table as he tried to digest the news. Jozef in an orphanage! Memories of unruly children and bullies slid through his mind. His aunt, dead! More memories, this time of a bright smile and a warm touch. And Uncle was living with someone else, a woman he suspected would take a shot of vodka over solid food. The coffee tasted bitter; he gulped it down.

"What's that woman doing here? She looks like a drunk." He could hear the indignation in his voice.

Uncle's face tightened. "Don't talk like that. Mag took care of me when I needed someone. I hadn't heard from you. Your mother had no interest. I was alone. Filled with grief." His facial muscles relaxed, and a tear welled up in one eye. "To make matters worse, I was broke and could hardly walk. I put Jozef in the orphanage and tried to face this place alone. But I couldn't. Mag came to my rescue. I wouldn't have survived without her. I needed help ..." His voice trailed away.

"What are you doing for money?"

Uncle shrugged his shoulders. "Mag gets a little clerking at an office. I find a day's labor every now and then. Hardly enough to put food on the table. Don't suppose you have extra." He glanced at Kaz with greedy eyes.

Kaz shook his head. He thought about the apples he'd eaten on the train. They were his only food for the past twelve hours. "You seem to have enough to buy vodka," he accused.

Uncle's head sagged. He didn't answer.

Kaz left the building with a troubled heart. He'd gone there in search of his aunt's smiling face and his uncle's unwavering gaze. All he'd found was a stranger with watery eyes and a man whose world no longer turned properly on its axis. After the unventilated apartment, the wintry air smelled fresh. It revived his spirits and ignited his determination to find work. He wasn't going to let circumstances trap him the way they had his uncle.

Chapter Eight

A gloomy fog of depression hung over Krakow. Factories laid off workers; businesses closed. Food prices plummeted to the point where peasants could no longer afford to harvest their crops and bring them to market. People suffered from hunger in the cities while food rotted on the ground in the countryside. Food lines sprouted along the streets. Some people joined the lines without any idea of what was being offered. It didn't matter as long as it lessened the hunger in their stomachs. It only took a few days for Kaz to realize that the job market was just as barren at home as it was in Gdynia. He and Charlie managed to find odd jobs offered by friends, but nothing permanent presented itself, and it was apparent that Charlie's grandfather couldn't feed them much longer.

Kaz had spent a discouraging day calling on company after company and was on his way home when he heard a ruckus on the other side of a wall beside a clothing factory. He turned a corner and discovered a man in his early forties holding a woman's arm with one hand and raising the other above his head in a threatening manner. She shrieked in alarm and tried to pull away.

"Let go of her," Kaz yelled as he ran toward them.

The man looked in his direction, his face distorted in anger. "This is none of your business," he snarled.

"It is if you intend to hurt that woman," Kaz replied angrily. "Let her go, now!"

Kaz's unexpected appearance had the desired effect. The man's grip loosened enough for the woman to yank her arm away. The man clenched his hands into fists and turned his full attention on his intruder. "I'll teach you to meddle where you don't belong," he growled.

Kaz never slowed his stride. He crashed into the man with surprising force, took a mighty swing and clipped him on the jaw, sending him sprawling to the ground. Kaz stood over the stunned man, his chest heaving in quick breaths. He noticed for the first time that his quarry wore trousers, rather than work pants, and a shirt with a collar. Whoever, he was, he wasn't a factory worker.

"You make one more fist, and I'll pound you into dust," he warned.

The man scrambled to his feet and glared at Kaz while he brushed the dirt from his clothes and tried to decide what to do. The heat in his eyes slowly faded.

"The hell with it," he muttered. With that, he stepped around Kaz and walked away.

The tension in Kaz's body relaxed. He turned his gaze toward the young woman who stood trembling nearby. He discovered a lithe figure wrapped in a dark blue, cotton dress with shoulder-length, black hair pulled off a delicate face whose severe expression suggested more anger than fear. He had the vague notion that he'd seen her before, but he had no idea where.

"You okay?"

"I am now." She brushed back strands of wayward hair with a graceful motion. "That man was horrid." Her delicate features blossomed into a radiant smile that made her dark eyes dance with pleasure. "Thank you for rescuing me."

"What was that all about, if you don't mind my asking."

"Oh, he works for my father. Or did. I just fired him. He managed our warehouse, but he's been falsifying shipment records."

Kaz was surprised by the young woman's poise. He guessed her age at no more than twenty. "Have you discussed this with your father?"

"I'm about to. We've suspected something was amiss. The numbers weren't adding up. I just reviewed the week's bills of lading and discovered four entries where the merchandise received by the shipper was less than the amount declared in our inventory. He was changing the numbers and pocketing the difference. I was so angry I fired him on the spot. My name is Daneta Rudnicka, by the way." She gestured toward the clothing factory. "My family owns this place." She assessed Kaz with a quizzical stare. "And who are you?"

"Kaz Kowalski." He suddenly felt shy in front of this self-assured young woman. "I just got out of the navy. I'm looking for work."

"Are you trustworthy?" She shielded her eyes from the bright sky with her hand and looked at him more closely.

Kaz was taken aback by the frank question. He straightened his shoulders. "I am," he responded forcefully.

"Good, then let's go talk to my father. We need a new warehouse manager."

Kaz followed Daneta into the factory where he was greeted by the chattering noise of dozens of Singer sewing machines run by a small army of women. The place smelled of freshly cut cloth and warm bodies. Kaz found the room cheery compared to the chilly air outside. Daneta led him up a flight of wooden stairs to a series of offices and supply rooms. She marched to the end of a hallway and opened a frosted glass door to reveal a spacious office. A grave-looking man with a full head of gray hair glanced up from his papers as they entered. He was dressed in a tailored, brown suit, a white, long-sleeve shirt with gold cuff links and a red, silk tie. It was the kind of clothing that Kaz associated with a gala event like a ball, not that he'd ever attended one.

"Father, I just fired Mr. Bordowski." Daneta said this forcefully, as if she would brook no argument. "He was stealing money just as we suspected. But when I told him to leave, he became belligerent and threatened me. This man came to my rescue." She looked at Kaz. "This is Kaz Kowalski."

Mr. Rudnicka peered over his reading glasses at Kaz. "Thank you, young man. Sometimes my daughter gets ahead of herself and finds herself in awkward situations. I appreciate your help."

Kaz saw how Daneta's neck reddened at her father's remark, but she held her tongue. "He's looking for work," she said in a calm voice, "and we need a new warehouse manager. I thought we should consider him."

"What have you done?" Kaz could see by the quizzical look on the man's face that he was skeptical. Kaz knew he probably looked too young for such a position. His short stature didn't help.

"I've driven train engines and worked a lathe. Most recently, I sailed in submarines for the navy."

Mr. Rudnicka arched his eyebrows. "Most impressive, young man, but the warehouse is full of rough necks. Do you think you could handle them?

"I'm used to dealing with those types, sir."

"You should have seen the way he took care of Mr. Bordowski," Daneta chimed in. "Stood up to him without hesitation."

Mr. Rudnicka stared at Kaz while he pondered his daughter's suggestion. "It would be premature to discuss a manager's position, Mr. Kowalski, but give me your references and come back in three days. If you check out, we'll discuss the matter further. We can certainly use a new hand in the warehouse."

Daneta gave him a shy smile as they left the office. "My father likes you. I can tell."

"Thanks to you. I appreciate your support." He hesitated, not certain how to explain his last name. "I grew up with my aunt and uncle and used their name: Kowinsky. However, in the navy I had to enlist under my father's name: Kowalski. I hope that won't confuse things."

"I'm sure not. I will tell father."

Kaz gave Daneta his references and left. His feet danced as he hurried down the stairs and exited the building. He had a job! He was certain of it. After weeks of fruitless searching, he couldn't help but be hopeful. Especially after the way Daneta had vouched for him. He recalled the timid smile she gave him as he departed. She was an interesting woman. One moment confident, the next, shy.

Kaz continued his search for work, but he knew the warehouse job was his only real chance. The three days crawled along at the pace of his old submarine. He found himself counting the hours and realized it wasn't just the prospect of work that bewitched him. He couldn't stop thinking about the headstrong woman with the delicate cheekbones and dancing eyes.

When he finally returned to the factory, Daneta greeted him. He tried his best to appear nonchalant, but he couldn't prevent a rush of blood from warming his face. He hadn't reacted that way to a woman since Christina. He was pleased to see a flushed look on her face, as well. Their eyes met briefly before she turned away.

"You've got a job," she announced as they mounted the stairs to the office. "Not sure what father has in mind, but we'll find out."

Kaz smiled and hurried after her.

"We'll start you in a training program," Mr. Rudnicka informed him without preamble. "You'll begin by stocking shelves and filling purchase orders. Get that under your belt and you will move to shipping. We ship all over Poland and to neighboring countries, but we also have many local customers who deal with us directly through the warehouse. So, you'll also be dealing with them."

He paused and assessed Kaz with a frank stare that reminded him of his uncle. "I haven't heard back from everybody, but the navy and the train yard give you high marks. I also like the way you present yourself. None of our current workers has the capability to be a warehouse manager, but I don't want us to get ahead of ourselves." He gave his daughter a meaningful glance. "As far as the other workers are concerned, you're just another floor worker, not a trainee."

Mr. Rudnicka picked up a sheet of paper from his desk and studied it. "There is one other matter which requires some delicacy. We know Mr. Bordowski was stealing from us, but we don't know if he was acting alone. He may have had accomplices. Part of your job will be to learn if there were others."

"You want me to spy on them?" Kaz shifted uncomfortably in his chair.

"Not spy exactly, but if there is a broader conspiracy of theft, we need to stamp it out. I want you to keep your eyes and ears open. If you spot any suspicious activity, you report it to me at once."

Kaz mulled this over. He'd never handled such a responsibility, and he wasn't sure what to think about it. Mr. Rudnicka was telling him to squeal on his fellow workers, and if he did so, they would know it. They would resent him when he became their boss. But if he was to assume a management position, he had to put the company's needs first. Stealing was stealing. He'd never approved of such behavior, and he didn't now.

Mr. Rudnicka interrupted his thoughts. "Six months should be long enough to see what you've got. You ready to get started?"

"Yes sir," Kaz replied firmly.

"You have a place to stay?" Mr. Rudnicka's question surprised him.

"Only temporary. I've got to find something."

"There's an apartment across the street from the warehouse that we rent to employees. Has its own kitchen. It's vacant right now, if you want it. The rent is below market, so you can save some money. In return, I would expect you to keep an eye on the place after hours. Have a look around in the evening to make sure everything is secure."

Once again, Kaz shifted in his chair. Mr. Rudnicka wanted him to act like a part-time night watchman. More specifically, he wanted Kaz to watch for any unusual activity in the warehouse. It meant more work, but he wanted the job, and the apartment would give him an affordable, convenient place to stay. It would also keep him closer to the young woman seated next to him, and he found himself drawn to that idea. He glanced her way and caught her eye. She blushed and looked away.

"The apartment sounds fine," he responded. "And I'll be happy to check on things from time to time."

"Good. I'll expect to see you ready to work at seven, tomorrow morning. Daneta will get you squared away." Mr. Rudnicka turned his attention to the papers on his desk. The interview was over.

"Why don't we invite Kaz for dinner tonight while he gets settled in?"

Mr. Rudnicka looked up, startled by Daneta's suggestion. "I'm sure Mr. Kowalski has things to do."

She turned her attention to Kaz. "Do you have plans this evening?"

He squirmed under the heat of her father's glare and tried to figure out his answer. The few zlotys in his pocket would barely cover food until he got his first pay voucher. He had no plans, other than another evening with Charlie. A home cooked meal sounded tempting.

"I guess I'm free. There's nowhere I've got to go."

"Good," Daneta exclaimed with a smile to her father. "It's settled then. Dinner is at six"

The Rudnicka's house, a large, two-story structure with a dozen gleaming windows, sat back from the street in the manner of a country home. It was located a few blocks from the factory on a broad avenue shaded by mature trees whose branches swept elegantly over the sidewalk. Kaz stopped briefly to admire the grand elegance of the place and to wonder how a small-business owner could afford to live there. He mustered his courage and strode up the concrete walkway to the heavy, oak front door.

His knock was answered by an elegant woman in her fifties wearing a black, evening dress accentuated by a pearl necklace. Kaz had rushed to Charlie's and retrieved his clothes so he would have something clean to put on, but his best shirt and pants looked shabby compared to the woman he faced.

"You must be Kaz. I'm Daneta's mother, Mrs. Rudnicka. My daughter told me about your bold action with Mr. Bordowski. Your intervention is most appreciated. Please come in."

Kaz entered a carpeted entryway and was shown into a sitting room filled with polished furniture and elegant lighting fixtures. Once again, everything about the place suggested the kind of prosperity enjoyed by the landowners and aristocracy, not a garment factory owner.

"Please sit down. Daneta will join us in a moment."

Kaz sat uncertainly on one of the fine, upholstered chairs and tried not to stare at his hostess. Mrs. Rudnicka had the same delicate cheekbones and angular face as her daughter. Neither was quite beautiful, but they both exuded a captivating charm when they smiled.

Kaz sensed that Mrs. Rudnicka wasn't sure what else to say. He fidgeted on the chair and tried to make conversation, but his tongue wouldn't cooperate. Tension filled the room. Kaz prayed that Daneta would appear and save him from his awkwardness.

Right on cue, Daneta swept into the room in a white dinner dress that was only slightly less formal than her mother's. The dress showed off her slender figure and thin, creamy arms.

"There you are. How are you two getting along?" She gave Kaz a brilliant smile that lit up her face. "Mother, have you offered our guest a drink?"

"I was about to." She looked just as relieved as Kaz by Daneta's arrival.

Everyone agreed on vodka martinis, and Mrs. Rudnicka made the drinks. Kaz wondered why Daneta's father was not performing the rituals.

"How do you like the apartment?" she asked as she handed Kaz his drink.

His mind whirled back to earlier that afternoon when Daneta had showed him his quarters: a bedroom and living room with a kitchenette and small bathroom included. It lacked the elegance of his current surroundings, but it was clean and well maintained. A faint scent of cedar odor suggested that the furniture had recently been polished. Its main view was of the factory and warehouse. To Kaz, it seemed like a palace.

"Very comfortable," he responded. "It suits me fine."

A maid entered and announced that dinner was ready to be served. Daneta took Kaz's arm and steered him into a spacious dining room with a mahogany table that sparkled under the lights of a chandelier.

"Well, Mr. Kowalski, I trust you have settled in." Mr. Rudnicka gave him a polite smile as he joined the group but did not offer his hand. "Be seated."

Kaz took the offered chair across from Daneta, with her parents at either end. The meal was surprisingly simple, beef and dumplings served in a big, ironstone tureen, but savory. Kaz had to restrain himself from taking a second helping before the others had finished their first. It had been awhile since he'd eaten so well. Polite questions were asked about Kaz's background. He felt it best not to go into too much detail, so he skipped the saga involving his mother. Kaz sensed that Mr. Rudnicka merely asked about his family out of courtesy and thought he looked rather bored until Kaz shared some of his stories about the navy. When he told them about sinking the boat towing the target vessel with a dummy torpedo, everyone laughed.

Throughout the meal, he made a studied effort to keep his eyes away from the dark-haired girl opposite him, but he couldn't help wondering if she was watching him. The harder he tried not to look at her, the more compelled he felt to do so. Each time he succumbed, he encountered her furtive glances cast in his direction. And each time their eyes met, she gazed back at him for a brief moment before dropping her eyes demurely. When the conversation turned to the day's business, Daneta turned her attention to her father and began a lively discussion about the number of sales made that day and the orders filled.

Kaz observed her with fascination. She was different from the girls he'd known. She wasn't as pretty as some, but that didn't matter. He found her poise and self-assurance sexy. She took a great interest in the business and seemed to have as much knowledge as her father about what had transpired. However, she blushed prettily whenever she saw Kaz staring at her. They continued to fight their battle of glances, each trying hard not to get caught looking, but each finding their eyes inevitably drawn to the other.

The conversation shifted to world matters, particularly Germany's increasingly aggressive behavior.

"Hitler's Nazi party continues to build Germany's military, but no one seems to notice," Mr. Rudnicka declared. "He's started an air force, called the Luftwaffe, in direct defiance of the Versailles accord, and has introduced conscription to expand the German army." He pushed the hair off his right ear as he spoke, his expression solemn. "What use does he have for such a powerful military force unless he intends to use it? And where will he attack first?" He looked around the table to make sure he had everybody's attention. "Why, Poland, of course! I don't trust this Hitler fellow. He claims to have no interest in war, yet his actions betray him. I fear it's only a matter of time before we are invaded again."

Kaz had not been following the developments in Germany, but he could see that Daneta's father was well informed, much like his uncle, and he tried to pay attention to what he was saying. He knew there were forces at work that could undermine Poland's fragile steps toward prosperity, and he shared the man's concerns. However, he found it difficult to concentrate on the man's apocalyptic words when Daneta's face danced before him. There were two conversations taking place: one verbalized by Mr. Rudnicka; the other a more subtle dialogue in the form of coy and furtive glances.

POLAND INTERRUPTED

Dinner ended abruptly when Mr. Rudnicka declared that he had business to which he must attend. He rose from the table and left the room without preamble. Everyone else rose as well. The maid appeared and began to clear the table.

"It's early yet." Daneta addressed her comment to her mother. "Perhaps, we can talk a bit in the sitting room."

Mrs. Rudnicka smiled and shook her head. "You two go ahead, dear. I have other things to do."

Kaz followed Daneta into the adjoining room and sat on the same chair as before. Daneta sat facing him on the couch and gave him a frank stare. "We've met before, you know, at school. It was many years ago. I was in pig tails then." She laughed and sighed. "I was the first one to reach you after you hit the railing behind the swings. But you were pretty groggy. I doubt that you remember me."

Kaz blinked in surprise. That was why she'd seemed familiar when he first met her. He did recall a girl frowning at him when he returned to his senses after tumbling over that railing, and helping him to his feet.

"I *do* remember. Well, sort of," he confessed. "Not the pig tails, but I do recall a very serious look on your face. Why didn't you say something sooner?"

"I'm not sure. It didn't seem like the right time until now." She shifted her position on the couch and changed the subject. "You mustn't mind my father. He gets a bit worked up when he talks about the Germans. If you believe him, they will invade us at any moment."

"He has a point, though. I know my uncle would agree with him. And based on my experience in the navy, I doubt Poland could stand up to the Germans for very long."

"Are you still fighting?" She shifted the subject again. "You used to get terribly angry."

"I try to avoid fights. I've learned I can't lick the whole world. But I won't back down if there's no choice."

Daneta glanced at the family phonograph in the corner of the room. "Do you like music?"

Another abrupt shift in subject, he thought. He was having a hard time keeping up with her.

"Of course."

"What kind?"

"Most any kind. Music you can dance to."

"I enjoy dance music," she agreed, "but I enjoy the classics more."

"I don't understand the classics," he admitted frankly. "Never listened to them at home."

"That's probably why. You have to sort of work at understanding good music. Then you come to like it more. It's not as simple as popular songs. Maybe I'll play some of my favorites for you some evening soon."

"I'd like that. I'd like to try."

"And maybe some evening you can show me your favorite music. We could go dancing."

Kaz was caught off-guard by her bold suggestion, and it made him a bit uncomfortable. He was used to initiating the conversation with women, not the other way around. Plus, this was the first time he'd visited a girl in her family's drawing room, and he wasn't sure what to say. He suddenly wanted to retreat to his room where he could think more clearly.

"That would be fun, but now I had better say goodnight. Tomorrow's my first day, and I want to get an early start."

Daneta walked him to the front door. "Good luck tomorrow." She opened the front door. Then she paused and looked at him. "I hope we will be good friends."

"I'm sure of it," Kaz gave her a weak smile. Good friends. That had been his relationship with Christina, even though he'd hoped for more. He wasn't sure what he hoped for with the dainty, self-assured woman standing before him, but he suspected there might be more at stake than just good friends. He retreated down the walkway and headed for his apartment.

Chapter Nine

The warehouse sat next to a broad, concrete yard where trucks arrived to pick up shipments and to make deliveries. Kaz could see it clearly from his apartment. He knew he was expected to keep a sharp eye on the place when it was closed for the night. The apartment gave him an ideal vantage point.

He had awakened early and now hurried down the wooden outside stairway to the ground floor. The sun that greeted him was a fiery ball rising through smoke pouring from hundreds of chimneys. As he walked across the pavement toward the warehouse, he noted that the large, sliding doors of the building were firmly closed; the place looked deserted. He knew it was not yet seven, but he was eager to get started. The crisp, morning air stung his nose and ears as he looked around. Suddenly, a small door popped open to reveal Daneta and her father.

Mr. Rudnicka looked at his pocket watch. "You're early, that's good. The others will be along shortly."

Daneta gave Kaz a brief smile, but it lacked the warmth of the previous evening. He could see that she was all business this morning.

Kaz followed them into a large, square building filled with a warren of metal shelves stuffed with boxes. A staging area near the two, sliding doors was a jumble of more boxes.

"We have two main sections to the warehouse," Mr. Rudnicka intoned. "The shelves where cloth, buttons, and other inventory are stored until needed in the factory, and the floor area where finished goods are sorted by customer and staged for shipping or pick up. This is also where we receive the raw materials. Your job will be to learn how the raw materials are labeled and stored and to move incoming fabrics and other merchandise onto the appropriate shelves." He pointed to a row of boxes as he spoke. "When materials are called for, you'll find and deliver the requested items to the factory. We make a variety of shirts, pants, dresses and uniforms. Some are custom orders. Others represent our regular product lines. The latter are shipped to stores. When each order is finished, you will move it to the warehouse and stage it for shipping. You'll be given a ticket to fill out for every transaction within the warehouse. Daneta will help you learn the paperwork. Once finished goods are signed over to shipping, you'll close out the ticket and send it to bookkeeping."

With that, Mr. Rudnicka turned and departed. Daneta saw Kaz's dazed look and gave him a warmer smile.

"Father likes to throw a lot of information at you. Don't worry. I'll walk you through each step. By the end of the day, you should have a pretty good idea how things work."

Loud voices announced the arrival of the warehouse workers. The sliding doors were shoved open with a screeching noise of wheels on metal that reminded Kaz of the train rushing past him in blood alley. When Daneta introduced Kaz to the men, suspicious glances were tossed his way. Kaz figured they'd heard about his confrontation with their former boss, and they were taking his measure. They were all in their thirties and forties. He realized how young he must look to them. There were six men in all. Three sported scruffy beards in need of trimming. All looked fit from the labors of working in the warehouse, but one stood out in Kaz's mind, a man named Marek, who looked particularly aggressive. He stood a foot taller than Kaz, and had a wrestler's build, although Kaz noticed that his flabby midsection showed the affects of too many beers enjoyed after work. If the man had a weakness, he thought, it would be his stomach.

Soon, trucks arrived to begin the day's cycle of pickups and deliveries, and the warehouse filled with a buzzing mixture of men's laughs and curses, heavy boxes thumping on the concrete floor and trucks sputtering to life under the weight of full loads. Dust showered the chilly air. Kaz was glad he'd worn his jacket, although most of the men had already stripped off theirs. One machine was of particular interest. The men called it a lift machine. It consisted of an open cage on wheels with a platform in front that could be raised and lowered on a vertical mast. This allowed the driver to move heavy boxes around the warehouse and to stack them or remove them from the shelves.

Daneta spent the morning showing Kaz the system for storing the materials delivered by trucks. When they broke for lunch, she noticed that he hadn't brought anything to eat and offered to share her sandwich with him.

"We can go over the tickets at the same time," she suggested.

They walked into the factory and climbed the stairs to a room with tables where workers could eat. Kaz tore into the half-sandwich that Daneta offered him while they discussed the tickets. Kaz tried to concentrate, but he found his eyes wandering to her lustrous, black hair and her intense expression. What was it, exactly, that he found so appealing about her? He couldn't be certain. She wasn't like the other women he'd known: nothing like Christina.

"When are you going to let me listen to your music?" he asked suddenly.

She looked up, startled, and blushed. "I was thinking about tonight. Father will be at his club and mother is busy. It would be a chance to spend some time together."

The smile that blossomed on her face chased away the tight lines around her mouth. It was like sunshine breaking through clouds. One moment she was prim and all business, the next, charming and coy.

Kaz returned her smile. "I'd like that."

Brahms. Beethoven. Mozart. The names floated through the air amid the musical notes produced by the violin strings, piano keys and wind instruments that filled the Rudnicka's sitting room for the better part of two hours. Daneta had led Kaz through a thicket of composers, musical periods and instruments with the deftness of a conductor waving a baton. To make matters worse, she had poured wine to accompany their musical feast: first red, then white. Kaz sipped the wines in concert with Daneta, but his mouth watered for vodka.

"Which piece did you like best?" Daneta asked.

"That last one ... by that guy, Tchaikovsky."

"The 1812 Overture. Yes, that one is very stirring. It was composed to commemorate Russia's brave stand against Napoleon."

"I liked the cannons," Kaz confessed.

Daneta let out a squeak of laughter. "I knew it. You men are all the same."

"And I liked the one by Beethoven."

"His fifth symphony. Yes, that is also very powerful. What about Mozart's Eine Kleine Nachtmusik?"

"A little too effeminate for me. What does it mean?"

Daneta gave a throatier laugh this time and touched the back of his hand. "You definitely prefer the heavier works. I shall play some Wagner next time. The translation of Mozart's piece is, A Little Night Music."

"A strange title."

"He wasn't sure what to call it, so he jotted those words down as a reminder to himself. He never changed them."

Daneta's mood suddenly shifted. "You'd better leave now,"

"Did I say something wrong?" Kaz asked in surprise.

"No. It's just that father isn't quite used to you yet. It's better if you go before he comes home."

"What about your mother?"

She'll tell father, of course. She leaves it to him to speak to me. But, I don't think he'll say anything as long as you're not here to confront him."

"I'm not sure what to make of him," Kaz admitted as they walked to the front door. "He seems so formal all the time. He never relaxes, lets his guard down."

"It's our history. The Rudnickas are a large family with many cousins, uncles and grandparents. Most are very wealthy. They own vast tracts of farmland and oversee armies of peasants who work the fields. Father is a very distant cousin, and a rather poor one compared to the rest. He wants to believe he holds a high position in society, but the truth is, we are looked down upon by most of the family. So, father puts on airs and acts as if he has a higher station in Poland's gentry. We're not poor, as you can see, but father thinks we are, and he resents his situation."

"I don't think he likes me."

"It's not a question of liking you. At present, you are no more than a servant in his eyes. That will change, at least a little, once you become a manager. You must be patient."

Daneta opened the front door, and before Kaz could leave, raised up on her toes and kissed him on the cheek. The sudden pressure of her lips on his skin surprised and unnerved him. He felt his face flush in a warmth of pleasure.

"Thank you for listening to my music tonight. I hope you enjoyed it." Her eyes searched his face.

"Very much," he responded with what he hoped passed for enthusiasm.

"I'm glad. Perhaps, next time, we can try some dance music. You can take me somewhere."

She closed the door without waiting for his reply.

Kaz walked back to his apartment in a state of turmoil. Daneta confounded him. One minute she was shy, the next quite forward; at times, a bit distant, other times, warm, almost passionate. It wasn't necessarily a bad thing. He kind of liked the uncertainty, but he never felt in control, which unsettled him. He was used to initiating things, not reacting to a woman's whims. It didn't matter. The kiss told him he would see more of her, and that their relationship was likely to grow in complexity.

A few nights later, Kaz arranged to meet Charlie at a nearby dance hall and invited Daneta to join them.

"You wanted to try some dancing. Here's our chance," he enthused.

Daneta looked less than pleased at the idea of going to a dance hall, but she agreed. Charlie met them there and presented his most charming behavior. Kaz could tell that Daneta liked him.

The dance hall was another matter. A cacophony of voices rose in waves to the raised ceiling; lungs sucked every ounce of oxygen from the room; the air was tainted with thick clouds of tobacco smoke; and everybody was swimming in vodka, with the result that people were quickly becoming drunk. Couples took to the dance floor like lost lovers determined to rediscover each other. Bodies clung together. Mouths sang songs to the music, slurped vodka, snaked tongues across necks and breathed into every ear. When a mouth kissed the wrong partner, a fight broke out. It'd been months since Kaz had visited such a place, and it felt like home.

Not so, Daneta. She stood stock-still and refused to move. It was as if someone had nailed her shoes to the floor. People shoved past her to reach the bar; she hunched her shoulders to ward off their bumps and blows. Her expression was severe. She appeared so tight-lipped, Kaz feared that she couldn't breathe. Two eager men advanced on her with offers to dance. Kaz had to push them away with raised fists.

"Come on, let's get out on the floor," he urged. "The music is great!"

Daneta didn't think so. "It's too fast for me. Can we wait for a slower one?"

Kaz grinned and raised his vodka glass. "Sure. I would enjoy a slow dance with you."

Right on cue, the music lost its upbeat tempo and segued into a song about love. Kaz put his arm around Daneta's waist and pulled her onto the dance floor. The warmth of her body against his sent a shudder through him, and he drew her closer. He half expected her to resist, but she clung to him. Once again, he was thrown off-balance by the shifting drama of her moods. One moment, she appeared so uncomfortable, he thought she'd want to leave; the next, she'd wrapped her arms around him in a passionate embrace. Her cheek felt moist against his, and her neck beckoned to him. He slid his mouth down until it caressed her skin. Again, he tensed in anticipation of rejection, but she surprised him, again, by joining his venture into the intoxicating world of wet skin and hot bodies. Their lips finally met in a kiss that sent the noisy room into retreat and left them alone on the floor. They held each other tightly until the music ended.

Daneta broke the spell when she leaned back with a gasp and stared at him. It was all Kaz could do to stop himself from pulling her back to him. He sensed another mood shift and held his breath.

"I can't stay here," Daneta yelled above the noise. She fanned her face with her hand. Her eyes darted away from him and sought the exit door. "It's too wild for me. I must go."

Kaz opened his mouth to encourage her to stay, but he said nothing. The look of desperation on her face told him that she'd had enough. He nodded and went to retrieve their coats.

The promise of spring was in the night air. It was nippy, but not as bitingly cold as before. Still, Daneta hung onto Kaz's arm as if there was a winter storm brewing. Disappointment hung in the air, but he couldn't help responding to her gesture. He put his arm around her.

"We had better say good night here," Daneta advised as they approached the house. "Father is home tonight. He doesn't know where I've been. I told him I was visiting a girl friend." She snuggled against him in the dark. "I hope you're not too angry with me about tonight."

Kaz shook his head. "No, it's fine. I know you didn't really want to go there."

"I did enjoy myself. It just became a bit too much for me. I'm not used to that sort of place. Maybe, we could try somewhere else. The Athletic Club is nice." She squeezed his arm.

Kaz had heard of the Club but never been there. He knew it was quieter than the dance hall and more formal. His clothes wouldn't do there.

"You'll need a new shirt and pants," she commented with a giggle. "I'll have to take you shopping. Let's go next week. My treat."

Kaz stiffened at the idea of a woman paying for his clothes, but he couldn't resist her enthusiasm. He *did* need some new things, but he would have to put his foot down about who paid for them. He was earning money now. He would pay his own way.

They kissed goodnight, and Kaz watched Daneta walk to her front door. It was a nice kiss, one might even call it lingering, but it lacked the passion of the earlier one on the dance floor.

The next few months unfolded in a flurry of fits and starts. Charlie announced that he was joining Christina in Warsaw, where she'd found a job and he had prospects at the same company. Kaz was sorry to see him go, but he realized that he no longer thought about Christina so much. The ache burning in him had all but vanished. He gave Daneta credit for that development. Despite their differing tastes, he enjoyed her company. They did go shopping for new clothes, and Kaz did put his foot down about paying for them.

"You look very handsome," Daneta remarked with her shy smile when she first saw him in his ironed slacks and shirt. "Now, you are ready for the Athletic Club."

Kaz's first visit to the Athletic Club was filled with contrasts. The Club was brightly lit and featured a broad, highly polished dance floor where couples could twirl and swing freely without banging into each other. Kaz's dance club was much darker, and people were squeezed together. The Athletic Club's patrons wore suits, pressed slacks and shirts, and gowns that hid a woman's figure. The men at the local dance club wore shirts opened at the chest and the women tight skirts that showed off their figures to advantage. Dancing at the Club was more restrained and the music less rowdy. Not to Kaz's liking, but he knew it made Daneta happy, and they still managed to find new ways to press their bodies together while dancing. They went three weeks in a row. Each time, the pressure between them built a little higher.

At the warehouse, Kaz quickly learned his duties and attacked them with enough energy to make his co-workers nervous. One morning after a week on the job, Marek approached him while he was stocking shelves.

"You better slow down." The menace in the man's voice got Kaz's attention. Kaz jumped down from the lift machine. His hands were suddenly moist from tension. He quickly wiped then on his pants and assessed the man.

"What do you mean?"

Marek pulled a red handkerchief from his rear pocket and mopped his brow, a ritual he repeated many times a day. The man was a heavy sweater. He eyed Kaz as he shoved the cloth back in his pocket.

"You're working too fast. Makes the other men look bad. They work hard enough, but they aren't in a race."

"This is just the way I work. I'm not racing anybody." Kaz glanced around and noticed two or three of the workers watching the conversation.

Marek tapped Kaz on the chest with his forefinger. "Race or not, you better slow down."

Kaz swung his attention back to Marek. He stared at the man's sagging stomach and wondered if it was time to test his fists on it.

There had been tensions between the two of them since the first day. Marek had been walking around the warehouse like he owned the place. It was obvious he wanted to assume the position of warehouse manager, and he somehow understood that Kaz stood in his way. Kaz decided against starting a fight. It wasn't the time. But he couldn't let Marek push him around in front of the other men.

He knocked Marek's hand away from his chest. "You ever jab me with your finger again, I'll mop the floor with you." He brought his face closer to Marek's and looked him square in the eye. Marek blinked at Kaz's unexpected response but held his ground.

"Just remember what I said." Marek stared back at him for several heartbeats before he turned and walked away.

Marek was the least of Kaz's troubles. Inventory was handled in such a slipshod manner that things were constantly being misplaced. He often found items on the wrong shelves. Daneta informed him that ticket orders did not always match production, but the mishandled inventory made it difficult to track each ticket. When she asked the men about missing merchandise, they just shrugged their shoulders and glanced at Marek. Bordowski had pilfered stock when he ran the warehouse. Daneta had managed to unravel that scheme by tracking specific orders through the warehouse, but Kaz suspected that some of the goods were still being stolen. He couldn't prove it. The lack of a well-managed inventory made it nearly impossible to track all the orders. The only way to be sure was to catch the thieves in the act. So, he sat by the window in his apartment at odd hours, certain that he would spot the culprits moving merchandise out of the place at night. Nothing happened. Night after night, the warehouse grounds remained quiet.

Kaz began to think that he'd simply misread the situation, even though his gut told him otherwise. Then, he had an idea. He was studying the jumble of code numbers printed on the boxes on the shelves when he remembered how the navy had used colored marking pens on the arms of the recruits to track them through the screening process. Why couldn't a similar system be used on the inventory and finished goods? Kaz went to work and quickly devised a simple method to identify each step in the factory and warehouse operations from raw materials to finished goods. When he showed his idea to Daneta, she beamed her approval and immediately escorted Kaz to her father's office.

"Why didn't we think of it?" Mr. Rudnicka's rhetorical question was asked more to himself than to the others. He nodded to Kaz. "It's simple, but it works. Good job. Just the kind of thinking I would expect from a future manager. I'll order colored labels at once."

Kaz basked in the glow of Mr. Rudnicka's approval and Daneta's smile as he walked back to the warehouse. He was in such a good mood that when she suggested they return to the Athletic Club after work, he agreed without hesitation.

The colored labels arrived later that week, and Mr. Rudnicka announced the new tracking system with Kaz standing by his side. Kaz felt the stares of his fellow workers digging into his skin. Marek's glare was particularly intense. Kaz didn't care. He intended to prove himself worthy of the manager's position, and if Marek got in his way, he'd be ready for him.

During the next few weeks, Kaz kept a sharp eye out for any suspicious activity in the warehouse, but the men went about their business at their normal, docile pace. Kaz couldn't uncover any hint of misconduct. He was beginning to think that he was wrong about the missing inventory when he noticed something. Boxes were being loaded onto trucks as usual, but he spotted a stack that was missing the labels used for finished orders. He watched them for the rest of the day, but nobody touched them. He thought they could have been set aside by someone too lazy to put them away, but something didn't feel right. The boxes had no business being where they were, and everybody was studiously avoiding them. The day ended without incident. The boxes remained untouched until the lights were turned off and the warehouse was locked up for the night.

Daneta had suggested that they go dancing again, but Kaz begged off.

"I want to keep an eye on things. Something doesn't smell right."

When she pressed him for an explanation, he shook his head. He didn't want to announce his suspicions until he had some proof. So, he stayed at home that night with the lights turned off and stared out his window at the warehouse. Time ticked past midnight. All remained quiet. Kaz shifted his shoulders to relieve the tension from his vigil. It was a clear night with stars sprinkled across the sky. No moon was visible, however. The warehouse was cloaked in shadows. It was nearly one o'clock, and Kaz was about to admit defeat when one of the shadows betrayed movement. Kaz's head shot up. He rubbed his eyes and looked again. No one was visible. Perhaps he was wrong. Then, a dark figure, a shadow within the shadows, shifted its position. He could barely make it out in the starlight. Suddenly, a second shadow slipped through the gloom and joined the first. The two figures worked their way past the large, sliding doors to the smaller door to the left. It was quickly opened. They had a key! The shadows disappeared inside.

Kaz hadn't planned what to do next. He looked around for something he could use to defend himself, and settled on a heavy, iron skillet. Weapon in hand, he rushed down the stairs and ran across the concrete square toward the warehouse. The figures were just emerging with boxes in hand when they heard Kaz's footsteps. Kaz's body was coiled for action, but before he reached the men, he saw a flash of light and heard a loud bang that echoed off the building and the pavement. And a bullet zinged past Kaz's ear! Gun, he thought wildly. They have a gun!

The skillet in his hand clanged on the concrete as he dove to the ground. The rough pavement chaffed his hands. He looked up in time to see the two shadows dropping their boxes and running toward the corner of the building. Kaz jumped up to give chase, but before he'd gone ten steps, he heard a truck engine churn to life. By the time he reached the corner, it had roared down the alley to the main street. The truck squealed its tires as it made a sharp right turn and disappeared. The thieves were gone.

He stood, chest heaving, and reflected on what might have happened if that bullet had come a little closer. He recalled another time a bullet had whizzed by him, that fateful day on the streets of Krakow when soldiers opened fire on a group of protesters. This was the second time he'd nearly been shot, and he didn't like it any more than before. He turned and walked over to the side door where several boxes lay in disarray. Even in the weak light, it only took a moment to confirm his suspicions. They were the same boxes that had been left on the warehouse floor. He could tell by the missing colored labels. Then, something caught his eye. He reached down and picked up a red handkerchief. It was Marek's! He had the proof he needed to expose the man.

Kaz's first instinct was to call the police, but he changed his mind. Instead, he hurried down the street to the Rudnicka's house and banged on the front door. Lights blinked on as he banged again. The front door flew open to reveal Mr. Rudnicka standing in his nightshirt.

"Kaz, what's the meaning of this?" he barked in an ill-tempered voice. Daneta magically appeared behind him, pulling a robe over her exposed shoulders. Kaz had to fight an unbidden urge to kiss her neck and arms. He focused his attention on her father and told him what had just happened. Mr. Rudnicka left Kaz standing on the porch while he and Daneta rushed upstairs to dress, then the three of them hurried to the warehouse. Everything was as Kaz had left it, except for the handkerchief that he still held in his hand.

Once he'd inspected the mess, Mr. Rudnicka did call the police, who arrived in less time than it took for Kaz to return to his apartment and retrieve a jacket to fend off the cold, night air. Daneta stood close to him shivering from the chill. He wanted to put his arm around her but dared not with her father hovering nearby. The police inspected the handkerchief and agreed that the evidence looked damning. It wasn't substantial enough to pin Marek to the scene, however. Anyone could own a red handkerchief. Still, Mr. Rudnicka was convinced. He stomped around furiously, declaring it was all the evidence that he needed to fire the man.

By the time the police had finished their investigation of the crime scene, daylight was pushing its gray arms across the sky. Mr. Rudnicka took possession of the handkerchief and told Kaz to see him in his office at seven. Kaz returned to his apartment to wash and to eat a quick breakfast of cold cereal, then hurried back to Mr. Rudnicka's office. Daneta was waiting with her father when he arrived. He tried to read her expression, but she wore her business-like frown, which gave no hint of what was to come. Mr. Rudnicka spoke without preamble, something Kaz noticed that he often did.

"Kaz, it's time we settled things. I like the initiative you've shown in the warehouse, and the way you dealt with our theft problem It's time I made you the manager. We'll announce it this morning, just as soon as I fire Marek." He held up the red handkerchief as he spoke.

Kaz smiled with relief. At last, he'd found a position with prospects and real responsibility. He had something to look forward to each day, and he had a home, of sorts, with Daneta and her parents. She was smiling at him, now, in a manner that told him he'd found a safe harbor in his stormy life. And he'd found a respite from the pain he'd suffered over the loss of Christina. Life suddenly looked very promising. Only one thing bothered him: Marek.

"Thank you, sir. However, wouldn't it make more sense if you made the announcement and I fired Marek? It would send a message to the rest of the crew."

Mr. Rudnicka sat back and pondered his suggestion. "Good point, Kaz. I like that. We'll take care of things right now. And you'll need to find a replacement."

"I've thought about that. Marek has assumed an unofficial role as the leader of the men, and he's let them work at a slower pace. The men like that, of course, but it's not very efficient for the company. I believe we can do the same work without hiring anyone else. I think we can wait until we have more business."

Mr. Rudnicka glanced at his daughter. "I believe you made a good choice when you suggested this young man."

She gave Kaz a knowing look. "In many ways, father."

Kaz took the red handkerchief from Mr. Rudnicka and stuffed it in his pocket while they headed downstairs to call the men together. As they gathered, Kaz kept a watchful eye on Marek, who fidgeted with his hands in the restless manner of someone who had something to hide. Normally, Marek gazed directly at Kaz, challenging him, but this morning he lacked his usual bravado. He stared off into space without talking to anyone, and when he turned away, Kaz noted that his back pocket was empty.

Kaz felt tension in his arms and legs, much like he had in blood alley. It was a good tension. It told him that he was ready to tackle the task that lay before him, to make the leap into a better future. He was ready for Marek.

When Kaz's promotion was announced, there were murmurs in the group. A few of the men tossed uneasy glances his way. He expected that and knew just what to do. As soon as Mr. Rudnicka was finished, Kaz walked up to Marek.

"You lost this last night." He pulled the red handkerchief from his pocket and tossed it to Marek, who caught it without thinking. "Go collect your pay voucher. You're fired."

Kaz turned his back on Marek and walked to the front of the men. He tensed, expecting Marek to charge after him, but nothing happened. It never failed to amaze Kaz how often bullies backed down when faced with a determined opponent. Marek stood, red-faced, at the back of the room, then turned and stormed out the door. "You haven't heard the last of this," he snarled as he left.

Kaz had heard that before, too. He faced the men.

"There are two things I want to make clear from the start. First, there has been some theft going on here in the warehouse. Marek just got fired for it, and I expect that to put an end to the matter. We now have an inventory system in place that makes it much easier to track merchandise. If anyone else if caught stealing, they'll be shown the same door as Marek. Second, we're going to pick up the pace around here. We can handle the workload with the crew we've got if we all put our backs to it. So, let's get to work."

Kaz didn't just give orders to the men; he led by example. He was the first one in the warehouse each morning, and he spent as much time on the floor as possible unloading trucks, stacking shelves and filling orders. He worked at a steady pace that was not so much hurried as busy. He never stood still. The men took notice, and their work performance rapidly improved.

His personal life was not so easy to manage. Kaz was still trying to unravel the mysteries of Daneta. They had little in common. That much was clear. She read books and listened to her classical music. He preferred evenings in bars with friends and co-workers. She liked to sip wine or even champagne. Beer and vodka were his drinks of choice, and he didn't mind downing more than a glass or two on a night out. And, of course, there were their differing preferences regarding the choice of dance halls. A rowdy nightclub was just fine with Kaz, but Daneta wanted him to learn ballroom dancing. She was eager to dance something called the waltz. Kaz found its rhythm boring, but he did his best to comply. He also made himself listen to the classical music she played for him. He had to admit that he was starting to get the hang of a few pieces, and he did rather like some of them, but he knew it would never woo him the way it did Daneta. She also enjoyed art galleries and museums and twice dragged him to exhibitions featuring some artist with whom he was unfamiliar. He took her to the Wawel Castle and proudly showed her the armory room, but he saw at once that there was little to hold her interest. She didn't care for war or its weapons.

The more he was around Daneta the more he also realized just how important the company was to her. She loved to talk about schedules and new clothing styles. She could spend hours pouring over the numbers in her journals with the company bookkeeper, a stiff, pompous man named Dominik. Kaz disliked the man from the first time he met him, but he suffered his airs in silence for Daneta's sake. Personally, he would have liked to introduce his right fist to Dominik's nose.

Despite their differences and the accountant's irritating demeanor, Kaz was drawn to the Rudnicka household. Since he'd proved himself capable of being a manager, Daneta's father had warmed to him, just as she had predicted. Mrs. Rudnicka also seemed to be more accepting of his visits, although she continued to treat him as something only marginally higher than a servant.

His main interest was Daneta. Her shifting moods fascinated him: one moment, coquettish, the next aloof, though never completely beyond his reach. That was part of her charm, he realized, her ability to draw him into her world of waltzes and art galleries with her pretty smiles. He was charmed, and he wanted her. However, that part of their relationship remained as elusive as the rest. They kissed when they were alone, and their bodies continued to seek each other's on the dance floor. None of those moments approached the desire they'd shared that first night at the dance hall, however. Kaz was beginning to wonder if they would ever experience that passion again, whether their relationship could grow beyond hand holding and kisses.

Until the night Daneta changed the ground rules between them.

It happened on an evening that began like so many others. Daneta's parents were gone and wouldn't return until late. Kaz was invited over to listen to music and to sip wine. He sensed a tension in Daneta's movements that he hadn't noticed before. Halfway through one of her favorite pieces by Mozart, she rose from the floor where she'd been sitting and closed and locked the door to the room.

"No need to be interrupted by the maid," she explained in her soft voice.

When she returned, she chose the large, comfortable couch and settled back into its pillows. Moisture glistened on her forehead like diamonds. Her breaths rose and fell in her chest. Her dress tugged across her bodice, revealing just enough cleavage to attract Kaz's eye.

"Join me here." Daneta tapped the cushion next to her with her hand.

Kaz emptied his wine glass and rose from the floor. He sensed that the mood was shifting onto unfamiliar ground. A small voice in the back of his head told him to be careful. So far, their relationship had been about as involved as the one he'd had with Christina, but something in Daneta's expression said tonight would be different. He knew that he should make his excuses and leave, but he couldn't bring himself to do so. Daneta's cleavage beckoned to him. The look in her eye entrapped him.

Kaz moved to the sofa and sat down. They began with sweet kisses. Soon, Kaz felt a heat rising in him that threatened to race out of control. His hands began to rove over her body. When he suddenly slipped his fingers into her cleavage, she gasped and pressed her hand on his. That was all the encouragement he needed. Any thoughts about

POLAND INTERRUPTED

control were abandoned. Any concerns about the differences in their lifestyles were forgotten. Any attempts to maintain their decorum were tossed aside. In a matter of seconds, they reached the edge of their known universe and jumped together into the abyss.

"Do you think I'll get pregnant?"

Daneta's voice snapped Kaz out of his reverie.

"I don't think so. Maybe. I don't know." He rubbed her arm to comfort her. "It isn't likely, but I guess it's possible."

Kaz had never thought about the consequences of his actions before. He suddenly felt a bit queasy.

"You're my first," Daneta continued in a matter-of-fact tone. "I've had other chances, but this is the first time I've really wanted to do it."

"What would happen if you did ... get pregnant? What would your parents do?" A terrifying image of Mr. and Mrs. Rudnicka storming into the room and discovering them flashed before him. He sat up and began to put on his shirt.

"We'd get married, of course. Daddy would be very angry, but he would insist upon it. Mother ... I'm not so sure. She might want me to get rid of it."

Married! Kaz had never thought about getting married. The idea intrigued him. Would that be so bad? He'd slowly immersed himself in Daneta's world and found warmth there, something that had been missing from his life. He liked his job, *and* Mr. Rudnicka, despite his gruffness. But how did he feel about Daneta? Was he in love with her? He couldn't be certain. Their sexual encounter had been very satisfying, although not as passionate as he'd experienced with some other women. He recalled how Alicja in the brothel had locked her legs around his body and squealed with pleasure. It was an unfair comparison, he realized. Daneta wasn't a whore. She was a novice, if her claim was to be believed. Maybe I *do* love her, he thought.

Kaz wrapped an arm around Daneta's shoulders and pulled her closer to him.

"What do you think about marriage?" he asked cautiously. "You don't have to get pregnant first, do you?"

Daneta put her own arms around Kaz and squeezed him tightly. "Of course not, silly. People just have to love each other." She gave him an inquiring look. "Do you love me?"

Kaz was no longer surprised by her directness, but the bold question still made his mouth dry. It wasn't just a question of love. It was a question of honor and doing what was right. Daneta wasn't like other women. With her, actions had consequences. It didn't really matter whether she got pregnant. All that mattered was that they'd been intimate together.

"I don't know much about love," he admitted, "but what I feel for you is real." He took her hand and held it. "I know I want you enough to marry you."

Daneta blushed crimson. Her lower lip trembled. She pressed herself against him. "Oh, Kaz, I want that too." She trembled violently and smothered his face with kisses. "I love you, Kaz. You make me happy. It's so wonderful. I can't wait to tell father and mother."

It hadn't been a formal proposal, but it was a proposal, none-the-less. How had it happened? His head was swimming

Kaz found himself sitting in the Rudnicka's dining room the following evening while the maid served dinner. He knew that Daneta had not yet told her parents about their plans or why she'd asked him to join them. The suspense from waiting for Daneta's announcement made him so fidgety he could barely control his knife and fork. To distract himself, he thought about the family's circumstances. As eloquent as the house appeared to Kaz, he realized that it fell far short of the small palaces where the truly wealthy lived, people like Daneta's relatives. And the maid, their only servant, was expected to cook, serve the meals, keep the house dust free and shine the floors. This did not discourage them from presenting themselves as landed gentry. Kaz feared that his low social status would abort any marriage plans, even if he had been promoted to manager.

They were halfway through the main course of veal and potatoes when Daneta raised her wine glass and cleared her throat.

"I have some wonderful news to toast. Kaz and I wish to be married. As soon as possible," she added.

Kaz watched Mr. Rudnicka out of the corner of his eye and saw a deep color rise in his face. His hand gripped his napkin as if he was chocking it.

"Are you insane? Married? To Kaz?" His questions dripped with sarcasm.

"Daneta, that's out of the question," Mrs. Rudnicka chimed in with an alarmed voice. "I'm already speaking to your aunt about an appropriate match for you. Someone with social standing."

"But I'm not interested in someone just because of his social standing," she cried. "I love Kaz, and he wishes to marry me."

"It won't do." Mr. Rudnicka thundered. "We have a reputation to uphold. You have a future to consider." He looked at Kaz for the first time. "Kaz is a good lad but hardly the match your mother has in mind."

"Your father's right, dear," Mrs. Rudnicka declared firmly. "It won't do."

Daneta shoved back her chair and rose to her feet. "Well, it will have to do. I might be pregnant!"

Mrs. Rudnicka slumped in her chair. Her husband glared at Kaz in disbelief. "I have trusted you and brought you into our home, and this is how you repay me?" he shouted. "Did you think I would do nothing? That you could somehow get your hands on our fortune?"

"Father, we don't have a fortune," Daneta responded in an exasperated voice. "And it's not his doing. I seduced *him*." With that, she rushed from the room.

Kaz stared at the parents in dismay. Mr. Rudnicka's tie had somehow come askew and flopped over his coat's lapel. His wife's carefully coiffured hair had lost its moorings and hung scattered about her forehead. The pair looked as if they'd been assaulted by a terrible storm, and he supposed they had.

He finally found his voice. "I know this is all unexpected, and I'm sorry. But we've been together a lot. We've gotten to know each other. And our feelings grew a lot faster than either of us intended. I respect you and your daughter. I want to do what's right."

Kaz followed Daneta from the room and found her waiting for him at the front door.

"Take me to your place. I can't stay here tonight."

She kissed him quickly and took his hand. Together, they opened the front door and plunged into the night.

It took three days for Daneta's parents to come to grips with the situation. Kaz was certain they would disavow the wedding, but Daneta's threat of pregnancy quickly caused fissures in their wall of objections and overcame their resistance. They might not like Daneta's choice for a husband, but they feared scandal even more. The thought of an unmarried daughter parading around with a great, cascading belly, announcing to the world that she would soon be an unwed mother, was more than they could endure. Her father caved in first, and hastily arranged for a simple ceremony.

Kaz went about his work in the warehouse during the upheaval and did his best to steer clear of Mr. Rudnicka. Kaz feared that if Mr.

Rudnicka saw him, he would be fired on the spot. Meanwhile, Daneta stoked the flames of her parents' anger by staying with Kaz in his apartment. It was an awkward arrangement. Daneta was clearly uncomfortable in such sparse accommodations, but she made the best of it. They arrived at an unspoken agreement to avoid any further sexual contact until things were settled. They curled up together in his narrow bed, but limited their romantic indulgences to a few kisses.

Mr. Rudnicka initiated the truce by marching into the warehouse and telling Kaz it was time to talk. Kaz followed him back to his office, where he was told to sit down, Mr. Rudnicka remained standing behind his desk.

"You won't have our blessing," he announced in his usual perfunctory manner, "but we can't let you disgrace our daughter."

"Daneta might not be pregnant ... "

"Doesn't matter. The damage has been done. The innuendos must be avoided. You two are to be married at once, so there can be no stain on my daughter. As far as the world's concerned, Daneta is still a virgin and will remain so until she's married."

Kaz knew the world to which he referred consisted of the family's wealthy relatives. As far as Kaz could tell, the Rudnickas almost never saw them, but that didn't stop them from seeking their approval.

They were married two weeks later on a rainy afternoon at nearby St. Joseph's Church. Charlie rode the train to Krakow that morning and stood as Kaz's best man. Woz sent his good wishes but couldn't get away from work. Neither could Christina, which disappointed Kaz. He would've liked her there so that he could bring closure to his feelings for her. He didn't bother inviting his uncle or mother. The former would have been an embarrassment and the latter would've had no interest. The sudden wedding announcement had undoubtedly sent a clear message as to the reason for the urgency, despite the Rudnickas' declaration that the young couple simply wanted to marry as soon as possible. Mr. Rudnicka's brother and wife were the only family on Daneta's side that attended. The one thing that Kaz remembered about her was her silvery hair, swept back in an elegant wave that framed her high cheekbones and her formidable Grecian nose.

It was an awfully small contingent for such a big church. The priest's voice echoed among the empty pews. Daneta looked quite pretty in a traditional, white bridal gown that had been measured and sown in record time. Kaz had chosen a ready-made, black suit that hung slightly too long on his short frame. The ceremony was lovely enough, although the priest had a disturbingly loud voice. 'I dos' were followed by a brief mass, then umbrellas were unfolded and everyone hurried into the stormy afternoon as if they couldn't wait to be rid of the place.

Chapter Ten

To keep up appearances, Mr. Rudnicka rented a spacious, elegant apartment for the newlyweds in an upscale neighborhood just far enough away to create some space between the two households. Daneta visited her parents several times a week, but Kaz kept a polite distance. He limited his appearances to formal dinners once or twice a month.

As the months passed, patterns developed. Kaz worked hard in the warehouse but felt little need to bring his work home with him. Once the place was closed for the night, he was ready to put the day behind him. At first, he was content to stay in their comfortable, new home. Daneta made dinner every night and after listening to some of her classical records, they explored each other's bodies in new and exciting ways. But he could only take so much Beethoven and Brahms. He longed to hear trumpets and saxophones playing to the harmony of street music and jazz. When they did go out, it was to a concert or a museum. Even the sex lost its magic after awhile. He'd never been in such a long relationship before, and he was surprised at how quickly the erotic pleasures of marriage lost their edge and became routine. At how quickly their springtime romance slipped into summer.

Kaz tried to shake off such thoughts and to rededicate himself to his new life. He drank the wine that Daneta offered him. He listened to the music she played. In the end, it wasn't enough. He wanted to join his old acquaintances for drinks, visit dance clubs and have fun.

Daneta had different plans. Her idea of having fun was working late and sitting down with the bookkeeper to review the day's business. Kaz thought that she spent too much time with the bookkeeper, a man he despised. There was nothing about him that Kaz could like. He was arrogant and skinny; his eyeglasses inched down his long nose, forcing him to constantly push them up again; and his eyes blinked like signals at a railroad crossing. Daneta found him witty and intelligent, which only irritated Kaz even more.

He began to take walks after dinner to clear his head. It was late summer by now. The evenings still held the warmth of the day's sun. It was a glorious time to explore the streets. Lights blinked on as daylight shuffled off to bed. The smell of flowerbeds laced the air with a chorus of aromas. He tried to interest Daneta in joining him, and she did on occasion. She even rested her head on his shoulder in a familiar way that he found charming. For those brief spells, romance regained the upper hand. Such moments were fleeting. Too often, Daneta was more consumed by the numbers swirling about in her head than she was by the prospect of watching the setting sun. Kaz would linger on the streets until after dark, then return to discover Daneta pouring over her ledgers.

It was only a matter of time before an open doorway to a bar filled with cheerful voices and clinking glasses drew him inside. He had two shots of vodka with his new friends before he left. Daneta seemed not to notice when he got home. A few nights later, he returned to the bar. This time, several ladies had joined the men. The mood was decidedly brighter, the ladies flirtatious. Kaz quickly downed his two vodkas and was sorely tempted to stay for more. The banter was filled with a spicy energy that tried to seduce him, but he knew he should go home. After a brief tussle with his conscience, he bade goodnight.

He returned home to a troubling scene: his wife and the bookkeeper huddled closely together reviewing a ledger in the dining room. Dominik looked up with his blinking eyes and stared uncertainly at Kaz, who wanted to storm across the room and pound the man with his fists. He stood trembling inside the doorway and struggled to control himself.

"What's going on?" he demanded.

Daneta had been so absorbed with her ledger, she hadn't heard the front door.

"Kaz, we were just looking at the week's numbers for the warehouse." She said this with her severe look. It told him she was all business. "The fabric inventory doesn't match what we've ordered. It's short by several boxes.

"Meaning?" He could hear the tension in his voice.

"We believe someone is stealing fabric before it gets to the factory floor," Dominik offered. "This isn't the first time the balances have been off. I've noticed it before."

Kaz swallowed a bitter taste as he eyed the two of them. He listened to Dominik's explanation, tried to understand what he said, but the words zinged past his ears with the force of stray bullets. All Kaz heard was an accusation that he wasn't doing his job. His mind whirled at the implication.

"We can discuss the matter after Dominik is gone." Kaz stepped aside to indicate that the bookkeeper should leave. Dominik started to gather the ledgers, but Kaz stopped him.

"Leave them here," he said curtly. "I'll review them with Daneta."

The bookkeeper nodded to them both and hurried to the front door. Once he was gone, Kaz turned his attention to Daneta, who was watching him with a troubled expression.

"That wasn't necessary. Dominik was only doing his job."

"You don't take up warehouse matters with him. You bring them to me," Kaz replied sharply. He immediately regretted his angry response when he saw Daneta tremble under the onslaught of his words. "I'm the one who has to deal with the warehouse," he added in a quieter voice. "Show me what you've found."

Daneta reviewed the numbers, and Kaz could see that she was right. The goods received didn't match the inventory in the warehouse.

"We've changed the locks. It's no longer possible for anyone to sneak in at night."

"Which means goods are being stolen during the day," Daneta added thoughtfully. She leaned close to him while they reviewed the numbers. He could feel her breath on his arm and smell the scent in her hair, both of which aroused him. Working together to solve the problem sent a spark of intimacy dancing between them. Daneta blushed coyly, just as she had done so often before they were married.

"But the color coding system makes it impossible for them to hide merchandise on the warehouse floor. It would be too easy to spot it, and I keep a close eye on things." Kaz was emphatic.

"Unless they got hold of the labels. Then, they could change the codes to make raw materials look like finished goods ready to be shipped." Daneta placed her hand on Kaz's, sending a new jolt of energy through him. "Where do you keep the labels? In you desk?"

Kaz nodded guiltily. "In one of the side drawers. I never expected anyone to be brazen enough to rummage through my desk."

"That's it, then. Someone is taking stickers and putting them on boxes to make them look like they're ready to be shipped. Then, they load them on one of the trucks making pickups, and they are spirited away right under our noses." Daneta squeezed Kaz's hand and stood back triumphantly. "Now, all we have to do is figure out who's the guilty party."

"That sounds too sophisticated for this bunch. Somebody has to be arranging things on the outside, somebody like Marek. I smell his hand in this."

Daneta nodded excitedly. "We have to prepare a trap to catch them. I can ask the distributor to put a small, black sticker on each box of fabric that they deliver. We can remove it from the boxes that go to the factory. But if any inventory is set aside in the warehouse and color coded for shipment, the sticker will still be there. When the stolen goods are loaded on a truck, we can have it followed to its rendezvous point. That's where we'll find Marek, or whoever is behind this scheme."

Kaz had to admit that Daneta had a good idea. He was amazed at how quickly she thought of it. He looked at her with new admiration and took her in his arms.

"You would make a good detective," he murmured into her hair.

"And that's what we need." She buried her face in his neck. "We need to hire a detective to follow the truck and deal with Marek."

Kaz had every intention of dealing with Marek himself, but at that moment all he could think about was taking his wife to bed.

The two of them presented their findings to Daneta's father the next morning, along with their plan to trap the thieves. Daneta made it sound like the plan was Kaz's idea, which he appreciated. He was still trying to get out from under her father's bad graces. Mr. Rudnicka was obviously pleased with their initiative. He gave Kaz a nod of recognition, and he agreed that they should hire a detective.

"He can use the apartment across from the warehouse. It'll give him a good vantage point. Kaz, you'll keep a close vigil on the men. As soon as you spot anything irregular, you can signal the detective."

The air was charged with anticipation. They were embarking on a great adventure, and it stimulated Kaz and Daneta in the most unexpected ways. It only took a look with an arched eyebrow or touch of the hand to throw them into each other's arms. Kaz no longer felt the need to visit the nearby tavern. Better still, Dominik stayed away.

Two days later, a delivery of new fabrics arrived, and their plan was set in motion. It was a large order, and it took all the men to remove the boxes from the truck and to store them on the shelves. Each box carried a new, black sticker in the lower right hand corner. Once the merchandise was put away, Kas began his vigil. He was careful to keep a safe distance from the new boxes, so he wouldn't alert the thieves or raise their suspicions.

POLAND INTERRUPTED

On the first day, six boxes were coded and delivered to the factory. None showed up in the shipping area. The second day also passed without incident. All the finished goods returning to the warehouse had the sticker removed. Kaz was beginning to fear that their scheme wouldn't work. Perhaps, they were wrong about the men. Or, someone had noticed him watching the inventory despite his efforts to act normal. His doubts grew as the third day stretched into the afternoon. However, all his doubts scattered when one of the workers, a close friend of Marek's, nonchalantly removed four boxes of raw fabric from the shelves. An hour later, they reappeared on the loading dock with colored tags showing them ready for shipment. All four boxes still displayed the new sticker. The boxes had not been to the factory floor. Soon, a truck arrived, and the driver presented paperwork to pick up several orders. The same employee that Kaz had observed earlier deftly slid the four marked boxes in with the other orders and loaded all of them into the truck.

Kaz stepped outside and signaled the detective, who hurried down the stairs and disappeared around the back of the apartment building where his car was hidden. As soon as the truck pulled away, Kaz raced to the detective's car and hopped into the passenger seat. He knew everybody at the warehouse was watching, but he didn't care. There was no way for anyone to warn the truck driver. The trap was about to snap shut. They set out at a safe distance and tailed the truck as it wound its way through traffic. Twice, Kaz thought they were too far back and were going to lose their quarry, but the detective remained calm. In no time, he had the truck back in his sights. They headed into a warehouse district near the Vistula River. The driver made one more turn past a local bar where music boomed out the door and parked a few doors away in front of a cinder-block building that boasted a small loading dock. The place smelled of burnt ash from a nearby factory. In a matter of seconds, Marek appeared from a small doorway, spoke briefly with the driver and began to unload the boxes. The detective told Kaz to stay where he was while he ran back to the bar to use a phone to call the police.

Kaz watched as Marek finished unloading the boxes and paid the driver some zlotys. The driver tipped his cap, got back into the truck and departed. Marek glanced around, more out of habit than concern, and lifted a roller door that opened onto a ten-foot by ten-foot storage room. Kaz was too far away to see clearly into the darkened room, but he was pretty sure there were more boxes from the warehouse. There were other containers, as well. Marek appeared to be doing business at more than one factory.

Kaz itched to get his hands on Marek, but he followed the detective's orders and waited. A song from the bar echoed down the street. It was the kind of music he would normally enjoy, especially when he had a beer in his hand, but now it irritated him. He didn't want any distractions. All his attention was focused on Marek. He opened and closed his hands in anticipation of facing the man. He hoped the police would let him take one good swing before they took him away.

Marek finished loading the boxes into the storage room. He pulled down the roller door and secured it with a padlock. Next, he took a key and locked the side door where he'd been waiting. He turned and started to walk away. He was leaving! Kaz stepped out of the car, heart thrumming, and looked around for the detective, who was still inside the bar. He thought about calling to him, but the music was too loud. It would drown his voice. He would have to stop Marek himself.

Kaz ran toward his quarry.

"Marek, you dumb, fat bastard, you're not going anywhere."

Marek looked back over his shoulder at Kaz in astonishment. "Where the hell did you come from?"

"It's not where I came from. It's who I came for."

Marek looked around for something to use as a weapon, but found nothing. Kaz slowed his pace and strode toward him. Marek balled his hands into fists. He took one step forward and threw a punch at Kaz's head. The speed of his attack caught Kaz by surprise. He attempted to duck, but the blow glanced off the side of his head, causing his eyes to water and his ears to ring. He staggered back a step to regain his balance. Another fist barreled toward him. This time, he managed to duck under the blow. The fist flashed past him. Marek's effort left him momentarily vulnerable, and that was the all opening that Kaz needed. He launched a series of quick jabs into his opponent's midsection. As he expected, it was too soft to withstand the power of his fists. A whoosh of air escaped from Marek, and he bent over, exposing his chin. Kaz scored a sharp uppercut to the man's jaw. Marek staggered. Kaz focused on his stomach with another series of blows. Marek sank to his knees, dazed and out of breath. Kaz was about to finish him off when the detective arrived with two police officers. Kaz stood with his heart pumping and his fist raised, ready to deliver a knockout blow. He barely heard the detective's order to stop. His ears were still ringing from Marek's first punch. He slowly lowered his fist and made way for the police officers, who quickly handcuffed Marek. They fished his keys from his pocket and marched him over to the storage room. The padlock was unlocked and the roll-up door was raised to reveal merchandise from several companies, including more boxes from the Rudnicka's clothing factory.

Kaz smiled with satisfaction. He knew he'd just earned his way back into Mr. Rudnicka's good graces.

Daneta's father was waiting for Kaz when he returned to the factory. He congratulated Kaz for his efforts on behalf of the company and invited him to dinner, a gesture that indicated at least a partial thaw in their relationship. Mrs. Rudnicka's response was less welcoming. There was no evidence of any thaw at that end of the dinner table. Winter still prevailed there.

Winter also began to spread its icy tentacles at home. The euphoria that Kaz and Daneta had experienced during their recent adventure subsided. The drama in their lives drained away and, with it, the spark that had driven them into each other's arms. The differences that had separated them before began to emerge, once more.

Kaz found himself immersed in a world of symphonies and sonatas, played on Daneta's record player after dinner and at live theater performances twice a month, where his mind wandered and his eyelids drooped. Then, there were the weekly sojourns to the Athletic Club, where they spent the evening dancing. Kaz was now recognized as a member of the Rudnicka family. He was greeted with respect by the staff and introduced to other couples whose backgrounds spoke of wealth and position in Poland's social hierarchy. He had little idea what to say to them and let Daneta carry their brief conversations. Daneta complemented Kaz on his improved dancing, but their bodies no longer pressed together with their previous hunger. Life, he concluded, was becoming dull. He made a valiant effort to appreciate this more refined way of life, but he longed for the boisterous voices and songs at the Old Hall and the other dance clubs he used to frequent. He wanted to drink beer, not Chablis, vodka instead of champagne.

Still, he might have found some way to adjust to his new life had it not been for Daneta's obsession with the family business. She discussed cash flow with her father at dinner, chatted to Kaz about personnel in the warehouse, and dissected sales data with anyone who would listen. As the months passed, she spent less time with Kaz and more time with the company ... and more time with Dominik, who reappeared, ledgers in hand, at least once a week. He would blink rapidly at Kaz before joining Daneta at the dining table to pour over the latest income and cost data. Kaz wanted to flee the house, but refused to do so when Dominik was there. He sat in the other room, instead, and tried to ignore their chatter. He refused to call it jealously, although it felt an awful lot like the turmoil he'd experienced when he saw Charlie and Christina together. One thing he knew for certain: the family business was invading their lives, and that *was* unhealthy.

Kaz tried to make his feelings known, but Daneta protested that the business was struggling due to the depression and needed her attention more than ever. Even when Dominik wasn't there, Daneta sometimes pulled out her ledgers after dinner to review the day's activity. Kaz fled the house on those nights, preferring the company of the nearby bar's patrons to that of balance sheets. The comradeship offered by his fellow drinkers was his only solace.

Insult was added to injury when Kaz returned a little early one evening from the tavern and saw Daneta's ledgers still sprawled across the dining room table. He casually inspected them and realized with a shock that they were connected to the warehouse inventory and shipping data. The ledgers for purchased fabric and sales lay next to them. Daneta was tracking his warehouse activity and comparing inventory records and shipments against purchase orders.

Daneta entered the room just as Kaz finished looking at the last ledger. He slammed the book down on the table and turned to face her. The smile on her face faded when she saw his angry expression.

"You're spying on me!" he declared.

"No I'm not." Daneta's face pinched into the severe look Kaz had come to know so well.

"Then how do explain these ledgers? You're checking up on me."

"I do the same with all the departments. Besides, that's how I discovered the thefts. That's why we found out about Marek. And I let you take credit for it."

Kaz opened his mouth to retort but closed it again. He knew she was right. She'd discovered the discrepancies in the books and devised the plot to uncover the thieves. He'd merely provided the muscle. The realization did nothing to improve his mood. He stormed out the front door and didn't return until the hour was late.

Daneta's moods began to affect Kaz's work. He no longer arrived with the energy he'd had before. He was more lethargic and less likely to admonish someone for sloppy or tardy work. The workers noticed and took advantage. Their work pace slowed, much as it had under

Marek's influence. Kaz felt the warehouse walls closing in on him. Marrying Daneta had seemed the right thing to do. He'd wanted to protect her honor, and he was drawn to the family, even if they hadn't accepted him with welcoming arms. The fabric business looked promising, despite the depression. He had a responsible position there. He had prospects. However, none of that could cover up the fact that his life felt as though it was over. It wasn't just the ballroom dancing at the Athletic Club or the concerts, or the classical music on the record player. It was with Daneta ... and it was with him. A brief whirlwind of passion had tossed them together, but they had never been consumed by the desire to hold each other for an eternity. Passion without love was a dimwit's journey.

Each disagreement was followed by a brief period of reconciliation, as they both tried to mend the fences that defined their relationship. These were pleasant times. They spoke softly to each other and shared warm moments of passion together. New tensions soon pushed them apart, however, and they entered a downward cycle of recriminations and despair. Each time they hit bottom, they would scramble out of the hole they had dug with their sharp words, and they would hoist themselves back into the warmth they still sought from each other. It was a steep climb, one that taxed all their strength. Inevitably, the ascent became too steep. Try as they might, they could no longer find the handholds necessary to reach the top. They floundered and slid back into the abyss.

One night, Kaz returned home to find Dominik and Daneta together in the sitting room listening to a classical record. Their journals lay scattered on the dining table in the adjoining room. Both bolted from their chairs with startled looks when he stormed into the room. Kaz nearly unleashed his fury but managed to rein in his anger. It would do no good to pummel the man with his fists. Dominik sensed the danger and fled from the apartment without bothering to collect his books.

Kaz turned his gaze on Daneta, who stood in the middle of the room with a perplexed expression that told him she didn't think she had done anything wrong.

"There's no reason to be angry. We were just taking a break."

"By sitting together and listening to music?"

"I wanted to play a new record. And Dominik likes this music."

Kaz heard the insinuation. He liked the music more than *Kaz*. "That still doesn't give you the right to entertain him when I'm not home," he shouted.

Daneta's lips tightened into a straight line. "I wasn't entertaining him. He's my employee. He comes here because I tell him to, not because he wants me." Her voice rose to a high pitch. "I'm not one of your women down at that bar you visit!"

Daneta charged past Kaz without looking at him, gathered up the ledgers and strode into the bedroom. The door slammed shut behind her. The door had never been closed before. Kaz got the message.

He spent a sleepless night on the stiff couch in the sitting room, wondering what to do. Marrying Daneta had been a bad idea, he realized. Not that she wasn't sweet in her own way. And she had tried to make the marriage work. They both had. But there was a gulf between them that couldn't be breached, and he doubted that they truly loved each other. Kaz had been a novelty that spiced up Daneta's circumscribed life. Daneta had been a breath of fresh air that he'd hoped would fill the void left by Christina. Neither of them had gotten what they expected. Kaz's life had not prepared him to offer the nurturing that she needed, and she couldn't free herself from the shackles of her colorless world.

Kaz didn't find any answers to his problems that night, but he decided it was time to start looking for them.

Chapter Eleven

The answer to Kaz's dilemma arrived a week later from an unexpected source. A truce of sorts had been declared since the night he'd slept on the couch. He made a conscious effort to be more attentive to Daneta's needs, and she resisted the urge to pull her ledgers out at home. Dominik had not made an appearance. When the night finally came that she insisted on spending an hour or two on company business, Kaz gracefully agreed and left the house with a promise not to be back too late.

The bar was filled with unfamiliar faces when Kaz entered. It was too early for the regulars to show themselves, so he plunked down on a stool at the bar and ordered vodka without ice. As he scanned the room, his eyes stopped at a ruddy face that was all too familiar.

"Captain Hermann," he cried as he crossed the room to his table. "What are you doing here? I thought you would never leave your old ship."

The captain returned Kaz's smile. "My boat left me. The navy decided to scuttle it. I figured it was time to call it quits, so I retired. Now I draw a small pension and live with my daughter and her family." He let loose a hearty laugh. "Damn, I still miss the sea, but life isn't so bad. What about you? You look prosperous for such mean times."

Kaz looked at his drink while he tried to think about what to say. "I'm married, now, and manage a warehouse. But I miss the sea, just like you. I'm thinking I need to make a change, but I don't know what to do. Jobs are so scarce. I couldn't just dump the one I've got unless I knew of something with promise. Preferably something on a ship." Kaz was surprised by his own words, but he realized that he had just verbalized something that had been forming in the back of his mind.

Captain Hermann rubbed his chin and looked absently around the room, his white brows knitted in thought. "I might know of something. There's a fella I met in Gdansk who's starting up a fishing fleet. Looking for able-bodied men. Prefers those with fishing experience, but I think he'd take someone who knows his way around a ship, someone like yourself."

Kaz sat back in his chair and downed the rest of his drink. He scratched his head while he thought a moment. "The only thing I know about fishing is what I used to catch with a pole in the Vistula River. But I'm a quick learner, and I know ships. I'd sure like to meet him."

"His name's Captain Jacob Prong. I'm to meet him here for drinks tomorrow night 'bout this time. Why don't you join us?"

Kaz nodded his head emphatically. "I'll be here. Don't you worry."

Getting away the next evening proved to be a little more awkward than Kaz had anticipated. Daneta decided it was time to go dancing again. To his surprise, she suggested returning to the dance club he liked so much, and she pouted when he told her he couldn't. He knew she was making an effort to appease him and he appreciated it. Not that it mattered. Her flag of truce wasn't going to change anything. He had to move forward with his life.

"I met my old sea captain from the navy. He needs a favor, and I promised to help him. I'm meeting him in an hour. Can we go tomorrow night?" It was a half-truth and half a lie. Kaz had never lied to Daneta before, and his face flushed with guilt as he met her gaze. If Daneta noticed, she chose not to say anything.

"Tomorrow, then," was her only reply.

Kaz arrived for his meeting on time. A few familiar faces were already lined up along the bar, but he ignored them and headed for the table where Captain Hermann sat with an angular man whose leathery face spoke of a great many years at sea.

"Kaz, sit down. This is Captain Jacob Prong. I've told him all about you."

Captain Prong was a thin man, but his handshake was strong. "Captain Hermann says I can rely on you. That's important. This will be a big operation, and I need reliable men.

"We're starting a joint venture between a Dutch firm and one from Poland. It'll be called the Polish-Holland Line and will consist of a fleet of trawlers based out of Scheveningen, Holland. We'll be fishing for herring along the coastal areas of the North Atlantic. The crews on the ships will be a mixture of Polish and Dutch. Someone like yourself will have to start at the bottom as a helper while you learn the fishing trade. Your pay will be low, but if the fishing is good, you have the prospect of a healthy bonus at the end of the season. At present, I'm recruiting a crew for a ship called the Meva. If the job interests you, you'll be expected to report in one week in Gdynia."

Kaz had never considered becoming a fisherman. He liked the idea of returning to sea, however, and fishing was as good a trade as any other. Besides, it would put some distance between him and Daneta, which was probably for the best.

"Count me in," he agreed. "I'll report to the Meva one week from today."

After they had finished their drinks, the two men left, and Kaz joined his friends at the bar. One of them, a young man called Pete, was in the middle of an argument with a rough looking character that Kaz had not seen before. Three other men stood nearby giving menacing looks. Kaz sensed trouble and quickly assessed the men at the bar. He counted four friendly faces that could be relied upon if things got rough. Before he knew it, fists were flying. Kaz ducked two blows and began swinging at anybody he didn't recognize. Others joined in the melee. He heard a shattering sound as a beer glass sailed past him and struck the wall. Two chairs flew through the air. Then, something struck him below his right eye. He slumped to the floor just as the lights went out. When he regained consciousness, he saw police officers sorting things out. Pete sat in a chair with a bloody gash in his forehead. Several combatants stood around nursing bruises. Kaz touched his cheek with two fingers and felt a twinge of pain. It wasn't bad enough to worry about, but he suspected he would have a colorful eye to show for his troubles. It was a heck of a way to finish his visits to the bar, but he couldn't help feeling exhilarated by the free-for-all. He'd landed a new job, and he'd managed to survive an old fashioned brawl with only minor injuries. All in all, it had been an exciting evening.

Kaz didn't bother to check himself in a mirror before he left the bar. Nor did he feel the need when he returned home. The shock on Daneta's face told him he most likely had a sizable black and blue bruise tattooed around his right eye.

"What happened?" she managed to gasp.

"A fight broke out down at the bar where I was meeting my friend. I have no idea why. I hit a couple guys in self defense, then somebody clobbered me."

Daneta touched his bruise gingerly. "You need some ice."

She retrieved a piece of ice from the freezer and rolled it in a dishcloth. "What happened to your friend?"

"He was gone by then. His name's Captain Hermann. I trained under him in the navy. He's found me a job on a fishing boat."

His casual statement crackled through the air with the force of a fast moving thunderstorm. Daneta stood in the doorway with the towel in her hand and looked at him in disbelief.

"Why would you become a fisherman? You have a good job."

Kaz took the towel from her hand and pressed it against his eye. "You know we haven't been good for each other, lately. We need some time apart. I need some time to think about things."

Kaz feared that Daneta would get upset and start to cry. Just the opposite happened. True to her nature, she straightened her posture, squared her shoulders and pressed her lips together in a thin line, giving him that familiar severe look he knew so well.

"If that's what you want, so be it" Her shoulders trembled, but she stood her ground. "Father will be disappointed in you. He likes you, thinks you have a good future here. You're letting him down."

"I'm not letting anybody down. I worked hard. It's just time to move on, at least for now. I enjoyed the navy. I liked being at sea. Maybe, that's where I belong."

"When do you plan to do this?"

"The ship's crew is being formed right now."

The storm Kaz had created crossed Daneta's face. "Fine, then. You can leave tonight."

Kaz started to object that he didn't report for a week, but he realized it would be better for everyone if he made other arrangements. He headed for the bedroom where he kept his old sea bag. He pulled it from the closet and stuffed his clothes into it without much thought about folding them. He just wanted to pack and be gone as quickly as possible. Daneta stood in the doorway and watched him. When he glanced at her, he saw that the firm line formed by her mouth had softened. She said nothing. The silence between them hovered in the air. There was no need for more words.

"Where will you go?" she asked at last.

"The ship is in Gdynia at the moment. I have enough money to stay someplace until I board it. It's called the Meva, by the way. It will sail out of Scheveningen in Holland. I'll mail you the particulars, in case you need to reach me for any reason."

Kaz took one last look around before swinging the bag over his shoulder and walking past Daneta to the front door. He didn't know what else to say, and he wanted to escape the anger in the room as quickly as possible.

"Good luck," she said softly.

Kaz took a long look at her before he shoved his way out the door.

Captain Prong met Kaz when he boarded the Meva with piercing, bright blue eyes, eyes that glittered from deep set, crinkled sockets, each topped with a tiny thatch of what looked like dried seaweed. There was no doubt as to the purpose of the ship. Even his unschooled nose could detect the odor of herring more than a city block to windward. The Meva looked sturdy enough, although sadly in need of a new coat of paint and a thorough scrubbing. He was led to the crew's quarters, which were located in a poorly ventilated cabin tucked under the forecastle. To reach it, he had to climb down a stepladder, pass through an open companionway, and claw his way past a burlap curtain. The floor, walls and ceiling were all made of rough, unpainted wood. In the center stood a small, wood-burning stove with a flimsy stovepipe rising out of it at a bizarre angle and meandering through a hole cut in the deck above. Rusty wire loops secured it in place.

Narrow, wooden benches surrounded the bulkhead on three sides. Bunk beds were built into the walls above the benches and fitted with sliding doors that could be closed when the bunks were unoccupied. The latrine was a fascinating piece of engineering. It was fashioned out of an old, wood-slat barrel without a top or bottom. A mottled, wooden toilet seat had been salvaged from somewhere and nailed to the top. The barrel hung suspended on two, short, boom timbers that projected over the stern rail. Standing at the barrel wasn't so bad, but when someone had to "sit on the throne," he hung suspended, feet dangling in the air, only ten feet above the pitching waves. In calm weather, the thing worked fairly well, but when the seas turned rough, with the ship pitching and tossing in a driving wind, it took all of a man's courage and agility to plant his bottom on that toilet seat!

The crew's quarters acted as galley, storehouse, dining room and recreation area, all rolled into one. The man they called cookie was a net man who hauled nets and gutted fish. When he wasn't performing those duties, he prepared the food, loosely referred to as chow, on the cabin stove. He did a passable job the first few days, because he was able to mix some fresh vegetables and salad in with the meat. After the first week, the crew made do with beans, flour and salt pork.

Breakfast consisted of a dish the cook called Dutch pancakes. He heated a huge iron skillet and dropped in a thick slice of salt pork. When the pork was browned around the edges and enough grease had bubbled out of it, he poured a half-inch layer of sourdough pancake batter over it. As soon as the dough was browned on one side, he turned the whole mess over and browned it on the other side. The result was a slightly burned, soggy pancake about half-an-inch thick that dripped grease and contained a half-fried slab of salt pork. As each pancake came out of the skillet, he flopped it onto a tin platter and sprinkled it with granulated sugar. A stack of four was considered breakfast for one able-bodied seaman. For anyone with a queasy stomach, however, the smell of cookie's pancakes was enough to send him scurrying on deck for fresh air.

The noon meal proved to be a bit better. The men worked in shifts and cooked their own fresh herring. The evening meal was normally a pot of beans with salt pork floating in it. Everything was either eaten or drunk from a crewman's bowl, a deep wooden dish issued to each man. It served as plate, cup, saucer and drinking glass, and each man washed his own bowl.

Kaz stayed on deck as much as possible while they headed for Scheveningen. The bracing wind and salty air raised his spirits, but in spite of his conviction that he'd made the right decision to go to sea, he still harbored thoughts about the life he'd left behind. He wasn't too worried about Daneta. She had her work, and her parents were close by. He thought she might move back with them, although she seemed to thrive on her own. He found to his surprise that he actually missed his wife a bit.

Captain Prong was a skillful skipper who commanded respect. His lanky body made a striking figure outlined against the sky when he stood on the bridge, his slicker flapping about the tops of his black rubber boots. He ordered a quick stop in Kiel so the men could buy any personal items they might have overlooked before continuing to the Netherlands. Kaz had just returned to the ship after posting a letter to Daneta with contact information when he noticed several mysterious crates being hauled aboard and stashed in the skipper's cabin. Kaz scratched his head, but for the life of him he couldn't figure out what was in those crates.

The ship moved out later that night, and by noon the next day ran into its first heavy weather, a raging Baltic storm. The little ship jumped and skittered across the waves like a frightened water bug, while its engines roared in an effort to keep the boat from being blown off course. Most of the crew, including Kaz, found their sea legs and rode through the storm undeterred. For a few, the experience was less satisfying, and they spent the next morning ignoring cookie's Dutch pancakes, preferring to lean over the rails, instead. The skipper addressed the situation by issuing a double ration of cognac to all hands. The liquor settled everyone's stomachs, and the crew was soon working at full strength.

One of the experienced members of the crew told Kaz that the mysterious crates the skipper had stowed away contained cognac. Apparently, good cognac was hard to find in the Netherlands, and the commander intended to sell most of his stash at a tidy profit. It was easy to smuggle the liquor into the country, because the Dutch harbor inspectors rarely bothered with small fishing vessels.

However, Captain Prong had not counted on a feisty, young inspector who seemed determined to do his job by the book. Shortly after the Meva's anchor rattled down in the harbor, one of the hands spotted a customs boat heading their way. The skipper shouted to the crew to get the cognac out of his cabin and to dump it over the side as quickly as possible. All hands raced to the skipper's cabin and started dragging cases of cognac to the rail on the opposite side of the ship. The men ripped the top off each case, grabbed a bottle in each hand, bent over the rail and smashed them against the hull. The poignant smell of expensive liquor filled the men's nostrils as they sadly watched the golden liquid trickle down the side of the ship. It wasn't long until one of the men decided to do something about it. Before smashing the next bottle, he pulled the cork and took a swig from it. The other men quickly followed suit. Soon everyone was taking two or three swallows out of each bottle before it was smashed against the ship's hull. By the time the agent came aboard, all evidence of the contraband was gone, and the men were swaying about like palm trees with silly grins on their faces. Two men on the bridge broke into song. They made up in gusto what they lacked in tune. And the cook appeared with an open bottle of cooking brandy that he kept in the galley. He held up the bottle and proposed that everyone toast to the Dutch customs. The agents left with a shake of their heads. It was doubtful they'd ever inspected such a dry ship with such an intoxicated crew.

The next few days in Scheveningen were busy ones. The ship had to be prepared for several rigorous months at sea. Engines were oiled and cleaned. Nets were checked and repaired. More provisions were brought aboard and stowed, including one case of cognac that was legally purchased for the crew. When all was ready, the skipper pointed the Meva's prow toward the rough North Sea and headed for waters off the southern Norwegian coast where he'd been told the fishing was good. The captain even produced one of the new bottles of cognac and passed it among the crew. It was a good omen, he said, to drink to a good catch. He got no argument from the crew.

It was the last carefree moment they would experience for the next three months. Kaz and the crew soon fell into a rigorous routine of Dutch pancake breakfasts, backbreaking work, and exhausted sleep, while always being immersed in the malodorous odor of fish. Kaz's job was to support the net men. That involved ten to twelve hour shifts of feeding the nets out so they didn't become snagged and hauling them in again.

The captain kept a tight rein on everybody. Disagreements were dealt with firmly. Fights landed participants in the brig for a night without a meal. The crew knew their jobs and worked hard, but they soon became a slovenly lot. The men slept, ate and worked on the run, with little time for personal hygiene. Many went days without bathing, and only a few bothered to shave. Faces swelled and turned blotchy red from constant exposure to the sun and wind. Hair and beards became caked with salt and sweat and stood out in all directions. They reminded Kaz of a pack of porcupines.

The workday began at two in the morning. The herring nets were attached to long lines that were as thick as a man's wrist and set so they could be trailed out behind the boat in a great arc. Once the nets were spun out and set, there followed a short period of waiting before the nets were hauled in again. During the lull, many of the men grabbed Cookie's Dutch pancakes and ate a quick breakfast. When the signal was given, Kaz and several others began pulling in the nets. Others lined up along the rails on either side of the ship to shake the fish into bins and fold the nets so they didn't snag. The heavy lines were coiled in the foredeck hatch, and the nets were hung to dry. Once the last net was in, Kaz had to begin feeding the dry ones out again. By the time they were set, it was six o'clock and it was time for more Dutch pancakes and bowls of coffee laced with cognac. Within the hour, all hands were called on deck to clean and pack the catch. Men sat on boxes or barrels alongside the huge bins in groups of three. Two of the men used short, thick knives to gill and gut the fish, after which the herring were tossed into barrels. The third man dipped coarse salt over them. When a barrel was filled, it had to be removed immediately to the cargo hold so the perishable fish would not be exposed to the sun.

By the time the last fish was packed away, it was time to commence retrieving the nets. The cycle of setting nets, retrieving them, cleaning fish and resetting nets went on endlessly as long as there was light to see. That translated into sixteen-to-eighteen-hour days in the summertime in Scandinavian waters. When darkness finally fell, the men tumbled into their bunks clothes and all. Within minutes they were snoring as loudly as those trains charging down blood alley.

Foul weather brought the only respite from the routine. Storms often made it too dangerous to remain on deck. Then, the men would batten down the hatches and huddle in their tiny cabin until it passed. Most took this free time to catch up on their sleep, but if the storm lasted long enough, they would wake up, drink coffee and either play cards or write letters. Boredom and body odors soon took their toll.

The men were generally grateful when the sun reappeared, even though it meant going back on deck to set nets and haul in fish. The air was fresh, and they knew that the quicker the hold was filled with herring, the sooner they could return to port.

When the cargo hold was finally filled, it was customary to head for the nearest port. It made no difference to the captain whether they docked in Holland, Sweden or France, just as long as there was a Polish-Holland Company agent available. After spending weeks at sea on a diet of beans, salt pork and fish, the men didn't care which country they reached, as long as there was fresh food available and they were free to spend time ashore. The Poles seemed to prefer the French ports of Dunkerque and Calais, but the Dutchmen hoped for Scheveningen or Rotterdam and the chance to spend a day at home.

After a day off, the crew faced a hectic schedule back on board. Captain Prong was always in a hurry to re-provision the ship so they could return to sea as quickly as possible. He knew that a fishing boat didn't make a dime in port, so he spent the time they were in port pacing back and forth and shouting orders to the crew.

"The season is too damned short to dally," he would remind everyone. "If we don't stay on schedule, there'll be no bonuses." He would continue to growl and curse until they reached the fishing grounds. Then, everyone was too busy to care.

One thing the men missed during their hectic days aboard ship was news from home, but the crews had developed ingenious methods to overcome this problem. It was common for as many as a dozen ships to be running at close quarters over a large school of herring. New arrivals were expected to share news with those who had been at sea for long periods of time. When two ships were running alongside each other, men would line up along the rail and shout messages back and forth with the help of megaphones. When boats were too far away, a man would stand on the foredeck by the captain and use flags to signal by semaphore.

Even the captain got into the spirit of things. On one occasion, a sister ship in the Polish-Holland Company came alongside, and its captain signaled that they had run out of cognac. Captain Prong told him to send a man over and he would supply a few bottles for them. Without hesitation, one of the men jumped in the water and proceeded to swim over to the Meva. The crew pulled him on board and tied four bottles to his belt, then lowered him back into the sea. He quickly swam back to his own ship and was hauled in, again. As the boats separated, one of the men braced himself on the swaying deck and signaled "thanks" in Polish semaphore.

Kaz expected to spend another three months at sea before winter set in, but it didn't work out that way. The Meva had docked in the French city of Dieppe to unload another hold full of herring and to make some minor repairs. The captain informed the crew that they would be on their way again by mid-morning the next day. Kaz joined the others for a night of drinks and fresh food in the taverns along the waterfront. Kaz's cheeks felt flushed from the vodka he'd enjoyed. He didn't want the night to end. So when some of the men headed back to the ship, Kaz decided to stay behind and enjoy a night in a clean bed with one of the local ladies who frequented the bars. The next morning, he woke up with a fever and stomachache, which he attributed to the previous night's festivities. He'd planned to enjoy a hot breakfast of potatoes and eggs before returning to the ship, but since his stomach wasn't cooperating, he got dressed and walked back to the docks, only to discover that the Meva had already sailed! He was stranded in France without his passport or other papers and not much money.

He hurried to find the Polish-Holland Co. agent and hastily explained what had happened. At first, the agent thought that Kaz had simply jumped ship. It took all of Kaz's persuasive powers to convince him that there had been a misunderstanding regarding Captain Prong's orders. All he wanted to do was return to the Meva. The agent informed him that there was a sister ship in port that might be able to get him back to his boat, but before he could do anything, Kaz rose from his chair, rushed to the bathroom and vomited. The agent took him to the hospital instead of the boat. After a series of tests, it was determined that he was suffering from a stomach ulcer. Kaz spent the next two days in bed. The sister ship sailed without him.

The doctor ordered him to rest for a few weeks and to stay away from salt pork or spicy foods. There was no other choice but to return to Poland. Kaz visited the Polish Consulate, who arranged for temporary travel documents that would allow Kaz to take the train to Krakow. The agent even advanced Kaz's train fare against his wages but informed him that he would lose his bonus since he hadn't completed his contract with the company. Kaz protested, but there was little he could do. He'd counted on that bonus to give him a head start on a new life. Now, he would have to start all over again. And without money, he had little choice but to return to Daneta, at least until he found a new job. He wired her to say he would be home in two days.

"What makes you think you can just turn up when you please?" Daneta stood in the doorway to their apartment with her arms folded across her chest and her lips pressed together. Her dark eyes darted across his face as she studied him.

"I'm sick." Kaz had expected to tell her his entire story, but in the face of her hostility, it was all he could think to say.

"What do you mean, sick? You look healthy enough to me." The eyes darted up and down his body.

"I have a stomach ulcer. I just spent two days in a hospital in France."

Daneta's hard expression softened. "How did you get an ulcer?"

"Too much worrying, I guess. I've lost my bonus, and I need to find a new job." He looked at her pleadingly. "I hoped I could crash on the couch for a week or so while I rest up and look for work."

Daneta remained in the doorway, but the tension in her shoulders lessened. She hesitated before pushing the door all the way open. "Come in, then. We can talk."

Kaz stepped into the familiar surroundings and experienced a sudden rush of warmth. Pleasant memories escaped from the corners of the rooms and washed over him. Despite their differences, the place hadn't been so bad. They had shared some good times there.

"You could return to the warehouse," she offered hopefully once they were seated. "Not as foreman, of course. That position is filled. But I'm certain father would hire you back."

Kaz winced at the idea. The last thing he wanted to do was to slip back into Daneta's world of Sunday night dinners with her parents and endless talks about the business.

"It's probably better if I stay out of your father's way, at least for now. Besides, I really enjoy life at sea. I want to see if there's another opportunity."

Daneta sighed her consent. "For a week or two, then. After that, I'm not so sure."

Kaz needed little incentive to look for work. The couch in the apartment was every bit as stiff and cramped as he remembered. Daneta was gone all day, and there was little to do. He took walks and tried to read one of Daneta's books. It only took a few days for boredom to set in. He was quickly regaining his strength, however, and that encouraged him.

Kaz tried to contact Captain Hermann in the hopes that he might know of another position on a ship, but he was nowhere to be found. He also telegraphed the Polish Holland Co. agent in Gdynia about possible assignments. The agent advised Kaz that there were no job openings at the moment, but he forwarded his job request to the Polish-British Steamship Company, which operated a cargo/passenger ship between Poland, England and France. The agent informed him that they might be hiring and promised to give him a good referral. Kaz sent a separate message to the steamship company but received no reply. He looked at his meager savings and tried to decide what to do. He was healthy enough to travel, but he had little money for lodgings and food. If he took the train to Gdynia, he would be taking a chance. The steamship company might not be hiring, or might have no interest in him. Still, it was a risk worth taking.

"Tomorrow, I'm heading for Gdynia." He thought Daneta would be pleased at the news, but she was strangely subdued.

"That was awfully quick," she commented.

"There might be a job available. The agent gave me a good referral, which could make a difference. But if I don't go there in person, I might lose my chance." He shifted his gaze from hers. "I'll leave in the morning."

"I'm a little sad to see you go so soon."

A barking dog woke Kaz during the night. He had no idea what time it was. The room was so dark he could hardly see a thing. His hearing was just fine, however, and when he detected the whispering sound of cloth near his couch, he sat up in alarm.

"Who's there?"

"It's only me," Daneta announced in a hushed voice. "Come."

She grasped his hand and urged him to stand. Kaz got up, puzzled. Daneta led him toward her bedroom.

"Are you sure this is a good idea?" he asked once he realized what she was doing.

Daneta pulled him to the bed and lowered herself onto the covers. She guided his hand beneath her silky gown to her breast. The softness of her flesh set him on fire.

"Don't say anything, Kaz. I need you tonight."

Neither spoke another word.

Kaz arrived at the Polish-British Steamship Company's headquarters in Gdynia late the following day. He promptly presented himself and asked to see whoever was hiring. He was shown to a chair in a waiting room, where he fidgeted for over an hour. The room had a prosperous air about it. The walls looked recently wallpapered, and there was the faint odor of fresh paint on the doors. His chair was cushioned and had armrests, something he hadn't seen very often. He surmised that the company was doing well.

The woman who finally came for him had the graying hair and fleshy figure of someone in her late fifties. Her stern expression reminded Kaz of Daneta's severe look. He didn't think that was a good omen.

"We received your message and the one from the Polish Holland agent. It sounds impressive, but we aren't looking for seamen at present. Certainly not fishermen."

Kaz sensed that the interview would end quickly if he didn't speak up.

"I'm not really a fisherman. My previous job was managing a warehouse. But I was in the navy before that and enjoyed life aboard ship. I just wanted to return to the sea, and the fishing job looked like the best way to do it."

The woman gave Kaz a fresh look. He straightened himself in the chair.

"Well, you present yourself well." Kaz perked up at the comment. Perhaps, he had a chance. "The only position we have vacant right now is in the steward department on the Abyssinia. The job entails assisting the cooks in the kitchen and cleaning the tables in the dining room. Is that something that appeals to you?"

It wasn't the kind of work that Kaz had in mind, but the job sounded a lot less demanding physically than being a fisherman on the Meva. Given his current health, it suited him just fine.

"Yes, if it gets me on your ship. I'm a hard worker and a fast learner. Hire me, and you'll see."

"I will speak with the department manager. Return tomorrow at ten. I'll let you know, then."

She was waiting for him with a sheet of paper when he came back the next morning. "I can offer you a six month contract. If you perform your duties properly, we'll discuss additional assignments. The company likes to promote from within."

Kaz read the document and signed where indicated. He exhaled a breath in satisfaction, pleased to be going back to sea.

Kaz boarded the Abyssinia in early autumn with a job that paid better wages than the Meva and a crew's quarters that were clean and comfortable. He had the top bunk in a small room that he shared with a young man named Simon, whose dark complexion and high forehead reminded Kaz of an illustration of an Arabian prince he'd once seen in one of Daneta's books. Space was cramped, but after the smells and snores aboard the Meva, it seemed like paradise. The only downside was the lack of prospects for a bonus, but at least he was assured of receiving enough wages to afford some new clothes, enjoy dinners and drinks ashore in the various ports of call, and still put aside some savings. He ate well and soon regained all his strength. His life seemed to have turned a corner, and for the first time in quite awhile, he was at peace with himself.

The Abyssinia was equal parts cargo ship and passenger line. Goods included tinned hams, bacon, butter and cheese. Fine liquors, including a much more costly brand of cognac than he'd enjoyed on his previous voyage, rattled invitingly in the hold. The cognac brought back fond memories of his time aboard the Meva, but his new captain saw no reason to offer such a luxury to the staff of the Abyssinia.

Kaz found the passengers even more interesting than the cargo. Most were families. The women wore tailored dresses that covered them from neck to toe, and the men wore black coats that framed bushy, gray beards. A few of the men wore top hats like the ones he'd seen in the Jewish cemetery in Krakow. He thought of the man who'd befriended him there all those years ago. There was no friendship offered in the faces of these passengers. The men squinted at Kaz with distrust as they huddled among themselves and murmured in hushed voices. The women wore gaunt expressions that hid any semblance of a smile.

The wealthiest families were tucked away in elegant, mid-ship staterooms that were off limits to most of the staff. The majority of the passengers shared more cramped quarters in the stern.

"They're Jews fleeing Hitler's Germany," Simon observed when he and Kaz took a quick break from their duties in the dining room to enjoy a cigarette and some fresh air. "See those satchels the men carry? They're filled with everything from diamonds to negotiable securities. These aren't tourists. They're refugees. Well off, perhaps, but refugees all the same."

"How do you know?"

"I'm a Polish Jew," he admitted, "I've spoken to a few of them. Listened to their conversations."

"Why would they leave their homeland? There's no threat of war."

"There is, actually. I've heard about a paramilitary organization called the SA that uses violent intimidation against the Jews in Germany ... beating them in the streets and smashing their store windows. The Jews are terrified, but nobody will help them." He nodded toward a group of passengers near the ship's stern. "These are wealthy Jews who have decided to leave. They've sold everything. One of them told me they had to pay a large fine to leave the country. Only the wealthy can afford such a fine."

Kaz stared at the people with curiosity. He'd been too caught up in his own troubles to pay much attention to what was going on in Germany, but he had to admit that what Simon told him didn't sound good. Could the Germans threaten Poland again? Poland claimed to have a modern army, but when Kaz thought back to his days in the navy, when their ship ran aground and their submarine sank the wrong boat, he had to wonder. A country that could spawn an organization like the SA shouldn't be taken lightly.

Mother nature marched her own army of turbulent, winter storms across the Baltic Seas as the Abyssinia plowed its way through the cresting waves between Poland, France and England. Each trip to England carried a fresh group of downtrodden passengers fleeing their homeland in Germany, and with them, fresh tales of horror. Jews had to wear the yellow Star of David on their clothes. The children were bullied and taunted at school, a problem that was soon solved when Jews were banned from all schools and universities. The SA stood outside Jewish shops and turned away customers. Placards were placed outside cafes, shops and public places, such as parks and swimming pools, declaring that Jews were not wanted or were forbidden. Government workers lost their jobs.

The biggest news whirled around something called the Kristallnacht, the night of the broken glass, when synagogues were burned, homes and businesses smashed and Jews killed. Thousands were arrested and disappeared. Rumors spread about a new horror: concentration camps.

Days passed quickly, and soon the rough, raw winds of the Baltic winter turned into zephyrs from the west. Spring rains turned the coastal hills along their route to brilliant green, and by the time the Abyssinia steamed into Gdynia harbor in late July, after ten months at sea, Kaz found himself actually looking forward to a visit in Krakow.

The mailbox at crew headquarters was crammed with messages accumulated over several weeks, including a pale, blue envelope that bore Daneta's delicate handwriting. Kaz held it in his hand, uncertain whether to open it. Was it a note welcoming him home, or something more serious? He carefully slit the envelope with his seaman's knife and extracted the neatly folded, blue paper. Daneta's message was brief and to the point.

Dear Kaz:

I am sure you will be surprised, and I hope pleased to learn that we have a baby daughter. She is a healthy little one, with blue eyes like yours, but with my dark hair. She was born May 25th, but I didn't wire you because I thought it best not to trouble you until you returned to Gdynia. In your absence, I had to give her a name and have chosen Edwina. I hope that is satisfactory for you. I am well and stayed for a while with my parents. I am back in our apartment, now, and have a nanny to watch over Edwina during the day while I work.

I look forward to seeing you soon.

Your wife,
Daneta

Kaz stared at the carefully crafted words in stunned silence. A steady buzz of voices surrounded him as his fellow crewmen searched for messages in the mailbox and talked about their plans during their time off. He barely noticed them. The sharp odor of shaving lotion on freshly shaved faces scented the air. He inhaled the fragrance with a deep breath while he scanned the letter a second and third time. Its message didn't change. He had a child. A daughter! The idea was so foreign to him, he could hardly wrap his mind around it. He and Daneta had not discussed having a baby since their marriage. Daneta was too caught up in the family business, and Kaz was still recovering from his childhood. When had it happened? He knew the answer ... that last night before he departed for Gdynia, when she took him into her bed. How ironic that one lost night could change the landscape of their lives so completely.

Kaz was filled with conflicting emotions. He knew he didn't love Daneta, and Daneta didn't love him. The baby wouldn't change that. Yet, he was surprisingly pleased by the news, and he looked forward to seeing Edwina.

The only train that he could catch to Krakow was a local that crawled through a long, dreary night and seemed to stop at every village and hamlet, including a layover of six hours when Kaz left the train and took a room in a nearby inn popular with sailors on their way to Krakow. It gave him time to think about his mother, who didn't want him, and his father, who denied his existence. That must not happen to his daughter. He and Daneta had to find some way to keep their family intact. But was that possible? How could they restore a love that never was? How did they rebuild a relationship that was doomed from the start? Would the arrival of Edwina somehow repair such an unworkable relationship? He didn't see how, but he was ready to look for answers.

Daneta opened the front door, her face flushed with anxiety. "I'm glad you came so soon."

He gave her an awkward embrace.

"Edwina's asleep. Come have a look at her."

They tiptoed into Daneta's bedroom, where Kaz found a little, pinched face peeking out from under her covers in a blue crib. The expression reminded him so much of Daneta's severe look, he nearly burst into laughter. He grew serious again. How were they going to deal with a child? What did Daneta expect of him? What would be his role as father?

They moved to the sitting room to talk. Kaz noted the familiar record player in its usual place in the far corner. It reminded him of the evenings he'd sat there trying to understand the classical music that Daneta loved so much. For Kaz, it was a symbol of the divisions between them.

"Kaz," Daneta began softly, "Since you've been gone, I've realized our marriage was never what it should be. I know that, now. I guess there's no reason to expect the arrival of Edwina to change things, but for her sake, we need to salvage as much of a normal relationship as we can." She looked down at her hands as she spoke.

Kaz glanced around the room while he tried to think what to say. There were new curtains. They made the room cheerier. "How do we do that? You've obviously given it some thought."

"Some," she agreed. "The one thing we must do for her is to sustain some semblance of a home ... of a family. At least during her most formative years."

"That's not easy when I'm gone so much." He stopped himself and rubbed his forehead in thought. "Wait, I get it. You want me to give up the sea and stay in Krakow."

Daneta nodded. "Not just in Krakow. Here, in the apartment."

Kaz leaned back in the chair as he absorbed her proposal. "But, I've got a steady job with the Holland-British Steamship Company. It pays good money. Returning here would mean giving that up. I'm not sure I want to go back to work for your father. Not in the warehouse."

"I wouldn't expect that," Daneta protested, "and it wouldn't be necessary. There's so much talk of war, the government is opening new defense plants near the city. I'm sure you can find good work there. Machinists are in high demand.

"And I will work, of course. I still love my job. While I was recovering from the delivery, I kept thinking about the business. I know that sounds absurd. I love my baby, but I missed my work."

It was growing dark outside. Rows of distant streetlights flared to life against the purple skyline of the city. Kaz gazed quietly through the opened curtains at the twilight.

"What about the baby? Who will tend to her?"

"I will, in the evenings and on weekends. The nanny, Mary, comes in while I'm at work."

Kaz shifted awkwardly in his chair. Nothing had changed between them. Daneta was still the same person. So was he. Trying to build some kind of life for Edwina wouldn't be easy. It was fraught with obstacles. He felt a sudden urge to flee back to the Abyssinia, but he realized that was no longer in the cards. He thought about the infant sleeping in the next room, and of his own childhood. He would not abandon her the way his parents had abandoned him. He was going to stay and to make the best of it. But there was still a big question to be answered.

"You say you want my back here, in the apartment. What do you have in mind?"

"We've used the back room for storage. I had it cleared out and put a proper bed and armoire in there. I've set the room up for you. We don't have to sleep together. You can come and go as you like. I won't get in your way. But I will expect you to spend time with Edwina. That way, things will appear normal, both to the baby and to the outside world."

Kaz realized that Daneta was as concerned about appearances as she was about his role as a father. It would be some time before the baby knew what was normal about sleeping arrangements. He could stay elsewhere; it would make no difference. She was worried about what her family would say, and the neighbors, and the people at work. With Dominik showing up God knows when, rumors would quickly spread. This way, she could retain at least a veneer of respectability.

The idea of living under the same roof in a platonic relationship sounded a bit bizarre. Eating meals together. Sharing the bathroom. It all seemed preposterous. How could they make that work? He needed time to think, but there was no time. He had to make up his mind, now, and he didn't want to start things with an argument. That wouldn't solve anything. He would have to go along with Daneta's plan, at least for a time, while he tried to figure out a more workable solution.

"Okay," he sighed. "We'll try it your way for the time being. See if we can make it work."

One thing he knew for certain. Edwina had been the result of a moment of weakness ... a one night stand, so to speak. He wasn't about to make that mistake again. He would stay out of her bed.

As he unpacked his clothes in the spare bedroom, he heard Daneta rummaging around in the kitchen preparing dinner. Once again, he fought the urge to catch a train back to Gdynia, to get back on that ship. He couldn't, of course. His fate was sealed. He was starting life over again, for the fifth or sixth time. He'd lost count. He would wire the company tomorrow and tell them he wasn't coming back.

Chapter Twelve

Daneta was right about the war effort. New factories were opening all around the city to produce arms for a potential conflict with Germany. With his experience as a machinist, Kaz had little trouble finding a full-time job with a company manufacturing machine guns and cannon parts for the army. The machinists were paid on a piecework basis, which suited him just fine. It was better than a bonus. He didn't have to rely on others to make more money. All he had to do was work hard and put in more hours. Within a few months, he was earning enough to splurge on simple pleasures, such as meals at a local restaurant and drinks at a tavern with his fellow workers. He made it a point, however, to return to the apartment two or three evenings a week in time to play with Edwina before she was put down for the night.

There was irony to be found in their situation, irony at how much Daneta's behavior had changed in reaction to the baby. She was no longer so obsessed with the company. The ledgers stayed closed. Dominik rarely came over. Concerts and dancing also lost their flavor. Daneta preferred walks to the park with the baby pram, instead, and more dinners at her parent's. Kaz joined her for an occasional stroll but stayed away from the family dinners. When they appeared together in public, Daneta played her role as a happy mother and wife to perfection. She smiled and greeted people in the neighborhood. She cooed at Edwina and encouraged Kaz to do the same. She took his arm as they walked. To the outside world, she and Kaz were a devoted couple.

Home was a different matter. Conversations were polite but limited. Daneta's manner was cool. They didn't touch. It was a platonic relationship at best, but it seemed to work. Edwina was thriving. She had doubled her weight and was beginning to sit up. She could roll over and slide along the floor on her tummy. Best of all, she was sleeping longer at night, up to six hours, which gave both Daneta and Kaz more time to rest. Kaz found Edwina's progress fascinating. He couldn't wait until she started walking and saying her first words.

Kaz would have considered his life tolerable, if it weren't for the clouds he saw forming on the horizon. It started with the sad news that Charlie's grandfather had died. Charlie and Christina came from Warsaw for the funeral. Kaz was glad to see his dear friends, even though it was for such an unhappy occasion.

"Kaz, you look just as ornery as ever." Charlie's bright eyes still held the promise of mischief, and his smile was as charming as ever.

"And you." They exchanged bear hugs.

"Hello, Kaz. We've missed you." Christina stepped forward and kissed him on the cheek. Her brown hair was cropped shorter, but it was still long enough to frame her oval face in a way that Kaz found magical. He inhaled the familiar fragrance of her shampoo. To Kaz, she was as alluring as ever. The old spark was still there, at least for him. He wondered why he couldn't find that spark with Daneta. Her delicate cheekbones and bright smile were captivating in their own way. In the absence of her severe expression, she was actually quite attractive.

After the funeral, they attended a wake at the grandfather's house. Kaz remembered fondly the brief time that he'd spent there while he and Charlie looked for work. It seemed a long time ago. For a while, conversations centered upon family topics and memories. It wasn't long, however, before discussions turned to the more sinister subject of war. Charlie's uncle, Stefan, got things rolling when he mentioned Hitler's recent forays into Austria and Czechoslovakia.

"First, Hitler marches into Austria, then into Czechoslovakia, and he annexes both countries. The British and the French do nothing about it. Now, he's setting his sights on Poland."

Poland, Kaz learned, had signed a non-aggression act with Germany in an effort to keep Russia at bay, but when Germany made demands for more influence over the portions of Poland inhabited by Germans, Poland refused. Now, Poland found itself in the cross hairs of its increasingly hostile and aggressive neighbor.

"I listened to one of Hitler's speeches on the radio the other evening. It was frightening," Uncle Stefan continued. "There must have been thousands of people gathered to hear him. Their roars of approval sounded like waves whipped up by a great storm. In a way, I suppose they were." He looked down at his drink and began to swirl it around in its glass.

"Hitler's just a pompous ass," someone else chimed in. "He talks big when he's pushing around smaller countries, but if he ever monkeys with Poland, he'll get his ears pinned back."

There were murmurs of agreement.

"I'm not so sure," Stefan countered. "Every time he makes demands, the other countries try to appease him. Then he gobbles up more territory. Look at Czechoslovakia. England and France agreed to let him have control over the borderland regions occupied by Germans, and they invaded the entire country. Now he has his eye on the region around Gdansk, our Polish Corridor as they call it." He looked down at the liquid swirling in his glass. "It's only a matter of time before we're all caught up in a great whirlpool of destruction."

"I'm inclined to agree." Kaz was surprised to hear his own voice. He'd never been very political or interested in foreign intrigues, but he'd heard lots of stories from the Jews being transported on the Abyssinia. "There are terrible things happening all over Germany, especially to the Jews, but to others, as well. I've been told Hitler is building a police state to control the people he considers undesirable."

"Aren't those just rumors?" Charlie asked. "Nobody knows what's really going on. And anyway, England and France would never let them invade Poland."

Kaz shook his head. "I've talked with many Jews leaving Germany. They've seen things first hand. Hitler's building an army that's much too strong for just self-defense. He means to use it."

The unexpected turn in the conversation had thrown a dark mood over the group. People shifted uneasily, uncertain what else to say. It was as though they were all standing on a flat prairie at harvest time and watching the onslaught of a giant tornado. It danced in the distance to the tune of its own terrible roar. Just like the roar of the German people shouting their approval for Hitler. Everyone could see it tearing up the cornfields in a great column of dust. Its effect was mesmerizing. There was nothing they could do to stop it, so they watched and prayed that it would move away. But it wasn't just dust and debris being tossed about. Humans were being torn from the earth as well. The human debris scattered before the storm told a story of mounting fury. At first, it had been the Jews, but now it included everyone who didn't agree with Hitler's vision: tradesmen, politicians, educators, leaders and soldiers from Czechoslovakia and Austria. Frightened fugitives were crossing into Poland, at first in groups of twos and threes, then tens, and now hundreds. All were being tossed into the void by the hurricane force winds rising from Hitler's Third Reich.

Czech soldiers were fleeing, also. They shed their uniforms and tried to lose themselves among the Poles in the small cities surrounded by farmlands. Those who made it as far as Krakow settled in makeshift camps with other refugees. They shared stories of the horrors they had endured, but they refused to divulge exactly where they came from, for fear word might somehow get back and cause trouble for those left behind.

Kaz had heard enough. It was time to go home. He bid goodnight and started the long, cold hike back to the apartment. As he walked along the deserted streets, he found it odd that so many of the people fleeing Germany were Germans! He couldn't imagine having to flee Poland. His mind was filled with thoughts of pain and sorrow; he found his feet moving faster.

Part II

Poland Interrupted

The Germans

Chapter Thirteen

Kaz was standing at the sink shaving when the first explosion shattered the calm, morning sky. The blast rattled the apartment windows and jarred the building so severely, he nearly dropped his razor. An accident in the rail yards, he thought. That must be it. He hardly had time to complete his thought before a second explosion hit, followed immediately by a third. He snatched his towel and wiped the lather from his face while he tried to collect his wits. Something was terribly wrong, and it had nothing to do with the rail yard! He ran into the hallway, where he came face-to-face with Daneta standing in the doorway to her room with Edwina cradled in her bare arms. Surprisingly, the noise had not disturbed the baby. Daneta looked cold and vulnerable.

"Kaz, what's happening?" Her eyes darted wildly about the room.

"Not sure. I think it must be bombs." He put his arms around her. "German bombs."

"War." Her body trembled against his. "It means war. What should we do?"

"I don't know." He tried to sound calm and reassuring, even though his heart was racing. "If it is Germans, they'll go after the rail yards and war plants, not neighborhoods like this one. We should be safe here, at least for now."

Just as he released Daneta, another explosion rocked the apartment. Edwina stirred. Daneta rocked her back to sleep.

"That one was closer," Kaz remarked. "About where my plant is located."

"How do they know where to strike?" Daneta whispered.

Kaz thought about that for a moment. "Spies. I expect some of those refugees that have been entering the country are German agents sent here to spy on us."

Thoughts swarmed through his mind. He stood in the hallway uncertain what to do. Panic rose in his throat. He'd just assured Daneta that they were safe, but he didn't believe it. Bombs were indiscriminate. They could land anywhere. Even the clothing factory! He ran to the sitting room and looked out the window. Smoke billowed into the morning sky from three, no four, locations. Another explosion startled him. The window shook so badly he thought it would shatter. He pressed his hands against it in a futile effort to control the vibrations.

"Get dressed," he called over his shoulder, "and feed the baby. I still think you are safer here than in the streets, but that could change. Pack some clothing in case you have to leave in a hurry."

Daneta nodded and disappeared into her room. Kaz dashed back into the bathroom to finish shaving, but his hand shook so badly, he couldn't control the razor. Twice, he nicked himself. He slammed the razor back into the cabinet in disgust and wiped the tiny dots of blood away with the towel. He held the edges of the sink with his hands and forced himself to take deep breaths. His mind calmed; his heart rate slowed. He began to think more clearly. If the Germans were bombing Krakow, they were attacking other towns and cities along the border with Germany, as well. Tanks and soldiers would be pouring across the frontier, and he wasn't certain that there was anything Poland's army could do to stop the assault, despite the chest pounding of its officers.

Kaz hurried to his own room and threw on his clothes. He had to find out if the war plant where he worked was still standing. He stopped pulling on the sweater he'd hastily chosen against the morning chill and thought a moment. When he and his comrades had been mustered out of the navy, the commander had told them that they were still part of the military. They were considered naval reserves, and if the country was ever attacked, they should report at once to the nearest naval unit.

Kaz walked to Daneta's room. She was in the middle of changing Edwina's diaper.

"I have to get to Gdynia. Report to the naval station there."

"Don't leave me here alone." Her voice was shrill with fear. Her fingers trembled as she tried to set the pin to hold the diaper.

"I'll walk you to your parents' house. Tell them to stay indoors and away from the windows. My guess is, there's an invasion underway, and it won't take the Germans long to reach Krakow."

Kaz held Edwina while Daneta threw clothes into a bag. When she was finished, Kaz returned to his room to gather his own clothes while she raced to the kitchen for baby food and something to eat. They settled for pieces of bread and rushed out the door. The sky appeared darker, more menacing, than it had in the apartment. Kaz looked to the east. A large cloud of smoke rose where his war plant was located, confirming his fears that the plants were being targeted. The bombing seemed to have stopped for the moment. People were emerging from their homes. They huddled in small groups and shook their heads as they looked around them in confusion. Daneta started to greet a neighbor, but Kaz hurried her along. They scurried through the streets, dodging cars and pedestrians, until they reached the front of her parents' home.

"I don't have time to come in." He gave her a quick hug of encouragement. "As soon as I know my situation, I'll get word to you. In the meantime, keep yourself and our baby safe."

He turned away and started walking in the direction of the rail yard. He prayed that the bombers had not destroyed everything.

More people were abandoning their homes as Kaz made his way along the streets. Some were properly dressed against the chilly, morning air; others looked like sleepwalkers as they stumbled over the pavement in their disheveled nightclothes. Some were simply too frightened to move their feet at all. To his amazement, Kaz saw a few people laughing! He heard them talking about military maneuvers, and he realized they were under the delusion that this was all part of some war game being conducted by the Polish air force. In their denial, they believed it was all make-believe. When an ambulance rolled past, siren wailing, they actually cheered, thinking it was part of the maneuvers. Kaz grimaced and moved on.

At the corner of Kopernik and Kacik streets, a break in the buildings provided a good view of the city skyline. Kaz stopped to scan the sky. Beyond the rising spire of an old church, the morning sun glinted off the wings of a silver airplane. Kaz had little knowledge of warplanes, but he felt certain that this one was not Polish. The plane wheeled into a graceful wingover and began a shrieking descent toward a city that was still caught with sleep in its eyes. Nothing stood in the way of the plane and its target. The plane plummeted almost straight down, until it disappeared behind the ancient steeple of the church. The sound of its engine died away as it evaporated into silence.

Thunk, thunk, thunk. Three muffled explosions sounded in the distance. Kaz imagined the bombs ripping a bridge to shreds somewhere along the Vistula River, or bursting through the roof of a factory. He pushed his way through the increasing crowds of people crying out for friends or relatives, or simply wandering aimlessly along the sidewalks. Power to the streetcars had been cut, stranding the vehicles and making it difficult for cars and ambulances to move about. No one seemed to quite know what to do or where to go. No one was laughing any longer. The realization that they were at war had overwhelmed them all.

Kaz wondered why the German Stukas were able to operate so freely without any challenge by the Polish air force. He could only assume that the first strikes had been at nearby airfields, rendering the Polish planes useless. No one rose to confront the Germans in the skies.

At last, the rail yards loomed into view, or what was left of them. He was greeted by a mass of rubble surrounding three large craters. The bombs had made precision strikes. Bodies lay about like broken dolls. An ambulance whined past him and weaved its way around the craters in an effort to reach the wounded, who groaned and called for help. Kaz was assaulted by the pungent odor of hot ash and burnt flesh as he rushed forward to help the ambulance personnel place two bloodied people on stretchers. He spotted one of the officers who patrolled the yard and ran to him.

"How can I get to Gdynia?" he asked.

The officer shook his head. "Last transmission before the bombs hit said that both Gdynia and Danzig had been cut off. The Germans have dropped men in by parachute and taken control. We were told to stop all trains headed that way." He looked around the yard. "Then, all Hell broke loose."

Two more ambulances arrived, and more wounded men were carried away on stretchers. Kaz surveyed the scene in numbed silence. What should he do? He thought about returning to Daneta and their daughter, but that was no answer. He needed to *do* something. He just wasn't sure what. In desperation, he decided to see what was left of the war plant where he worked. He stumbled out of the rubble and headed west.

The streets were filled with chaos. No one was sleepwalking any longer. Voices shouted in agony. Crowds rushed about in disarray, uncertain where to go. People covered their ears with their hands against the sound of the bombs, which had started falling again. Cars made little progress in the crush of humanity. Some were abandoned in the middle of the street. Kaz picked familiar side streets that were not as crowded. Memories of his boyhood days rushed back to him, memories of dodging down narrow streets on his way to the Wawel Royal Castle. Those had been carefree days. Given the current circumstances, it seemed likely they were gone forever.

Kaz breathed a sigh of relief when he turned a corner and saw the war plant partially standing. He hurried inside and found men with shovels trying to clear the debris. Most of the machines appeared undamaged. He spotted his supervisor and ran over to him.

"What can I do?"

A small grin broke out on the man's tired face. "Kaz, glad to see you're okay. We're clearing the area so we can start production again. The army's going to need every gun and shell we can make. Luckily, they provided us with backup generators, so we can operate without power. Grab a shovel and get to work."

Kaz joined the other men and spent the rest of the day clearing the wreckage. By nightfall, the place was clean enough to start the machines again, but production was limited. Sections of the production line had received too much damage and could not keep up with the other operations. Men were moved from station to station along the line to fill the gaps with extra handwork. It was slow, hot, backbreaking labor, but it had to be done. They worked through the night and into the next morning, pausing only long enough to gulp down large cups of coffee and to devour the few sandwiches that volunteers were able to bring. When they finally stopped long enough for a few hours sleep, Kaz collapsed on the floor.

The next two days were a nightmare of confusion throughout Poland. Orders were issued, countermanded, and issued again. Rumors flew through the air. Communications were disrupted all over the country, making it difficult to get orders to the troops. The army took over the railroad operations, but the Nazi bombers had done their job. Tracks had to be repaired, and schedules were bogged down. That made it difficult to move badly needed ammunition and supplies, or to shift troops quickly enough to stop the rapier-like thrusts of Germany's new kind of war: the Blitzkrieg. One rumor had it that Polish garrisons in Gdynia and on the Hel peninsula were standing fast against an onslaught of elite, German, armored divisions. Every Polish city along the western and southern borders was being pounded by the relentless Stukas. They plunged from the sky in great clouds, swarming like silver locusts and smashing Poland's historic buildings.

Amid the rumors and confusion, Kaz and the others worked on, and despite problems with supplies and balky machinery, they managed to produce a great many spare parts and finished guns. But the Germans were getting closer.

Three days later, the head manager called the workers together.

"We're moving the plant to a safer location. Trucks will arrive after dark to haul everything to a place east of the rail yards where the tracks have been repaired. There, we'll load our parts and equipment on flat cars provided by the army. We need to be up and running again in three days, so start packing our supplies and parts, and dismantle the machinery."

The men looked at each other. None of them had the strength to do what had just been commanded, but none of them complained. They knew it had to be done.

By nightfall, everything was ready. The men silently loaded the trucks and rode across the city in total darkness. The streets were nearly empty of people by now, but the trucks still had to weave their way through a maze of destroyed or abandoned vehicles. At times, the men had to jump down to push rubble and twisted metal aside. It was slow, dogged work, but by midnight, they had reached Wieliczka Station, the place where they were to rendezvous with the train. The station had been badly damaged by the bombs, but the tracks had been repaired. An hour later, a train squealed and groaned as it rolled to a stop in the darkness. No lights were visible. It was a ragtag mixture of old boxcars and flatbeds that looked as battered as the streets of Krakow, but the engine hissed with the promise that it would deliver the machinery to its new home.

The men began the process of transferring everything to the rail cars. It was morning by the time they were finished. They didn't dare move the train in daylight while they were so close to the city, so they covered the cargo with tarps and spent the day eating and sleeping. People gathered along the tracks in hopes of claiming a space on the train so they could escape the terror raining down on Krakow. They reminded Kaz of the men he'd seen waiting to jump the rails in blood alley.

When Kaz fell asleep, he dreamed about men leaping in front of fast-moving trains.

Chapter Fourteen

Just after dark, the long, overloaded train crawled out of the ruins of Wieliczka Station, each flatbed and boxcar crammed with dismantled machinery and refugees. More people clung to every handhold they could find on the sides and roofs. The war plant men and the workers assigned to repair the tracks had declared the first car off limits and barricaded the door. It was reserved for them. For a short time, the train moved at a steady pace, but as they approached the wrecked station at Bochnia, they ground to a halt behind another train waiting for track repairs. Passengers on top of the boxcars huddled together and tried to sleep, while those clinging to the sides dropped into the ditches alongside the tracks and bedded down in the grass. Up ahead, men with lanterns moved about fixing the tracks.

With each passing hour, the situation grew more bizarre. People walking along the adjacent road saw the stalled trains and hurried over to find a place on board. Those already there tried to shoo them away, but the interlopers wouldn't be denied. Fights broke out. People were shoved aside or pulled from their handholds. Some even began throwing pieces of machinery off the flat cars to make more room. Kaz and the other workers had to guard the equipment and turn away those who couldn't find space. It was early morning before the train shuddered to life and began to roll down the newly repaired tracks.

Kaz felt badly exposed as the train gathered speed and moved through the countryside. He scanned the sky for planes, certain that at any moment, they would become a target for the Stukas. All was quiet. They passed villages that were untouched by the violence. Farms sat in serene silence, unaffected by the horror surrounding them. The morning sunlight was bright, yet the air was crisp. Kaz wrapped his arms around himself for warmth. He felt as though he was sleepwalking through a dream that at any moment would spiral into a nightmare. Thoughts of Daneta and Edwina drifted through his dreams. He hoped that they were safe. There would be no way to get in touch with them for the moment. It dawned on him that his stomach was starting to growl with hunger. It was nearly a day since he'd last eaten. Soon, everyone on the train would be hungry. What were they going to do about food?

Without warning, the train ground to a halt, again. The engineer and train workers jumped down to inspect a section of rail. After some discussion, they reboarded. The train inched forward until it had passed the doubtful section, then gained speed. An hour later, the train stopped, once more, and the men piled out. Kaz joined them.

"What's wrong?" he asked an official in a rumpled uniform. "There doesn't appear to be any bomb damage."

"Sabotage," the man replied in a sharp tone. "We were warned about German agents operating in this area."

"In Krakow, too, I think. They were spotting our war plants for the bombers."

The man nodded. "We suspect they came in dressed as German refugees."

Kaz was headed back toward his boxcar when he thought he spotted a familiar face among the people gathered two cars away.

"Simon? Is that you?" Kaz called in disbelief.

A smile beamed across the young man's face. "Kaz, I never thought to see you again."

They shook hands and embraced. Simon's face was cut and bruised, his wiry hair matted to his forehead, his clothes torn in several places.

"What happened?" Kaz asked as he inspected his friend.

"I had taken a leave from the Abyssinia to go see my father, who is ill. I was on the last train out of Gdynia when the bombs started falling. German soldiers were floating down from the sky in great clouds of cloth, but we made it out before they could close down the rail yard. Later, our train was bombed." His face twisted at the memory. "I was riding in a car with a young woman. She was Jewish, like me. We were talking, getting to know each other. Then, our car was hit. She was seated by the window. The whole side of the car exploded, and she disappeared. I was thrown across the aisle. My ears rang so loudly, I couldn't hear a thing, but I managed to crawl out of the wreckage and run away. I never saw the girl again."

"Where are you going now?"

"Don't know. Wherever this train takes me."

"I'm trying to reach Starachowice. Me and my fellow workers." Kaz gestured toward the front boxcar. "We're hauling this machinery to start a new war plant there. You have any experience with machinery?"

Simon shook his head.

"Never mind. We can use another pair of hands to unload and assemble the pieces when we get there. Come with me." Kaz led Simon to the front car and introduced him to the others.

"Simon is a friend of mine. I figure we can use all the help we can get, so I asked him to join us."

There were murmurs of agreement. "Make yourself at home." "There's always room for a friend."

Simon smiled his thanks.

The train moved forward in starts and stops. Each time the wheels squealed to a halt, officials jumped down and inspected the tracks. Sometimes, they were only delayed a few minutes. Other times, the delays ran to an hour or more. At each stop, some of the chilled, cramped passengers took advantage of the pause to jump down and run to the bushes where they could relieve themselves. When the train lurched forward again, those caught with their pants down had to make a mad dash to regain their places on board. Before long, some of the elderly got left behind and families became scrambled as people lost track of loved ones. Part of the problem was that all the cars looked alike. There were no particular markings to distinguish one from the other. Passengers jumped onto the wrong cars, then began frantically looking for family members. Mothers anxiously called for children. Fathers darted from car-to-car and peered into the dark interiors in a desperate search for familiar faces. Grimy cheeks and foreheads, blackened by the soot from the train's engine, became harder to recognize.

Kaz soon grew used to the steady click-clack of the train's wheels churning along the rails. It soothed him to the point of drowsiness, and his head began to loll. His thoughts returned to Krakow. He wondered how his uncle and mother were coping with the mayhem, if they were still alive. He silently wished them well despite their disinterest in him. And what about his wife and child? He couldn't quite bring himself to think of them as a family, his role with Daneta hardly felt like husband and wife, but the arrival of Edwina had brought them closer. Their relationship had always been a duet of ups and downs. One moment, he wanted to draw her closer; the next, he wanted to push her away. It'd been an emotional ride that had exhausted him. There was no understanding it. All he knew for certain was that in a moment of weakness, they'd produced a child, a baby that now bound them together in a loveless marriage. Kaz rubbed his temples and sighed. Pursuing such thoughts made his head throb. He shifted his position against the boxcar's wall and let his head loll some more.

In the early afternoon, the train pulled into the station at Tarnow, a major switching station on the Dunajec River. It had taken forty hours to travel a distance of seventy-five miles. Part of the station lay in ruin. Bodies could be seen where they had been trapped in the rubble. Other bodies were laid out on the platform and covered with tarps. Flies buzzed everywhere. Kaz swatted them away as he surveyed the carnage.

"This doesn't look like a bomb attack. It's confined to a small area and most of the roof is still intact."

"It does look strange," Simon agreed. He flagged a station attendant who was wandering past. "Can you tell us what happened?"

"Somebody blew the place up with dynamite about an hour before the Germans started dropping bombs." He rubbed his hands to keep them warm. "Seems he set down a suitcase full of explosives and left. One of the passengers noticed it, but nobody was the wiser. Damn thing went off right in the middle of early morning rush hour. Killed or injured a couple hundred people and cut off the rail line for several hours."

Another German agent, Kaz thought. The whole offensive had been carefully orchestrated.

While the train waited for clearance to leave Tarnow, some of the hungry passengers hurried into the town in search of food. Many didn't make it back in time, and the train left without them. Their places on the cars were immediately taken by others who'd been milling about the station.

As the old train labored east, a warm breeze chased away the morning chill and brightened the prospects for a fruitful day. There had been no reports of sabotage along this section of track, and they proceeded through the countryside at a good clip. Kaz watched the trees and fields speeding past with a sense of contentment. He inhaled the musty odor of freshly plowed earth and marveled at the bounties of life. It was the first time he'd felt at ease since the morning of the German invasion.

His repose abruptly ended when he heard the distant roar of aircraft engines singing their song of havoc and destruction. German bombers swept in from the south in irregular waves. They were flying high, headed for more important targets elsewhere, not a lonely train fleeing across the plains. Everyone exhaled a sigh of relief when they passed overhead and disappeared into the brilliant, blue sky. Another wave appeared, and this time two planes broke away from the formation and began a strafing run. Bullets tore a straight line through the plowed earth. The line was aimed right at the train. It reminded Kaz of the wakes caused by those dummy torpedoes fired from his submarine. Only these weren't dummies. They were live rounds meant to kill anyone in their path. The engineer tried to increase his speed to disrupt the plane's line of fire, but it was no use. Large caliber bullets ripped through two of the middle cars. Screams told everyone that blood had been spilled. A father's head had exploded. A small girl had collapsed with a great hole in her chest. Others suffered gashed arms and broken legs. It'd been a casual assault. The planes returned to their formation without a backward glance. Their brief sport had torn families apart and shattered lives.

Another formation roared into view. This time, a plane released a bomb aimed at the train's engine. It missed by only a few yards, showering everybody with a cloud of blackened earth. Kaz wondered why they didn't drop more bombs. He could only assume that they were saving their ammunition for fatter targets. Luckily, the train's boilers were undamaged.

The train stopped to take on water at a small town near Tarnow. Volunteers formed a bucket brigade to get water to the boilers. When planes appeared, everybody dropped their buckets, jumped into a nearby ditch and covered their heads. It was a useless gesture in the face of bombs and large caliber bullets. The planes droned overhead without incident. Once they were gone, the men hurried back to their buckets and resumed their efforts to fill the boilers.

Toward evening, the train shuddered to a halt in a town near Debica. Bombs had blown apart a section of track, and workers said it would be two or three hours before repairs were finished. For some reason, the bombers had also taken quite an interest in the town itself. Nearly all the buildings had experienced some damage; many had been reduced to rubble. Kaz learned from one of the survivors that the military had kept weapons stored nearby and maintained a communications center there. More evidence that the German commanders had been informed of the military's presence ahead of the invasion.

"I think it's time we found something to eat," Simon suggested.

Kaz nodded in agreement. It had now been two days since they'd had any real sustenance. "There's some farm houses across that field. Let's go have a look."

As they approached the houses, Kaz saw that it was a dairy farm, or had been. No cows were visible. Two of the out buildings had been badly damaged, but the main building was intact. A small vegetable garden, the kind a child would grow, thrived in the front yard. They both called out a 'hello.' When no one answered, they stepped inside. Scattered clothing, open drawers and tipped over cupboards attested to a hasty and chaotic departure. Simon went to investigate the other structures while Kaz rummaged through the cupboards. To his surprise, several cans of cured pork shank tumbled out of a cabinet and rolled across the dusty floor. Kaz's stomach did summersaults. He hastily looked for something with which to open the cans and settled on a sharp knife lying on the sink. He was about to plunge the knife into one of the can's lids when Simon appeared in the doorway, accompanied by the sound of clucking chickens.

"Look what I found." He held up two hens by their feet. Their wings flapped endlessly as they protested their ill treatment.

"And I discovered some cans of pork, but let's save them for later." Kaz tossed them in his knapsack.

"I'm not supposed to eat pork." Simon eyed the knapsack.

"Why not?"

"I'm Jewish. Pork meat is considered unclean."

"Maybe, but it's better than starving." Kaz pulled one of the cans out of the knapsack and inspected the label. "Besides, it says it's cured. I don't think cleanliness should be a problem."

Simon shrugged. He took Kaz's knife and slaughtered and plucked the chickens while Kaz raided the garden for potatoes and onions. Next, Simon cut the two birds into quarters and washed them at a backyard pump. Finally, he struck a match to some firewood he'd stacked in a small pit, filled a kettle with water, threw in the birds and the vegetables, and set the kettle on the fire to cook.

"That's going to make a fine stew when it's done," Kaz commented. He sniffed the cooking odors and nearly grabbed one of the quartered birds and ate it raw. "Where did you learn how to prepare a meal like that?"

Simon grinned. "We lived next to a chicken farm when I was a kid. We were kind of poor, so when the farmer had an injured bird, he'd give it to us. He claimed he couldn't sell it, but I think he was just being generous. My grandmother chopped their heads off with an ax and taught me how to prepare and cook them."

It was getting dark enough for some of the train passengers to notice their fire. It wasn't long before a small group of men, women and children ventured into the backyard. Tensions rose as everybody looked at the kettle of food. Voices murmured. Kaz's first instinct was to chase them away, but he knew he couldn't. There were too many of them, and if he raised a ruckus, it would only attract others. He calculated that there was enough food to go around.

"Make yourselves to home," he offered. He was quickly surrounded by a circle of grimy faces who eyed the kettle with hungry anticipation.

Other than a crying child, a strange silence descended upon the group. No one said a word. Most were simply too tired and hungry to speak. Some were so dazed, they couldn't work their mouths to form words. Everyone sat and stared at the bubbling kettle, transfixed.

Kaz estimated that the food needed another half hour to cook, but his thoughts were interrupted when a sharp hissing sound broke the silence. It was followed by the familiar chugging noise of the train's engine stirring to life.

"The train's started," someone shouted from the shadows.

People stood up, uncertain what to do. If they waited for the food, they would miss the train. If they ran for the train, they would face another night of hunger. Feet shifted nervously; indecision paralyzed them.

"I wouldn't be too concerned," Kaz advised. "That train isn't going very far. There's been too much bombing activity in the area. It'll have to stop again before long. We can catch up to it in an hour or two. Anyway, the stew's about done. Better to walk on full bellies than to ride on empty ones."

Two men ignored Kaz's advice and hurried off. The rest raided the farm house for bowls or empty tins that could be used to hold the stew. They settled back down and resumed their vigil by the kettle.

Kaz counted the people around the fire: two women with small children, two others old enough to be grandmothers, and several men of varying ages. Twelve in all, not counting Simon and himself. There would be more than enough stew for everyone. He listened as the sounds from the laboring train faded in the gathering darkness and hoped he was right about its progress. He didn't relish joining all of the people walking along the roads.

Simon's voice interrupted his thoughts. Dinner was ready. A merry song of clanging tins and bowls filled the air as everyone shoved their containers into the kettle and scooped up as much of the savory meat, vegetables and broth as they could muster. The brew was steamy hot, but Kaz didn't care. He puffed and sipped and puffed some more, swallowing the meal as fast as his raw throat allowed. When the bowl was empty, he plunged it back into the kettle for more.

More faces appeared around the fire. The train had halted less than a mile down the track, and word had spread about the kettle of stew in the dairy farmer's backyard. The clanging music of metal against metal grew louder as more people jockeyed for position with cups, spoons, or any other receptacles they could find to capture a little of the remaining melange. When Kaz looked at the desperate faces around him, he felt guilty that he'd eaten so well. Still, he and Simon had been the ones to organize things. It was only fair that they gained a little profit for their efforts. Everyone got something. The hunger that had been written across their faces receded. People pulled coats and scarves around themselves with a look of satisfaction.

Kaz dozed, then started awake at the forlorn howl of a lonely dog. The fire had died to embers. A sharp chill now permeated the air.

Simon nudged Kaz's leg. "Best be getting back to the train. No sense walking any further than we have to."

Others stood and slapped the dirt from their clothes. Kaz helped a mother raise her child into her arms. When everyone was ready, they set off to find the train.

At mid-morning the next day, the train passed through Debica, a small, prosperous city with several church steeples pointing to the sky. The station lay in ruins, a familiar sight by now, and many of the switches were jammed. However, the main line was clear. The tracks were lined with people who wanted to flee further east, away from the advancing Germans. They shouted and waved as the train sped past, but it never faltered. There was no room for more passengers and no need to stop.

Once again, a feeling of contentment seeped into Kaz's psyche. There had been no sign of enemy aircraft that day. He and Simon had those cans of food tucked away. The train was making good progress. Contentment wrapped its arms around hope. It was a false hope, he realized. It was only a matter of time before his dreams were shattered by the reality of war.

And shattered they were. It began when they reached the little town of Ropczyce, where bombs had rendered a river bridge too weak to bear the weight of the train. A crew was trying to shore up the trestle with supports, but repairs wouldn't be finished before morning. Even then, there was some doubt as to whether the bridge would hold. The men left in search of food, while mothers, children and elderly anxiously waited. Children whimpered in their sleep. Old lungs wheezed in the cold, night air. Women, who'd probably never snored in their life, did so now.

Kaz and Simon walked down the tracks to a quiet spot where they could open one of the cans from the abandoned dairy farm. Simon had kept the knife he used on the chickens. He quickly punctured the lid and peeled it back. They devoured the meat. Simon no longer protested about pork being unclean.

Early the next morning, the crew declared that work on the bridge was finished, but they wouldn't guarantee that it could hold the weight of the train. It was agreed that everyone should traverse the bridge on foot before the train chanced a crossing. The passengers hurried across the deep span to the other side, where they stood and watched with trepidation while the train groped its way over the dangerous trestle. The braces quivered, but to everyone's relief, they held. A resounding cheer split the air when the last of the cars was clear of danger. The train workers laughed and slapped each other's backs. It was a small triumph, but at that moment, it rang the gong of glory.

Kaz noticed that some of the families with very young children or older loved ones left the train in search of food and lodgings in the town. Perhaps, they felt safer, now that they had traveled east. Or, they'd simply lost the will to push any farther. Either way, there were fewer people clinging to its roofs and sides as the train snorted like a great fighting bull and strode forward toward the morning sun.

Kaz's misgivings were renewed when a wave of bombers flew overhead, racing the train to the horizon. Not a good sign, he mumbled to himself. It was only a matter of time until their train became a target, once more. It seemed as if all the planes in Germany were following the train's route, and he wondered why.

"Simple," Simon replied to his musings. "The Germans need landmarks to guide them. All they have to do is follow the trains. Our rail system is like a giant map that leads them to every city and industrial plant in Poland."

Great, Kaz thought. Here they were trying to run away from the Germans, and all they were doing was showing them the way!

Soon, another formation of bombers appeared, and this time two Stukas tipped their wings and banked into a turn to begin a strafing run. Kaz held his breath as the bullets pummeled the earth. Unlike the previous attacks, this one targeted the engine. The bullets screamed with fury as they ricocheted off the steel surrounding the engine's cab. The train lurched to a stop, knocking anyone who was standing to the floor. The planes' engines roared loudly as they passed less than a hundred feet above the train and flew away. Voices shouted. Workers jumped from the boxcar and ran to the engine. Kaz followed.

"What happened?" he asked the coal stoker, who stood trembling off to one side, his face blackened by coal dust and distorted by fear.

"The engineer's dead. Bullets were flying everywhere. It's a miracle I wasn't hit." He sat down on a nearby rock and tried to gather himself. Kaz remembered the two times a bullet had narrowly missed his head. He understood the man's feeling of helplessness.

"Can you drive the train?" Kaz asked.

The stoker shook his head no.

Kaz walked forward and pulled himself onto the boarding rung where he could peer into the cab. The engineer was slumped forward, his hand still clutching the brake control. Shrapnel had blown away the top of his head; the interior was splattered red with blood. An odd odor filled the cab that reminded Kaz of wet varnish. He had to fight a surge of nausea. This was war, he thought. It was a brutal, violent business, and it made him realize how hard it was going to be to survive.

Two men gently removed the body from its seat and handed it down to workers on the ground. A crowd had gathered around the train workers below while they discussed what to do.

"He was a good man," one of them lamented. "And now there's nobody to drive the train. We're stuck."

Kaz stepped down and joined the group. "I used to drive trains. I can handle it."

"Don't remember seeing you." One of the men looked at him with skepticism.

"I ran trains out of Krakow. Haven't done so in a while. Not since I got laid off in the depression. But, you guys get the cab cleaned up, I'll drive your train."

"All right, then. It looks like you've got the job."

The men used hot water from the boiler to wet rags and wipe down the equipment. It was unpleasant work. Kaz watched them and reprimanded himself for stepping forward. All he wanted to do was make weapons for the Polish military, not put himself in the line of fire. His heart was hammering the way it did on those previous occasions when he'd put himself in the hands of fate and risked his life. Was he doing so again? Was this another attempt to end a life that left him unfulfilled? He didn't think so, but he couldn't be certain.

The men finished their cleaning, and Kaz looked over the controls. Miraculously, nothing had been damaged. The only thing that bothered him was the lingering odor. It smelled of death. He hoped it would dissipate once they were underway. He pulled the whistle to clear the tracks of people milling about, opened the cylinder cocks and pushed the throttle forward. The old engine groaned, and with a mighty quiver began to roll down the tracks.

The rest of the day sped by without incident. They stopped at a station, as yet undamaged, where they left the engineer's body and filled the water tanks. Kaz's neck muscles ached from the constant vigil of watching for more planes. He was thankful when night fell. He slowed the train's speed to four or five miles an hour and ran without lights. The stoker and Kaz both strained their eyes as they peered into the darkness and tried to determine if the track was passable. They stopped once for more water and again to wait for a switch to be repaired. Kaz fondly recalled the excitement of driving his first trains under the watchful eye of the engineer. He wished he could relive that excitement now, but all he felt was the disquieting tension of someone caught in the cross hairs of an invisible assailant.

As they approached the city of Przeworsk, Kaz suddenly saw flares drifting across the sky to the southeast. The direction of the flares alarmed Kaz. Had the Germans somehow launched an offensive from Czechoslovakia? Kaz estimated his location to be about 150 miles east of Krakow and 50 miles north of the Czech border. If the Germans had initiated an attack up the valley along the San River, they could form a vast pincer movement. It would allow their armored units to close the jaws of a giant trap on Warsaw by attacking central Poland from the east as well as from the west. Kaz had no training in army tactics, but he saw what a fantastic maneuver that would be, one for which the Polish army would be ill prepared. It also meant that Kaz's train was headed straight into the teeth of a German offensive.

"That looks like trouble," he commented to the stoker.

The young man nodded, but before he could speak lights flashed on the tracks up ahead. Kaz debated whether to speed up or to stop. It seemed unlikely that German ground troops would have reached this area just yet, so he had to assume it was Poles. He throttled back the engine and halted the train. The lights of Przeworsk were barely visible over a low range of hills outlined in the distance.

Men in Polish army uniforms appeared alongside the train. A man in a colonel's uniform approached the engine cab.

"Why are we stopping?" Kaz called down.

"I assume you saw those flares a few minutes ago."

Kaz's heart jumped. "Yes, why?"

"Those were signal flares from spotter planes directing a German ground attack. It's likely there are German armored divisions just a few miles ahead of us. They're reported to be moving up the San Valley." The Colonel studied the sky to the east where more flares had appeared. "Last I heard, they were approaching Jaroslaw. They may have taken it by now."

"I feared as much," Kaz replied.

"If that's the case, they'll be in Przeworsk in a matter of hours. Your train is headed right for them."

"We're trying to move war plant machinery to a new location at Starachowice. What should we do?"

"Wait here while I check with my superiors." The colonel hurried away and disappeared into the darkness.

Kaz climbed down from the cab and informed the war plant personnel what was happening. "I don't think we're going to Starachowice anymore."

"Where to, then?" one of the men asked.

Kaz shrugged his shoulders. "To hell, for all I know."

That got a few grim chuckles. Everyone realized that hell was only a few miles away. Kaz climbed back into the cab and shut down the valves, then joined the workers and soldiers who were sprawled in the ditch beside the tracks. They smoked and chatted while they waited.

"I thought we were going to fight Germans," one of the soldiers commented. "All we seem to be doing is staying out of their way. Or, at least trying to."

"Their tanks are a lot faster than ours, and they control the skies," another replied. "It's pretty hard to fight against those odds."

They watched in silence as a new round of flares burst in the sky. They seemed closer.

Before long, the colonel reappeared. "We think it's best to move the train into Przeworsk while we prepare to defend the city. That way, your passengers can look for shelter. I'm not sure what to do about your equipment. It doesn't seem likely you'll be able to assemble it here, and there's no good alternative at present."

"Maybe, we can scatter the pieces around town and hide them." Even as he suggested this, Kaz realized how impractical the idea was. He stubbed out his cigarette and climbed back into the cab.

He guided the train into the gloom of a city that had covered its windows with blankets, turned off the street lights, and done its best to hide in the dark. Heavy guns thumped in the distance. More flares glared in the sky to the southeast. They were definitely getting closer.

Kaz knew that dawn was only an hour away. Then, the bombers would come. He also knew it would be suicide to leave the train at the station. That would be one of the first targets the planes would hit. So, he parked it near some overgrown bushes on a side rail about a mile down the track and told the men to cover it with tarps. It wasn't much of a solution, but it was the best he could do.

Meanwhile, soldiers arrived and moved about the train informing passengers of the situation. They were advised to walk into the city to look for shelter. Many of the residents had offered to open their doors to the refugees. Otherwise, they could stay on the train and take their chances. There was no food there, however, and if the bombers sniffed out the camouflage, the train would be easy pickings.

Kaz and Simon decided to walk into town to assess their prospects. They still had two cans of pork but decided to save them for later. Daylight was creeping over the low hills. They could see that the place was well looked after. Streets were swept; shutters were painted; and gardens were pruned. The residents clearly took pride in their city.

As they approached the town center, they became aware of a ruckus behind a coal shed. Angry voices echoed off the surrounding buildings, but Kaz couldn't see what was causing so much anger. Suddenly, a mob of men surged into the square just ahead of him. The men in front escorted two very pale looking individuals whose hands were tied behind their backs. They wore loose-fitting civilian jackets, but their trousers had the crisp, khaki look of military clothing.

At the same time, the colonel Kaz had met at the train rounded a street corner on the opposite side of the square, flanked by two soldiers. He stopped to survey the situation.

"Where did these men come from?" he asked.

"They're German agents," a voice declared from the crowd. "We're going to hang them."

"They parachuted into a farmer's field east of here before sunrise," another added. "The farmer spotted them and called us. We caught one near where our troops are building defenses for the city. The other was headed for the rail yards."

The colonel eyed the intruders carefully. "They must be paratroopers of the Luftwaffe. You can't hang them."

"Why the hell not," a man behind the prisoners snarled. "They were going to destroy our city!"

"Nonetheless, they are prisoners of war. They need to be dealt with by our military. You'd better hand them over to me."

"But they're not in uniform," the man persisted. "That makes them spies, and we'll treat them like spies."

"There are rules of conduct for war," the colonel insisted. "Rules that must be followed by both sides."

"Rules?" The speaker stepped forward with an old gun in his hand and faced the Germans. "What do they know about rules? They came here to kill us. But we're going to kill them first."

Another joined the leaders with a rope in his hands. "I say, hang 'em."

The crowd pushed forward amid a sea of rising voices. "Hang them," was repeated again and again. The colonel hesitated in the face of the angry mob. It was clear that he didn't know what to do. On the one hand, he had a duty to uphold the dictates of war; on the other, he feared that he might not be able to control these men, in which case, it would be better to step aside.

The two Germans looked about, bewildered. One had the smudged, scratched face of someone who'd been shoved nose first to the ground. The other sported crisp blond hair that had hardly been disturbed by all the fuss. Neither looked older than twenty. It was apparent that they didn't know what was being said, but when they saw the rope, their eyes widened with fear. They didn't need to speak Polish to understand the argument.

The men in the crowd milled about with vengeance in their eyes. Kaz could see that they were not going to be deterred by the Colonel's plea to observe some rules regarding the conduct of war. They were frustrated, angry workers, the kind Kaz had supervised at the clothing factory, and they wanted blood. The crowd edged closer to the Colonel and his men, who tried to stand their ground.

Just as Kaz feared that the confrontation would explode into violence, a distant rumbling noise distracted the men. It sounded like the murmur of voices, metallic voices. Kaz looked to his left and saw the long guns of a dozen German tanks crawling over the tops of the nearby hills. They were several thousand yards away, but there was no mistaking the bright, red-hooked cross of swastikas painted on the grey-green monsters cresting the hill.

"Szkopy," someone shouted in the crowd. "The szkopy, they come."

Cannons roared from the Polish defensive positions that had been set up on the edge of the city, followed by puffs of smoke and explosions among the tanks. One tank took a direct hit. Its treads unraveled and it stopped. Others received glancing blows that hardly slowed them. The men stood and watched, dumbfounded, as the tanks returned fire in a series of booming volleys. Kaz's view of the Polish guns was obstructed by buildings, but he feared the worst. More tanks appeared on the hills. They thundered forward with the steady progress of locust devouring everything in their paths. Nothing was going to get in their way.

The muscles in Kaz's stomach tightened. Despite the attacks by the Stukas on his train, the war had remained somewhat impersonal, until now. It had been something from which one could hide with tarps. The tank assault taking place in front of him was different. There was no place to hide from those great, mechanized beasts. He looked around for the colonel, to ask him what to do, but he was gone, along with his soldiers. The mob was scattering, as well. In a matter of seconds, dozens of angry men had turned into frightened souls who were rapidly disappearing from the square. Only he and Simon remained, along with the two German paratroopers who were left standing unguarded in the square. The two men looked uncertainly at Kaz, then turned and ran off at an awkward gait with their hands still tied behind their backs.

"Where should we go?" Simon queried as he watched them run. The tanks had had the same effect on him as they did on everyone else.

More cannon shots boomed across the battlefield. Two more tanks were hit, but others replaced them. The tanks were sweeping down the hill and approaching the town. People could be seen running wildly from the fields toward the protection of the city's walls. It was a false sense of security. It wouldn't be long before tank shells began pounding the buildings.

Kaz felt his heart racing as he pondered Simon's question. He could hear the metallic squeal of tanks' treads as they moved closer. The staccato sound of machine gun fire erupted, adding to the cacophony of battle sounds, which were growing louder. People fleeing from the tanks were entering the square and running in different directions. Kaz wanted to run, also, but where?

"We can't stay here, that's for sure."

"Why don't we just take the train and go back the way we came?"

Kaz shook his head. "Too late for that. We'd have to turn the engine around. It would take too long. No, our best bet is to head south through the San Valley. If we stay away from the tracks and main roads, we might be able to slip past the Germans and make our way back to Krakow."

"What about Warsaw?"

"We want to stay as far away from Warsaw as possible. That's where all the Germans are going."

"But that's near where my family is. I've got to find them."

Kaz placed his hands on Simon's shoulders. "Go if you must. I'm headed the other direction. Good luck."

There was no more time to wait. Kaz raced across the square in the direction of the train tracks. More people were crowding into the marketplace. Troubled voices echoed around him. Cannon continued to thunder on the outskirts of the city, evidence that the Polish army was putting up a fierce resistance. He recognized faces from the train, but he ignored them and moved on. Greeting people would only slow him down. He ducked into a street and kept running. By the time he reached the train, his lungs were bursting. He bent over and put his hands on his knees while he caught his breath. People were still moving about the train cars. Most were older; the younger passengers had gone. Those who remained were either too frightened or too tired to leave. He wished he could help them but knew he couldn't. There was no time. The ground was already shaking from the advancing tanks. Soon, they would reach the station. Then, it was only a matter of time until they discovered the train.

Kaz saw familiar faces ahead of him, a machinist named Justin who had worked with him in the war plant, and a woman called Ilyna who had worked in the office. Justin was a bit older, possibly in his forties, but with his stocky build and powerful arms and legs, he looked fit. Ilyna was a bit stocky as well, with reddish-blond hair and a turned-down mouth that gave her a pouting look. Justin had ridden in the front car with the other machinists, but Ilyna had stayed in another boxcar with an older couple. Kaz could see by the way she kept glancing around that she was badly frightened.

"We're looking for Ilyna's parents," Justin said by way of greeting. "Have you seen them?"

Kaz shook his head no. "You can't stay here any longer. The Germans are not far away."

Tears welled up in her eyes. "They were supposed to wait for us here, but they must have gotten scared. Now, they're gone."

Justin put his arm around her shoulders to comfort her. Kaz had never noticed them together at the plant, but their behavior suggested that some intimacy existed between them, perhaps initiated by the shock of war.

"We were thinking of heading south. Try to work our way back to Krakow"

"Me to," Kaz replied. "The Germans are going to be too busy consolidating their positions and attacking Warsaw to worry about us. I figured if I stayed to the back roads and farm fields, I should be able to reach Krakow in two or three days."

"We should go, then." Justin's words were meant for Ilyna, who nodded as tears rolled down her face.

Kaz looked her up and down. "Wouldn't hurt to have company, as long as we can all keep pace. If anyone falters, I'll have to move on."

"Agreed."

Kaz pulled himself into the train's cab and found his knapsack where he'd hidden it in the coal bin. He slung it over his shoulders, dropped back to the ground and pointed toward a ditch that ran alongside the train. The other two nodded. They scrambled down the embankment and followed the ditch away from the station. If there were any advanced troops behind them, the train's cars would shield them from view. At the end of the train, they turned up a ravine and headed for a stand of trees. Once they reached the cover of the trees, Kaz looked back to see if any German soldiers had spotted him. To his amazement, he discovered more than a dozen train passengers in a ragged line hurrying for cover behind him.

"Where did they come from?" he asked Justin.

"Saw us leave the train and decided to follow, I guess."

"Damn, they're too old. They'll never keep up."

The stragglers puffed their way to where Kaz and his new friends were hiding and plopped down on the ground. Most of them were in their sixties and seventies; none looked fit enough for the journey. Kaz pawed the ground with his foot while he tried to decide what to do. If he abandoned them, they could find their way back to the train. The Germans would have little interest in them. They would be safer in town than trying to run across farm fields to God knows where. He turned and faced them.

"We're going to be moving at too fast a pace for you to keep up, and we can't wait. We have too much ground to cover." His words sounded harsh, but he didn't know what else to say. "You'll be safer here. The Germans won't bother with you. They're looking for people like us." He pointed to Justin and Ilyna.

"The Germans are a brutal race," one of the men cried. "All we want to do is find a place to hide until our soldiers drive them back where they came from."

Kaz shook his head in wonderment. They thought the Poles were going to win the war. Despite his instincts to run and survive, he didn't know how he could just leave them. Their dirt-streaked faces were filled with fear and despair. Kaz heard the metal creaking of a tank's treads charging along the train tracks. Suddenly, its cannon boomed. What had it fired at, he wondered? Polish troops? The train? He pictured people screaming, stumbling to get away. He looked at Justin and Ilyna for help. They just shrugged their shoulders. They didn't want to be the ones to decide.

There was only one solution.

"We'll take you as far as the first village, but you'll have to stop there." He heard murmurs of consent. He only hoped that there were no Germans waiting for them when they got there. Kaz rose and headed through the trees in the general direction of the San River valley. The others followed. He had no map, but he figured the valley would guide him. If they stayed north of Jaroslaw, which the Germans had already captured, and followed the valley, they should find the road to Belzec. Once there, they would be able to get a better idea of their chances. It didn't seem likely that the Germans were leaving many soldiers to guard the smaller towns or villages. They needed them for their assault on Warsaw. If he could get to Belzec, Kaz was pretty sure that he could bypass the German sweep. He shared his thoughts with Justin and Ilyna as they walked.

"It's a good plan," Justin agreed. "And there are plenty of villages on the way. We should be able to find a safe place to leave our fellow passengers."

Kaz looked back and saw to his dismay that he was already outpacing the rest of the group. Against his better judgment, he slowed a bit. They'd better find a village soon, he thought. Otherwise, the afternoon sun would take its toll, and they had no water.

They left the forest and entered a field of wheat that stood high enough to give them decent cover. Kaz thought about what he knew of Germans as he walked. The few he'd met seemed rather stiff and formal, not that easy to warm up to, except in a bar. Once they had a few drinks in them, they became quite jovial and friendly. He'd found them meticulous in their work. They paid attention to details. It was their meticulous nature that bothered him. He could see it in their planning for the current invasion, and he feared it would make them a deadly enemy.

As he expected, the heat took its toll as the afternoon progressed. They had to make frequent stops. Each time, the older people sank to the ground in a state of exhaustion, their breaths labored from the exertion and the lack of water. The latter problem resolved itself when, about six o'clock in the evening, they reached the banks of the San River. Even Kaz eagerly plunged his hands into the swift current to gather drinking water and to splash the wonderfully cool liquid across his face. Once he'd satisfied his thirst, he turned his attention to a bridge spanning the river about a mile upstream. It was an old, stone bridge, the kind used by farmers to bring food to market in the town that spread its venerable arms along the other side of the river. He saw no military activity, but he urged the group to stay hidden along the riverbank while he and Justin moved closer to investigate. He hoped the town would provide sanctuary for the group. Kaz could see that the bridge was still intact, a good sign, but he worried there might be German sentries posted out of sight.

A German voice danced across the water as Kaz and Justin crawled along the riverbank. The light was fading, but they were now close enough to make out the figures of two guards leaning against the bridge. Smoke from their cigarettes billowed in a light breeze and floated away. Rifles leaned in a casual manner against a stone abutment. Kaz and Justin looked at each other and shook their heads. They turned around and headed back to the group.

"There are German guards," Kaz announced when they reached the others. "We'll have to keep moving."

By now, the followers were on their last legs. They had collapsed on the ground, ready to call it a night.

"We can't go any further," one protested.

"We must take advantage of the dark to get past the sentries." Kaz studied the group as he spoke. Some had taken off their shoes to rub sore feet. Others lay sprawled along the riverbank where they'd fallen. None showed any signs of moving. "Okay, we'll rest one hour. Then, we really must go. Those who can't make it will have to take their chances in the town."

It was the best he could offer. He had no watch, but he thought the time interval sounded reasonable. There were a few groans, but nobody complained.

Only a sliver of light from a new moon showed them the way as they trudged through a farm field out of sight from the bridge. Kaz kept the moon to his left to guide him. People were beginning to falter, but he urged them to continue for another mile. He was about to call a halt for the night when the group stumbled upon a mound of potatoes taller than a man's head, and a similar mound of wheat. No one had eaten anything substantial in the last twenty-four hours. They all stopped in their tracks and stared at the two mountains of food, uncertain of what they saw.

"It's either a miracle or a mirage," Ilyna whispered.

Kaz stepped forward and touched one of the potatoes. "They're real all right. What are they doing here?" He glanced around quickly, thinking it might be a German trap.

"They're for anyone who wants them," a voice boomed from the shadows, causing everyone to jump.

Kaz whirled around and found himself staring up at a mountain of a man who stood as tall as the mound of potatoes. He was dressed in a loose-fitting, long-sleeved tunic made of coarse, white linen. It was cinched around the waist by a broad, black belt. Heavy, black, woolen trousers tumbled out from under the tunic, nearly reaching a pair of bare feet the size of small hams. An open vest of tanned sheepskin dangled about his powerful shoulders, its color nearly matching the skin on the man's rounded face. A battered, gray felt hat sat precariously on top of his oversized head.

Kaz looked around instinctively for some weapon with which to defend himself, but the man's white teeth gleamed in a smile that told him there was nothing to fear.

"I'm called Stanislaw." He extended a huge paw.

"I'm Kaz." He grasped the offered hand, which completely enveloped his. "Do you live around here?"

"My house if just beyond that grove of trees." He gestured over his shoulder. "This is my farm."

Kaz introduced the other members of the party and briefly explained their situation.

"Follow me to the house. We can get something to eat and sort things out."

As they walked up the rutted wagon road leading to the farmhouse, Stanislaw explained that his family had fled up north when news of the German invasion came over the radio. He'd remained to look after the livestock.

"Haven't spoken to anybody in two days, but I've kept a close watch on the soldiers in the town. There's only a handful. Most have moved on, to continue the assault, I imagine."

They arrived at a spacious, rambling farmhouse built from home cured bricks and wood. There were more than enough chairs in the living room and around the kitchen table for everybody to sit down. Most did so with a sigh of relief. After the day that they'd endured, the farmhouse felt like a fairy tale castle. There was a large fireplace against the far wall that spread its warmth through the house. A pair of deer antlers hung on one wall. A moose head hung on the other.

"You like to hunt?" Kaz asked by way of making conversation.

"My father. I never liked to hurt anything."

A gentle giant, Kaz mused. Perhaps, they *had* tumbled into a fairy tale.

"There's a bathroom off the kitchen and another down the hall you all can use to clean up. Meanwhile, I'll throw some food together."

Kaz watched the food preparations with amazement. From the smokehouse out back, he produced a plump ham and some fresh-smoked sausages; from the cellar he retrieved three bottles of red wine; and from the root cellar in the hill behind the house, he brought a heavy jar of cool buttermilk and a cloth of aged cheese. He fired up the kitchen stove and slapped slices of ham into two skillets. The odors of hot meat and bubbling fat quickly filled the room. Mouths were soon watering to the point of drooling. Next, he went to the pantry and selected several loaves of crusty bread. He piled all the food on the large kitchen table. Finally, he set out plates, cups, glasses, knives and forks while the slices of ham simmered in the iron skillets on the stove. When everything was ready, he summoned everyone to supper.

Kaz and the others tried to be polite, but they couldn't help themselves. They all piled into the food as if they feared that it might disappear at any moment. It reminded him of a funny story he'd once heard in a bar about four gentlemen sitting down to a dinner that included five pieces of ham sitting in a serving dish. Each took one piece of ham and ate it while politely ignoring the last piece, which still sat in the serving dish. Suddenly, the lights went out. There was a moment of silence followed by a terrible scream. When the lights blinked back on, they saw one gentleman's hand on top of the meat with three forks stuck in it! That was how the meal progressed. No one was going to leave a slice of ham or a crust of bread lying around. No one was going to wait for the lights to go out.

"Those piles of food down the road. What are they for?" Kaz finally asked.

"Oh, those." Stanislaw chuckled. "I put them there for anyone who happened along. I figured people were going to need to eat, and I'd rather those in need get it than the Germans. They've left me alone so far. Too busy attacking elsewhere. But sooner or later they'll show up here, and when they do, I imagine they'll clean me out."

His face turned red with anger. "I'd rather feed good Poles than those lousy szkopy."

Kaz smiled and nodded his agreement. "We saw a few soldiers guarding the bridge into town. I assume there are others."

"Not many, but more will come. Then, they will get around to farmers like me." He poured more wine into Kaz's glass. "Right now, I'm more worried about the Volksdeutsche from the settlement over near Biela Gora. Those jackals will be nosing around soon."

"Who are they?"

"Germans who settled here over the past few years. They showed up during the depression and started buying up farms that were going broke. Pretty soon, there was a whole community of them. They're good farmers, but they remain very loyal to their homeland. Some say they're fanatics. All they talk about is how good life has become under Hitler." Stanislaw removed the skillets from the stove and sat back down. "I don't know the details, but many believe they were given money by the German government to come here. They all claim to have Polish ancestry."

"Will they support the German invasion?"

Stanislaw shrugged. "Who knows? It seems likely, seeing how much they talk about their country. Some say there are more settlements like this one. They could provide a very effective occupying force to help the army control us."

Kaz pondered this news. Once again, he thought about the meticulous nature of the Germans he'd met. Here was a good example: an invasion of German farmers to support the invasion of German troops. It wasn't as far fetched as it sounded.

"We have to move on in the morning." He glanced toward the passengers from the train. "But we can't take the older people with us. We'll be moving too fast."

"Your friends should be safe here for a few days, at least. And there's plenty of food. You're welcome to stay, too, if you change your mind about going."

Kaz shook his head. "Thanks, but we want to get back to Krakow, if possible. Before the Germans cut off all the roads."

"You should probably push on to Rawa Ruska. I have a brother there who can help you. He'll know if the roads are open. Sometimes, I still get news on the radio from Warsaw. It seems the Germans are focusing most of the army there for a final battle. If so, many roads to the south will not be well guarded. It may be possible to get through."

"That's what we hoped. It sounds like our best option."

"Well, stay the night. I'll give you more food to take with you in the morning."

A loud banging noise startled Kaz out of a heavy sleep. It took him a moment to gather his thoughts and to realize that someone was pounding on the front door. Early morning light filtered through the window's curtains above his head. The sweet smell of cooked ham still hung in the air. Stanislaw stumbled into the living room in his nightshirt. He shuffled to the door and flung it open.

A small man about Kaz's height, but much thinner in build, stood ramrod straight in the doorway. When he saw Stanislaw towering above him, he had to tilt his head so far backwards, he nearly tipped over. The man was dressed in an ill-fitted, gray-green shirt and jacket that made Kaz think of a homemade Nazi uniform. The analogy was reinforced by the way the man combed his hair forward on his forehead and by his attempt to grow a sparse mustache on his upper lip. He looked like a comic opera version of Der Fuhrer. Three other men with pistols jabbed in their waistlines stood in the yard behind him. There was nothing comical about those men. The stiff looking man's hand darted into the pocket of his jacket and withdrew a folded piece of paper. He quickly unfolded and consulted it.

"Are you Herr Scepurik?" He asked this in a voice that was intended to sound authoritative, but lost its base and ended in a loud squeak.

"I am."

The little man shifted his weight on the porch's heavy, wooden planks. He smoothed the paper against his chest and commenced to read it.

"All occupants of this house must report themselves to the Kommandant of the village of Swidnik by noon tomorrow. Those who fail to comply will be dealt with when the legions of the Wermacht arrive later this week."

After carefully refolding the paper and returning it to his pocket, he glared at Stanislaw. "Do you understand this order?"

"Yes."

"Very well, see that it's obeyed." He turned on his heel and strode off the porch. The three men followed him as he marched down the rutted road toward the next farmhouse.

Stanislaw closed the door with a resigned shrug of his shoulders. "It's already happened."

"What?"

"They've come."

"The Germans?"

"The jackals."

"I would've liked to punch that little bastard in the nose."

"You saw the others. They all had guns. And there's plenty more men where they came from."

"They're the farmers you talked about?"

Stanislaw nodded as he walked over to the fireplace, picked up a poker and sifted through the dead ashes. "They're from the Volksdeutsche colony. I recognized the leader. I've seen him in town but never spoken to him." He chuckled. "I think I gave him quite a shock when I opened the door."

Kaz couldn't help smiling. "He nearly fell over backwards."

"I have that effect on people."

"Well, you should've chased them off your land. I doubt they would've shot you."

"It doesn't matter. I think this war will be over very soon. The Wermacht will overrun us, and we'll learn to follow German orders. I doubt they'll take our farms as long as we do what we're told. They're going to need food, lots of it. But they *will* take all those potatoes and wheat out by the road, and a lot more."

Stanislaw motioned for Kaz to follow him to his bedroom, where they could talk privately. "I don't know what will happen to your friends. It might take a few weeks, but I'm sure they'll be relocated. Where, I don't know."

"I thought about that when I looked at those thugs in the yard." Kaz looked over at the bed. It seemed too small for such a large man. "Things are happening too quickly. The three of us need to leave, now, and move as fast as we can. Are you still willing to house them until the Germans arrive?"

The big man nodded his head emphatically. "Of course, they're Poles."

Chapter Fifteen

The group was reluctant to see Kaz and his friends go, but they knew there was no choice. The three of them threw as much food as they could carry into their knapsacks and, with directions and an address for Stanislaw's brother, raced off across the fields toward Rawa Ruska. Kaz couldn't help worrying about what would happen if they ran into German troops, but the freedom of being on the move again raised his spirits. Other than a few Stukas flying overhead, there was no sign of the war. The world seemed at peace.

Kaz's sense of tranquility vanished within the hour when the roar of German armored divisions --- trucks, tanks and towed cannons --- filled the air with such a din, it drowned out the noise of the German aircraft flying overhead. He hid with Justin and Ilyna in bushes below the crown of a hill where they would not be outlined against the sky and watched the procession, which stretched for a mile or more along the main highway.

"They must be coming from Rawa Ruska," Justin said in awe. "How do we avoid them?"

"I'm not sure," Kaz replied through gritted teeth. "These damn Germans seem to be everywhere." He rolled over on his side and propped his head in his hand. "All we can do is wait for them to pass, then see what happens."

It was an hour before the last armored vehicle rolled past them and disappeared in the haze of dust and exhaust fumes generated by the convoy. When it appeared safe, the three of them ran over the crest of the hill and hurried on their way toward Rawa Ruska. They arrived on the outskirts of the city in the late afternoon, but they hesitated to enter for fear of German sentries. So, they scurried from side street to side street in an effort to locate any German soldiers. The more they looked, the more dumbfounded they became. It appeared that the city was empty of Germans. Instead of being greeted by soldiers, they found quiet, tree-lined streets where homes and shops stood intact. Even the railway station was undamaged. There was so little evidence of the war, it seemed as if the Germans had never been there. What could have happened, Kaz wondered?

After asking directions, they retraced their steps and found themselves at the doorstep of a unassuming, clapboard, two-story house situated five blocks from the train station. The man who opened the door looked nothing like the gentle giant who was his brother. He was slight of build, his face was ruddy, his cheekbones were more angular, and he stood more than a foot shorter.

"We're looking for Pawal Scepunik," Kaz announced.

"That's me." The man looked at him quizzically.

"Oh." Kaz hesitated. "We just came from your brother's farm. I guess I was expecting somebody bigger."

Pawal laughed. "You're not the first to admit that. Stanislaw is my half brother. We have different fathers." He opened the door wider. "Come in."

After introductions, Kaz got to the point. "We're trying to get to Krakow. Do you have any information on German movements? Earlier in the day we saw a couple of armored divisions heading north."

"It's very confusing. The Wehrmacht rolled in here three days ago and looked like they planned to stay, but early this morning they packed up and left. I've been listening to updates on the radio. Come and join me."

They spent the next two hours eating their food and listening to the reports broadcast on the radio. Slowly, a picture of the war emerged. As they had guessed, Poland's air force had been destroyed on the ground, and Germany's Stukas were free to bomb Warsaw, Krakow and other cities. Warsaw was now surrounded. Polish forces were badly outgunned, and their supply lines were severed. Yet, they were putting up a fierce defense of the city and were inflicting heavy losses on German troops. It seemed a hopeless cause, but the Poles did not intend to go meekly.

Then, devastating news. Russian troops were entering Poland from the east. They had already struck the exposed flank of the Poles in Warsaw. The Germans were moving troops forward to secure their victory, and that left cities and towns like Rawa Ruska open to the Russians. Russian forces were now crossing the Polish border and taking control of several cities.

"That explains it," Pawal shouted. "There have been rumors of the Russian army massing nearby. The Germans have moved their troops out and the Russians are taking over. They'll be in Rawa Ruska by tomorrow."

Kaz sat in stunned silence while he digested the news. He knew Poland was finished. It was only a question of where he wanted to be when the dust settled, and that decision was an easy one. The Germans were brutal, but the Russians were barbaric. If he was going to face an occupying force, the Germans were the lesser of two evils. And he still wanted to get home to Krakow. He wanted to see Daneta and his daughter.

"We have to leave tonight," he announced to Justin and Ilyna. "We've got to move as fast as we can."

They both agreed.

"Pawal, you're welcome to come with us."

He shook his head. "My home is here and my brother is nearby."

Kaz understood. Family was important in times like this. He and his companions quickly repacked their knapsacks, said their goodbyes, and hurried into the darkness. They spent that night and the next day walking along dusty back roads past farms and villages. On three occasions, they nearly stumbled upon small units of German troops, but they were able to hide until they passed. There was no sign of Germans in any of the villages. They were able to move about unchallenged. Several of the villages had put up barricades, comprised of furniture, sandbags and farm equipment, and mustered hunting rifles in anticipation of a confrontation with the Germans. With the radio reporting the resistance by Polish soldiers in Warsaw, they'd gotten it into their heads that they would do the same. Kaz didn't bother to point out the futility of their efforts in the face of tanks, Stukas and cannons.

At one point, they were stopped by a band of self-appointed national guards and held for two hours on the suspicion that they were German spies. Fortunately, Kaz still carried his card showing that he'd been in the Polish navy. They thought it might be a forgery, but Kaz stuck to his story. They finally relented and let them be on their way.

A few hours later, they came upon an open-air car with bald tires and dented fenders that was loaded with Polish soldiers. The car skidded to a halt alongside them, raising a cloud of dust.

"Have you seen any German troop movements along this road?" demanded a young lieutenant seated in the front.

"We saw a dozen or so Germans yesterday quite a ways east of here, but none today," Justin replied.

"What about Polish units. Have you met any?" The lieutenant removed his field goggles and wiped the lenses with a handkerchief that was so dusty it made little difference.

Kaz shook his head. "Not since we left Przeworsk."

"Damn," the lieutenant muttered as he replaced his glasses. He turned to one of the soldiers holding a light machine gun in the rear seat. "They must've been cut off somewhere between here and Jaroslaw. We'd better double back and see if we can catch up with the 72nd."

The car turned around and roared off down the road. Kaz gazed after it until it disappeared over a rise. It was apparent that the young lieutenant had no idea where to go or what to do. Kaz suspected that that was true for most of the Polish army. Troops were scattered across the landscape in disarray.

The trio continued on their way and made steady progress until early afternoon when they reached a highway that cut across their route. They stopped in a tree line a quarter of a mile away and watched as German vehicles roared up and down the road.

"There's no way around it," Kaz observed. He wondered where the lieutenant and his car of soldiers had gone.

"Maybe we should wait until dark," Ilyna suggested.

Justin and Kaz agreed. They settled down behind some bushes and rested. The food Stanislaw had given them was running low. Soon, they would have to scrounge for food from the farms they were passing. The sooner they got moving, the better.

Headlights moved up and down the highway in a steady pattern that reminded Kaz of raindrops. The traffic ebbed and flowed, but it never completely ceased. He sat next to his companions and waited.

"How will we ever get across?" Ilyna asked with despair.

"Be patient. Even the Germans have to sleep," Kaz assured her.

From the position of the new moon, Kaz guessed that it was after midnight before the trucks and cars dropped from a steady hum to the occasional grind of shifting gears.

"It's time," Kaz decided. "Let's move."

They worked their way through the underbrush to the side of the road. After all the activity, the night seemed eerily dark and quiet. They listened for any sounds of approaching vehicles, hitched up their courage and ran across the concrete to the safety of a farmer's field. A rush of adrenaline swept over Kaz as he raced up a dirt road past a potato field. He heard the pounding of Justin's and Ilyna's footsteps close behind him as he headed toward the dark outline of a farmhouse where he hoped to find sanctuary. They were greeted by two burly dogs who growled and snapped as they strained at their leashes. Lights flashed on in the farmhouse, and before the three could decide what to do, two men stepped onto a broad porch with pistols in their hands. Bright lanterns in their other hands illuminated the yard. Kaz and his companions stared at the guns.

"Stay right where you are." The command was in Polish, but the accent was German.

"We got turned around," Kaz offered. "Can you tell us the way to Krakow? We're trying to get home to our families."

The two men conferred with each other in German. "We'll let the authorities decide what you should do."

Kaz's heart rate jumped in alarm. These were German farmers, just like the jackals who visited Stanislaw's farm. His mind whirled through his alternatives. He could run, but he knew the dogs would be set loose. They would most likely tear him to pieces. The pistols made it impossible for him to charge the men. They would cut him down before he got ten feet. He looked at Justin and saw him sorting through the same alternatives and outcomes. After all he'd just been through, he had to accept the fact that he was now in the hands of the Germans. His only hope was to talk his way out of this mess. There was no choice but to do what these men ordered. He cursed his stupidity and his bad luck.

Kaz and his companions were forced to lie face down on the ground while their wrists were bound behind them with sturdy ropes. They were thrown in the back of an old farm truck and driven back to the highway. A rush of cold air chilled Kaz to the bone, although he suspected his shivering body had more to do with his predicament than the night air. The truck roared down the highway for several miles until the lights of a village hove into view. They stopped in front of an old warehouse that had been converted into a jail and interrogation center. Kaz was separated from his friends and pushed into an office without windows. His shoulders ached from having his hands tied so tightly behind him. To his relief, one of the guards untied the rope and handcuffed his hands in front. He was made to sit at a small desk with a German officer facing him. A guard with a rifle stood at attention in the far corner. The officer was unarmed. He yawned and scratched his head. He looked tired and bored. Kaz could see that the officer didn't want to be there anymore than he did. Both wanted to find a soft, warm bed.

The interrogation began in a friendly manner. Kaz was relieved to discover that the man spoke Polish. Kaz gave his name and explained how he'd come to be there. He figured the truth was his best hope. He prayed that Justin and Ilyna had reached the same conclusion. Otherwise, their stories wouldn't match.

"Come, come," the officer cajoled. His expression grew increasingly lively as the talk progressed. "You can't expect us to believe you are just running around the countryside trying to get home. You were caught in the middle of the night."

"We were trying to avoid being arrested," Kaz confessed.

"You were hiding from us, you mean."

He nodded. "We didn't think you would take kindly to us moving about."

"You were right about that." The officer leaned forward and stared into Kaz's eyes. "Many of you soldiers are throwing away your uniforms and trying to hide among the locals. You must think we're stupid not to know that."

"But I've already told you that I was in the navy. I was mustered out two years ago. I can show you my identity card for the naval reserve." He fished awkwardly in his pants pocket for his wallet and opened it. He shoved the card across the table.

The officer looked at the card and pushed it aside. He waved at it with the back of his hand. "Yes, I see you have one, but it is easy enough to forge such a document."

"Not in such a short period of time."

The officer smiled at the comment. "Well, you don't have to convince me any longer." He rose without another word and left the room. Kaz listened to his retreating footsteps. They stopped amid the murmur of voices. A moment of silence was broken by the brisk staccato of boots marching his way.

An overfed man in the gabardine tunic of a Gestapo officer entered the room. He, too, had a smile on his face, but his was as thin as ice. Unlike the army officer, this man had a gun in a holster on his hip. Kaz shivered when he looked at him. He sensed that the pleasantries were over.

"So, you do not wish to reveal your regiment or its location."

Kaz wasn't sure whether he should respond. He remained silent.

"Is that not so?" The smile was made even thinner by raised eyebrows. It was the most evil smile he'd ever seen.

"The only Polish soldiers I've encountered passed us in a car yesterday. They seemed headed for Warsaw." Kaz forced himself to sit straight and to retain a calm exterior. His insides were running riot, but there was nothing he could do about that.

The officer turned and said something to the guard, who came forward with a chain in his hand and motioned for Kaz to stand up. Kaz complied. The chain was passed quickly through the handcuffs and pulled upward. The guard stood on the chair and hooked the chain to a large nail that had been pounded into an open beam overhead. When he was finished, Kaz was standing on his toes with his arms raised tightly above him.

The officer went to a cupboard and pulled out a rubber hose about four feet in length. He glared at Kaz. "You have one last chance to save yourself."

Kaz wanted desperately to say something ... anything ... to satisfy the man, but he didn't know what that should be. It didn't matter. Before he could respond, the officer stepped forward and struck Kaz across his back with the hose. The pain was so unexpected and sharp, he nearly cried. The hose struck again, this time on his aching shoulder. Another blow was delivered to his chest, then one to his face. Pain radiated from each strike as if a series of earthquakes had been unleashed in his body. More blows fell in quick succession on his head, stomach, arms and legs. His voice croaked when he cried out. His breathing became labored. His mind reeled. He no longer stood on his toes. He hung from his wrists and slowly rotated in reaction to the punishment. His mind began to hide from him. His thoughts were no longer coherent. All he could do was focus on the pain and embrace it. It was all he knew to do.

Kaz was convinced that he was about to die when a soldier rushed into the room and spoke to the officer in an urgent voice. Kaz's body was screaming at him, and his eyes were closing. He forced them open so he could see what was happening. The officer stormed out of the room without another word. The guard who'd strung him up hurried over to Kaz and released the chain from the nail. Kaz collapsed on the floor in a heap. Hands grasped his arms, sending fresh waves of pain through his body, and he was dragged down a hallway to a larger room, where his handcuffs were removed and he was shoved inside. The door slammed behind him. A heavy bolt slid into place. Weak light filtered around the edges of a window that had been boarded up. Kaz managed to raise himself into a sitting position so that he could get his bearings. There was no furniture. Metal shelves lined the walls. Boxes were piled at the far end. It looked like a storage room.

The piercing pains were starting to recede into aching fields of misery that shouted at him when he moved. He ignored them and pushed himself to his feet. Whatever interrupted his torture had saved him from something far worse than what he felt now, but he knew it was only a temporary reprieve. The officer with the icy smile, or someone like him, would return, and that prospect terrified him. He had to force himself into action while there was time. He searched with his hands along the wall by the door for a light switch and found one. When he snapped it on, a weak overhead light filled the main part of the room. He tested the boards covering the window. They were firmly secured by large nails. He would need a crowbar to wrench them loose. There was nothing in the room that would give him that kind of leverage, unless ... He turned his attention to the metal shelves, which were reinforced with cross braces on the back. He could see that the braces were secured with metal screws. If he could remove the screws, he could free one of the braces and use it like a crowbar.

He searched the shelves until he came across a metal flange with a firm edge. Voices in the hall made him pause. If they opened the door now, he was finished. The voices moved past the door and faded. Kaz grabbed the flange and inserted it into the head of a screw. It fit snugly. Kaz's hands shook when he applied pressure to turn the screw. Pain radiated down his arm. He persisted. Soon, the screw was rotating freely. He repeated the process on a second and a third screw. He held the brace with his left hand while he removed the last screw so that it wouldn't clatter to the floor. Then, he limped across the room and forced the brace under the first board. The dull ache in his arms and shoulders sharpened into pain when he applied pressure. He ignored his discomfort and bore down on the brace. The nails groaned as they gave way. More voices passed in the hall. Kaz ignored them and kept working. The board came free and light poured into the room, early morning light that told him he had to move fast. He quickly removed two more boards and released the window's latch. The window slid upwards with little complaint. Somewhere, a door banged. It was only a matter of time, minutes perhaps, before someone came looking for him He had to hurry. He dragged a box under the window for height, and with a feeling of exhilaration, hoisted himself through the window to freedom.

Kaz found himself in a side yard filled with scrap wood. He listened intently for any sounds of voices or people moving about. All was quiet. The morning air was cool. It refreshed him and succored his badly bruised body. His thoughts turned to Justin and Ilyna. Where were they, he wondered? Had they been tortured as well? It seemed likely. He wanted to find them, to help them, but that would be a fool's errand. If he didn't leave now, he would be discovered and returned to that frightening room. He had to flee. Surprisingly, he discovered his wallet in his pocket. He had no idea how it got there. Had the guard returned it? His naval identification card was lost, however. It told the Germans who he was. It made him a fugitive, and like any fugitive, his only hope was to run.

Kaz took a deep breath to calm his nerves and hobbled into the village. No one was on the streets. Kaz stayed close to the buildings, ready to leap into a doorway or down an alley at the first sign of movement, but except for a crowing rooster, the village was not yet awake. He wished he could knock on a door and ask for some water and bread, but he feared running into another German jackal. So, he ignored his hunger and thirst and hurried into a stand of trees that hid him from the road.

Before long, he came upon a creek where he quenched his thirst. He thought about the dogs at the farmer's house. He hadn't heard any barking nearby, but if the Germans came looking for him, they might use dogs. The creek wandered in the direction that he wanted to travel, so he removed his shoes and walked in the ice-cold water for a mile or more. He hoped it was far enough to throw off his trail from those farmers' dogs. The day looked promising. The sky was a soft, hazy blue. No clouds covered the rising sun. No Stukas ruined his view. And it was less than 200 miles back to Krakow. Nothing to it, he thought. Not after what he'd been through. He kept walking.

Chapter Sixteen

Kaz stumbled into Krakow fifteen pounds lighter than when he'd left. His first impression was the presence of German soldiers. They were everywhere. They strode down the streets and drove around in cars like they owned the place. The Poles walked with their eyes cast down. They looked defeated. The bombing campaign had taken the fight out of them. Kaz bristled at the sight of the intruders, but he didn't dare confront them or venture down the main boulevards. He was unshaven, unwashed, and his clothes were filthy. His face was black and blue from the beating he'd taken. He smelled and looked like a bum. The Germans would pick him up in no time. So, he slipped down familiar back alleys until he reached the apartment he'd shared with Daneta.

He remembered the last time he'd returned to Krakow during the depression. His first thought had been to see his uncle and aunt. That had been his home. Only his aunt had died and Jozeph had been sent to live in an orphanage. Now, he had a new home and a child of his own. Yet, he approached the apartment with the same trepidation that he'd felt before. There had been little warmth in either home. He didn't expect that there would be much now. He wasn't certain if Daneta would even be there. He'd left her with her parents. It was likely that she was still with them. He knocked just in case and was surprised when the door opened. Daneta stood there staring at him with the same horrified expression as the time he returned home after the barroom brawl.

"Kaz, what's happened to you?" She flung her arms around his neck without waiting for an answer and gripped him with all her strength. "I've been so worried."

The warmth of her greeting overwhelmed him. He pushed aside all his doubts and fears and held her close. It was a moment to be cherished. After all that had happened, he couldn't help but savor it. For a brief span of time the Stukas were gone. So were the tanks, and the dogs, and the Germans. There were no more Gestapo officers or rubber hoses. There was only the warmth he so badly needed. Once before, he'd asked himself if his feelings for Daneta meant that he was in love, and he couldn't answer. It was the same, now. No matter.

Whatever it was, it drew him to her and succored his wounds, just as the cold water had done in that creek.

Daneta kissed him fiercely and stood back to assess him. She reached out and touched his face. "What did they do to you?"

"I was tortured," he replied with a sob. "I guess I'm lucky to be here at all."

Daneta wiped tears from her eyes. "I feared the worst. I thought you were dead."

"Where's Edwina?" His eyes swept past her into the apartment for some sign of his daughter.

"She's with my parents. I only came back to get more clothing." She pulled him into the room with a smile and closed the door. "You need a bath."

"And fresh clothes." He laughed. "I'm a mess, I know."

"What happened to your face?" Daneta's eyebrows knitted into a look of concern.

"I'll tell you everything after I bathe."

"I will run you water and scrub your back."

Daneta cried when he undressed and she saw all of his bruises. She left the bathroom while he soaked in the tub. When she returned, her eyes glistened with the promise of her naked body.

"Move over," she demanded in a husky voice.

Kaz vaguely recalled that he'd sworn not to do this again, but that was before the Stukas, and the tanks, and the Germans. War had changed the rules. There was no more future, only the here and now. The Germans had brought him death and destruction, but they had also brought him something he desperately wanted: the warmth of a woman who needed him, at least for the moment.

Kaz made room for his wife to slide in beside him, and in no time, they were making love with more passion than he'd ever known in his long, lonely life.

"Do you think they're looking for you?" Daneta asked. They were seated on the couch in the living room. Despite the intimacy they'd just shared, they sat a foot apart, uncertain whether they should touch or not. Kaz had shared his story, including his harrowing escape from the Gestapo officer who'd beaten him.

"Possibly. I'm a very small fish in their sea, but they don't like losing prisoners, and they have my naval ID card. There's no address on it, but they know I was trying to reach Krakow. They could check with the city clerk and track me down."

"Everyone has to register with the new government the Nazis are setting up in Wawel Castle."

Images flashed through Kaz's mind of rooms filled with sacred documents, statues, art treasures, and those marvelous suits of armor that had dazzled him as a boy. They represented a thousand years of Poland's history, and now they were under the control of Hitler's forces.

"A new government?" he queried.

"Yes, under a man named Hans Frank. It will govern central and southern Poland. There are rumors that they plan to deport all but the most able-bodied Jews. They're already rounding up many of them and sending them to rural areas outside the city where they will be put in labor camps."

Kaz's mind reeled from so much information. "What labor camps?"

"I don't know much about them. They're supposed to be located around Poland."

Kaz thought about his friend, Simon, and wondered if he would ever see him again. "They're keeping the strongest Jews in Krakow and sending the weaker ones to labor camps? That doesn't make sense."

"I know, and that's not all." Daneta looked around the room. "They also plan to evict many Poles from their homes to make room for arriving German officers and their families. We're going to lose this apartment. That's why I'm here gathering my clothes. I have to stay with my parents. Father has arranged for us to keep our home. In return, a high ranking German officer is staying with us, and we're making clothing for the Jews being moved to labor camps."

Kaz couldn't believe what he was hearing. Things were moving much too fast. He thought about his experience with the Gestapo. He could still the feel the blows tearing his body apart. His skin burned with anger. Hot words vaulted off his tongue before he could retrieve them. "You father is making a pact with the devil. No matter what you call them, those labor camps will be nothing more than brutal prisons. How can you be a part of that?"

Daneta bristled at his accusation. "That's not true. They're to be housed and fed. In exchange, they'll make shoes and cooking utensils and other things needed by the army."

Kaz scoffed and pointed to his bruises with a shaking hand. "You see what that Gestapo agent did to me, and I'm not even a Jew. What do you think will happen to them?" His voice rose. Tension crackled between them.

Daneta bowed her head with the grace of a ballet dancer. Tears rolled down her cheeks. "I don't know what you expect of us, Kaz. All father is trying to do is hold together some semblance of our life."

"But not at the expense of the Jews. It's a terrible bargain."

"They will survive, just as we must. That's all Father wants, for the family to survive. That includes you and me and Edwina." Daneta sucked in a sob as she spoke.

Kaz's anger subsided. He put his arm around her shoulders and pulled her trembling body closer. "I know. I'm sorry. All any of us want right now is to survive." He thought about his baby daughter. "When can I see Edwina, by the way?"

She shook her head. "I don't know. Not until you register, I think. That officer who's staying with us will ask too many questions.

"I'm not sure I should register just yet. Maybe, I'll wait awhile. See if anybody comes around asking about me. I don't want to face the Gestapo, again."

"What will you do?"

"First, I'll go see Charlie and find a place to stay. Then, I'll figure something out. I'll get a message to you at the factory." The tension between them had dissipated, and so had their intimacy.

Daneta moved away. "Do you have any money?"

"A few zlotys left in my wallet. Not much," Kaz admitted.

Daneta jumped up from the couch and hurried to the bedroom. She returned with a fistful of zlotys. "Take these. I have more at home."

She gave him a weak smile as they walked to the front door. "It was a relief to see you again, Kaz. I'm so glad you're okay." She touched the bruises on his face. "Take care."

"I will, I promise." Kaz returned her smile, looked cautiously along the hallway and hurried down the stairs.

No one answered Kaz's knock at Charlie's apartment, so he left a note and retreated to wait at the Pod Krzyzykiem, a local bar in the stare miasto or old town section of Krakow. The bar's name meant 'under the little cross,' and was derived from the tavern's proximity to a street-side shrine called 'of the man of sorrows.' For centuries, the Polish intelligentsia, including university students, revolutionaries and patriots, had gathered there to discuss and plot Poland's future. It was there that the ideas of freedom and independence were debated, often clandestinely, over steaming mugs of mead. It was there that followers of the famous major general, Kosciuszko, supported Poland's independence from Russia in the ill-fated uprising of 1794. It was there that Kaz would decide his future under the iron thumb of Nazi Germany.

There were less than a dozen people in the room when Kaz entered. He sat at a back table where he could watch the door while he nursed a beer. His hands twitched whenever someone entered. It was odd to feel so exposed. Just the way a fugitive would react, he thought. So far, there had been no evidence that anyone was looking for him, yet he couldn't stop himself from staring at every stranger in the room.

His mind tumbled back to Daneta. He didn't know what to do about her. She was the same person as before, yet the war had tossed them together like two tumbleweeds in the wind. The result had been another passionate moment together. Would it produce another child? He hoped not. There was too much else to worry about ... too many questions ... too much uncertainty. Still, he couldn't help but revel in that moment. He'd needed it. They'd both needed it.

His thoughts scattered when he saw two figures back-lit in the open doorway of the bar. He knew at once that it was Charlie and Christina. He leaped to his feet and hugged them both with a cheerful shout, then stepped back and appraised them. He sensed a tension in Christina that he'd never seen before, and the mischief in Charlie's eyes was gone, replaced by a harder edge that spoke of a life turned inside out. They joined him at his table and ordered beers.

"What happened to your face?" Christina queried. She inspected his bruises with concern. Kaz caught her eye. Was there any spark left in his feelings for her? He didn't think so. To his surprise, an image of Daneta in the bathtub swam into his thoughts. He shook his head. His world was revolving in strange ways he couldn't completely understand. Maybe it was the war, or, maybe, he was just moving on.

He glanced over at Charlie.

"I had a run in with a Gestapo officer," he responded. "These are the result of his interrogation methods." He told them about his escape. "I don't know whether I'm a fugitive or not. I've decided to wait a few weeks before I register for work with the Germans. I want to make sure nobody's looking for me."

"That might be wise," Charlie agreed.

"In the meantime, I need a place to hide out. My apartment is being requisitioned by the Germans." Kaz's words were tinged with anger.

Charlie studied Kaz. "I know someone who can help, but first we need to talk about other matters." He stared around the room. "There's a great history to this place. Would you like to be a part of it?"

"What do you mean?" Kaz glanced at Christina. Her expression remained serious.

"Poland is forming a government in exile," she said in a low voice. "It's to be headquartered in Paris, at least for now. An underground is being established in Poland to work with the government on opposing the German and Russian occupations."

"We're setting up communication lines to send information about German movements and to receive orders for field operations," Charlie added.

" What do you mean by field operations?"

"Sabotage, that sort of thing."

Kaz leaned forward in his chair and planted his elbows on the table. "My god, you're talking about forming a resistance movement right here in Krakow."

"All over Poland, actually." The hard edge in Charlie's eyes expanded until it filled his pupils. "We intend to bring as much trouble and grief to these bastards as we can."

Kaz sat back in amazement. His whole body was thrumming at the news. Was it possible? Could an underground movement of upstarts like Charlie and Christina take on such a formidable enemy?

"How do I get involved?" he demanded.

Charlie's face broke into its old, familiar grin. It was the first time he'd truly smiled since he arrived. "I'll vouch for you. The higher ups will want to check you out, of course, but with my recommendation and your run in with the Gestapo, you'll have no problem."

Charlie wrote down a name and address on a bar napkin. "This is a safe house where you can hide out until you're cleared. Memorize the address and destroy it. I'll let them know you're coming. Wait for an hour before you go."

They rose from the table and embraced again. "I can't believe we're doing this, how far we've come. It feels good to have some purpose other than just surviving."

"It'll feel even better when you get your first assignment. Be patient, though. It might take a few days. These people are very thorough."

Kaz grinned. "I can wait as long as it takes to get back at those cockroaches."

After Charlie and Christina were gone, Kaz sat back down and ordered another beer.

He avoided the main streets where he might run into curious German soldiers and headed toward the eastern part of the city. His feet marched with a purpose he hadn't felt since he'd escaped the Gestapo. Poland had been interrupted, again, and so had his life, but he no longer scurried along the pavement like a fugitive. He was about to become a soldier in a new army, one that would confront the Germans, and the Russians, and fight to return Poland to its people.

Kaz found the apartment building in a run down section of the city. He climbed two flights of narrow, dark stairs and knocked on a freshly painted, brown door that showed the heavy brush marks of a halfhearted job. A radio from an adjoining unit cast subdued dance music into the hallway.

A woman who appeared to be in her early thirties answered his knock. Her dark hair had been hastily pulled back off her forehead and secured in place by a pin. Her beige blouse and gray skirt suggested someone who worked in an office. She looked at him with expectant, olive-green eyes.

"I'm Kaz Kowinsky. Charlie sent me."

Recognition flashed across the woman's face. "Of course. Come in."

Kaz entered a small living room crowded with chairs and bookshelves. Papers were scattered across a wooden table that had somehow found room to hold the clutter.

"I'm Agata. My husband, Zdisek, will be home soon. I understand you need to stay out of sight for awhile." She indicated a chair and sat across from him. Her eyes cut into his in a disquieting manner.

"For a few weeks, yes. I need to find out if it's safe for me to register. The Gestapo may be looking for me."

The olive eyes continued to scrutinize him. "What Charlie has done is highly irregular. Sending you here, I mean. He must trust you very much."

"We've been best friends since we were boys." Kaz hesitated, not certain how much to say. He decided to plunge right in. "He mentioned something about an underground movement. I told him to count me in."

"One thing at a time." Agata's voice remained aloof, although her facial muscles relaxed into a hint of a smile that caught the corners of her mouth and pushed them upwards. She looked prettier when she smiled. "First, we need to learn if you are on any wanted lists. We have contacts in the clerk's offices. It shouldn't take too long to find out whether anyone is looking for you. In the meantime, you can stay here."

Kaz recalled Daneta's comment about families being forced to share living quarters. "Are other families staying here, as well?"

"No, that would be awkward. We've had the city records fixed to show there are three families here, and we keep some clothing and toiletries lying about in case the Germans wish to have a look."

She stood up abruptly. "Well, make yourself at home and stay away from the windows. We'll sort you out soon enough."

Kaz spent the next three days thumbing through books and magazines in an effort to keep from going stir crazy. He'd never been much of a reader. He preferred action rather than sitting around. Time ticked by much too slowly. He paced a lot. Despite Agata's order to stay away from the windows, he couldn't help hiding behind the curtains and watching the Jews moving about in the Pordgorze district that started just a few blocks away. Every day, more Jews arrived with their belongings piled in carts and stuffed in travel trunks. German soldiers prodded them along like cattle.

People visited the apartment at all times of the day but stopped before the ten o'clock curfew took effect. Kaz had to stay in his room during those occasions, so he never met or saw the visitors. Agata's husband, Zdisek, had the powerful arms and legs of a wrestler. He proved to be just as serious as his wife, although he did like to drink vodka and to discuss politics in the evening. Kaz found his company stimulating.

"We used to travel all over Europe before the Germans came. Now, we like to stay closer to home." He sipped his vodka and leaned on the kitchen table. He preferred the kitchen to the living room. "How about you? Have you had a chance to travel?"

"Czechoslovakia when I was little, and around Poland. I was in Rawa Ruska a few days ago. The Germans had just abandoned the city and turned it over to the Russians. I ran for my life."

Zdisek chuckled. "Yes, the Russians. They're a different breed from us Europeans."

"I believe forming an alliance with Stalin was a wise move," Kaz offered. "It allows Hitler to seal the eastern frontier without committing any troops. But it won't last."

"Why not?"

Kaz sipped his vodka thoughtfully. "Because Hitler doesn't intend to share his glory with anyone, especially not the Russians."

"I agree. Still, Stalin has a large army. It might be difficult to keep him at bay."

"Hitler will find a way."

They drank in silence.

Charlie visited on the third day to tell him that he'd passed the screening process and would be woven into the resistance network just as soon as they confirmed his status with the Germans. Kaz expressed surprise that no one had interviewed him.

"Agata assessed you. She's got a keen eye. If you get the okay from her, you're as good as in."

He learned that Agata and her husband ran a travel business from a small storefront. They had one employee, but booked little business other than for German officers. They didn't make much money, but they didn't care. The company was a front for their real business, making life miserable for the Germans.

On the fourth day, Kaz got the good news. "No one's looking for you," Agata informed him, "either at your old apartment or at city records."

Kaz perked up. At last he could get out of the apartment and do something. "What can I do to help you?" he asked.

"First, you need to get registered with the German authorities. You said that you were a machinist and a train engineer. Emphasize the latter when they ask for your occupation. It would be useful to have somebody who can travel around the country without raising suspicion."

Kaz marched into the registration office the next morning and applied for a job as a train engineer. When the interviewer asked him why he hadn't come in sooner, he explained that he'd been out of the city when the war started, and he had needed a few days to get back. The interviewer asked surprisingly few questions, and Kaz volunteered nothing. He was ordered to report to the rail yards that afternoon.

Kaz was astonished at the level of activity when he returned to his old workplace. Dozens of men were repairing and refitting locomotives damaged by the brief war. Boilers needed mending. Wheels had to be realigned. Tie-rods replaced. It was evident that the Germans were eager to restore Poland's rolling stock back on its rails as soon as possible so they could more easily move personnel and equipment around.

He couldn't help but smile when he looked over at the forge where he'd worked and remembered Filas jumping up and down after grabbing the red-hot handles of his tongs. That seemed a lifetime ago. Now, he was a train engineer and a newly minted member of the Polish underground.

His first assignment was to pilot a "stone train" from Krakow to the granite quarries at Skarzysko-Kamienna and back again. He learned that some of the Jews shipped into the countryside had been put to work there. The rock was being transported throughout the Reich to repair cities and to build walls and prisons.

The train's engine was a tired old beast that looked as though it had been resurrected from the scrap heap. The hopper cars that would hold the rocks weren't much better. They were dilapidated relics with faulty brakes and loose couplings. They didn't look sturdy enough to haul coal dust, let alone blocks of granite. To further complicate things, the route wound through rugged hill country with grades steep enough to test even a sound engine. And, to make matters worse, he'd never taken that route before. He had no information regarding the locations of signals, the sharpness of curves, or the changes in grades. He was expected to "drive blind" in an antiquated steam engine towing cars that should have been retired years ago. When he introduced himself to the fireman, Kaz discovered that he'd never made the trip either. The only good news was that they would make the run to the quarries with an empty payload. It would give them a chance to learn the most dangerous characteristics about the route before loading in tons of granite for the return journey.

The Germans didn't care to hear about these problems. They only wanted to see results. So, off they went, riding their ancient steed into the pages of history. In addition to shoveling coal into the firebox and attending to the boiler, the fireman was responsible for releasing sand onto the tracks to maintain traction on steep inclines. He did this by pulling a lever attached to a container filled with sand. Kaz worked out a simple system of signals for the fireman so he would know when to use the sand and how much to apply. Kaz waved his gloved hand to alert the fireman to start the sand, then raised or lowered his thumb to increase or decrease the flow. It was important to release the right amount. Too little sand, and the wheels would spin out of control; too much sand and the wheels would grab too quickly and put undue pressure on the old train's couplings, causing cars to separate with disastrous results.

POLAND INTERRUPTED

The journey to the quarries proceeded without incident, although there was plenty of cause for concern. They had to pass through a series of tunnels where the earth overhead was saturated with water. The moisture dripped on the rails, making them wet and slippery. When the wheels began to spin, Kaz signaled the fireman, who released sand until the train was brought under control. Their system worked well enough with a light payload, but Kaz worried about the return trip when they would be loaded down with rocks. There was one section in particular that worried him, a very steep grade that entered a tunnel. The train's engine would be trying to maintain traction on the tunnel's wet track while the hoppers carrying the rocks were still defying gravity on the steep slope. Kaz did his best to memorize that stretch and placed a very large check mark in his mind to beware of that grade and tunnel.

The fireman built up a good head of steam for the return journey, and things progressed as expected until they approached the portion of track that Kaz had noted. He pressed the throttle forward to gain as much speed as possible up the steep incline. Everything seemed normal until the engine reached the top of the incline and entered the tunnel. The instant the drive wheels hit the wet tracks, they began to lose traction and their speed slowed. Kaz opened the throttle cautiously, but the heavy load created too much drag on the train. The wheels responded by spinning faster and the speed continued to decline. Kaz feared the sand would not be enough. If he didn't stop the train, the cars might pull the train off the tracks and down the mountain. He frantically reached for the brakes, but the fireman misinterpreted his hand motion as the sand signal. He tugged on the sand release lever and flooded the rails with sand. The train lurched wildly, causing Kaz to miss both the brakes and the throttle. Every bolt, nut and plate in the old engine groaned, and a shower of sparks shot out from behind the wheels. With a tortured screech, the train's wheels gained traction and the engine lunged forward. Miraculously, the train held together as they were propelled through the tunnel at a high rate of speed. Kaz managed to grab the controls and to throttle back. When they rolled out the other end of the tunnel, they found themselves under a peaceful canopy of stars. They'd made it up the grade, and the wheels were still on the tracks.

Kaz slumped back in his chair and looked over at the shaken fireman, uncertain whether he should smile or holler at him. When he saw the man's face -- soot-covered, with widened eyes that looked like two hen's eggs frying in a pan -- he let out a whoop of laughter.

"You look like you stepped on a sleeping bear."

"Damn near pissed in my pants," the man responded with a sheepish grin.

Relief gave way to alarm when Kaz heard a loud snap. The entire left side of the engine suddenly tipped up so violently, he thought they were about to flip on their side. He braced himself for the impact, but gravity took over and the wheels crashed back down on the tracks with a rending roar. For a few blissful moments, they rolled along normally, then up they went again, and the whole frightening process repeated itself. Kaz gripped the brake lever as hard as he could and managed to bring the train to a halt before it did further damage. Now, however, a loud hissing noise replaced the sound of grinding metal. The noise told him that steam was escaping from one of the boilers. A quick look at the pressure gauge confirmed his fears. Both men jumped from the train and ran. When they were a safe distance up the tracks, they stood with hands on hips and waited until the hissing had subsided.

Kaz flipped on his torch to assess the damage. On the left side of the engine, the tie-rod that connected the piston to the drive wheel had broken. The portion still bolted to the drive wheel had flopped in an arc and stuck into the ground as the wheel rotated. The train's forward motion had raised the wheel like a giant crutch and shoved the left side of the train upward until it nearly reached its tipping point. Once the wheel had passed over the rod stuck in the ground, the whole mess came crashing down again.

"It's a miracle the wheels stayed on the track," Kaz mused. "Not that it matters much. We aren't going anywhere."

The engine was covered in cinders from the violence of the broken rod. Pieces of shattered metal littered the roadbed. Kaz walked around the engine to inspect the other side.

"The tie-rod on this side is dangerously bowed as well," he pointed out to the fireman. "This engine was an accident waiting to happen."

"There's a town with a station a few miles down the tracks. I can run there and wire for help," the fireman volunteered.

"That's a good idea. I'll stay here and keep an eye on things."

The fireman grabbed his own lantern and headed down the tracks. Kaz returned to the cab and settled down for a nap while he waited. He'd hardly closed his eyes when he heard boots crunching the cinders in the roadbed less than a hundred feet ahead of him.

Kaz bolted upright. "Who's there?" he demanded.

"Hello, friend." A low voice rumbled from the darkness. The voice sounded Polish. "Looks like you've got trouble."

Kaz turned on his lantern and whipped its beam of light toward the voice. The light revealed three men dressed in dark clothing standing beside the tracks. Two of the men held rolled up burlap bags under their arms. At first, Kaz thought they were peasant farmers, but when he looked more closely at the lead man, he changed his mind. It wasn't the man's broad shoulders that got his attention, although it was obvious that hard muscle lurked beneath his jacket. Nor was it the unusual hat he wore, a hat with no rim in the back and a visor in the front that stuck out like a duck's bill. Nor was it the shock of red hair that revealed itself when he removed the hat and rubbed his scalp. It was the gun dangling casually from a strap on his shoulder, barrel pointed toward the ground, that got his full attention. It wasn't a hunting rifle. It was military issued.

"Where did you get the hat?" It was a stupid question, but Kaz couldn't help himself.

"Gift from an American friend. Told me men who wore them played a game with a bat and a ball. Gave it to me when he returned to his own country."

The latter comment was accompanied by a sigh of regret. The man studied the train. Kaz heard a cicada singing somewhere in the nearby brush. The man pointed the gun barrel toward the locomotive.

"Looks like the szkopy will have to do without their rocks for awhile."

Kaz steadied his nerves as he stared at the weapon. It would do no good to run, and he didn't think the men meant him harm. "I'd say so. We broke a drive rod. My fireman has gone for help."

"We saw him. You from around here?"

"Krakow."

The man stepped closer.

"What do you want?" Kaz asked nervously.

The man pointed toward the tender. "We thought the szkopy might spare us some coal." A smile creased his face.

Coal! The man wanted coal. Kaz found the idea hilarious, but he didn't laugh. He stared at the three men more intently. Realization overcame his doubts. He knew who these men were.

"You're with the new resistance movement."

"What makes you say that, friend?" The smile disappeared. Hands tightened on the rifle. The air grew heavier.

Kaz raised his hands, palms forward, to show he meant no harm. "I am, also. I've just joined a cell in Krakow." He pointed to the tender. "Take all the coal you want."

The tension dissipated. "Thank you, friend."

The other two men unrolled four burlap sacks, grabbed the boarding rung and hoisted themselves into the tender. One began tossing large chunks of coal out of the coal bin; the other swept the coal into the bags with his hands. Soon, the bags were bulging. The men carefully tied the tops of the bags and handed them down. A horse suddenly snorted in the darkness, and another man stepped into the light leading a brown mare. The horse's hooves clip-clopped along the tracks. The men hoisted up the heavy bags and hung them from the saddle. Then, the men and horse disappeared into the night. Except for the man with the gun, who lingered.

"I know your cell leader, but we never mention names to strangers. Tell them that Simon the Red says hello."

"That's a colorful name," Kaz commented.

"It helps distinguish me from Simon the Black, who operates elsewhere."

"Around Warsaw?"

"At times."

Simon! Could it be? "And he has black, wiry hair?"

The man nodded.

"I think I know him. If so, he's a good friend."

"Tell me your name."

The request was in direct violation with the man's previous comment about not sharing names with strangers, but Kaz didn't see the harm in it. He had aleady revealed his name, and they were obviously on the same side.

"Kaz Kowinsky."

"I'll pass your name along. Good night my friend." The man turned and disappeared, just like the horse.

Chapter Seventeen

When Kaz returned to Krakow, he braced himself for a tirade from the German lieutenant in charge of the rail yard, but the officer's response to the news about the train was surprisingly mild. The broken drive rod showed considerable metal fatigue. It was quite possible that the heavy load triggered the breakdown. Neither Kaz nor the fireman mentioned the sand incident in the tunnel. The German investigators grumbled about sloppy Polish maintenance and dropped the matter.

Within a few days, Kaz was assigned a newer and more powerful locomotive. It towered over the older engines. He named it Tatra after one of his favorite mountain ranges near the border with Czechoslovakia. The brief hiatus gave him free time to visit Daneta and Edwina. It also brought him face-to-face with Major Werner Schmidt who was now living in the Rudnicka household.

"I understand you drive train engines." The officer spoke reasonable Polish. He sat with his legs crossed on the living room couch and drew smoke into his lungs from a German cigarette ensconced in a filtered holder. The smoke escaped like steam when he exhaled.

"Yes sir." Kaz sat across from him while he waited for Daneta and the baby.

"An important job for someone so young."

The officer's tone of voice had just a hint of accusation in it. It reminded Kaz of the interrogation room where he faced the Gestapo agent. He squirmed under Schmidt's watchful eye.

"I began driving trains before I was twenty." He hoped it didn't sound like bragging, but he didn't know what else to say.

"Yes, well ... " Another stream of smoke erupted. "The point is, you are in a position to see a lot, traveling around the country the way you do." He smoothed his pants leg and eyed Kaz closely. "There are rumors, more than rumors, of armed resistance among your countrymen. And spying. Such behavior will not be tolerated."

Kaz had heard about the new laws being implemented against the insurgency. For every German assaulted, ten Poles were to be picked at random and shot. Any insurgents captured would be interrogated until they divulged the names and locations of their comrades. Kaz had no doubt about what that meant. They would be tortured. He thought about the rubber hose he'd faced and shuddered. Major Schmidt noted his reaction.

"A most unpleasant thought, I know, but one you can do something about."

Kaz stared at the man, confused. What did he mean?

"Do you play chess, Kaz Kowinsky?"

Kaz shook his head.

"A pity. It's such a challenging game, much like war. It requires great patience, yet it can be terribly violent. Sometimes one must sacrifice pieces in order to win."

Kaz tried his best to look attentive, but he didn't have the faintest notion where the conversation was headed. The major let silence build between them before continuing.

"When you see any suspicious behavior, you will report it to me. I will want names, places and dates. What people plan to do. Where. When. That way, we can cut off the heads of these snakes before they cause trouble. That will save Polish lives. People will not need to be shot. And ... " he slowly looked around the room, "your family will be safe. No one will need to be sacrificed."

Kaz's shirt began to stick to his back as he listened. His hands grew clammy. He felt his veins throbbing with hot blood. There was no mistaking the major's meaning. He expected Kaz to spy on his comrades! And if he failed to deliver, Daneta and her family would suffer.

Schmidt excused himself when Daneta entered the room with Edwina flailing in her arms. Kaz took the baby and kissed her on the forehead. He tried to relax, but tension filled his chest.

"You look worried, Kaz. Is anything wrong?" Daneta glanced at him with concern.

Kaz shook his head. He didn't want to worry her about what Schmidt had said. "I'm okay. Your German guest makes me nervous, is all."

"He's been very polite and friendly. A gentleman."

A gentleman with the venom of a cobra, Kaz thought to himself. He would have to discuss this development with Agata.

"Yes, we've heard about Major Schmidt. He's cunning and very dangerous. We know he has the Rudnicka factory making prison clothing for Jews." Agata stared at Kaz with her olive eyes. They were standing in the hallway facing each other. "There has been talk about eliminating him."

"I fear that would compromise the Rudnickas." Kaz tried to sound objective, but his mind was tumbling through the alternatives, none of which looked promising. "I don't want to endanger my wife and baby."

"I understand. The parents, however, have gotten very close to Schmidt. Perhaps, too close." Silence hung between them. A car backfired on the street, jolting Kaz. Voices murmured behind closed doors in the living room where a meeting was taking place.

"There is another possibility. Come with me." She threw open the doors to the living room. Two men sat with Zdisek in quiet conversation. They looked up at the unexpected intrusion.

"Sorry to interrupt. This is Kaz. I believe my husband has mentioned him to you. He has come to us with a development that could give us an unexpected opportunity."

Agata repeated what Kaz had told her.

"We have a list of men whom we know to be traitors, men who are working for the Germans in return for favors. The Rudnickas are on that list, although we don't believe they are actually spying for the Germans. I propose we leave the family alone and use Major Schmidt to rid ourselves of traitors who *are* spying for the Germans. We plant evidence and Kaz reports them to the major."

"That's a wonderful plan," Zdisek enthused. "We let the Germans get rid of our traitors for us." The other men agreed.

"Good. It's settled, then. We leave the family alone and feed the major misinformation about our traitors."

For the next few weeks, Kaz hauled troops, supplies and building materials along a route between Tarnow, Debica and Krakow. He became intimately familiar with German operations around this sector of Poland and tried to learn about their plans. He also got to know a man whose heavy build reminded him of Marek. Kaz nicknamed him Big M. Big M maintained the locomotives. He was affable and always joined the other rail men for drinks after work. But he also asked questions about Jews who had not reported to the Germans and about the resistance. On several occasions, he was seen talking to a German officer who was known to be making inquiries about the Polish underground. Big M was high on the insurgency's list of traitors.

Kaz had not seen Daneta since the night he'd met Major Werner Schmidt. He knew she wondered what was wrong, but he didn't want to face the man again until he had something to report. That moment arrived the night he returned from a run to Debica and found Agata waiting for him.

"We've hidden dynamite in the traitor's cellar," she informed him with a look of satisfaction. She put a hand on his arm. "It's time for you to visit your family and to tell Major Schmidt about him. Tell Schmidt he's planning to blow up a troop train. Tell him that he needs to act right away."

Kaz changed his clothes and hurried to the Rudnicka's. He was relieved to see two soldiers guarding the house. It meant that Major Schmidt was home. Mr. Rudnicka let him in with a look of displeasure and told him to wait in the parlor. Laughter floated from the living room. Kaz recognized Mrs. Rudnicka's voice intertwined with the major's.

Daneta appeared in the doorway.

"Kaz, I haven't seen you for weeks. I thought something was wrong. Where have you been?" Concern mixed with displeasure in her voice. It was the perfect match to the frown he'd seen on her father's face. He suddenly felt uncomfortable. The warmth of his earlier reunion with Daneta in the apartment had slipped away into the fog of memories.

"I've been terribly busy with train runs. The German's haven't given me a moment's rest. And one of the trains broke down. Nearly had a bad accident."

"Oh." The word escaped from her lungs in a breath of air — light, floating. But he could hear the worry in it. It made him feel better. "Tell me what happened."

He described the incident in the tunnel, but said nothing about Simon the Red.

"Kaz, you must be careful. You're a father, now."

"And a husband." He smiled weakly.

"That, too." She glanced nervously toward the living room. "Edwina's already asleep. Should I wake her?"

"No, don't do that. Actually, I need to speak with Major Schmidt for a moment. Could you tell him I'm here?"

Surprise lit up Daneta's face. "The Major? Whatever for?"

"Something he asked me to do. I'll wait here while you get him."

Daneta hesitated, then turned and disappeared into the living room. Kaz stood with his hands behind his back and listened to hushed voices. A chair moved. Werner Schmidt strode from the room.

"Mr. Kowinsky. How nice to see you, again."

Kaz dispensed with the pleasantries. "Perhaps we should step outside."

"Of course." The major led the way onto the front porch. Stars had blanketed the sky when Kaz first set out that evening, but clouds now hid most of them.

"Do you have something for me?" the major asked expectantly.

Kaz handed him a slip of paper with Big M's real name and address on it. He cleared his throat and forced himself to remain stoic. "I overheard this man talking about blowing up a train full of German soldiers. He's gotten hold of some dynamite and has it hidden in his cellar. I snooped around and got his address. I believe he intends to do something in the next few nights."

Major Schmidt stared at the paper thoughtfully. "Very good, Mr. Kowinsky. I will have this checked at once." He turned his stare to Kaz. " This is a good start. Keep it up. Remain vigilant. So you won't have to sacrifice any pieces."

He gave Kaz a cobra smile and returned to the house.

Autumn faded into winter, then spring. Kaz continued to run trains out of Krakow and found enjoyment doing so, even though it was for the Germans. It gave him a sense of freedom, and it helped the underground. He was able to pass along valuable information about German troop movements, and it put him in contact with Pols who were aiding the Germans. So far, Agata had been able to discredit three of these traitors, and Kaz had passed along their names to Major Schmidt. All three had been arrested and hauled off to prison. Agata was pleased with the results. Driving the trains not only gave Kaz a sense of purpose, it was a way to hide from the world, but the world wouldn't hide from him. First, Germany invaded Denmark and Norway. Then Belgium, Luxembourg and France. The Germans tried to suppress news in Poland about their military adventures, but word quickly spread. Germany was no longer a country trying to protect its borders. It was a dragon devouring everything in its path. Nazi troops quickly entered Paris, and Poland's government-in-exile fled to London. Even there, it wasn't beyond the reach of the German Luftwaffe. The exiled government had hardly settled in before Germany began bombing England.

The news not only destroyed Kaz's bubble, it destroyed the hopes of the Polish people. France and England were considered allies who would eventually come to Poland's aid. Now, France was defeated, and England was being pummeled from the air. Who would save Poland?

Some prayed for the Americans to intervene, but they'd shown little taste for war.

Yet, even before these historical events broadsided Kaz's world, another grim story was unfolding that would tarnish Polish history for a generation, and Kaz found himself caught right in the middle of it. It began one morning when he was called into work early. A light, freezing mist shrouded the rail yards. The stationmaster met him at the dispatch gate.

"You're to dead-head your engine to the Krakow-Podgorze station on the west side of the city. You'll pick up a special train there bound for Rzeszow."

The order was unusual. Eastbound trains were customarily assembled at the Krakow-Plaszow station on the east side of the city.

"Why the reversal of procedures?"

"You'll be told all you need to know when you get your train."

Kaz shrugged his shoulders and rubbed his hands as he walked briskly to his engine. The fireman was already aboard waiting for him. He eased the big engine out of the yard and headed west. When they reached the station, a German sergeant joined them, and they were shunted off onto a weed infested siding normally used for loading livestock. Kaz scratched his head in confusion but said nothing. After traveling some distance and negotiating a complicated series of switches, they backed into a deserted siding somewhere between stations. Three more Germans boarded, only these were SS men. All carried light, sub-machine guns. One joined the sergeant in the cab; the other two climbed onto the tender.

"No one leaves the train without permission," the SS man in the cab warned them. He took up a position behind Kaz and his fireman and ordered him to back the engine along the siding.

Kaz slowly opened the throttle, and the engine obeyed. Soon, a line of boxcars loomed in the mists behind them. It was a forlorn looking location, well away from the main train tracks. Kaz applied the brakes and brought the engine to a halt at the point where the lead boxcar coupled to his engine. Kaz estimated that there were forty boxcars in the train. They were old, unpainted, dilapidated. He'd seen cars like these before. Usually, they were shoved off on an unused siding where they sat abandoned. Not so, these cars. They were still being used to haul something.

A brakeman appeared and signaled that the train was ready to roll. Kaz stood up to go inspect the coupling, but the SS man stopped him with the nose of his sub-machine gun. He said something in German. Kaz didn't need a translation. He sat back down.

The brakeman hoisted himself into the cab. "I'm Polish but I speak German. I'll ride with you and translate." The cab was getting crowded.

"What's in those boxcars?" Kaz asked in a quiet voice.

The brakeman shook his head. "You don't want to know."

Before Kaz could probe further, a soldier at the rear of the train appeared and waved a red lantern. They were clear to go.

"Where are we headed?" Kaz directed his question to the SS man.

"Not for you to know," the brakeman translated. "You drive the train. Let them worry about the destination."

Kaz peered into the gray mists as he cautiously moved through a maze of rail yards south of Krakow. They skirted the city and chugged into open country. Once they were clear of congestion, they rolled along at a good clip. They passed towns and smaller cities without slowing down. It was as if they had been given a green light all the way through the heart of Poland. Kaz still wondered about the train's purpose, but he decided not to pry while they were all jammed in the engine's cab. He'd wait until he could talk to the brakeman alone.

In the town of Sedziszow, a yardman flagged them down and informed them that repairs were being made on a switch. They would be delayed about an hour. Kaz was stiff from sitting at the controls. He wanted to stretch and to see for himself what he was hauling.

"I need to walk around a bit and go relieve myself."

The brakeman spoke to the SS man, who conferred with his associates on the tender.

"It's okay," the brakeman informed him. "Just stay away from the boxcars."

Kaz jumped to the ground and sauntered down the line of cars toward a clump of bushes. Many of the cars were converted cattle cars with narrow openings between the slats. He thought that if he got far enough down the line, he might be able to peek inside, but he quickly abandoned that idea when he looked up and realized there were armed guards seated on several of the roof tops! Why so much security, he wondered? It was then that he heard coughs and soft voices coming from inside one of the cars. There was a plea for water, a cry to be let out. Kaz's instinct was to unlatch the big doors in order to slide them open, but he didn't dare. He could feel the guns randomly pointing at targets. He was certain some of them were pointing at him.

Kaz went about his business and tried to think what to do. He was hauling a mass of humanity God knows where. The idea appalled him, but one look at those SS guards on the roofs told him there was nothing he could do. There had been talk about prisoners being relocated to labor camps. Mostly Jews, although he'd been told that other poles were included. Captured insurgents, for example.

Kaz ignored the brakeman's warning and walked closer to the boxcars as he returned to the engine. Gnarled hands clutched at the slats as he passed. Wrinkled, bearded faces pressed into every opening. Bodies were packed so closely together, there was no room to sit down. Those who were too weak to stand leaned against their neighbors for support. A strong odor of lime tainted the humid air. Moans of the sick and the old mingled with the whimpers of children in a sorrowful chorus. An old lady stood in grim silence against the slats and pulled a tattered, gray shawl more tightly around her shoulders. Beside her, an old man in a black skullcap and striped prayer shawl intoned a religious dirge. The old man stopped his prayers and looked at Kaz with pleading eyes. Long, orthodox braids dangled from his head. He slowly pulled a small, leather pouch from the inside lining of his coat. "I have gold," he whispered in a croaking voice. "Bring water for us, and you may have it. A thin arm pushed the pouch between the slats. He was trying to buy water for everyone on the train!

"Keep your gold. I'll see if there is any water."

Before he could move, an SS guard stepped up beside him and grabbed the pouch from the old man's hand. The hand disappeared back inside just before the German slammed his rifle butt into the slats. He shouted something and spit on the slats. Laughter spilled from his mouth along with one word, "wasser." He pointed at his saliva and laughed some more while he motioned for Kaz to be on his way. Kaz obeyed with a heavy heart. He estimated that there were 2,000 passengers on the train. It seemed there would be no water for any of them that day. Even their gold couldn't save them.

There were no more stops along the route, no more opportunities to inspect the boxcars or to see how his passengers were faring. He seethed inwardly at what he'd seen, but he maintained a stoic composure. There was no way to help these wretched people, and he needed to stay out of trouble. Otherwise, he would be no good to anyone.

At last, Kaz was ordered to stop the train at Ugnev station, where the cars were unhooked and coupled to another train run by a German military crew. Kaz was assigned to a train loaded with wheat and vegetables that was bound for Krakow. He knew he should feel relieved to be rid of the burden, but the faces continued to haunt him all the way back to Krakow. He needed to talk to someone about what he'd seen. It was either that or go mad.

When he finished the run, he left word for Charlie to join him at the bar where they'd met previously. Kaz had already downed three shots of vodka by the time Charlie arrived. It took two more shots before he could talk about what had happened.

"I still see the pleading eyes of that old man with the pouch of gold. They torment me. He was ready to give away his life's savings for a drink of water, for himself and for the others."

Charlie drank his beer and ordered a second one. "It's those damned SS officers. They treat all of us like scum."

"They were being sent to a labor camp. What's going to happen to them there? Half the people on that train weren't fit enough to do any real labor. Hell, the way they were being treated, they were lucky to be alive."

"Maybe, they won't be much longer," Charlie intoned in a flat voice. "Maybe that's what the Germans want, for them to die."

Charlie's statement slammed up the side of Kaz's head with the force of a sledgehammer. He began to turn his empty vodka glass around and around on the table with his fingers. He wanted another drink, but he knew his face was already flushed. It wouldn't do any good to get too drunk. He shook his head to clear his mind.

"I don't know if I can face another trainload like that, Charlie. Not if I'm driving people to their deaths."

Charlie put his hand on Kaz's in a gesture of commiseration. "Talk to Agata. She knows a lot about these things. Maybe, something can be done."

Agata stared at Kaz with her olive eyes. As always, her hair was pinned back in a haphazard fashion. Her blouse was slightly wrinkled and her skirt was hastily patched in two places where moths had feasted on the material. Everything about the woman suggested there was little time for herself. Her husband didn't seem to mind. He rubbed her shoulders and brushed her sleeves with an affection that Kaz wished he could demonstrate toward Daneta. He pushed his thoughts aside. He needed to do something about the faces floating in his mind.

"You must follow orders," she said in a flat voice. "It's distasteful work, I know, but it must be done. You're in a unique position to give us badly needed information and to help us rid ourselves of the traitors in our midst."

Agata's pep talk didn't slay the demons dancing inside his head, but they did shore up his resolve. Whatever transpired, he would have to see it through.

The next week passed with nothing more eventful than a trip to the rock quarries and scheduled runs along his normal route. Each time he got his orders, he cringed in anticipation as he scanned the cargo list and destination. He carried coal, not people, canned goods, not humans, rocks, not Jews. He was assigned everything but people. He began to hope that the nightmare was behind him. That all changed when he returned from a twelve-hour shift and found the German dispatcher waiting for him in the Krakow rail yards.

"Turn your engine around," he commanded. "You're to dead-head over to the west side of the city and pick up a train there. These men will accompany you." He nodded toward an SS officer waiting impatiently by the tracks with two soldiers.

Kaz understood at once what the load would be. His mind reeled at the prospect. "I've just finished a long shift," he protested. "I need rest. Otherwise, I might miss a signal or nod off. It's dangerous."

"No matter. You're our lead engineer for special assignments. There's no one else available that we can trust. This train must go out tonight. You are to report immediately."

"What about food? I haven't eaten."

"Wait here." The dispatcher disappeared into his office and returned with a box of sandwiches and two bottles of beer. "We have thought of everything."

The man's stony expression told Kaz that there was no use protesting further. He had no choice but to obey orders. He took the sandwiches but ignored the beer. He was going to need his wits about him. He needed coffee, not alcohol.

He proceeded through the same maze of switching stations as before and arrived at the weed-infested side yard. The ghost train awaited him. This time, he made no effort to see what was in the old boxcars. He ignored the heavily armed guards seated on the rooftops. He made no inquiries.

The brakeman who had translated on the previous run didn't join them. Kaz learned that the SS officer spoke sufficient Polish to give him directions. They rolled through the countryside at night with little conversation. Kaz concentrated on staying alert. He took only small bites of the sandwiches he'd been given. His appetite had deserted him.

Kaz swore under his breath as he followed the route outlined by the SS officer. Knowing what he transported made him sick at heart and discouraged. There seemed to be no way to stop the Germans. They were too damned efficient, for one thing. He could see that the transfer of Jews was conducted under the personal direction of the Gestapo, and they were ruthlessly thorough in their operations. There had been a few scattered attacks on trains like this one, but little had been accomplished. Trains were delayed, and Poles shot, but the Jews were still delivered to their fates. It was going to take more than a handful of insurgents to do any real damage. Kaz desperately wanted to do something that would make a difference. His only hope was that Agata and her gang knew what they were doing.

Near dawn, Kaz eased his train onto a siding near a town called Szopienice, where he was told to uncouple the engine. He saw a military crew standing by with another engine to complete the journey. He knew the town was located near a new camp being developed by the Germans. Only this one was not called a labor camp. It was referred to as a concentration camp, and its name was Auschwitz.

Chapter Eighteen

The rock quarries were a massive undertaking. Giant pits had been dug into the earth, and trucks roared back and forth as they hauled granite, freshly carved from the mountainside, to the train's waiting hopper cars. Laborers swarmed over the debris with picks and shovels. The men reminded Kaz of worker ants attacking a garbage bin. The surrounding hills were being eaten away by dynamite blasts and giant bulldozers. The air was filled with fine rock dust and the heavy sounds of granite yielding to the insatiable appetite of German machinery.

Kaz enjoyed his runs to the quarry. He and his fireman had time to relax and eat their lunches while the freight cars were filled with boulders the size of streetcars. He gulped a bottle of beer and surveyed the carnage. In another six months, the hills would be gone and the quarry reduced to a skeleton crew.

"I'll miss this place when it's closed," he commented to an office worker who often joined them with a sandwich or cup of stew brewed by his wife.

"It won't happen for a while yet." The middle-aged clerk took a bite of his sandwich and washed it down with coffee from his thermos. Kaz liked the man, despite the fact that there didn't seem to be an abundance of brain tissue in the attic. He wasn't bad company.

"Anyway, you'll be back soon enough."

"Why is that?" Kaz's curiosity was peaked.

"Saw the schedule for next week. They're expecting a priority load. Your name is on the manifest. You'll be running the train."

"What's a priority load?"

"Dynamite for the quarry and Jews to do the heavy lifting."

"How many Jews?"

"Couple hundred, maybe more. Bringing them from Krakow."

Kaz's mind sorted through this unexpected information. It was the first time he'd been told in advance that he would be transporting Jews. Perhaps, there was some way to sabotage the train and free them. He couldn't wait to share his news with Agata.

The gleam in Agata's olive eyes told Kaz that she was very interested. She mulled over the news. "I need a couple of days to pull people together," she said at last. "Be here Thursday night at six."

"I can't guarantee when I'll get back from my run. They never tell me my schedule until I show up for work. I only learned about this priority load because some clerk opened his mouth when he shouldn't have."

"Do your best. Our plans will include you."

Kaz fidgeted through the next two days, fearful of a last minute change in schedule that would send him to Auschwitz. He would never get back from that run in time. To his relief, his route didn't change, although a delay on the appointed day put him an hour behind schedule. He rushed to the apartment in the hope that he wasn't too late.

Agata greeted him at the door with a furtive glance down the street. Her expression was tense, but her pupils danced with anticipation. She wore her usual gray skirt, although this one showed no signs of moths. Either gray was her favorite color, he decided, or she preferred all her outfits to be the same so that she wouldn't have to waste time every morning deciding what to wear. Kaz realized that he was getting distracted. He returned his focus to Agata.

He started to apologize for being late, but she stopped him. "It's good you're here now. We're just finalizing our plans for the operation. Come join us."

She ushered him into the living room where he found Zdisek standing with a man that Kaz recognized at once by his closely cropped, red hair.

"Hello, friend." The tall, angular man smiled.

"Simon the Red! I never expected to find you here." Kaz shook his hand as if he *were* an old friend.

"We snuck him in before curfew last night." Zdisek offered Kaz a glass of sherry.

"And I must leave tonight. It's dangerous for me to spend too much time in the city."

"Then, we'd better finish our business," Agata suggested. Everyone sat down. "We've been able to confirm that a special train is scheduled for the quarries early next week. The load is secret, but if the clerk Kaz spoke to is correct, it'll include dynamite and Jews.We're going to attack that train."

Agata paused and turned her gaze to Kaz. He could feel his pulse rate jumping. "And it's vital that you're the engineer on it."

Kaz sat up straighter in his chair. "The clerk saw my name on the schedule., so it shouldn't be a problem."

"Remember the tunnel where your train broke down?" Simon asked with a wink.

Kaz nodded sheepishly.

"We'll block the entrance to that tunnel, and we'll be waiting in ambush. The moment you stop the train, we attack."

"What do I do?" Kaz asked.

"You'll have a gun. Your assignment is to shoot any Germans in the cab with you."

Kaz's mouth went dry. He'd never shot anyone, and for a brief instant he wondered if he could. Then, he remembered the Gestapo agent with the rubber hose. It was all the incentive he needed. "What about the fireman?"

"You'll have a new fireman who's one of us. It's his responsibility to shoot the guards on the tender. That will leave us free to concentrate on the guards on the rest of the train."

"And the Jews? What happens to them?"

"They're all able bodied men selected for the quarries. Some may want to run, but we hope most of them will join us." Simon paused, then pushed ahead. "The fireman will leave with us when we're done, but you'll stay behind. Which means we'll have to knock you out and put a gash in your skull."

Kaz's facial muscles tightened as he tried to process what he'd just heard. "You want to bash me in the head?"

Simon gave him a warm smile. "Sorry friend, but we have to make it look like you were wounded during the battle. Grazed by a bullet."

"The Germans will suspect you anyway," Agata interjected in her usual, cool voice. "You must expect to be interrogated."

The rubber hose loomed in Kaz's mind, only now it wasn't an incentive. It was a dark shadow that threatened him with painful memories. The whole operation was getting out of hand. It was one thing to spy on the Germans and to give them misinformation. It was quite another to shoot them and to be beaten over the head and tortured. His first instinct was to say no, to politely decline their invitation to mayhem. Then, he thought about the Jews he'd seen in those boxcars and the ones he would be saving from the quarries. And he thought about Edwina and what kind of life she would live under German rule. It seemed there was little choice. If he didn't join the battle and take his medicine, he wouldn't be able to live with himself. Besides, he'd just been thinking about how little was being accomplished. Here was a chance to help Simon the Red and his brave followers. Here was a chance to put his life on the line once more, only this time for a worthwhile cause.

"Okay, let's do it," he declared. "When do I get my gun?"

"It will be brought to you the night before," Agata assured him. "But first, we have to move you to a new apartment, so there's no trail for the Germans to follow back here. We have a place arranged for you nearby where you'll be safe."

The ornate, brick apartment house on Tatrzanska Street jutted up from the face of the hill like a great, red wart. It towered above the surrounding structures, and except for the spire of St. Joseph's Church, commanded an unobstructed view of the new Jewish quarter sprawling to the south of Kaz just one block away. He unpacked his duffle bag and made himself at home. He heard children yelling and parents admonishing them. It reminded him of his Uncle's apartment. It'd been some time since he'd thought about him. He supposed he should make some effort to see his Uncle, but he hardly had time to visit Daneta and Edwina, and he had little interest. It was best to keep his mind on matters at hand, matters like getting a gun and shooting Germans.

The next few days followed their normal routine. He made daytime runs and returned to his new apartment at night. He hadn't heard from Charlie but knew he was just as busy. He thought about visiting Daneta but didn't feel like facing Major Schmidt so close to his upcoming mission.

Boredom was about to set in when he heard a knock on his door. He opened it to find Charlie standing in the doorway with a wide grin on his face. He held a package in one hand and a bottle of vodka in the other.

"Thought you might want a nightcap before your big adventure." He looked around the apartment with a nod of approval. "Nice place. You're coming up in the world."

While Kaz retrieved glasses for the vodka, Charlie unwrapped his package, revealing a handgun.

"I haven't been told anything. Just to bring you this." He put the gun on the kitchen table and sat down.

"We're going to save some Jews." Kaz joined Charlie at the table. Charlie filled the glasses with vodka.

"Better if you don't tell me too much. Keep things compartmentalized. That way, I can't say anything if I'm caught, and vice versa." He threw down the first drink in a single gulp. "I guess it's okay to talk about Christina. She's headed back to Warsaw. Her grandmother is sick. But it's also an opportunity to pass information back and forth with a group of insurgents there."

"Would that be Simon the Black, by any chance?"

Charlie nodded. "You've heard of him?"

"I think I know him. We worked together on the Abyssinia and met up again at the start of the German invasion. He's a Jew."

"An angry one from what I understand. His parents were shipped to one of those labor camps where they died. Now, he leads a band of rebels that has made a series of raids on German outposts. They hide in the forests around Warsaw. He's gaining quite a reputation."

"Just like Simon the Red," Kaz laughed.

"I heard you met him, also."

"When my train broke down on the way back from the quarries. He took some coal."

Charlie picked up the gun and inspected it. "Looks like you're getting into something more than just running trains."

"I'm learning that there's no halfway in this underground business. You're either all in or your out."

"You were always the daredevil, Kaz, so I'm not surprised that you're all in."

"It's like blood alley all over again, only this time the train will be shooting back."

Charlie stood up to leave. "Whatever you're doing, stay safe. You're my best friend, and I don't want to lose you."

"Nor you."

They hugged at the door before Charlie slipped into the night.

The next morning, Kaz reported for duty at the rail yard with a forced smile on his face. He tried to look nonchalant, but he felt everyone's eyes upon him. The weight of the gun in the bottom of his backpack tugged at his shoulder straps. He'd never been searched before, and he knew there was no reason for today to be any different. Then, why were his hands shaking? Why did he believe that people were looking at him? They weren't, of course. He knew that. He just couldn't control the tension in his body, or the guilt in his head.

"You've been assigned to a quarry run today, Kaz," the dispatcher called out to him.

Relief swept over him. They weren't going to look at his backpack … or arrest him. Things were going as planned.

"Only, your fireman is sick. We got you a replacement."

Kaz looked at the hard, unfamiliar face standing near the engine. He knew that the man also had a gun, and Kaz could tell from his icy stare that he was all business.

A long line of empty hopper cars was strung out behind the engine. The string was interrupted in the middle by three boxcars. Those would be the Jews, he surmised. Another boxcar clung to the end of the train. That one would contain the dynamite. He was relieved that it wasn't closer to the engine, just in case there were any accidental explosions during the firefight. German soldiers sat with machine guns on the rooftops. Two more were stationed on the tender. If all went according to plan, they soon would be dead.

"We have extra boxcars this time," he commented casually.

"Not your business," the dispatcher replied. A SS officer and another soldier approached the train. "These men will accompany you to the quarry."

Kaz knew the drill from his runs to Auschwitz. He glanced at the SS officer and looked away. If all went according to plan, the officer and the soldier would soon be dead, shot by his own hand. He boarded the train and dumped his backpack against the wall beside his seat. Then, he unzipped the main flap and pulled out a pack of cigarettes. The handle of the gun was hidden just inside the flap where he could easily grasp it when the time came. His hands had stopped shaking, he noticed. A steely calm had descended on him. It was as if he was back in blood alley, waiting for the train that he knew was coming, waiting to embrace it. His fear was gone. He looked at the SS officer again and thought about the rubber hose. He would be ready when it was time. He offered the officer a cigarette, who declined with a stiff shake of his head. Kaz gave him a thin smile.

The cars screeched and groaned as he eased the train out of the yard, then settled into a steady, clanking rhythm as it picked up speed. It was a clear day, a good day for a firefight. He hoped the sun would be in the machine gunners' eyes. Kaz glanced at his watch. It would take an hour to reach the tunnel. He spent the time rehearsing what would take place when the train stopped. He wouldn't move until he heard the first gunshots. Then, he would reach into the backpack, grip the handle of the gun, and raise it out of the bag. He would shoot the soldier first. He had a gun, but his attention would initially be drawn to the gunshots coming from the ambush positions tucked into the mountainside above the train. Next, he would turn to the SS officer. The officer had a pistol on his belt, but it was held in place by two straps. It would take him a moment to free it. That should give Kaz the time he needed. Finally, he would turn his attention to the tender to make sure that the fireman had killed both soldiers stationed there.

Kaz smiled serenely. It was a good plan.

However, when the train rounded a curve and the tunnel was revealed, the plan flew out the window. He could see the boulders blocking the tracks, but when he grabbed the brake control and started to slow the train, the SS officer whirled on him.

"Nein," the officer shouted. "Schnell. Schnell."

The officer wanted Kaz to speedup and smash into the boulders! Kaz shook his head violently and gripped the controls as hard as he could. The wheels screamed against the metal rails as they continued to slow. The boulders loomed larger, but he knew there was enough time to stop. He caught movement out of the corner of his eye and realized that the officer was pulling his pistol from its holster. Instinctively, Kaz let go of the brake and grabbed his gun. The engine crashed into the boulders and ground to an abrupt halt. The impact nearly threw Kaz from his seat. The officer stumbled and banged into the control panel. The unexpected collision gave Kaz just enough time to raise his weapon and fire it before the officer could recover his balance. A sharp roar filled the cab, much like a thunderclap overhead. A look of disbelief swept over the SS officer's face. He fell against the controls and slumped to the floor.

Kaz's attention turned to the soldier, who'd been knocked over by the train's crash. He was scrambling back to his feet, his rifle swinging upward into a firing position. Kaz shifted his aim and fired at the soldier, but he wasn't sure he'd hit his target. More claps of thunder roared through the cabin. He was vaguely aware of the fireman exchanging gunshots with the two soldiers on the tender. A sharp pain streaked down his arm as hot metal creased his shoulder. The soldier in the cab had shot him! Before he could react, blood burst from the forehead of the soldier. He'd either been struck by a bullet fired from the tender or by a round from one of Simon's men. The soldier slumped and disappeared from view. Kaz was spun sideways by the impact of the bullet ripping through his flesh. He dropped the gun and gripped his arm.

A fuselage of shots was raining down from the mountainside. The machine guns on the boxcars clattered in response. Kaz was overwhelmed by the noise. It echoed off the mountain into the cab where it ricocheted about. Only, it wasn't just noise bouncing off the walls. Bullets were spraying the cabin, as well. Terrified, Kaz ducked behind the boiler and prayed it wouldn't blow up. The air was dancing with lightning and thunder. He wanted to pull his jacket over his head and disappear, but that wasn't possible.

The firing stopped as abruptly as it had begun. An eerie calm floated through the pall of gunsmoke that filled the cabin. Kaz looked around in amazement. The fireman lay dead on the floor, as did the SS officer and his soldier. He couldn't see the two soldiers on the tender, but there was no sign of movement. Simon's men were rushing down the steep slopes of the mountain and boarding the train. Frightened horses whinnied as they were coaxed out of the tunnel and urged toward the boxcar containing the dynamite. The screech of rusty wheels announced that the doors on the boxcars housing the Jews were being opened. Kaz staggered forwad and watched as men in striped shirts shielded their eyes and stepped uncertainly from the dark cars into the daylight.

Kaz's own eyes began to water. He wasn't sure if it was the result of the pain from his wound or the relief at finding himself alive. Simon and two of his fighters swung into the cab.

"You were hit," Simon remarked as he inspected Kaz's arm. "A flesh wound. It missed your arteries."

Kaz winced but said nothing.

"The bullet wound is a nice touch. It adds credibility to your story. But we can't dress it. It has to look like you were left for dead." He looked over at the fireman's body. "Too back we lost this one. He was a good man."

Simon turned to his fighters. "The shots will have been heard in the village down the tracks. German soldiers will be here soon. So, we have to move fast." He returned his attention to Kaz. "No time to talk, I'm afraid. We still have to knock you out as planned. Sorry about that."

Before he could protest, Simon signaled to one of the fighters, wno slammed the butt of his rifle into Kaz's head. His world went dark.

As Kaz slowly regained consciousness, his first thought was how much his arm and his head hurt. He heard footsteps pounding up metal rungs as men scrambled into the cab. Voices echoed around him. German voices. He opened his eyes and discovered several soldiers inspecting the bodies. One of them exclaimed something when he saw that Kaz was alive. Strong arms lifted him to a sitting position. His head swam. Someone spoke to him.

"I don't understand you," he replied in polish.

"Who are you?" a voice responded. He saw a SS officer approaching him. His face was both grim and angry.

"I'm the engineer. My train was attacked." He winced when he moved his arm. Blood was streaming down his face from the wound on his head. "I was shot."

"Yes, I see that. Who shot you?"

"I'm not sure. They blocked the tracks with rocks and started shooting when I tried to crash through the barrier." Kaz glanced around him. All the weapons were gone, including his pistol. Simon must have taken them.

"Your wounds are not very bad," the officer said with skepticism. "You will come with us, back to Krakow for questioning." Kaz was put in the back of a truck that had been driven up from the village on the railway tracks. The SS officer rode in a separate car.

It took two bruising hours to reach the outskirts of Krakow. Kaz endured the ride with gritted teeth. His arm felt as though it had been burned by Filas's hot tongs, and his head throbbed without mercy. He expected to be taken to the Gestapo headquarters, but he found himself being driven to the north side of the city, instead. His heart missed a beat when they stopped at a complex of three and four-story brick buildings. He recognized it at once as the Montelupi, previously the Polish National Guard Armory, now a German prison. It was used for political prisoners, resistance fighters, and other trouble makers. They were interrogated there, then transported to a labor camp or shot.

Kaz was taken into the bowels of the place and pushed into a room with no heat or windows and only one dim bulb flickering in the ceiling. A short, wooden bed with one, thin blanket crouched against the wall. A tarnished, metal pot had been shoved under the bed. From its foul odor, Kaz had no trouble figuring out what that was for. The place offered all the comforts of a medieval castle.

He sat on the wooden bed and inspected his arm while he waited. The gunshot wound had crusted over, but it still ached and he worried about infection. His head's drumroll had settled into a dull throb. He heard cries of anguish far down the corridor and shuddered to think what was to come. It was impossible to keep track of time. There was no reference point for how quickly minutes turned into hours. He shivered and decided to move about the room to warm himself. His breaths formed brief pillows of fog as he walked. When a key finally clanged in the metal lock, he welcomed it, even though he knew it was the precursor to mental torment and physical pain. Two guards cuffed his hands in front of him and marched him down a colorless corridor to a ten-foot by ten-foot room furnished with a metal table and two metal chairs. Like his sleeping room, it was windowless and chilled to the point of frost. Kaz immediately looked around the room for a rubber hose and was relieved not to find one. A guard forced him to sit on one of the cold chairs, where he was left to shiver for an interminable length of time. He dozed fitfully in the chair.

Kaz snapped awake when the door clanged open. A SS officer entered the room with a pad of papers in his hand and took the chair opposite him without saying a word. He glanced at the papers and looked at Kaz with a scowl. The muscles in Kaz's neck tightened. The officer had a jagged scar down his left cheek that made Kaz think of a lightening bolt.

"How is it you are alive when everybody else is dead?" It was a blunt question accompanied by a piercing glare.

"I don't know. Dumb luck, I guess."

The SS officer obviously didn't like the answer. The scowl on his face deepened.

"The fireman was killed, why not you?"

"I think the attackers believed I was dead, also."

"Why didn't you run the blockade?"

"I tried to, but I feared if I crashed into the rocks with too much speed, it would derail the train. I was in the process of slowing the train when I was shot in the arm. Then, something struck my head. Everything went blank. That's the last thing I remember."

"What is your name?" The sudden shift in the line of questioning caught Kaz by surprise. He hesitated.

"You do remember your name?"

"Kaz Kowinsky."

The officer referred to his papers. "And where do you live?"

Kaz gave him the address on Tatrzanska Street.

Again, the officer inspected his papers. "You have just moved there. Where were you before?"

Kaz's mind was in a whirl. His head still ached, which made it difficult for him to think straight. He knew he didn't dare mention Agata's apartment. There was only one hope. "My wife, Daneta, and our baby are staying at her parent's house. I visit them when I can. We had an apartment, but it was given to a German officer and his family. So, I've been moving around, staying with friends."

The officer jotted something down.

"There's a Major Schmidt staying there," Kaz added. "You can verify this information with him."

The questioning continued for some time. It was methodic, relentless. How did he get his job at the rail yard? Who were his friends? Why didn't he live with his wife at the parent's house? Was he ever in the military? Where was he when the Germans came? Kaz's mind grew fuzzy. His head pounded with each new question.

At last, the SS officer stood up and strode from the room without comment. A guard marched Kaz up the drafty corridor to another door, where he was joined by half-a-dozen prisoners. They stood silently and waited until the guard motioned for them to take off their clothes. Once they had complied, the guard gave the clothes to another soldier who disappeared with them down the corridor. The other prisoners, men in their thirties and forties, looked as confused as Kaz felt. He tried to speak, but the guard shouted at him. Kaz shivered and wondered how long they were expected to endure this treatment.

The answer came a few minutes later when the guard opened a door leading to a dark, lifeless courtyard comprised entirely of cement. Kaz blinked his eyes in surprise when he realized there was no daylight. Night had crept into his little world without him knowing it. The outside temperature was well below freezing, and a cold blast of air greeted them as they were led out of the building. The corrridor felt like a sauna by comparison. The guard pointed across the courtyard at a low, poorly lighted building and indicated that the prisoners should go there to shower. They stumbled, naked and barefoot, across the cement and entered a room with a row of shower heads protruding from a concrete wall. Kaz turned on his shower and felt the thin stream of tepid water with his hand. It felt warm in contrast to the air, but when he forced himself under the water, it still chilled him to the bone.

The guard pointed to a small bar of soap in a wire basket and said in Polish, "Jew soap." He laughed as each prisoner took his soap and cleansed himself. Kaz's brain was too frozen to understand what the guard meant. He knew better than to ask.

The men hurried back across the courtyard dripping wet and gathered in the corridor for another gap of time until their clothes, damp and steaming, were unceremoniously dumped on the foor in front ot them. The men made a mad scramble for the pile, each trying to identify his own. Despite their dampness, Kaz's clothes felt blessedly warm when he pulled them over his shaking body. Next, the men followed the guards down a stairway to another corridor defined by a series of rooms with bars on them. The men were each herded into a separate cell and told in Polish not to talk.

As Kaz entered his cell, he noticed another prisoner, a tall, thin man with a limp, being escorted to a cell at the far end of the corridor. There were no other prisoners at that end of the cell block, and Kaz wondered why the man was being isolated. He wanted to call out to him, but two guards took up positions in the corridor to enforce the 'no talking' command.

Kaz soon forgot about the other prisoners as he huddled on a low bunk bed in a hopeless effort to warm himself. Eventually, he fell into a fitful sleep. However long he slept, it wasn't long enough. The crisp, metallic sound of keys opening his cell jarred him awake. He was given a thin soup of potato peels to eat, then he was led back up the stairs to the ten-by-ten room, where the interrogation process repeated itself. Why didn't he die with the others? Why didn't he run the blockade? Who were his friends? Why didn't he live with his wife? What did he do in the navy? Kaz tried to remember what he'd said before, tried to give the same answers.

Again, he was returned to his cell. Again, he was awakened after insufficient sleep, given potato soup and led up the stairs. His brain was numb from the cold and the lack of sleep. The ordeal was taking a heavy toll on his body and on his mind. It wouldn't be long before he went crazy.

This time, however, something different happened. During the questioning, an orderly knocked on the door and entered the room. The SS officer was clearly annoyed by the interruption. The orderly whispered something in his ear and hastily departed. The perpetual scowl on the officer's face darkened.

"It appears that you have powerful friends, Mr. Kowinsky."

Kaz blinked and looked at the man, confused. "I've told you who my friends are."

"So you have. Including Major Werner Schmidt, it appears." The officer stood up, straightened his uniform and glared at Kaz. "You have been released."

Kaz staggered to his feet, uncertain what he'd just heard. "Why?"

"Because you have friends," his interrogator replied as he turned to leave. "You are free to go."

Guards ushered him through a maze of corridors and out into a brilliant sunshine that nearly blinded him. He was reminded of the Jews leaving the boxcars by the tunnel, how they raised their hands to ward off the sun. Kaz was doing the same. A car waited for him by the outside gate and drove him through the delicious scenes and sounds of familiar streets to the Rudnicka's house. As the car pulled into the driveway, Daneta rushed out the front door, threw her arms around him and kissed his cheeks. It was a fairytale ending to a dark nightmare. He feared that at any moment the door of his prison cell would clang shut and he would be jarred awake from this wonderful dream. When he squeezed Daneta's warm body against his, he expected her to disappear in a puff of smoke. Nothing of the sort happened. Sunlight flooded over him and birds twittered in the nearby trees. Daneta's breath tickled the skin on his neck. Her arms gripped him around his waist. Somehow, the nightmare was over. He was safe.

Other than the maid who was feeding Edwina, the house was empty. "Father spoke to Herr Schmidt, who agreed to have you released," she explained while she led him to the bathroom and filled the tub with soothing, hot water. "Although, I don't think it was simply father's request that did it. The major was genuinely interested in you." She looked at him, puzzled. "You seem to have some sort of relationship with him. I've been hesitant to pry. Are you working for him?"

Kaz let out a breath of air that sounded like a sigh. He didn't dare tell her about the insurgency or the traitors' names that he was feeding Schmidt. "He wants information from time to time. I've agreed to supply it in return for your safety."

Daneta looked at him in surpise. "What do you mean? We're not in any danger."

"We all are. I know you like the idea of him living here. It gives you a sense of security. But he's a very dangerous man, and he would turn on you and your parents in a heartbeat if it suited him. You must be careful. Don't reveal things that could be used against you."

"I can't believe it," she said as she turned off the water faucets. "He seems the perfect gentleman."

"Don't tell your father what I've said, Daneta. If word got back to Schmidt, we could all be in trouble. Me most of all."

"I'm worried about you, Kaz. You keep getting in trouble. Please take better care of yourself."

"I'll try, believe me. But these are dangerous times."

Daneta inspected Kaz's wounds, took iodine and bandages from a cabinet over the sink and cleaned him up. The iodine seared his flesh, but he didn't complain. The pain felt good. It meant that he would soon heal.

"Put the bandages on after your bath," she commanded.

Kaz half expected Daneta to return while he was in the tub and was disappointed when she didn't. He wished he understood their relationship better. Or Daneta. Most of the time she kept her distance, but when he was in trouble, she was like a warm sponge that wrapped itself around him and succored him. When he finished his bath, he put on the bandages and the bathrobe she'd given him and walked down the hall to her bedroom. The door was ajar just enough for him to peek in and see her lying on the bed.

"Come here," she demanded in her familiar, husky voice, the same voice he'd heard the last time they made love.

He obeyed.

Chapter Nineteen

For the next few months, Kaz enjoyed the luxury of an apartment to himself. He didn't know how Agata managed it, but it seemed to be a small reward for his role in the train ambush. Simon had recruited over two hundred Jews to his army and had obtained a large supply of dynamite that he was now using to blow up German trains. Most important, Kaz had not revealed Agata's base of operations. She knew he was someone on whom she could rely. He even had some free time to visit Daneta and Edwina. And, on occasion, Daneta came to his apartment alone for a few hours of abandonment. Theirs continued to be a strange relationship. He understood that in normal times they wouldn't have stayed together as a married couple, but the war and German occupation had flipped their worlds upside down. As usual, Daneta initiated their interludes, and he responded.

At the foot of Tatrzanska Hill, the Nazis were constructing a wall surrounding several blocks to the south and to the east that were designated as the Krakow Ghetto. The original ghetto, located on the other side of the Vistula River near where Kaz had lived with his uncle and aunt, was almost a city within a city, a Jewish sanctuary since medieval times. The Jews named it Kazimierz in honor of Kazimierz the Great who had walled it off as an independent city and presented it to the Jews. Its medieval flavor remained unchanged until the Germans arrived in 1939. They decided that the Kazimierz Ghetto was in too valuable a location to be inhabited by Jews, so they were now creating a new ghetto in the Podgorze section of Krakow by erecting walls between the buildings and bricking in the windows facing the surrounding neighborhoods. Four, gated intersections manned by guard towers provided the only ways in and out. The result was a massive prison compound several square blocks in size that began just one block from Kaz's living room window.

The Germans began by rounding up Jews from all over the city and herding them into the new compound. Next, they shipped Jews in from the rest of Poland. Nearly every day, trainloads of new arrivals were prodded along Kalwaryjska Street past the large, tree-lined square that sprawled before the ghetto gate. At sundown, the long shadow of

St. Joseph's main spire crawled across the square and pointed the way through Kalwaryjska gate like a black finger of doom.

The ghetto soon teemed with five times its normal population. Those who were already housed in apartments had to crowd together to make room for the new arrivals. Usually, this happened peacefully, but sometimes nerves became frayed and tempers flared. Arguments ensued. Day after dreary day, they kept coming, the young, the robust, the aged, the lame. Men, women and children. Silent, terrified, and exhausted, they shuffled through the gate toward an unknown fate. Once inside, they went about the grim business of surviving there.

Squads of uniformed Sonderdienst, Polish Nazi police of German origin, were conscripted to perform guard duty. They walked the perimeters with orders to shoot anyone caught trying to leave. The German soldiers were brutal in their behavior toward the new arrivals, but it was the Sonderdienst who were the true sadists. Each day, a squad would enter the ghetto streets, point to an apartment building and shout commands in German. Terrified residents of the designated building scrambled out like mice disturbed from a nest and assembled in the street. While half of the squad searched the apartments for hidden weapons or contraband, the rest conducted a shakedown of the people in search of valuables. Anyone found with a gun or knife was shot on the spot.

Hostages were often selected at random to be questioned or for work details. Those selected were prodded at the end of bayonets into rows of three to be marched away. If someone was too frail, or failed to move quickly enough, he or she was shot. Loved ones standing along the curbs did not dare to attend to the dying. They couldn't even sob or wail for fear that they would meet a similar fate.

Once the hostages were gone, a truck rattled down the cobblestone street followed by Polish laborers. The laborers tossed the bodies into the bed of the truck without making eye contact with the living left behind. Only after the truck and laborers had turned a corner and exited the ghetto did the ghostly faces along the curb give up their vigil and return to their building. Several of the apartments had more room that night, but not for long. The vacated space would soon be filled by more arrivals and the cycle would repeat itself.

Kaz said little about these incidents to Daneta. It wasn't something he cared to talk about, and he knew it would upset her needlessly. One afternoon when she joined him at his apartment, however, she got a front row seat to an astonishing scene. It began when she observed two Sonderdienst guards patrolling along Wieliczka Street. Here the buildings stood four stories tall. The windows on the lower floors had been bricked in, but a few on the top floors were only shuttered. Brick layers had not yet gotten to them. The two guards suddenly stopped and looked up at a fourth floor window where a heavy, wooden shutter stood open.

Instinctively, Kaz tried to draw Daneta away from the window, but she shook him off and stared at the two men.

"Close that window," one of the guards shouted.

The second guard took aim with his rifle. Daneta grabbed Kaz's arm as she watched. An elderly woman appeared in the window and reached out to grasp the loose shutter, but before she could close it, the sharp crack of a gunshot rang out. The guard with the rifle laughed as the figure crumpled from view.

"I said close that window," the first guard shouted again.

Silence. For a long moment, nothing stirred. Then, slowly, the hooked end of a walking cane protruded through the window and snagged the offending shutter. A quick jerk slammed the shutter closed with a heavy thump. No sound came from within the apartment. No voices were heard. No one cried out. The discordant noise of the rifle shot had long since echoed away. There was only silence. Another space had opened in the ghetto.

The silence was finally broken by the clump of the guards' boots as they resumed their rounds. In a few days, the window would be filled with bricks and that afternoon's deadly encounter would be forgotten, except for Daneta and the man with the cane. They were two strangers who would never meet, but they shared a stark moment when the dead departed from the living.

Chapter Twenty

Victorious armies marched on full stomachs, or so the old axiom said. In Poland, that meant eating lots of bread. Poland was well-known for its bread, most of which was made by grinding wheat into flour on querns that were handed down for generations. A quern consisted of two round, flat stones that had been worn smooth by decades of use. Grain was spread on the bottom stone and ground into flower by the top stone, which was turned by a wooden handle inserted into a small hole. All Poles knew about querns, even a city-raised boy like Kaz. They had achieved near metaphysical status due to the finely textured bread baked from the flour milled by those querns. The Polish were famous for their bread, and that started with the art of the quern.

"We have to save the querns," Agata announced with a particularly urgent tone in her voice. She was seated with Kaz, Charlie and two other men in the living room of her apartment. "The Germans plan to destroy them so that farmers can't bake their own bread. That way, the Nazis will control the food supply. They intend to gather the wheat harvest, have it ground at distribution centers, and return just enough flour to the farmers to sustain them. They will keep the rest for their army, and there'll be nothing left for Simon or the other resistance fighters."

The heavy hand of the Nazis was slowly choking the life out of Poland. Polish citizens needed permits for everything, even bicycles. No one was allowed to drive a car, and precious few licenses were issued for trucks. The latter were mostly granted for the movement of wheat and potatoes from the farms to German-controlled warehouses in the cities. Poland was now forced to feed the German army as well as its citizens. The districts overseen by the General Government headquartered in the Walwel Castle fared somewhat better due to the area's large agricultural economy. Food needed to be distributed quickly and efficiently, so some of the restrictions were eased. That included Krakow, where Kaz and the others were able to move about with a certain amount of freedom.

Agata turned her attention to Kaz. "The time has come to move you into field operations. We need to get you released from your current job driving trains."

Kaz was taken aback by the idea of leaving his position. He loved his job. "What would I be doing?"

"Smuggling weapons and food to the fighters, for one. Documenting troop movements and Nazi activities for another. Our fight has become more complex and more dangerous. We need people like you and Charlie to take a more active role."

Kaz considered the proposition and had to admit that he found it appealing. His old, daredevil spirit was ignited by the thought of doing something that involved more action. Things had been a bit dull since the train ambush, and he didn't want to drive anymore trains to Auschwitz. There was only one problem.

"I don't know if the Germans will let me go from the trains. They're short on engineers."

"We've thought about that." Agata handed Kaz a slip of paper with a name and address on it. "We have a doctor who'll give you a medical report stating that you're no longer fit to drive trains. Have you ever been sick before?"

Kaz was uncomfortable at the idea of being seen as weak or unfit. He'd always been in good health. He was about to say no when he thought about how his fishing career had ended.

"I once had a stomach ulcer."

"Perfect. I'm sure the doctor will be able to work with that."

Kaz visited the doctor the next day and was given a quick exam. When the doctor learned about his stomach ulcer, he grunted approvingly and wrote up a report indicating a recurring condition and recommending complete rest. Kaz showed the report to the dispatcher at the rail yard and was told to take it to the German army medical center. Kaz protested that he'd already been examined, but the dispatcher ignored him. He had to be checked by a German doctor before he could be released from duty. Kaz worried that the Germans would see through his subterfuge.

He thought about hurrying back to Agata's doctor, but realized that strategy wouldn't help. The dispatcher had already rejected the doctor's report. Presenting himself to the German doctor didn't seem promising either. He was trapped. He needed a different plan, something more subtle. He thought for a moment. Perhaps there was a way. He'd found the Germans to be a bit stubborn at times. Tell them one thing, and they would believe another. Claim he had an ulcer, and they would most likely conclude that he was just fine. The answer was to use the German's recalcitrance to his advantage..

"I don't know what this is all about," he protested to the German doctor as soon as he was admitted. "I'm in perfectly good health. I just want to get back to my train."

The doctor didn't speak fluent Polish, but he made it clear that he would be the one to decide what Kaz could or couldn't do. When he pressed Kaz in the abdomen, Kaz winced just enough to appear as though he was hiding something. The doctor probed some more and jotted down his notes on a report attached to a clip board. Then, he handed it to Kaz and told him to go see the eye doctor.

"There's nothing wrong with my eyes," he remonstrated. "I want to get back to work."

The doctor waved him away without further comment.

Kaz knew that his eyes were fine, but he decided to continue his charade just in case the first doctor decided to send him back to his train. He deliberately misread several of the letters on the charts, trying to make just enough errors to suggest that his eyes were weak. Next, came the depth perception test, a critical phase of the examination for an engineer. He carefully misaligned just enough pegs to make it look as though he was having some difficulty. He sat back, crossed his fingers and waited.

"I see you work for the railroad." This doctor spoke fluent Polish. "What do you do?"

"I'm an engineer."

"When was your last eye exam?"

"Before the war. I passed a very simple exam when I enlisted in the navy."

The doctor looked at Kaz with a thoughtful gaze. "Have you ever missed a signal or had an accident?"

Kaz thought about the crash in the tunnel when the rod broke. "Only once, but that was due to a mechanical problem," he hastened to add. "My eyes are fine."

"I'll be the judge of that." He looked at his notes and adjusted his glasses. "I can't certify your health based on these tests. You could cause a serious accident."

"But trains are my livelihood. What about glasses?"

"We haven't enough glasses for our soldiers. What makes you think we would waste them on you?" The doctor spoke with such distain, Kaz knew it was time to shut up. He accepted the report and left.

Kaz returned to the rail yard with his report. Within an hour he'd been paid for time worked and released.

The farmer's truck followed a path defined by a pair of weak headlights as it bumped along a rutted road through the surrounding farmland. It was close to midnight, and Kaz was worried about being stopped by German soldiers. He sat in the passenger's seat and looked out the window for any signs of trouble. Charlie drove the truck as fast as he dared along the uneven road. They both had forged papers in their pockets giving them authorization to drive to a storage facility where they were supposed to pick up a load of wheat that was destined for the hungry German army in Krakow. First, however, they had to make a side trip to a forested area where a large cache of querns was hidden. They planned to take the querns to an old barn outside the city where Simon and his men would be waiting. That was why they were following an unpaved side road and why they were worried about being stopped. They weren't sure how they could explain themselves if they were discovered making a detour.

At last, they reached a dark stretch of forest where two men with lanterns were waiting to guide them. They followed a narrow, twisting path through stands of cedars and pines to an abandoned cabin. The floor boards of the cabin were hastily removed to reveal hundreds of querns. To Kaz, they looked like ancient tombstones resting on their sides. Everyone pitched in and hauled the querns to the yard, where they were spread evenly across the bed of the truck and covered with a tarp. Once the job was finished, three men with guns hopped in the back.

"We'll ride with you to the grain depot, in case there's any trouble. It's only a few miles."

This was the most dangerous leg of the journey. Once they loaded the bushels of grain over the querns, their hidden treasure should be safe. But first, they had to travel several miles with nothing more than a tarp hiding the querns from curious eyes. Kaz had no doubt that there would be a firefight if they were stopped. He constantly twisted in his seat and watched for Germans. He noticed that Charlie appeared quite calm by comparison. He also scanned the road for any signs of trouble, but he did so with an untroubled air of certainty that whatever happened, they would prevail. Kaz was relieved that they didn't have to put Charlie's faith to the test. They soon ducked down a gravel path and stopped outside a barn that leaned so far to the right Kaz wondered if would still be standing once they removed the wheat.

Kaz breathed a sigh when the last basket of wheat was loaded into the truck and they were on their way. There were still things that could go wrong, he knew. It was past midnight. They had to reach Simon's hiding place well before dawn so there would be time to unload and reload the truck and to send the fighters on their way while it was still dark. Road blocks or other delays could prove fatal. So, it was with a thumping heart that Kaz spied lanterns floating in the road ahead of them, signaling them to stop. Charlie braked in the middle of the road, indicating that he expected to be quickly on his way. Two German guards approached on either side of the truck. One spoke to Charlie in German. Charlie knew enough of their language to explain that they were transporting wheat to Krakow. He produced his papers as he spoke and gestured for Kaz to do the same. The guards inspected the documents and promptly handed them back. For a moment, Kaz thought they were in the clear, but that hope faded when the first guard demanded that they get out of the truck and open the canvass flaps covering the back. They complied. The truck was filled to the top with baskets of grain. It would take half an hour for Kaz and Charlie to unload everything. He could see by the frown on his face, that the first guard was trying to decided what to do. Kaz gripped a knife he kept hidden in his pocket. He wasn't going to be taken without a fight.

The guard randomly picked three baskets from different parts of the load and indicated that Kaz and Charlie should unload them. Then, he plunged his rifle barrel into the grain in the first basket and shoved it around. He repeated this process with the other two. Satisfied, he indicated that the baskets could be returned to the truck. Kaz gladly followed his orders and hopped back into the truck. There would be no need for the knife tonight.

They rolled down the road to their rendezvous without further delay. Kaz could see that it was a strategic location for Simon and his men. Rolling hills and forest started less than a mile away and led into the Tatra Mountains where the fighters could quickly become lost among myriad canyons and bluffs. Simon was waiting for them with two dozen men and horses. All held rifles and carried pistols in holsters attached to their belts.

"Hello again, friend."

"You can call me by name," Kaz offered.

"Better not to. The Germans know about me, but not you. It's best to keep it that way, if possible."

The men quickly unloaded the truck and bundled the querns into saddle bags that hung over the horses. Next, they tied several baskets of grain behind the bags. The rest was put back in the truck.

"I wish we could take more," Simon remarked as they prepared to leave, "but we have to leave some for the Germans. Otherwise, the farmers will get in trouble."

With that, they spurred their horses and disappeared into the black night on their way to the Tatra Mountains.

All Kaz could think about when he got back to Krakow was crawling into his bed to sleep. The sun had risen, and the streets were busy. He was about to climb the stairs to his apartment when he saw the apartment manager hurrying toward him. The man pounded along the pavement on short legs and waved his hands urgently.

"I don't know what you did, but you're hotter than a frying pan."

Kaz had hardly spoken to the man since he moved there and was surprised by his familiarity. Sleep fled Kaz's body; his senses went on high alert.

"What do you mean?"

"A SS officer and two soldiers came here yesterday afternoon and again last night. One of the soldiers stayed to watch the place, but he left a couple hours ago. Gave me a number to call the moment I saw you."

"How do you know they were looking for me?"

"Had your apartment number and your name. Demanded to see your rooms."

"Thanks for alerting me." Kaz's heart was pounding as hard as the man's footsteps. Something was wrong. He looked around nervously.

"Hell," the man responded with a pinched face, "I don't have any use for those szkopys. Whatever they want you for, I expect they deserved it."

"I need to get my stuff. Do you think it's safe?"

"You hurry up. I'll keep an eye out. If I cough, take the back stairs and come around the side of the building. I'll signal you when it's safe to leave."

Kaz rushed up the stairs and entered his apartment. He saw at once that furniture had been moved around. In the bedroom, drawers had been opened and the mattress flipped off the bed. Kaz grabbed his duffel bag and threw clothes into it as fast as he could. Next, he ran to the bathroom to gather his razor and toothbrush. He was about to head out the door when he heard a distinct cough from the landing at the bottom of the stairs. Kaz froze and listened. Heavy boots scuffed the wooden stairs two stories below him. There was no attempt at stealth. The soldier had no idea that he was there.

Kaz tiptoed down the hall to the back stairs and descended as quietly as possible. He slipped through the side yard to the front of the building and peeked around the corner. He was breathing so heavily, he feared the whole neighborhood could hear him. He shifted the duffel bag on his shoulder and forced himself to calm down.

The little man was standing idly near the bottom of the stairs, his hands at his sides. Kaz scanned the street for other soldiers but spotted none. Then, his eyes saw it. Leaning against the tree by the curb. A shiny bicycle. Not just any bicycle. A bicycle belonging to the soldier. Kaz knew instantly what he had to do.

The moment the apartment manager motioned for him to run, he raced to the bicycle, hopped on and madly pedaled away with the heavy duffel bag dangling from his back. He looked around, half expecting to see the soldier taking a bead on him with his rifle, but all he saw was the manager doubled over with laughter as he headed back to his own apartment. The breeze created by his momentum refreshed his tired body. Freedom blew gently through his hair as he pumped the pedals. He hadn't felt this good in a long time.

He felt light headed and wanted to laugh, but the seriousness of his situation sobered him. The Germans were looking for him, and he was riding on a stolen bicycle without a permit. Not only that, the two wheeler was new and shiny. It would draw immediate attention. He could be stopped at any moment and arrested.

Kaz quickly turned a corner and disappeared into a narrow side street where he was less likely to be noticed. He stopped near a large, trash container and pondered what to do. Why were the Nazis looking for him? Had the SS officer from Rawa Ruska caught up to him? Or did the Germans have more information about the train ambush? It didn't matter. Kaz knew that either way, he was in trouble.

German voices echoed down the side street as two soldiers strode purposely past the corner where Kaz was hiding. He quickly stowed the bicycle behind the trash container and walked away. He had to find Agata and discuss what to do.

"It was Major Schmidt," Agata informed Kaz. They were seated in the living room of her apartment. He'd arrived there, breathless and sweating, after abandoning the bicycle a mile away and slipping through the back streets. "I fear he has figured out our ruse."

"What should I do?"

"Stay away from the Rudnicka household. He'll have the place under twenty-four hour surveillance."

He thought about Daneta and the baby. "What about my family?"

"You can't go near them. If you try to approach them at home or work, even on the street, you'll be caught and they will be in trouble. You must disappear from their lives."

Kaz felt the air rush from his lungs, and with it, a sense of loss, as if he'd been shipwrecked and thrown up on some forgotten island. It was unfair to ask him to give up what little family he'd managed to scrape together. It wasn't idyllic, but he was a father, and he didn't want to simply disappear as his own father had done. Yet, that was exactly what Agata said he must do ... give Daneta and Edwina up and slip away without leaving a trace. Otherwise, he would be in danger. *They* would be in danger.

Agata cupped her hands in her lap and leaned forward as if she were about to share a dark secret. "You've become too valuable to be lost because of a silly mistake, Kaz. It's time for you to go underground."

"I thought that's what I was doing."

Agata shook her head. "I'm talking about something more permanent. Wait here."

She hastened from the room and returned moments later with a box in her hands. Inside the box were blank travel documents, permits and passports. A smaller box contained dozens of rubber stamps.

"We can forge any document issued by the Germans, including identification papers. We have lists of people taken from birth records in a dozen different cities, and from church and city hall documents. Each name includes their birth date, hair and eye color, approximate weight and height. These are all people who moved away from their birthplace and either died or emigrated out of Poland before the Nazis arrived. We will match you with a good likeness. By tomorrow, we'll have new identification papers and travel documents for you. You can stay here for the night while we make arrangements."

That was it, then. Kaz Kowinsky would cease to exist, just as Kaz Kowalski had done years before. Kaz returned to his old room and tossed his bag on the bed. He was getting tired of all the moves. He felt like a gypsy living his life without permanence of address or belongings. He tried to imagine a more stable life, one that included Daneta and Edwina, but that was not to be. He seemed destined to keep moving from place to place, changing his name, never putting down roots. Maybe, his fate would be different if the Germans were gone, but that seemed unlikely. They had become a fixture in everybody's lives, and they showed no sign of leaving.

Poland couldn't dislodge the Germans by themselves. The country's only hope had been that someone would come to their rescue, but who? Germany had already invaded Denmark and Norway. Those countries had fallen like pearls from a broken necklace. Next had come Belgium, Luxembourg and the Netherlands. More lost pearls scattered across the landscape of Europe. And what of France? FRANCE! They were supposed to be Poland's ally. They had an army. They'd built the Maginot Line, a series of fortresses, bunkers and rail lines along its border with Germany. In the end, it did little good. The Wehrmacht punched holes through the vaunted Maginot Line, rolled into France and occupied Paris within a month. Then, there was Great Britain, whose navy and air force were among the finest in Europe. They should have confronted the Germans, but they chose appeasement with Hitler and paid a heavy price. Now, the Luftwaffe was raining bombs down on the British people.

That left the Americans, Poland's remaining hope. If they got involved, Europe might yet be saved from the fiery dragon that had already consumed half the continent. The war was not popular in the U. S., however. Its citizens preferred to sit back and watch while Germany and its allies consumed its neighbors. If the invasion of France and the bombing campaign in England couldn't spur them into action, Kaz worried that nothing would.

In the meantime, the Germans continued to tighten their noose around Poland.

Kaz fidgeted in his room, pacing, sitting, then pacing, again, his mind in turmoil. What to do about Daneta? If he followed Agata's advice, he might never see his child again. If he didn't, he would put everyone at risk. Yet, how could he just disappear? That's what his real father had done, and Kaz had sworn that he would never do that to Edwina. There was only one way he could think to make contact, and he would need Charlie's help.

The next morning, Charlie joined Kaz at the apartment to discuss Agata's plans for the two of them. She joined them in the living room.

"Kaz, here's your new identity papers." She inspected them before handing the documents to Kaz. "They are very good. Even the Gestapo would be fooled."

Kaz looked at his photo and his new name: Kaz Gorski. It was an ugly name. Kowinsky had style to it, as did Kowalski. Gorski sounded like a blunt instrument used to hit somebody over the head. He had to admit, though, that the papers looked real. They even had a few creases and smudges to indicate use. He was satisfied

"We need eyes on the Wawel Castle to keep track of who's coming and going there," Agata continued. "Charlie and Kaz, that assignment falls to you. We're moving you to our safe house overlooking the castle."

"Don't worry," she hastened to add when she saw the disappointment on the two men's faces. "There'll be field assignments, as well, but reconnaissance is important. We need to know what the Germans are up to."

As soon as they were finished with the meeting, Kaz pulled Charlie aside.

"I need your help. The Germans are watching Daneta in the hopes that I'll show up. I can't contact her, but I need to let her know why I'm disappearing. I don't want her to think I'm just abandoning her and my daughter."

"Kaz, you know I'm glad to help, but what can you do?"

"I believe I can get a message to her through the bookkeeper, Dominik. I just need you to deliver it."

Charlie looked surprised. "The bookkeeper? I thought he didn't like him."

"Can't stand the man, but he won't betray Daneta. If you take a letter to him at the factory, he'll pass it on, and the Germans won't be the wiser."

Charlie grinned. "Of course I'll do it. I love pulling the Germans' whiskers without them knowing it."

Kaz spent the rest of the day trying to put his thoughts down on paper. In the end, his message was a simple one.

Dear Daneta:

It is hard for me to put thoughts to paper, so please excuse my poor efforts. You know by now that Major Schmidt is looking for me. You may not know that he has you under close surveillance. That is why I must write to you instead of coming myself.

If I am caught, I will be put in prison and possibly shot. So I must disappear. How long I will be gone is hard to say, but I doubt that I can come back as long as the Germans occupy our country.

I know our marriage has not been a successful one, but we have created a wonderful child that I shall cherish in my thoughts. Please take good care of her and know that I am not abandoning either of you.

I hope we will see each other again someday soon.

Kaz

Chapter Twenty-one

A convoy of trucks loaded with soldiers and pulling cannons roared past Kaz and Charlie as they made their way across the Vistula River to a three-story, corner apartment building on the fringe of downtown Krakow. Cars with German officers zoomed along the cobbled streets. A sense of urgency permeated the air. Kaz realized that there had been a bit of a lull the past several months while the Germans consolidated their gains elsewhere in Europe. Now, they were on the prowl, again.

The apartment building to which they were assigned had once been an elegant residence. Now, it looked tired and in need of a fresh coat of paint. It was built around a courtyard garden and was guarded by an iron fence with a gate that opened onto the street. The apartments formed an elaborate puzzle of iron balconies that reminded Kaz of a picture he'd once seen of the magnificent buildings along the Grand Canal in Venice, Italy.

"Looks pretty fancy," Kaz commented as they approached the main gate, "but old."

"It's older than you know. Agata told me that Copernicus once lived here. That would have been in the early 1500's!"

Kaz nearly choked with laughter. "He was probably the last one who painted the place."

They entered the courtyard and mounted an iron stairway to a second floor balcony that extended around the enclosure. Charlie stopped at the first apartment, fished a key from his pocket and opened the door.

"Welcome to our new digs," he announced with a formal bow.

The windows of the small parlor offered a sweeping panorama of the city and a splendid view of Wawel Castle. The massive castle sat on its hill like a man-made Gibraltar basking in the late afternoon sunlight. Its front gate was clearly visible from the apartment window.

"We'll have no problem seeing who comes and goes," Kaz commented. "But it seems like simple duty after ambushing trains and rescuing querns."

"It's important duty, but you're right. Agata knows we can do much more. That's why she chose us. Follow me."

He led Kaz through a sizable kitchen to a back bedroom and walked over to a paneled wall. When he tugged on the molding above the panel, it came loose. Charlie removed it and slid the panel open. Kaz couldn't believe his eyes. There was a small, windowless room tucked into the extreme back corner of the apartment.

"This was once the maid's quarters, but we found a better use for it." He snapped on an overhead light to reveal a single chair and unmade bed surrounded by stacks of rifles, machine guns, pistols, boxes of ammunition and more boxes with grenades. "We'll be smuggling these to Simon and others in the next few days."

Kaz whistled. "I'm impressed. How did you get these?"

"We raid the German armory from time to time. It sits on top of some old catacombs which give us access without being seen. We go in late at night and only take a few weapons at a time. Not enough to be noticed. So far, they haven't missed anything."

Kaz picked up one of the rifles and inspected it. It looked lethal enough, but he preferred a handgun. It was easier to hide and more effective at close range. He'd learned that much during the train ambush.

"It must be tricky getting this stuff in here without being seen."

"There's a back stairway. We bring them in that way, very quietly at night. Once we have a good supply, we pack everything in crates of food and ship it out. We have three trucks with forged documents that let us move around." Charlie grinned. "What do you think?"

Kaz continued to look at the cache of weapons with amazement. "It's quite an operation. Much more extensive than I thought. I imagine there must be more groups like this in Warsaw and other cities."

Charlie nodded. "The underground isn't just a handful of fighters hiding in the forests or mountains. It's also a network of smugglers and spies."

Kaz noticed parts for a shortwave receiver and transmitter lying on the bed. "Who uses that?"

"A man we call Willard. He's on his way here as we speak. Willard sends and receives messages from all around southern Poland and coordinates them with operators in other sectors. He tracks things like troop movements, arms shipments and military operations. That information gets forwarded to Simon the Black, Simon the Red and others who use it to plan sabotage activities and ambushes, like the one you were involved in." Charlie spread his arms wide. "This is the main base of operations for Krakow. We're standing at the epicenter of the underground movement in the city."

"I thought that was Agata's role."

"Agata's group is very important, but she's more involved with planning. This is where the operations are carried out."

"Do we still report to her?"

"Agata's husband, Zdisek, actually runs this part of the underground, but he and Agata coordinate everything."

Willard arrived without fanfare a short while later. He had a narrow head and long nose that made Kaz think of a greyhound. As far as Kaz could tell, he never smiled. Willard was a big man in every sense of the word, but when he worked with his shortwave equipment, he moved with the grace of a ballet dancer. He gently moved the equipment to the kitchen table next to a window, switched on the receiver and opened the window just enough to slip an antenna outside without it being noticed. Next, he donned a headset and carefully rotated knobs until he found the frequency he wanted. When he was satisfied that all was in order, he went to work sending and receiving messages. His language consisted of numbers and letters. Kaz listened, fascinated. He knew Willard was talking in code; to Kaz, it sounded like gibberish. He was surprised when Willard shut the equipment off after only a few minutes.

"There are trucks roaming the streets with receivers scanning the frequencies and listening for unsanctioned chatter," he explained. "When they discover a suspicious signal, such as ours, they try to triangulate it to learn our location. That takes some time, so we arrange a schedule that varies from day-to-day, and we keep our conversations brief."

Charlie pulled a bottle of vodka from a kitchen cupboard and poured everyone a shot. "What are you working on now?"

"We're trying to gather intelligence about a new weapon being developed by the Nazis. It's called a flying bomb, or V-bomb."

Kaz took a gulp of his drink. "What's so special about that? We have flying bombs now. The Luftwaffe if dropping tons of them on Britain."

"Those don't fly. They just fall. The V-bomb is attached to a rocket that can be fired from land and fly a couple hundred miles to its target. No airplane or pilot required. All we know so far is that they're being tested and might soon be ready for production. It could change the whole balance of the war."

"Nobody's mentioned them before. Are they being tested in Poland?"

Willard shook his head. "Not so far. Everything is being conducted in Germany. But we think the Germans may set up production plants in Poland to keep them away from British bombers. If they do, we want to know where they are so we can sabotage them. The program has a high priority with Hitler, from what we understand."

Charlie twirled his glass, as was his habit. "And if they are planning to do something in southern Poland, there'll be meetings at Wawel Castle."

"Precisely. That's why Agata sent you here."

The next few months were filled with tedious spying interrupted by clandestine forages into the Polish countryside, where they smuggled weapons and delivered food supplies. Kaz and Charlie spent hours peering through powerful field glasses, observing and recording the military rank and number of officers entering Wawel Castle, as well as other visitors in civilian clothing. They kept a keen eye out for anyone who might appear unusual and were rewarded one day when a tall, elderly man, in a coat that fit him so poorly he looked like a beggar, was escorted into the castle by two SS officers.

"Something odd just happened," Kaz announced to Charlie. He described what he'd seen.

"It does sound strange," Charlie agreed. He took his pair of field glasses and joined Kaz at the window facing the castle.

For the next two hours, they kept a watchful eye on the main gate, worried that they would miss the old man's exit. Several more SS officers entered the castle grounds, but there was no sign of the man for whom they were looking. A half-hour later, their patience was rewarded.

"There he is," Kaz nearly shouted. He focused on the man's face. His eyes were large and round, but placed off-center. His facial skin sagged over sunken cheeks, and he walked with a labored stride that suggested his limbs were sore.

"I think I saw this man at Montelupi when I was held prisoner there. I didn't see his face, but his unusual height and limp look very familiar. He was all by himself in the last cell at the end of the corridor."

The same two SS officers put him into a car and drove him away. Before they left, Kaz got a good look at their faces. One of the officers sported a jagged scar on his left cheek, the same scar he'd seen on the officer who interrogated him at Montelupi!

"I recognize that SS officer from the prison. There's definitely something going on. I've got to get this information to Agata." Kaz set out for her apartment at once while Charlie continued to monitor the castle.

"This is exciting news," Agata beamed. "You've just described Professor Jasinski. We've wondered what happened to him."

"They're keeping him at Montelupi where I was interrogated. I know I saw him there, and I recognized one of the SS officers from there, as well."

Agata's eyes widened in surprise. "That is interesting. Jasinski is a world renown mathematician. He's also Jewish. Willard picked up some chatter about him on the shortwave. We believe the Germans are using him to further their work on the V-bomb. If they took him to Wawel Castle, something important is being planned. We have to get him out of that prison. The information he could give us on the V-bomb program would be priceless. But we need to know exactly where they're keeping him."

"I can show you. All I need is a layout of the grounds." Kaz took a pencil and paper from the table and made a quick sketch. "The building holding the prisoners has a concrete courtyard. The cells are in the west side of the building down one flight of stairs. My cell was about here." He make a small circle. The professor's was here." He drew another circle at the end of the row of cells. Get me a layout of Montelupi and I'll show you the building."

Things moved quickly over the next three days. A man who used to work at Montelupi when it was an armory met with Kaz, and they quickly identified the frightful building where Kaz had been interned and interrogated.

"That would be the only building suited for prisoners," the man confirmed. "The police used it to hold petty criminals when the main jail was overcrowded."

Two others reconnoitered the grounds at night to determine the locations and strength of prison guards.

"It's lightly guarded," they reported. "Only a dozen men after midnight. Two of them walk the perimeter once every hour, which will give us enough time. There's a breach in the back wall where some construction work is in progress. It's only secured by a temporary, wooden barrier which can be scaled easily. The Germans are not too worried about security."

On the third night, four men trained in night raids gathered at Agata's apartment to review the final plans. Kaz was asked to join them. No names were exchanged.

"There's no moon tomorrow night which will give us excellent cover." The speaker was a leader who Kaz had never met before. He was lean and quick in his movements. His eyes flickered with the gleam of a panther on the prowl. "We'll come down the Vistula River in a small boat and land it here." He pointed to a location on a field map. "From there, we can use a network of back streets to reach Montelupi. Once we breach the wall, we need to kill the men guarding the prisoners quickly and quietly. Only knives and choke wires can be used. If shots are fired, we'll have to abandon the mission and return to the boat. We can't get involved in a fire fight in the middle of Krakow."

He turned to Kaz. "Where did the guard keep the cell keys?"

Kaz thought a moment. "On his belt. They dangled from it."

"Okay. The keys shouldn't be an issue. But if they've moved the professor, we'll have a problem. We have to be very quiet. We can't just walk down the hallway calling his name. It'll rouse the other prisoners."

"Aren't you going to release them?" Kaz asked. He imagined himself back in his cell waiting to be freed.

"Not if we can help it. There would be too much noise and confusion. Other guards might be alerted. The mission could fail."

"I believe we have a simple way to identify Jasinski," Agata interrupted. "The professor has written extensively about a mathematical calculation known as Pi. It's an endless series of numbers. The professor uses the first three numbers, 3.14, as a sort of pseudonym. Use those numbers to identify yourselves. If it's him, he'll respond."

Agata turned her attention to Kaz. "You'll meet the men at the back wall with a truck. The truck has a false panel in the front that Professor Jasinski can slide behind. When you close the panel, no one can detect it unless they get in the truck and inspect it closely. Tomorrow, I'll give you directions to a farmhouse near a supply depot in Radom where we'll hide the professor until more permanent arrangements can be made. If you get stopped, your papers will show that you have a permit to pick up food from the supply depot for delivery to Krakow."

She rose from her chair. "Good luck, men, and God speed."

Kaz wasn't sure about God, but he knew it was a good evening for a cat fight. He was standing by his truck and listening to two male cats screaming and spitting at each other in the darkness of a moonless night. They each wanted the other's blood. His own blood was thundering through his veins, just as it had before he'd driven his train into that ambush on the way to the rock quarries. He stared over the back wall at the ominous shape of the building where he'd been held, and he trembled, not from fear, but from the memory of the bitter cold he'd endured while imprisoned there. Half-a-dozen lights fought the shadows surrounding the buildings in the complex. As he listened, the two cats continued their turf battle. Their howling voices ricocheted among the buildings like stray bullets. He was starting to worry that the ruckus would rouse the guards when the mood changed. A low growl rose up and faded away. No one answered. The night grew quiet. A victor had been crowned.

Kaz glanced at his watch. It was nearly one o'clock. The team should be arriving any minute. He stared hard at the shadows around him and nearly cried out when one of them shifted its shape. The four men appeared before him as if by magic. They were dressed in black – shirts, pants, shoes. They were thieves of the night, and they were there to steal one of the Nazi's most prized possessions, a mathematician who could calculate the flights of rockets.

Without a word, they waited until the two sentries passed by on their hourly walk around the perimeter, then they quickly scaled the wooden barrier in the breached wall and disappeared. Kaz checked the time: 1:30. Minutes ticked past. Tens of minutes. One-fifty. Two o'clock. Two-ten. Where were they? Suddenly, a dozen prisoners scurried over the wooden barricade. When they reached the ground, they scattered in all directions. Next, the four men could be seen lifting an elderly man over the barrier. They half-carried him to the truck. Kaz could see by the sunken cheeks that it was the professor. His frying pan eyes flew around in wild abandon.

"What went wrong?" Kaz whispered in the tone of an angry parent.

"He refused to come," the lead man answered. "Kept insisting that the Nazis would kill his family. Made so much noise, he woke the other prisoners. We had no choice but to release them. I was about to clip this one on the chin when I remembered Agata's advice. As soon as I said the Pi numbers, he calmed down."

The professor whimpered something about his family, but before he could say more, one of the men clamped a hand over his mouth. Everyone froze as the two sentries swung past on their hourly rounds.

When they were gone, Kaz gripped the professor by the shoulders and looked at his face. He was relieved to see that his eyes had settled down. "Professor, we are going to take you to a safe place where you never have to help the Germans again. Then, we'll look for your family."

It was a lie. Kaz knew that his family was either in a ghetto or a concentration camp, by now. It was unlikely that they could find or save them. But he had to give the man some hope, at least until they reached the farm house. Reality would sink in later.

The men lifted the professor into the back of the truck. Kaz took his arm and guided him to the open panel. "You're going to lie down in there and not make a sound. Any noise will bring the Germans. Then, you'll return to your cell and your family will never see you again."

The man slowly nodded. "I understand. You are trying to help. And I know there is not much hope." Shoulders slumped, he stepped behind the panel with the air of someone ready to submit to his fate and lay down in the narrow space. Kaz closed the panel and hurried to say goodbye to his co-conspirators. The men dissolved into the night just as magically as they'd appeared.

Kaz wished he could drive his truck down the back streets, but he knew that would look suspicious. He drove down the main boulevards and held his breath. Charlie had given him a pistol when he left. Its weight felt comforting in the pocket of his coat, although he didn't dare use it in the city. There were far too many Germans around for that. He kept his eyes riveted for signs of trouble but saw none and rolled into the countryside unchallenged.

He was nearly halfway to the farmhouse when he spotted a road block up ahead. He cursed at his luck. It was too late to turn around. All he could do was pray that the professor would keep quiet and that he could bluff his way past the guards. He did have papers, after all.

Two soldiers waved him over to the side of the road and indicated that he should get out of the truck. Blood was rushing through the narrow canyons of his veins as he got down, just as it had during the prison break. He handed them his papers, put his hands in his coat pockets and opened his coat to show that he had nothing to hide. The index finger of his right hand curled around the trigger of his gun. If they demanded to see his coat or inspected the truck too closely, he would shoot them both right through the pocket. It would put holes in the coat, but he didn't care. One soldier looked at the documents while the other walked to the back of the truck and lifted the flaps. He shined his lantern into the truck and slowly scanned the interior. Kaz's finger tightened on the trigger. The soldier dropped the flaps and returned to where Kaz was standing. The first soldier handed Kaz his papers and indicated that he was free to go while the other raised the temporary barrier that blocked the road. Kaz hopped into the cab of the truck, his fingers sticky from the tension, and started the engine. He wanted to roar off down the road but forced himself to drive away at a more normal rate of speed.

It was dawn by the time he reached the farmhouse. Two men were waiting for him, a father and son. They helped the professor out of the truck and led him into the house. Kaz accepted their offer of coffee and a slice of bread, then hurried on his way to the supply depot, thankful to have made it through the night. The professor watched him go with wide, worried eyes. He said nothing further about his family.

Not all of Kaz's missions were so successful. He made an abortive trip up the Vistula River and rode a bicycle to Stalowa Wola where he was supposed to gain the release of a prisoner from a forced labor camp. A Pole who worked there was willing to help the underground. Kaz gave him money to bribe a camp guard to secure the prisoner's escape, but after waiting two days, it became apparent that something had gone wrong.

"The guard took the money, but the prisoner has been moved to another location. The guard refuses to give back the bribe. I can't make a fuss, or he'll turn on me."

Kaz couldn't help wondering if his contact had simply kept the money for himself. There was no way to find out. He had to abandon the mission and return to Krakow empty handed.

On another occasion, he was sent to a deserted Jewish prison camp at Sandomierz to locate a cache of money that an elderly Jew was supposed to have hidden in a hollow bedpost of a bunk bed. It was mid-winter, and when Kaz arrived, he discovered a desolate cluster of unpainted shacks surrounded by a tangle of rusted barbed wire. Before approaching the camp, he set up an observation post inside an abandoned shack a short distance away and studied the place through binoculars. A mass of footprints in the snow around the main gate area indicated that the place had only recently been evacuated. There was no chimney smoke or sign of movement. After an hour, Kaz entered the camp.

The place had been systematically gutted of anything of value. All that remained in the buildings were scraps of wood, a few shreds of clothing and remnants of cooking fires. Snow had drifted in through the broken windows. Despite the swirling breezes moving through the buildings, an odor of urine and unwashed bodies lingered in the air. It wasn't hard to imagine what a hell it must have been for those trapped there.

Kaz found remnants of bunk beds but no money. Either the prison guards had discovered it, or Agata's sources had been given bad information.

Yet, despite these setbacks the resistance flourished. The Germans demanded total submission to their draconian rule, and the Poles refused. Independent cells such as Agata's and Zdisek's sprang to life throughout Poland. Dozens of partisan groups like Simon the Red and Simon the Black sprouted in the fertile soil of rebellion and took to the forests and mountains where the Germans had to fight them on the partisans' terms. Trains were derailed. Convoys of troops ambushed. Military camps attacked. Large swaths of forests, including those near Krakow, were considered so dangerous by the Germans that they abandoned them. There was no central command or leadership directing the operations, yet everybody understood the goals: resist the enemy at every opportunity and undermine their efforts to control the country.

Chapter Twenty-two

The venerable train lurched and rocked along a section of mended rails east of Tarnow. Partisans had recently attacked a German troop train along that stretch and blown up the tracks. They had been hastily repaired, and the patched section caused the train to sway as it puffed its way through the night. Remnants of a rain storm pelted the windows, their sound drowned by the constant creaking of the rail cars. Kaz knew it was cold enough outside to numb his fingers, but inside it was surprisingly warm, due to the crowded passenger cars. More than one hundred hot, odorous bodies were jammed into a space in each car designed for half that number. The effect was over-powering, much like sitting in a room with an oven cooking soured onions and garlic. Many of the seated passengers dozed fitfully and murmured in their dreams. Those standing swayed stoically to the train's motions, hoping that a seat would become available at the next train station when some of the passengers departed.

Kaz was one of the lucky ones. He had a window seat from which he watched the hooded lights of Wonjniez station flash past in the night. For a brief moment, rivulets of rain drops on the window pane were transformed into dancing diamonds that quickly faded away. The dozing man next to him sagged against his shoulder in a familiar manner. Kaz pushed his head away with a shrug and turned his attention back to the fathomless night.

He was returning from a successful mission that involved shepherding two Jewish resistance fighters to a contact outside of Warsaw where they could join a group of like-minded partisans. Their goal was to encourage resistance in the labor camps and ghettos. Eventually, they hoped to smuggle guns into the enclaves. They would operate separately from Simon the Black's men, but they would coordinate their efforts toward their common goals. Kaz wished he could see Simon, but he knew that wasn't possible. Simon was hidden in the forests where only a handful of men could find him.

Kaz carried separate identification papers for his outbound and return journeys. His picture remained the same, but his name and profile changed. It was a new system designed by Agata to cover their travel routes in case of scrutiny at check points.

A lot had happened during the past nine months. In early June, Wawel Castle had buzzed with military activity. Officers of all ranks poured through the gates, accompanied by support personnel carrying rolled up maps, briefcases and folders. It was all Kaz and Charlie could do to keep track of the various officers and their staff. Reports from other outposts around the city told of increased troop movements, tanks loaded on trains, and squadrons of Stukas staged at nearby airports. Whole divisions rumbled through southern Poland. Something big was about to happen, and Poland was right in the middle of it. What was going on?

The answer revealed itself three weeks later when Agata made the startling announcement that the Germans had invaded Russia. With the support of its Allies -- Finland to the north and Romania, Hungary, Slovakia, Croatia and Italy to the south -- Hitler had attacked on a broad front from the Baltics to the Black Sea. One of the main corridors for this frontal assault was through Poland. Germany and its Axis allies achieved such a strong tactical surprise, they overwhelmed the Soviet army and destroyed its air force on the ground, just as they had in Poland. Germany's blitzkrieg attack proved as devastating in Russia as it had been elsewhere. Millions of Soviet soldiers were cut off from reinforcements and surrendered. German forces reached the gates of Leningrad by late September and the villages surrounding Moscow by December.

Despite these lightening quick advances, the Soviet army did not crumble. Stalin demanded that his military forces stand and fight to the last man. Deserters were shot. Resistance stiffened. The Russian army dug in. German troops were unprepared for a longer war. They ran low on food, fuel and ammunition as they outran their supply lines, leaving them vulnerable to counterattacks on their flanks. The Germans began to flounder.

Two pivotal events took place within hours of each other. Russia mounted a counterattack that broke the assault on Moscow, and halfway around the world, the Japanese bombed an American naval base on an island in the Pacific Ocean. The base was called Pearl Harbor. Within days, President Roosevelt declared war on both Japan and Germany and prepared to send troops to England.

Kaz couldn't believe the news. The Japanese had dragged the Americans kicking and screaming into the war!

A sudden lurch indicated a downshift in speed as the city of Tarnow loomed into view. Those standing were catapulted forward as they clutched wildly for handholds. Hands found what they could and feet braced against the train's unexpected motion. Iron wheels screamed on the rails; the balky train ground to a halt. The man next to Kaz lifted his head and looked around with eyes swollen from sleep. His thin hand darted to a stubbly chin that was the color of ashes. He stroked it while he tried to assess what was happening.

Kaz looked out his window. Clouds of steam pouring from beneath the train momentarily obscured his view. When it cleared, he saw the flickering lights of hand torches and heard the crunch of heavy boots on cinders. The doors at either end of the passenger car burst open. A man clad in the black uniform of the Gestapo stood in the forward doorway. His right hand gripped a pistol, his left a leash restraining a large, German shepherd. The dog bared its teeth and pulled on the leash. People in the aisles squeezed against each other in an attempt to move away from the growling animal. Those in seats cowered against their backrests. Those at the back tried to turn and leave by the other door, but a Wermacht rifleman clad in an iron helmet blocked their way. The submachine gun he held at the ready looked even more menacing than the dog.

"On your feet," the Gestapo agent shouted in Polish. "Everybody out."

He pulled the dog back from the doorway and began shoving passengers out the door. People moved reluctantly forward. Here and there a window was pushed open and a bag tossed out in a futile effort to hide contraband. Kaz was near the back, which gave him time to make a quick mental inventory of his small bag and pockets. The bag held nothing but a rain slicker and a spare pair of socks and a shirt. His pockets held a little money, his papers and his I.D. card. It was the papers that worried him. His return papers were tucked in his shirt pocket, but he still carried his outbound papers in a hidden compartment in his jacket. He was in no danger as long as the guards didn't perform a strip search, which was unusual. However, it was also unusual to stop an entire passenger train like this. If they did a thorough search, he could be in trouble. There was no time to get rid of them now. He'd have to wait for a better opportunity.

Kaz followed the others out of the car and joined a line formed loosely along a ditch. Kaz thought about dropping the papers in the grass behind him. Not a good idea, he decided. There were too many guards watching the passengers, and the papers had his picture. He couldn't let them be discovered before he was released.

A commotion two cars away grabbed everyone's attention. Guard's voices shouted over the loud roar of gunshots. Screams followed. The man next to Kaz stood tall enough to see over the other passengers. He clicked his teeth in agitation.

"What happened?" Kaz asked with alarm.

"A woman tried to roll under the rail car and escape out the other side. The guards shot her."

A partisan, Kaz thought. She didn't have the right papers, and she didn't want to be caught and tortured. He shifted his weight uneasily and reviewed his options. There seemed to be little choice but to follow orders and bide his time.

The guards prodded Kaz and the others along a loading platform and through a pair of large, sliding doors into a cavernous, lighted room that smelled of dead meat and sawdust. It appeared to be a warehouse used to store the carcasses of a slaughterhouse. Along one wall, rows of beef and pork halves hung from hooks, waiting to be processed and shipped. Metal tables gleamed beneath the meat.

The auditorium-sized building was constructed of wood, except for a ten-foot high, concrete wainscoting around the lower walls. Combined with the concrete floor, the place acted like an echo chamber. Voices caromed off the surfaces around Kaz. Chairs scraped the floor. Rough shutters covered a series of high, recessed windows that would provide light during the day. The area to the left of the sliding doors had been partitioned into an office and a conference room. Along the wall opposite the office, several Gestapo officers milled around tables as they prepared to interrogate the passengers and to review their travel documents. Lists of names lay on the tables. Kaz wondered if his real name was among them.

He looked around the room but saw no place to discard his extra travel documents. He moved to the far wall and sat on the floor under one of the recessed windows. There was a window sill five or six feet above his head. It looked like his best option. It was unlikely that his papers would be noticed there if they were lying flat on the sill. He couldn't do it now, however, not while the guards were watching. He would have to wait for a distraction.

His fellow passenger from the train sidled up next to him and sat down. "You got a handkerchief?" he asked in a low voice.

Kaz looked at the man with surprise. "Why?"

The man rubbed his stubbly chin just as he had on the train. "I need to wrap it around my hand like a bandage. To hide this." He pulled a small wad of zlotys from his pocket. "They're all I've got, and I don't want those szkopys taking them."

"Just put them in your shoe."

The man shook his head. "First place they'll look. I've seen them shake down people before."

Kaz didn't want to give up his handkerchief, but he didn't know what else to do. He reached into his back pocket and pulled it out. "Here. It's been used a little."

"All the better," the man grinned. He flattened the zlotys against the palm of his hand and wrapped the handkerchief around the hand. "Can you tie it for me?"

Kaz complied. People were starting to line up at the tables to be interviewed and to have their papers examined. He observed the process with trepidation as the first train passengers were screened. He was relieved to see them cleared without a body search. Perhaps, he could keep his other documents. No sooner had he thought this than a man was pulled aside and marched into the conference room next to the office. More followed. They were mostly younger men like Kaz. His heart rate accelerated as he watched. He knew that they were looking for partisans and would interrogate those men much more thoroughly.

The man with the zlotys stood up and moved to the line. Kaz followed him with his eyes as he stepped up to one of the tables and handed over his papers. At first, all seemed in order. The SS officer reviewed the documents without comment and seemed prepared to return them when another officer stepped forward and pointed to the handkerchief. The man explained in broken German that he'd injured himself, but the officer would not be dissuaded. He indicated that he wanted the handkerchief removed. When the man hesitated, the officer reached out and ripped the cloth from his hand. The zlotys fluttered to the floor. The man's shoulders sagged as he looked at his tormentors. His hand darted to his chin. The officer stepped around the table and struck the man across his face with a short riding whip. The man sank to his knees. The German shouted at him to pick up the money and took it from him when he was finished. He struck the man on his upper back and forced him to his feet. A guard grabbed the back of his shirt collar and marched him into the room with the other detained passengers.

Kaz silently thanked the man for his folly. It provided the diversion that he needed. All eyes were turned to the drama being played out at the table. In one, swift motion, Kaz pulled the extra papers from his jacket and laid them on the window sill above his head. He quickly walked away and joined the others in line. When his turn came, the officer reviewed his documents with great patience. He compared the photo and looked over the profile that accompanied it.

"Why are you on the train?" the officer asked in broken Polish.

"I was visiting my girl friend. I'm on my way home to Krakow."

The officer seemed satisfied, but before he could hand back Kaz's documents, the other SS officer stepped forward and indicated that Kaz should be taken to the waiting room. Kaz cursed his luck as he joined the others. He was caught in one of the German's random security sweeps and didn't know if he could escape it. The man who lost his zlotys walked over and handed Kaz his handkerchief with a shrug. Neither spoke. There was nothing to say.

More men and a few women were pushed into the room. The place was beginning to feel as hot as the train. Finally, two guards shouted at them and marched them out to lorries waiting to transport the group to an old school building near the center of Tarnow. They were led down a corridor to another large room where more tables had been set up along one wall. The doors were closed and guards posted outside.

Kaz studied the room. There were now at least a hundred people in the group. They moved about and murmured in hushed voices. No one knew what to expect. Several tall windows caught his eye. They started three feet above the floor, and he estimated their height at about ten feet. All were covered in black paint which prevented any light from entering or escaping the room.

"Those windows were painted when the Germans were bombing us. They're latched from the inside but not locked."

The voice startled Kaz. He turned to see his new acquaintance standing next to him.

"What makes you think so?"

"I used to teach in a building like this one. Same kind of windows."

"Aren't there storm windows on the outside?"

"Yes, but they're just latched like these. These windows swing in. The storm windows swing out. There's usually enough space between them for a body to squeeze in. Close the inside window, then open the storm window. That way there's no light visible. With luck, nobody will see you."

"You propose to just climb out the windows and walk away?"

The man nodded.

Kaz scratched his head. The idea intrigued him, but the downside wasn't too appealing. If he was caught, he would probably be shot. However, the upside meant escaping the prospect of a labor camp. Climbing out the windows sounded like it was worth the risk.

Kaz wandered over to the nearest window and opened the latch. Sure enough, the window swung inward. He opened it a few inches and looked behind it. He saw another latch on the outer storm window, just as the man had predicted. There were no locks. Kaz noticed two or three people nearby watching him. He quickly closed the window and returned to his fellow conspirator.

"You're right," he said in a low voice. "The only problem is, we don't know what's out there."

"We're near the street. Probably a yard area and a sidewalk."

"And a guard with a gun!"

"They'll most likely be guarding the doors. Anyway, it's pretty dark. I'm going to run around the back of the building."

The man stepped over to the window and unlatched it. Kaz looked around. The doors to the room were still closed. No guards had yet entered. He cursed under his breath, picked up his small bag and followed. He held the window ajar just enough for both of them to squeeze into the gap between it and the storm window. A few people murmured as he pulled the window shut behind him. He prayed they would keep their mouths shut until he was gone.

The man waited several seconds, then unlatched and slowly opened the storm window. "The coast is clear," he whispered.

He slipped out the window and Kaz followed. The man crouched down in the shadows next to the building. "I'm going in that direction," he whispered and took off at a low gait toward the back of the building.

Kaz took a few steps after him but stopped when he saw a dozen teenage students walking along the sidewalk leading past the front entrance. He couldn't see the entrance from his view point, but he knew that guards would be stationed there with rifles at the ready. It seemed like lunacy to consider exposing himself to those guards, but the idea of hiding in the group of students felt safer than running around the building. He made an instant decision and walked over to the group. For once, his short stature was an advantage. He blended right in. The students were laughing and talking. The boys took no notice of him as they sauntered along the pavement flirting with the girls. The guards stared at them with bored expressions as they passed.

Kaz was about to congratulate himself when voices shouted and shots rang out from the side of the building where the man had gone. The students screamed and scrambled for cover. The two guards ran around the corner of the building and disappeared.

Kaz ran with the students until he passed the front steps, then he forced himself to slow down. Two SS officers raced up the steps, but their attention was focused on the doors to the building. They ignored the students and Kaz. The doors opened, and they disappeared inside. Kaz walked away at a rapid pace. He never looked back.

Was the man dead? He assumed so. His mouth went dry when he thought how close he'd come to his own death. If those students hadn't come along, he would surely be dead, now. He wasn't, however, and he celebrated by taking in great gulps of the cold, night air. It revived him and settled his nerves. The air tasted like freedom. It was the third time he'd been incarcerated and either been released or escaped. He felt like a cat with nine lives: he had six more to go.

Chapter Twenty-three

Kaz shivered uncontrollably. He was seated, naked, on a creaking, wooden chair in a concrete hallway. The doors at either end were wide open, allowing drafts of winter air to buffet his chest, arms and legs. His feet dangled just inches off the floor. All the toes were numb, as were the fingers of his hands which were tied behind him. He tried to remember how he'd gotten there, but his mind was as numb as his toes and fingers. The corridor looked familiar. He forced himself to untangle the maze of blood vessels running through his brain and to think. The corridor reminded him of Montelupi Prison. That was it! He was back in prison, but how had he gotten there?

The brisk clip of boots echoed down the hallway behind him. He twisted his head and caught sight of a SS uniform. The officer stepped in front of him with a rubber hose which he smacked against the palm of his left hand. The man was right handed, Kaz thought stupidly. The officer shouted at him in German. Kaz shook his head to indicate he didn't understand, but that only infuriated the man more. The officer brought the hose crashing down on Kaz's shoulder. The hose was frozen.

Kaz cried out in pain and stood up. Somehow, his hands had come free, and he managed to ward off the next blow with his arm. The arm trembled as pain streaked through muscle and bone. Kaz shouted louder and prepared to attack his tormentor.

Then, he snapped awake.

He was standing beside his bed, chest heaving, his hands bunched into fists and his legs spread wide apart. Befuddled, he frantically looked around the room. The icy air was gone. In fact, his undershirt was drenched in sweat. Slowly, his breathing returned to normal. He lowered his fists and sat down on the edge of the bed.

"You okay in there? What's all the yelling about?" Charlie's voice brought him back to reality.

"I was dreaming. Had a nightmare."

"It must've been one hell of a nightmare. You were shouting." Charlie's face appeared in the doorway. "Who was after you?"

"That damn SS officer with the rubber hose. Only I was in Montelupi. At least I think I was."

Kaz worked his shoulders up and down and plucked the clammy undershirt away from his skin. He got to his feet and walked past Charlie to the kitchen. "I need a drink."

Charlie followed him. "You look like you saw a ghost. I've never seen you so white."

Kaz pulled a bottle out of the cabinet above the sink and poured himself half a glass of vodka. He took a quick drink and sat down at the table. Charlie joined him and filled two fingers of the liquor in an empty jelly glass. They sat in silence for a few moments.

"I don't like it," Kaz commented.

"Don't like what?"

"The dream ... or nightmare ... or whatever you want to call it. I think it's a bad omen." Kaz took a cigarette from the pack on the table and lit it.

"Lot's of people have crazy dreams, Kaz. That doesn't make them bad omens."

"This one felt different. That SS officer was too real. The prison corridor was too real. I've never experienced anything like that before. When I woke, I was ready to kill somebody."

Charlie rose from his chair. "I think what we need right now is some hot food. I'm tired of the sandwiches. It's pretty quiet. Let's go down to the Little Cross and get something to eat. You'll feel better with some hot borscht in your stomach. Get your coat." Charlie said this as he put on his jacket and headed for the front door. "It's my treat."

They were halfway down the stairs when they ran into George Blaszek, the apartment caretaker. George walked with a limp from a wound he'd received in the first world war and had trouble breathing. He knew Kaz and Charlie kept strange hours but never tried to pry into their affairs. They felt George was someone they could trust.

" You boys going dancing?"

Charlie laughed. "Not tonight. Just dropping by the Little Cross for a late dinner. Can we bring you something?"

George shook his head no. "You take your time. I'll keep an eye on the place."

Winter lay like a white quilt that mantled the courtyard and surrounding streets. Kaz's breath formed puffs of white clouds when he spoke. They reminded him of his beloved trains.

"Is everything stowed away properly?"

Charlie gave him a curious, sidelong glance. "Of course."

"And the panel is secured in the back bedroom? The radio equipment is safe?"

"Yes, for Christ's sake. What's wrong with you?"

"I told you, I have an uneasy feeling."

"That dream really has you spooked." He threw his arm around Kaz's shoulders. "Nothing's going to happen. Tonight is no different than any other night."

A few scattered lights twinkled in the blacked-out city, but despite the moonless night, the snow made visibility rather good. Buildings along the main thoroughfares loomed as silhouettes against the sea of white that covered everything. The city was so quiet, they could hear the nearby Vistula River sloshing against the shore. The fresh snow squeaked beneath their boots. They turned into an alley and headed for Stadum Square.

"Only a week until Christmas," Charlie mused as he looked up at the stars. "I wonder what the new year will bring."

"I just hope it's not trouble."

"You and your trouble," Charlie scoffed. "You need to relax and get drunk."

"I need to see Daneta and Edwina," Kaz announced suddenly. "I've been thinking about it for some time."

"Agata would be pretty angry."

"Agata doesn't need to know. It's my business, not hers."

"It's hers if you get caught." Anger tinged Charlie's voice.

They stopped in the shadows of a side street and waited for a German convoy to pass before they sprinted across Planty Boulevard and darted into an alley. They entered the restaurant by the back door and took a curtained table near the rear entrance. Only a dozen customers sat at scattered tables. Prior to the German invasion, the restaurant had been a favorite gathering place for Krakow's intelligentsia. Now, it served more than a few members of the underground, who often came later in the evening after the regular patrons had finished.

The menu was much more limited than it used to be, but the waiter managed to fetch them an ample amount of steaming mashed potatoes, beetroot soup and little dumplings stuffed with boiled plums. Since Kaz and Charlie were regular customers, the waiter also brought a jar of honey, and a small plate of ginger cookies, a specialty of the house. Both men piled into the food as if it were their last meal and finished everything, right down to the cookie crumbs. When the waiter returned with the check, Charlie handed him a sheaf of bills folded around a pack of Czech cigarettes.

"Your tip is inside," Charlie commented as he lit a small cigar. He knew the waiter loved Czech cigarettes.

"Thank you," the man beamed as he left the table.

The food settled Kaz's nerves considerably. The more he thought about his dream, the more stupid he felt. Charlie was right. It had just been a crazy dream.

Charlie leaned back and puffed on his cigar. "Damn good food." He belched to emphasize his statement.

Kaz was about to admonish him for his poor manners when the curtains surrounding their table suddenly opened, and George Blaszek stuck his head through them.

"Thank God I found you," he gasped as he strained to catch his breath. It was apparent that he'd been running. "You can't go back to your place. There's trouble."

Kaz straightened in his seat. "What do you mean, trouble? What kind?"

"Germans," George announced between heavy breaths. His eyes widened as he said the word, and he licked his lips. "I don't know what's going on, but they were looking for you."

"What happened?" Charlie demanded. His face was red with anger. "Tell us exactly."

George pulled his mittens off his hands and snatched the fur cap from his head, revealing wisps of white hair. "I heard a truck roar up outside. When I looked out the window, I saw soldiers running up the stairs. They went straight to your apartment and banged on the door. When you didn't answer, they took a small ax and smashed the door open. They destroyed it."

George glanced nervously behind him. "They ransacked the place. Took some things, papers mostly, and left. As soon as they were gone, I came here. I didn't dare go look in your apartment. They are surely coming back."

Charlie jumped up and grabbed George by his shoulders. "You sure you weren't followed?"

The man nodded vigorously. "I used back alleys the whole way here. Nobody saw me." He licked his lips again and shifted away from Charlie's iron grip. "What did they want? Why would they destroy the door like that?"

Charlie took George's hand and shook it. "We're not sure, but thanks for warning us. Now, you'd better return home and go about your business. Stay away from that apartment, though. You don't want to run into those Germans."

George agreed and hurried out the back door.

"Were our binoculars left out?" Kaz queried after George was gone.

"No, they were stowed away in the back room, but there were lots of time logs and notes lying around on the kitchen table. Plenty to tell them we were spying on Wawel Castle. Something or somebody gave us away. It's only a matter of time before they find that hidden room."

"We better see if Agata is safe."

"And check in. Decide what to do."

The two men rushed from the Little Cross.

The winter night may have seemed white and glistening on their way to the restaurant, but it looked dark and threatening on their return. They stood shivering in the alley across the street from Agata's apartment and watched for any sign of suspicious movement or activity. The cross street was empty. No trucks or cars were visible. After watching for nearly half an hour, they slipped across the boulevard and crept up the stairs. Charlie and Kaz both pressed their ears against the door and listened for any unusual sounds. They were greeted by silence. Kaz could wait no longer. He tapped lightly on the door. Nothing moved inside. He tapped louder, more persistently. Again, they waited. A floor board suddenly squeaked. Someone was moving through the hallway.

"Who's there?" Agata queried in a low voice.

"It's Kaz and Charlie," Kaz responded. "There's trouble."

She opened the door just wide enough to let them in, then quickly shut and locked it. A dim light shone from the living room. The black out curtains had prevented them from seeing it across the street.

"What's happened?" she asked urgently.

Kaz repeated George's story. "We haven't gone back there, but we think the safe room is still intact. George didn't see them taking anything other than our note pads and papers."

Agata thought a moment, then responded in her usual, decisive manner. "If your place has been compromised, mine is probably next." She pondered a moment. "Go back to the Little Cross. Talk to the owner, Bartek. Tell him I sent you. He'll let you stay there tonight. Zdisek and I will join you tomorrow, once we've sorted things out."

The restaurant was closed by the time they returned, but their loud knocking soon brought Bartek to the door. Once they identified themselves, he let them in and showed them to a back room with a couch and thick floor rug. They flipped a coin. Charlie got the couch, Kaz the floor.

"We've got to go back there," Charlie whispered as they both tossed and turned. "Our travel documents and new IDs are in that safe room. And money and guns. *And* the shortwave radio. Too much valuable stuff to let the Nazis get their hands on it."

"We'll discuss it with Agata tomorrow. See if she thinks it's safe."

But Agata didn't come the next day. When Kaz asked Bartek, he shrugged his shoulders. There had been no word. By nightfall, the two men were so restless, they couldn't keep out of each other's way.

"I'm going back there tonight. You with me?" Charlie asked as he paced the room.

"Hell, yes. Anything is better than sitting around here any longer."

They left by the back door and followed the familiar alleys to the safe house, where they hid across the street and watched for German guards or any activity inside their apartment. After an hour's surveillance, they slipped through the shadows to George's apartment and tapped on the door. George let them in with a nervous twitch in his right eye.

"Have the Germans been back?"Kaz asked without formalities. "Are there any guards we haven't noticed?"

"You can't see it from here in the dark, but they've boarded up the door. No one can get in. I guess they didn't want any nosy neighbors poking around in there." George's voice trembled, and he glanced toward his door. It was obvious he didn't want them there. "I haven't seen any guards."

"Damn it," Charlie exclaimed, startling both George and Kaz. "We'll have to rip those boards off."

"You would need a crow bar, and it would be much too noisy."

"Charlie thought a moment. "There's a transom above the door. Did they board that up, too?"

George scratched the wispy hairs on his head. "I don't think so. Just the door."

"Did they take anything else from the apartment?"

George shook his head. "Not that I could see."

Charlie looked at Kaz. "They'll be back tomorrow to do a more thorough search. We've got to act now. I can get through that transom if you hoist me up. I can use a chair to get back out." He turned to George."We're going to get some personal things out of there tonight. Then, we'll be gone. You won't have to worry about us anymore."

George smiled with relief.

They slipped across the courtyard and up the stairs to the apartment. Kaz gave Charlie enough of a boost to pull himself through the transom, then stamped his feet in the cold while he waited. He thought about the dream. It *had* been a warning, an omen. The more he thought about it, however, the more uncomfortable he felt. It was only a premonition, but something about the events of the past twenty-four hours didn't fit. Something wasn't right. He suddenly had an overwhelming urge to get away from there as fast as he could.

Charlie returned to the doorway. "Here's the money and forged documents," he announced as he pushed them through the transom. "The shortwave is too big. We'll have to leave it."

Kaz hurriedly gathered two rolls of money and the papers and slipped them into his coat pockets. "Get out of there, Charlie. You've done all you can." All he could think about was the frozen, rubber hose crashing down on his shoulder. The dream wouldn't leave him alone.

"I want to get some of those guns and ammunition first.. We can use them."

"Charlie, no ..." Kaz started to protest, but he was too late. His friend had disappeared back into the apartment.

The loud roar of a truck engine suddenly filled the quiet street below, followed by the appearance of a troop truck pulling up and screeching to a halt in front of the building. Soldiers jumped out the back.

"That sounds like trouble." Charlie spoke urgently through the barricaded doorway. "What's going on?"

"Soldiers. They're headed into the courtyard right now. Get out of there, Charlie."

"It's too late to use the transom. Take the back stairs to the alley. I'll see if I can get out the back window and jump."

"That's two stories."

"Never mind. Go! Now!"

Kaz saw the soldiers starting up the stairs. It was all the incentive he needed. He ran in a crouch to the back staircase and took the stairs two-at-a-time to the first floor. Voices shouted down the stairs behind him. Nails and boards screamed as a crowbar ripped off the wooden planks barricading the door. Kaz ducked into the alley and watched in horror as beams of light flashed through the back window. The soldiers were already in the apartment! Two soldiers rushed down the back stairway and spotted Charlie opening the window. Kaz shrank back in the shadows, his mind reeling in disbelief. One of the soldiers fired a warning shot into the wall below the window. Charlie stopped his efforts and stood outlined by the bouncing lights behind him. A rifle was raised. The butt of the rifle slammed into Charlie's head, and he slumped from sight.

Kaz knew that if he'd had a gun, he would have shot those two soldiers and tried to rescue Charlie, but he had no weapon other than his useless fists. He also knew that if he didn't run now, he would be discovered and join his lifelong friend in an interrogation room where that frozen hose would beat him to death. He had no choice. He had to flee.

With a silent sob, he turned, raced down the alley and disappeared around the corner. As he picked out a route back to the restaurant, questions and doubts tumbled through his mind. Had George squealed on them? No, George had done everything he could to save them. Had there been a lookout stationed where they couldn't see him? That seemed more likely. Perhaps, it was the same man who gave them up in the first place. If that was true, it had to be someone inside the resistance, but who? And why hadn't Agata met them as planned? Had she been captured? If so, where could Kaz go?

The first, feeble rays of morning sunlight touched the steeple of a nearby church. The steeple turned pink and gold. Smoke drifted into the sky from a thousand chimneys and hung in a gray pall over the awakening city. A flock of pigeons rose against the eastern sky and swung north toward the open fields beyond Wawel hill in search of a morning meal. Their wings flashed white and gray above the snow-covered roofs that defined Krakow's skyline. How peaceful everything looked just then. What a contrast to the jungle of violence he'd just escaped. How different his world was from the one facing Charlie. The nightmare had come true for his friend. He would never understand how, but it had happened.

The back door to the restaurant was unlocked, just as he and Charlie had left it. Kaz entered quietly but quickly became aware of voices coming from the dining room. He looked in and found Agata, Zdisek, and Bartek seated at a table. Agata saw Kaz's anguished expression and stood up.

"What's happened? Where's Charlie?"

Kaz could hardly pick up his feet as he stumbled toward Agata and flung his arms around her. The sobs he'd been holding inside of him finally escaped in a deluge of grief.

"The Gestapo's got him," he intoned between shuddered breaths.

Agata's shoulders sagged. She released Kaz's arms and stepped back to look at him. "You went back to the safe house."

Kaz pulled the wads of money and documents from his coat pockets and dumped them on the table. "Charlie wanted to rescue everything, but the Germans came back. He was trapped in the apartment. I barely got away." Guilt tinged his voice. "I told him to get out sooner, but he wouldn't listen."

Agata led Kaz around the table and sat him down next to her husband. She leaned into him, her olive eyes focused on his.

"Kaz, I feel as much pain as you, but I can't let it get in the way of what must be done. We're at a critical junction. Someone has betrayed us. Enough people have come and gone to give us a long list of suspects. The important thing now is damage control. Fortunately, we are compartmentalized. Our cell has been exposed, but the others haven't. That's because only Zdisek and I know about them."

Agata sat down across the table from him. She put her elbows on the table and clasped her hands in front of her. "Thanks to your quick warning, we were able to move all of our files and documents before the Gestapo came looking for us. And from the looks of what you've brought us, Charlie cleared out everything that might be used to identify you. The Germans still don't know who you are, which means you can go back into the field. Zdisek and I will have to change our identities, but once we've set up a new base of operations, we can function as we did before."

Agata's piercing gaze had its desired effect. The fog lifted from Kaz's brain. He concentrated on what she was saying. "So it's business as usual."

"Not as usual, but we are still in business." She gave Kaz her hint of a smile. "That is, if you still want to be involved."

Kaz thought about that. Was this his chance to walk away? But where would he go? What would he do? He was a fugitive. The Gestapo was looking for him. Major Schmidt was looking for him. His whole life revolved around the insurgency now, and in Charlie's absence he needed it more than ever.

"Of course I'm in," he declared.

"You can stay here for a day or two, while things are worked out." It was the first time Bartek had spoken. "You'll have to stay in the back room during business hours, but you'll be safe there."

Kaz returned his attention to Agata. "What about Christina? Someone has to notify her."

"That's already being taken care of. She'll change her identity just like you."

Kaz was thinking about Christina's emotional state of mind, while Agata was focused on more practical maters. She might be in danger, too.

"Is there any way I can contact her?"

Agata shook her head. "It would be too great a risk." She reached out and touched his hand. It was a gesture she'd used before, touching him to reassure him. "Let us deal with it."

For the next twenty-four hours, Kaz lived in limbo – sleeping and reading in the back room during the day, and wandering through the darkened restaurant at night. It gave him time to relive his life with Charlie, from their fight in the school yard when they first met, to his envy when Christina chose Charlie over him, to their adventure in blood alley, to the time they spent together spying on Wawel Castle and saving querns. He thought a lot about Daneta, as well. Despite their differences, he still felt something for her, her and Edwina. It had been a long time since he'd last seen them, and he had no idea when he could again. Not while Major Schmidt lived in the Rudnicka's house. Not while Kaz remained a fugitive. Not while the Germans controlled his country.

Agata returned the second night wearing a beige dress and a coiffure of curls. The difference in clothes and hairdo was startling. Kaz couldn't help staring at her, but she chose not to notice. They sat down at a table next to the bar and shared glasses of vodka. Agata touched her hair as if unsure what to make of it herself.

"Part of your new identity?" Kaz asked in a nervous tone of voice. He was desperate for word about Charlie.

Agata gave her hint-of-a-smile."It doesn't suit me, but I'm stuck with it, at least for now." She placed her elbows on the table and leaned forward. Kaz held his breath. He knew she had news.

"We believe Charlie is in Montelupi Prison. That's what one of our informants tells us." She saw the expression of hope on Kaz's face and pressed on before he could ask questions. "Since our successful raid there, security has been beefed up considerably. It's like a fortress, now. There's no way to mount a rescue attempt."

Memories of arctic cells and sleepless nights blurred with the frozen rubber hose from his dream. Kaz bit his lip.

"We'll keep an eye on things, but there's little we can do" She sat back and took a sip of her drink. Her olive eyes watched him intently.

"Right now, I'm just as concerned about you. You need to get back to work. It will help you with your grieving."

As always, Agata's gaze was sobering. Kaz pulled his thoughts away from Charlie and concentrated on what she was saying.

"To be safe, we want to get you out of Krakow for a while, and we need a new agent to relay vital information between Krakow and the partisans. Groups like Simon the Red. Our previous agent died recently."

Kaz nearly choked on his drink. Agata anticipated his reaction. "He wasn't killed by the Germans. He was an older fellow who lived in the Tatra Mountains. He had a heart attack. We want you to take his place. We're making arrangements with the local police to set you up as an agricultural worker who travels back and forth between towns in the mountains and Krakow. We've found a farm in the Podhale area where you can stay while we finalize things. Shouldn't take more than two or three weeks."

Kaz sat back and smiled for the first time in two days. The idea of working in the Tatra Mountains was very appealing. He wouldn't mind taking a break from Krakow. There were too many haunting memories.

"It sounds perfect."

"Good."

Kaz expected her stand up and leave, but she remained seated.

"There's one more thing." Agata hesitated, something she rarely did. Kaz sensed more unwelcome news. He watched her fiddle with her drink.

"The Nazis are taking over more of the factories. Giving ownership to Germans and throwing out the Poles. Major Schmidt has been shielding the Rudnickas, but last night, one of the other partisan cells in Krakow attacked his car and shot him. He still lives, but he's in serious condition." Agata looked Kaz square in the eyes. "Daneta and her family have been taken into custody for interrogation."

There it was, again, that terrible word: interrogation. The word echoed in his mind as he tried to grasp what Agata was saying. The word pounded in his ears. People didn't just go into interrogation. They were beaten with rubber hoses or frozen half to death. Often, they didn't return.

"And what about Edwina?" His voice croaked as he asked the question.

"We have no idea. The baby is undoubtedly in the hands of the Nazis. If Daneta is released, they will probably be reunited. If not, who knows? Perhaps an orphanage. Or an adoption by a German couple. These things happen all the time."

Kaz drank his vodka in silence. Agata had placed a cool hand of condolence on his shoulder and left. Bartek had locked up and was gone. Only shadows and a light dripping noise from the bathroom sink accompanied him through his dark thoughts. He wanted to stay, to rescue both Charlie and Daneta. He wanted to find Edwina, to steal her away from the Nazis' clutches. He wanted to join forces with Simon and sweep down from the mountains to exact revenge on Schmidt and all the Nazis. He wanted to do anything but sit in the shadows drinking vodka alone.

Chapter Twenty-four

The Tatras thrust their craggy, limestone fingers up through the fir-mantled Carpathians to form a nearly impassable barrier along Poland's southern border. Sloping northward from the base of those snow-capped peaks lay the Podhale, a rich, agricultural district that sat astride the twisting, black Dunajec River. Translated literally, Podhale meant "below the mountain meadows." The economic and cultural center of the rugged Podhale was Nowy Targ, a rural city of fifteen thousand hardy people.

Beyond Nowy Targ to the south, a single rail line twisted upward to Zakopane, a prewar mecca for winter skiers and summer hikers. However, wartime travel restrictions had long since reduced the area to its primary function – trading center for the Gorale, a handsome, mountain people whose isolated habitat and fierce fighting spirit had traditionally shielded them from invaders. Many thought of them as the "true Poles." They raised sheep and goats in remote valleys, plied the wild rivers on rude, log rafts, and traveled dusty roads in heavy, wooden carts. Gorale men wore beaded, fringed sheepskin jackets and snug, white, homespun wool trousers, split at the cuff and piped up the side with scarlet ribbon. Their rounded, black, felt hats were worn low over wild hair that bore a resemblance to the straw thatch on their cabins. They were a quiet, self-reliant people who lead a semi-nomadic life, free and proud. Visitors from America likened them to the Indians that originally inhabited so much of the United States.

The Gorale had never known serfdom, never been conquered by Huns, Tartars, Mongols or Crusaders. They had no fear of Poland's newest invader, the Nazis, and they dealt with them accordingly.

Kaz rode the train to Zakopane, where he was met by Andrew Donek, the farmer who would hide him for the next few weeks, and taken by wagon along a rutted road to his temporary home – a rustic cabin and farm in the back country on the north edge of the Podhale. There, he was greeted by Andrew's wife, Julia, a plain looking and plain spoken woman who didn't smile easily. They were both getting on in years, and the farm showed evidence of mild neglect – fallen fence posts, worn harnesses and rusted plowshares. Kaz needed to keep his mind off of his personal troubles and welcomed the chance to do some physical labor. He mended fences, repaired a leaking roof, oiled and sewed harnesses and sharpened the aging plowshares. His few weeks turned into four months, but the Doneks didn't seem to mind. They appreciated his contributions. Kaz received occasional messages from Agata to sit tight. It was taking a little longer than she had anticipated to arrange for his new job position and identification.

"The Germans seem to be taking over Polish farms," Kaz commented one night during dinner. "Aren't you worried about being thrown off your land?" He thought about the German farmers he'd seen taking control of Polish farms in other parts of the country.

"The Germans don't bother us too much. We are Gorale. If anyone tries to take our farms, we'll fight to the death." Andrew pointed in the direction of the heavy forests that began just a few miles to the south. "And we wouldn't be alone. Simon the Red lives in those forests, as you know. The Germans don't dare pursue him there, and he would come to our aid."

Julia nodded in agreement. "We tolerate the Germans. They have enough power to control the bigger cities. They have much less control over our smaller towns and farms. They take a portion of our crops to feed their men, and we put up with that. But if they ever try to take our farms, blood will flow."

Kaz smiled at the steel edge to Julia's voice. They might be an older couple with a few rotted fence posts, but their ancestors had been warriors and they would be again, if need be.

"By the way," Andrew added almost as an afterthought, "your new job assignment has been approved by the Germans. Looks like you'll be moving on."

Kaz looked up from his plate. "When?"

"Tomorrow. Somebody is coming for you in the morning."

Kaz looked around the cabin with a mild feeling of regret. He'd come to enjoy his stay there and was sorry to leave on such short notice. "It's been good getting to know you. Hope we'll meet again."

"Oh, we will," Andrew asserted. "We're one of your contacts. You'll stay here when you go to Krakow and use our shortwave radio."

Kaz chuckled. "I'll be damned. Here, I've been living with insurgents all this time and haven't known it."

Andrew gave him a sheepish grin. "We couldn't say anything until arrangements were finalized, in case something went wrong."

A lone rider on horseback approached the main cabin early the next morning, leading a second horse by its tether. "Looking for Kaz Kowinsky."

"That's me." Kaz stepped onto the porch. His body tensed. "Any news on my friend, Charlie, or my family?" Kaz had only received one message from Agata two months ago. Both Charlie and Daneta had disappeared into the bureaucratic nightmare of the German prison system. Charlie had been moved from Montelupi, but nobody knew where. It was thought that Daneta was being held at a women's prison on charges of conspiracy in the attack on Schmidt. Edwina had been whisked away to an orphanage.

"Sorry." The man shook his head. "I've just got instructions for you." He didn't introduce himself. Kaz wondered if that was an oversight or on purpose. "Mind if I come in?"

They all gathered around the kitchen table, and the rider produced a rough map of the area. "This is the road to Rabka where you'll be going. It's a half-day's journey from here. I'll guide you for the first hour. We'll meet a man from the agricultural department driving a truck with an insignia on the cab. That's the man you'll be working with. He'll drive you the rest of the way."

Kaz packed his belongings and said goodbye to the Doneks. He'd only been on a horse a few times with Charlie when they were much younger and was relieved to learn that he wouldn't have to ride the animal all the way to Rabka. He knew he would be saddle sore if he did.

They took off through fields that were already tinted pale green by sprouting wheat. Only in the deepest hollows between the rolling hills did the dark earth show through. Here and there irregular mottled stains appeared where residual water from melting snow had lain and dried, leaving a scum of hard mud crisscrossed with tiny cracks. Frogs croaked loudly in scattered ponds, and the brilliant sun warmed Kaz's back.

From time-to-time, a monstrous Krupp truck hurtled past them, the open flaps in back revealing its load of soldiers and arms headed for the Ukraine. Alternatively, empty trucks rumbled in the opposite direction to pick up more men at the military depot in Rabka. The continued assault of heavy wheels on the dirt road had pulverized its crown and turned it into a river of ankle-deep powder that billowed and swirled in the wake of each passing vehicle.

A farming village of half-a-dozen homes emerged from the dust. It wasn't big enough to be called a town or to merit a name, yet that was where they stopped. They sat far enough back from the road to avoid the worst of the dust and waited. Flies buzzed around Kaz's face and ears. Cicadas sang in the tall grass blanketing a nearby hill. Kaz found his guide with no name to be a man of few words, so he contented himself by looking at the sweeping vistas of farmland flowing in every direction from where he sat and smelling the recently turned, perfumed top soil that surrounded him. He was no farmer, but he could see that it was planting season. He pulled a container of water and a sandwich provided by the Doneks from his duffel bag.

Kaz's reverie was interrupted by the sudden appearance of a small truck which roared down the road and stopped in a swirl of dust near where they sat. A small insignia on the cab door indicated that it was the agricultural vehicle for which they were waiting. A man nearly as short as Kaz and wearing an enormous, green felt hat hopped down and waited expectantly for them to join him.

"Kaz Kowinsky?"

"I'm Kaz." He shook the man's hand.

"I'm Tolek Swiba." Tolek turned to the other man. "Thanks for bringing him. I'll take it from here."

The man nodded, tipped his hat to Kaz and departed. Kaz would never see him again or learn his name.

"We've got a ways to go, so we better get started. We can talk on the way."

The truck proved to be almost as uncomfortable as a saddle. The springs in the seat were so stiff, Kaz found himself shifting constantly in an effort to find a softer position. The engine whined as though a hive of bees had been turned loose under the hood. And the truck's suspension proved to be just as stiff as the springs under his seat. They jounced along the uneven road with the bumpy gait of a runaway horse. Kaz began to regret eating that sandwich.

After a few miles, he found himself settling into the truck's rhythm, and he was anxious to learn more about his new assignment. "What's in Rabka?"

"An agricultural research center that I run." Tolek swerved to avoid a pot hole. "The Germans want to get more production out of the farmers' fields. My task has been to develop new methods to increase crop yields by providing better irrigation, controlling harmful insects and using improved fertilizers."

Kaz braced for a bump in the road. "But I don't know anything about farming. How am I supposed to help?"

Tolek laughed. "The Germans overseeing my work don't know a damned thing either. All you need to do is look like you know what you're doing. *Your* job is to pass information back and forth between the partisans hiding in the mountains around here and Krakow.

Tolek drove for a few minutes in silence while he negotiated a particularly rough section of road. "My research is ongoing, but where I need help is teaching the farmers these new methods. I'm setting up meeting sites in villages and towns, and I've produced a simple pamphlet that explains what I'm doing." Tolek slowed as a large Krupp truck filled with soldiers rolled past in a storm of swirling dust. "I'll train you in the methods I've developed. Nothing too complicated. Just enough so you can answer basic questions the farmers will have. Then, you'll drive from farm to farm and invite the farmers to come to one of my meetings where I'll show them how to increase their crop yields. 'Invite' is a polite way of telling them that the Germans expect them to attend."

"So, I'll be running around talking to farmers, but what I'll really be doing is passing messages. How will I do that?"

"We've set up a few drop points. The Doneks are one. They have a shortwave radio that will allow you to communicate with Krakow. Others include dead drops: a loose brick in a wall or a knot that can be removed from a hole in a tree trunk. That sort of thing. And once a month, you'll deliver a report to the Germans at the agricultural office in Krakow. It's the perfect setup. You'll have complete freedom of movement and will be able to operate right under the Germans' noses without them suspecting a thing."

Kaz smiled at the idea. "Sounds perfect. I like thumbing my nose at the Germans."

Tolek laughed. Kaz liked his easy laugh. "One more thing. We told the Germans that you're my brother. We have new documents for you … for Kaz Swiba." Tolek laughed again. Kaz joined him.

By the time they reached Rabka, the sun was well past its zenith and hurtling toward the distant horizon. It wouldn't be long before dusk settled over the city. They came to a stop in front of a rambling building attached to several acres of hot houses filled with corn, wheat, potatoes and other crops.

"The hot houses let me work year 'round. Now that spring is here, I'll be using the open fields out back a lot more." Tolek led the way into the building. "Before we get settled, let me introduce you to Wilk."

He opened the back door and was greeted by a large wolfhound who pulled at the end of a tied rope and growled uncertainly at Kaz. His eyes smoldered with grey-green fire. He had a regal head and black, silky fur that shaded to silver along his sides and went grey-white under his belly.

When Kaz raised his hand to waist level, the dog's ears went back, his tail dropped, his eyes narrowed and his growl increased in intensity. He faced Kaz boldly, ready to defend himself.

"Looks like he's been abused."

"Not by me, but I think you're right. I got him off a German soldier for two bottles of vodka. The German claimed he found him running loose on the Russian frontier during a recent battle. He had explosives taped around him."

Kaz lowered his hand and stepped a little closer. "Explosives? Why?"

"We think he was an anti-tank dog. The Russians trained them to run under tanks by tossing food under them. Pretty soon, the dogs would run under any tank they saw looking for food. When an enemy tank approached, the Russians strapped explosives to the dogs, set timers and let the dogs loose. They would run under the tank and blow it up. I guess the timer didn't work on Wilk, so he survived."

"That's a hell of a story. I can't imagine treating a dog like that." Wilk continued to growl as Kaz got closer.

"Here, give him this." Tolek tossed Kaz a piece of sausage. "You feed him, he'll love you forever."

Kaz got down on his haunches and reached out with the meat held by the tips of his fingers. "You sure he will only take the meat?"

"Yeah, he's pretty careful about that."

Sure enough, the dog stretched out his long mouth and snatched the sausage cleanly from Kaz's fingers. "He's quick."

Tolek strolled over and ruffled his fur. "Stick out your hand and let him sniff it."

Kaz extended his hand, fingers lowered, and took a breath as Wilk continued to growl. After a moment's hesitation, however, the dog sniffed his fingers and licked Kaz's hand.

"He can still smell the sausage," Tolek laughed. "You just made a friend for life."

During the next two months, Kaz settled into his routine, traveling through the countryside and calling on farmers. He passed messages through the dead drops and twice spent a night at the Donek's farm where he used the shortwave radio to send coded messages. One of his clandestine recipients was Willard, who now operated a new shortwave from an undisclosed location in Krakow. Kaz was glad to know that Willard hadn't been caught as a result of the raid on the apartment.

Kaz also made two trips to Krakow to deliver reports to the German Agricultural Command Center. He didn't see Agata on the first trip, but received a message prior to his second one to meet her at the Little Cross restaurant. Unsettling memories washed over him as he entered the poorly lighted establishment. The low light was designed to keep identities as private as possible. Kaz recognized Agata by her curls. She was slowly sipping a cup of coffee in a corner booth.

"Why meet here?" he asked after he had slid into the booth opposite her and exchanged greetings. "Isn't this too public?"

"The informer didn't know about this place. So, we decided to keep using it. It makes an excellent contact point. It's off the main streets and small enough to avoid attracting attention. We maintain surveillance in the area to make sure no Germans come sniffing about."

Agata gazed at Kaz with her hypnotic, olive eyes. "We caught the informant, by the way. It was a visitor from Warsaw. He was compromised by the Germans over some stupid theft where he worked. We let him lead us to his German contact in Krakow and killed them both."

Kaz found the news comforting, although it couldn't assuage the burning pain in his stomach. "Still no word on Charlie?"

"No. We think he's been sent to a labor camp, but we don't know for certain. We don't even know if he's alive or dead."

"And Daneta?" He held his breath.

"Still in the women's prison. We do know that she's been moved into a section used for long-term prisoners. It doesn't look like they are going to release her anytime soon." It was a stark comment that shook Kaz's soul. The pain in his stomach burned hotter. He'd always admired Daneta's spirit, but he didn't know how she would survive in a place like that.

"I guess there's no way to get to her." It was a question, a desperate one, but he said the words in a flat tone that suggested he already knew the answer.

Agata shook her head decisively, which made her curls bounce. "And there's no sign of your daughter. We can't find her in the orphanages. That doesn't mean she's not there. We have very few resources in those places."

"But if Daneta's considered a prisoner, not just a suspect being interrogated, then Edwina might be given to a German family," Kaz muttered to himself.

"That's possible," Agata agreed.

Kaz blinked. Even the low light in the restaurant was suddenly too bright. He had promised himself to take care of Edwina, but he'd failed. The prospects of ever seeing her again were dimming day-by-day.

Agata set her coffee cup on the table. She was suddenly all business. "We haven't much time. I have schedules for three troop trains headed for the Ukraine over the next week. Germany is trying to bolster its forces. If we can interrupt those trains, it'll hurt the Germans' efforts in Russia."

Kaz tore his thoughts away from prison cells and children's homes. It was time to go to work.

Whenever Kaz returned to the agricultural research station, Wilk was there, waiting to raise his spirits. The dog was capable of acrobatic feats that would have made him a star in any circus. One of his most amazing stunts involved his leaping ability. Tolek had built a six-foot, wire fence enclosure attached to the main building where Wilk could greet visitors with his fierce growl but couldn't harm anyone. Tolek only put him there when he was too busy to keep track of him. Wilk was content to sit behind his barrier and survey the world, that is until Kaz arrived. Wilk would start barking, stand up and in a single bound, clear the fence. Then he would attack Kaz in a tail-wagging, tongue-licking frenzy. Kaz laughed heartily at the welcome. He could never understand how the dog could jump so high from a standing start, and why he never bothered to do so except when he came home.

"Kaz, you should take Wilk with you on some of your day trips," Tolek suggested. He loves to ride in the truck, and he pines for you when you're gone too long."

Kaz ruffled the dog behind his ears. "That's a good idea. I could use some company."

Tolek's smile disappeared behind a more serious expression. "I had a visitor today. A SS officer."

Kaz snapped to attention. "Not a Major Schmidt."

"No, no." Tolek could see the fear in Kaz's face. "This man was named Schneider. But he's snooping around. Asked a lot of questions about our station here and your work with the farmers. Looking for partisan activity, I suspect. I got the impression he might know something. You better be careful."

"Always am, but I'll take extra precautions."

Two days later, Kaz decided to take Wilk on his run. Wilk sat in the front seat next to Kaz and stuck his head out the open window, his eyes narrowed and his fur flying away from his face as the wind from the moving truck greeted him. Kaz's first stop was a dead drop in a stone wall next to a small, wooden bridge that spanned a creek running past a nearby farmhouse. He'd already called on the farmer on a previous visit, so he saw no reason to bother him today. He looked around carefully as he pulled to a stop a hundred meters past the wall on the opposite side of the road. When he was satisfied that nothing was amiss, he put Wilk on a rope leash and got out of the truck. As he started to wander down the road past the farmhouse, Wilk tensed and rumbled a low growl. The dog's ears sprang up and his tail dropped, all signs that something troubled him. Kaz looked at the thick bushes ahead of him, then bent down to tighten a shoe lace while he glanced toward the wall. He'd developed his own system to warn him if anyone had tampered with a drop. Each drop was different. In this case, he always turned the stone covering the drop two inches off center so that a small crack was visible. It only took an instant for him to see that the stone was fitted tightly into the wall. The crack was gone.

A blood vessel in his neck began to throb. All the muscles in his back tightened. He rubbed Wilk under his chin and slowly stood up. His instinct was to get back in the truck and drive away as quickly as possible, but he realized that would only confirm his guilt. If someone was watching him, he had to do something that seemed normal. So, he walked Wilk a little further, then returned to the truck. He put Wilk in the cab and rolled up the widows. Lastly, he took a folder of papers and headed back to the farm house.

The farmer's wife answered his knock almost at once. Kaz realized that she'd been watching the whole charade. He forgot her name, but he remembered her blushing face and lively smile.

"Hi. I told your husband I would drop off a paper about irrigation. Is he here?"

"He's in town getting supplies. Come in."

She waved him in with her hand and closed the door the moment he was inside. "There's a couple of Germans over in those bushes watching my house," she exclaimed. Fear creased the corners of her eyes.

"I thought so. My dog warned me."

"What do they want? I was about to saddle a horse and go find my husband."

"Don't do that. They're looking for me, not you."

"Because you hide things in that wall down by the creek. I've seen you."

Kaz hesitated, uncertain what to say. He knew that his face must be reflecting the surprise he felt at her revelation. He had always thought he was being very discreet, but it was obvious that he wasn't as clever as he thought. After a moment's pause, he realized that he had little choice but to trust her. He nodded.

"For the partisans." It was a statement, not a question.

"For the partisans."

"Well, I wish you would throw those damn Germans out of our country. I'm sick and tired of having them here."

"We're trying," he said with a relieved smile.

Her face remained creased with worry, but her eyes brightened. "Well, I'm glad you're doing something."

He was about to hand her a pamphlet on irrigation techniques when Wilk started barking. Kaz ran to the window and looked through the curtains.

"The Germans are coming." He whirled around and raced back to the woman. "Do exactly what I tell you. Unbutton your blouse."

The woman looked at Kaz, horrified. She stood still. Kaz reached out and quickly released the first three buttons on her blouse while she tried to swat his hand away. Footsteps pounded up the three steps onto the wooden porch.

"There's no time." Kaz jammed his right hand under her blouse and grasped her breast. She wanted to cry out, but Kaz had already snaked his left arm around her waist and pulled her to him in a tight embrace. Then, he pressed his lips against hers in a passionate kiss just as two soldiers and a SS officer burst into the room.

Kaz and the woman jumped back from each other in a haze of hot breaths and disheveled hair. Her chest rose and fell as she tried to compose herself. Her right hand flew to her partially exposed breast and shoved it out of sight while her left hand fumbled with a button.

The SS officer was about to shout an order at them, but when he saw the scene, his mouth turned up in a knowing smile.

"What have we here?" he mused.

Kaz looked down at his feet, abashed. "Nothing, sir. I was just dropping off a pamphlet that I'd promised."

"About what, lechery?" he demanded with a smirk.

Kaz caught the woman's eye and was relieved to see recognition in her face. She understood what he'd done and why.

"No sir. It was just something that came over me. It was my fault, not hers." He sounded contrite, but he winked at the SS officer as he spoke.

"What *is* your business here?" The officer's tone became official.

Kaz showed his ID and pamphlets and told him about the work to increase farm production. It was obvious from the officer's smirk that he was less interested in Kaz's explanation and more interested in the farmer's wife. He stared at her with such a frank assessment, Kaz feared that the officer might tell Kaz to leave so that he could sample the goods for himself. He returned Kaz's documents, instead, and indicated to the soldiers that it was time to go.

"Please forgive my behavior," Kaz pleaded as soon as the Germans were gone. "I was thinking fast and didn't know what else to do. I hope your husband will understand."

"I'll certainly tell him about the Germans, but perhaps I'll skip some of the details." She straightened her blouse as she spoke. "Sometimes marriages work best when a few things are left unspoken. He does have a shotgun and a temper."

"I'll leave that to your judgement, but I sure would appreciate it if you could avoid the part about the shotgun." He said this with a weak smile. "I'll try not to bother you again."

Kaz hurried to his truck without a glance at the wall and drove away as quickly as he dared. The Germans were nowhere to be seen, but he feared they might still be watching. As soon as it was safe, he turned down a back road and headed in the direction of the station. He rubbed Wilk's head as he drove.

"Wilk, you just earned your weight in sausages."

"We've got trouble," Kaz announced to Tolek without preamble. He described what had just happened.

"Damn. I knew it the minute that SS officer showed up here. Our cover's been blown." Tolek thought a moment. "We'll need to change our base of operation. Look, the monthly report is almost done. I'll finish it tonight, and you can take it to Krakow tomorrow. I'll work on options while you warn Agata."

Normally, Kas would have stopped at the Donek farm to use the shortwave and to rest overnight before continuing, but he and Tolek agreed it would be safer to skip that leg of the journey and to make a run straight to Krakow. It was late by the time he arrived, and he was exhausted from the long, dusty drive. He drove to the Little Cross, parked the truck in the alley and slipped in the back door. He signaled to Bartek and collapsed at a corner table. Only a handful of people were eating at that hour. The cooking odors reminded Kaz that he hadn't even thought about food all day. His stomach complained loudly at the oversight.

Bartek seemed to read his mind. He threw together a plate of beef and potatoes, grabbed a bottle of vodka and two glasses and joined him.

"Our cover is blown," Kaz said as he piled into the plate of food. "I've got to warn Agata."

"I'll get word to her at once. Why don't you use the backroom tonight? The place is about ready to empty out, and I know Agata will want to see you." He poured two glasses of vodka and slid one across the table to Kaz, who gulped it down.

"That would be great." He waited until everybody had gone, then settled into the familiar room. In bed, his mind returned to the day's events, to how lucky he'd been and how Wilk had saved him. When he thought about grasping the farmer's wife's breast, he chuckled. It hadn't been a bad ploy. Perhaps, he could use it again sometime.

When Kaz stumbled out early the next morning in search of coffee, he was greeted by Agata's olive eyes. The effect was startling. It snapped him awake, but he still poured coffee into a large mug before he joined her at a table.

"Tell me what happened."

Kaz described the SS officer and the stakeout at the dead drop. Agata agreed that they should move their operation to a new location. Tolek would know what to do. She had news as well. The Russians had turned the tide and were pushing the Germans out of their country. And America was sending troops and armaments to Great Britain. It was only a matter of time before they invaded Europe. She withheld the most damaging news until last. It was the kind of news one dreaded and never anticipated, the kind of news that would haunt Kaz for the rest of his life.

Daneta had died of pneumonia in prison.

Chapter Twenty-five

There was a mild buzz in Kaz's ears that wouldn't go away. It started the morning Agata told him about Daneta. A month had passed since then. Tolek had arranged for a new operation in animal husbandry centered in Nowy Targ. It was a bigger operation than the experimental crop program in Rabka. Their job was to manage the inventory of livestock owned by the farmers in the Podhale district. The Germans wanted to keep their thumb on the farmers and to prevent them from sharing their hogs, chickens and cattle with the partisans. Their new task didn't make Kaz or Tolek very popular with the peasants and landowners, but Tolek quickly devised a bookkeeping system that allowed the farmers to hide a few wayward animals. It also didn't take them long to realize that Kaz and Tolek were working with the partisans, not against them. Distrust melted away, and Kaz was able to set up a new network to pass messages, including a shortwave radio hidden in a farmer's barn.

Tolek reported to a German officer by the outlandish name of Herr Krieslandwirt, whose stomach and posterior were almost as wide as his title. Kaz quickly nicknamed him Kaiser behind his back, and Tolek concurred. The man had little knowledge of animal husbandry or accounting, but he was meticulous in his record keeping. Tolek knew that he was not to be taken lightly. His primary responsibility was to audit Tolek's books and to make decisions about which animals should be retained by the farmers and which would be slaughtered. As with other agricultural programs, Herr Kaiser's goal was to leave enough livestock to allow for adequate breeding and to keep the peasants from starving. The bulk of the food went to feed the German army. However, Tolek's bookkeeping system hid enough inventory to leave a little extra for the farmers and for the partisans. It was, in effect, a black market taking place right under the Germans' noses.

Kaz threw himself into his work, but none of his efforts could ease his depression or stop the buzzing in his head. It reminded him constantly of Daneta and Edwina. Twice, Kaz managed to forward inquiries to Krakow regarding his daughter, but there was no new information. Edwina had disappeared completely. The likelihood that his daughter was in an orphanage declined with each passing day. That left only one possibility. Edwina had been adopted, stolen from Kaz's life without a trace. The idea that he would never see Daneta or his daughter again overwhelmed him with grief. It hollowed out his will to live. The only way he could cope was to go about his business and let his survivor instincts take over. He rarely smiled, and he distanced himself from those around him. Even Wilk sensed his loss and tried to comfort him. Kaz ruffled his hair, but he couldn't cope with emotions or pity, not even from a dog. He just wanted to be left alone.

The livestock office occupied half of the first floor of an old, three-story, red-brick building that fronted on Nowy Targ's famous market square. Tall windows along the west wall overlooked Szaflary Street and provided a ringside seat for the passing parade of life in the city, including one of the world's most unusual, historic fairs. By four o'clock on market days, farm wagons loaded with produce from every corner of the Podhale creaked along the cobbled streets and took up stations around the square. Every available space around the old brownstone town hall in the center of the square was filled, and the overflow of traders choked the side streets. The place was a bedlam of bartering amid rows of animals, coops of fowl, piles of vegetables, sacks of grain, heaps of clothing, cheese, flowers, fruits, trinkets, and wagon loads of rock salt hauled all the way from the Wieliczka mines.

The presence of so many transients made Nowy Targ the perfect meeting place for the partisans who hid and operated in the Tatra Mountains. Here, a man could move among the throngs of buyers and sellers, meet friends, exchange information and pick up the black market goods arranged by Tolek and Kaz without being noticed. Nowy Targ was also less than fifteen miles by mountain trail from the Czech border, which made it an ideal location for smuggling refugees out of the country, especially Jews.

Sometimes, the partisans would intercept one of the supply trains headed from Nowy Targ to Krakow. Schedules of these trains were kept secret, but Kaz and Tolek always knew when one was about to depart. Activity would intensify around the loading docks: milk containers stacked, sides of beef bundled, bags of grain piled. Kaz would send word to the partisans, and the train would be ambushed. They only struck every third or fourth train, enough to keep them in supplies, but not enough to raise suspicions. The train's guards had the good sense to throw down their weapons and hide in the underbrush while the robbery was in progress. The guards were badly outnumbered, and the partisans had a fierce reputation. If the guards resisted, they knew that snipers firing from the surrounding hillsides would wipe them out.

Eventually, the German army ran out of patience and sent troops to capture or kill the partisans. Each time, a warning would be forwarded to the livestock office and the partisans notified. They would disperse and hide until the Germans called off the search. Farmers kept them informed of the troops' movements via the message network run by Kaz. Many picked up hoes and joined the peasants in the farmers' fields. Others simply melted away into the unforgiving terrain. After a week of fruitless searching, the troops would leave. Once they were gone, the partisans retrieved their weapons and contraband from caches dug into the steep hillsides and covered by tangles of brush and were on their way. Ferreting them out, especially when they knew the Germans' every move, was about as successful as capturing flees in a dog kennel. The partisans could disappear in one location and reappear in another so effortlessly, the Germans were kept in a constant state of confusion and frustration.

Kaz no longer made regular runs to Krakow. He moved back and forth between the central office and a new sub-station in the mountains east of Nowy Targ. The sub-station was located near a small village and allowed Kaz to reach the farmers in the outlying areas. The journey from Nowy Targ was made by horseback with a heavily-laden pack animal in tow, following the road to Czorsztyn. From there, he set off on a secondary trail through a winding mountain pass.

His objective was a cottage perched high atop a fir-covered slope overlooking the lands of Czorsztyn Castle which lay in ruins in the valley below. Upon arrival, Kaz ducked beneath a wild rose vine that crept around the edges of the cottage's front door and entered the cottage. Low ceilings framed a main room built from stone, kitchen, parlor, dining area and two bedrooms. The small windows in the main room commanded an inspiring view of a canyon that had been carved by the Dunajec River sweeping down from the Tatras. On the far side stood the castle ruins, which marked the border with Czechoslovakia and guarded a trail used by traders from the east for more than a thousand years. Czorsztyn's rulers had once grown rich extracting tribute from wealthy merchants who passed there on the way to Krakow with treasures from the orient. On the near side of the canyon stood the grand villa of Czorsztyn's current owner, Drochojewski, the last remaining descendant of the noble Polish family of that name. The villa was reported to have enough rooms to entertain a hundred guests, a great ballroom and a theater where operas and plays were performed. Drochojewski, now an old man, would hire troops of traveling musicians and actors and invite wealthy families to attend. Guests were met at the train station in Nowy Targ and transported by carriage to the villa, where they were entertained and dined for a week at a time. That all ended when the Germans arrived, but Drochojewski still clung to the remnants of the family's traditional way of life. He kept highly spirited horses, supervised the fermenting of fine wines from grapes of his own vineyards and, when he could find a worthy opponent, played a crafty game of chess.

On his first trip, Kaz spent two weeks calling on farmers and gathering intelligence from the partisans to pass along to Krakow. Kaz relished the days he spent outdoors in the mountains and his evenings in the solitude of the cottage. It was the catharsis he so badly needed to calm the turmoil inside his head. Slowly, the buzzing faded, and he heard the sounds of life once more. The Tatras became his wellspring; they gave him the will to move on with his life.

He was sorry to leave and looked forward to returning. He was packing up on his last afternoon in preparation for his horse ride back to Nowy Targ when he was surprised by a knock on his door. He opened it to find a peasant standing there in baggy pants and wrinkled shirt. The peasant introduced himself and presented Kaz with a handwritten invitation for dinner that evening at the Drochojewski villa. Puzzled, he dressed in his cleanest set of clothing and rode his horse down a narrow trail past rows of meticulously cultivated grape vines to the villa. A livery man took his horse when he dismounted and led it away to the stables. The villa, painted white with a red, tile roof, stood three stories high and spread out on both sides of the main entrance with the grace of butterfly wings. He walked under the portico, grasped a large, round door knocker and gave it a solid rap. The knocker emitted a musical, metallic ring.

The door was promptly opened by a tall, bony woman whose regular features were slightly impaired by a pair of protruding front teeth.

"My name is Kaz Swiba," Kaz said, using his assumed name. He handed her the invitation.

"Please come in." She led him across a marbled entryway to a large study with a massive fireplace, above which hung a large, coat-of-arms announcing the Drochojewski legacy. Paneled walls framed immense paintings of long ago battles and the posed figures of men Kaz assumed were Czorsztyn ancestors. Heat from the fireplace radiated to all corners of the room, but not so the light. Shadows hid features that he could not see.

An elderly man with a mane of gray hair and thick glasses hobbled into view with the aid of an elaborately carved, wooden cane. He was impeccably dressed in woolen slacks, a silk, white shirt open at the collar and a dinner jacket "Welcome, Mr. Swiba. Please join us in my study."

It took Kaz a moment to realize that there was another man seated in the room. His face was hidden in shadow, but Kaz instantly recognized him by his shock of red hair.

"Hello again, friend." The warm voice was as familiar as the hair.

Kaz stepped forward and shook his hand. "What a pleasant surprise." He glanced around at his host in confusion. "How do you know each other?"

"We have known each other for many years," Drochojewski replied. "Simon comes from a prominent family. Now, we work together, doing all we can to disrupt the Germans." He poured a glass of red wine in a hand-blown crystal glass and handed it to Kaz. "This is from my vineyards, a fine Cabernet. I hope you will enjoy it."

Kaz had never been much of a wine drinker, but he had to admit that it tasted very smooth. "I had no idea you were involved with the partisans. No word has reached us in Nowy Targ. Or here, for that matter."

His host smiled broadly, as if he was about to wink. "I prefer to keep a very low profile. The Germans pretty much leave me alone up here. This is partisan country, after all. But I maintain a reputation of impartiality which sits well with our unwanted guests. I profess to prefer my horses and vineyards, and they seem to respect my social standing. It makes the perfect cover to aid Simon and his men." He swirled the wine in his glass with a deft touch and took a dip. "And I've had my eye on you and your associate since you arrived last month. I was hesitant to approach you, but Simon convinced me that you were safe. He has told me about some of your exploits. We can use your help."

Kaz lowered his eyes modestly. "I've always stood ready to do what I can for the resistance."

"And you have lost a good friend in the process."

Kaz was startled by the comment. "You know about Charlie?"

Drochojewski gazed at Kaz with sad eyes. "I know a great many things, including what happens to our compatriots. Charlie was interrogated at Montelupi Prison, then we believe he was shipped to Auschwitz. There is no coming back from there."

Kaz's heart sank at the news. An image of Charlie's mischievous smile swam before his eyes. "We suspected as much, but we didn't want to give up hope."

"Hope is a luxury we're not allowed, I'm afraid, but come." He put his free hand on Kaz's shoulder and guided him toward the dining room. "We shall discuss important matters over dinner.

They sat down to a dinner of fresh salad, rare, T-bone steak, baked potatoes and green beans. Kaz had not eaten so well in years. While they ate, Simon shared a few stories about recent raids and efforts to smuggle Jews into Czechoslovakia. Drochojewski waited until they were nearly finished with dinner before he got down to business.

"The Germans have been pushed out of Russia and the British are bombing the western part of Germany. It's only a matter of time before the Americans invade from England." He cut a slice of his steak as he spoke. "Yet, the Germans continue to put pressure on Poland. There is a new program called recolonization that is evicting Polish peasants from their farms and villages and relocating them. Many are being shipped to Germany to support the war effort. Others are being sent to labor camps. It's estimated that forty or fifty thousand people have already been affected, and the Germans are nowhere near finished."

"We believe the German program may be headed our way," Simon interjected. "There are growing troop movements nearby, and trains with empty boxcars are being staged in Krakow. Those trains could be in Nowy Targ in less than two days."

Kaz sat back in his chair. Just when he thought he'd found peace, he was reminded of the war. There was no escaping it, not even in these pristine mountains. "How can Tolek and I help?"

Drochojewski set down his knife and fork and leaned toward Kaz. "We need your eyes and ears in Nowy Targ. If they plan to invade us, there will be a buildup of forces: soldiers, weapons, supplies, troop movements, train activity. We need accurate accounts of all their operations. I will set up a message link with you, so you can forward this information to me. I, in turn, will see that it gets to Simon. Can you help us?"

"Hell yes," Kaz exclaimed. Drochojewski's request filled him with a new sense of urgency. The prospect of working with Simon, again, energized him. And he found the odd man seated before him inspiring. "What will you do with the information?"

"Resist," Simon said bluntly. "Ambush their troops. Sabotage their trains. These are our mountains. Our land. We have always stopped them here. We'll do so this time, as well."

Kaz left the villa with a new resolve. He would do everything in his power to prevent the Germans from succeeding in their nefarious plan. He would take up a gun if necessary. He owed it to Charlie.

No sooner had Kaz's life found its footing than it turned an unexpected corner. He had just returned from his sojourn in the mountains and was telling Tolek about his unexpected meeting with Drochojewski and Simon the Red. They were seated at the table eating sandwiches. The food reminded him of his recent banquet at the villa, and his mouth watered.

"Kaz, I think you ought to take charge of that operation, with my full support, of course. You know Simon, and it sounds like you've made a good contact with this Drochojewski fellow."

"I'd like that. I want to do everything I can to help Simon and his men."

"There's one more thing," Tolek continued. "Our operation just got bigger. In addition to the livestock and poultry, we now have to tally grain crops, hay and dairy products. So, we've arranged for another worker, also a partisan supporter. She originally came from Krakow." Tolek paused while he took another bite of his sandwich. Kaz waited expectantly. "You may know her: Christina Nowak."

The name struck Kaz with the force of a thunderbolt. Christina's oval face and slightly flared nose surfaced from his memories in a shower of sparklers. It was as if a ghost had suddenly inhabited his body. His skin tingled as though he'd been caught in a snowfall. Christina was coming to Nowy Targ!

"When?" His voice echoed in his ears.

"Tomorrow. I'm to pick her up at the train station at noon."

Kaz's heart pounded against his rib cage so loudly, he could barely think. "Let me do that. She's an old friend."

Tolek appraised Kaz's eager response. "I don't recall you mentioning her to me."

"Last time I saw her was before Charlie disappeared. It's been awhile."

"Fine by me. God knows, I've got enough to do around here."

Kaz was all fingers and toes the next morning as he left an hour early for the train station. Tolek watched him go with a chuckle. "The train's never early, only late." Kaz ignored him.

True to Tolek's word, the train was an hour late, which gave Kaz ample time to pace the platform and mull over his response to Christina's unexpected arrival. It was clear by his reaction that something was going on, but what? He'd just lost Daneta and Edwina, and he still grieved for them. Yet, the prospect of seeing Christina again left him breathless. Did his feelings for her really run that deep, or was she simply a ghost of memories past? The questions bounced around in his head. He had no answers.

At last, the train chugged into the station in a white cloud of steam. Kaz watched expectantly as people began to climb down the metal steps to the platform He felt a moment of panic that she wouldn't appear or that he wouldn't recognize her. But recognize her he did. She strode purposely along the platform among the other passengers with a small suitcase in her hand. When she spied Kaz, she hurried to him and dropped the luggage. They greeted each other in a tangle of arms and hugs, neither saying a word.

"I'm so glad you're here, Kaz," she breathed, at last, when she stepped back and looked at him. A winsome smile briefly pushed aside her serious expression, then retreated. "We've both lost so much." She searched his eyes with hers.

Her comment reminded him of his recent conversation with Drochojewski. "The news about Charlie isn't good," he said quietly.

"No, it isn't." Christina's serious expression deepened into despair. "There's really no hope left. Once he left Montelupi, things were decided. He was either sent to a labor camp or Auschwitz. Either way, he isn't coming back."

Kaz didn't bother to respond. There was nothing that he could add. He became aware of a hissing sound emitted from the train's engine and the crush of passengers. He could smell the warmth of their bodies as they poured around him. Eager voices greeted one another. Trains were the vehicles of happy arrivals but, also, sad departures. Kaz was feeling both at that moment.

"Come on." He picked up Christina's suitcase and inspected it. "Not very big."

"I travel light these days."

"Well, hopefully, you won't need to travel again for awhile. Let's get you to your new home."

Wilk greeted Kaz with his usual enthusiasm, then turned his attention to Christina. Normally, he would have growled and approached her with suspicion, but he seemed to understand that she was Kaz's friend. After a brief inspection and sniffing process, he stopped in front of her and raised his tail in a sign of acceptance.

Tolek welcomed her aboard with enthusiasm. "We need the help." He looked inquisitively at the two of them, trying to read their body language. Kaz could tell that Tolek was dying to learn more about their previous relationship, but he was in no mood to disclose anything further at that time.

After Christina had a chance to settle into her new quarters, they gathered for coffee while Tolek outlined areas of responsibility. He and Kaz would continue to manage the livestock. Christina would handle the crops and dairy products. Their conversation grew quieter when they discussed the partisans. Herr Kaiser was gone for the day, but it was always wise to assume that other ears were listening. Kaz explained the black market at the Nowy Targ market place and the raids on supply trains.

Christina nodded with approval. "We ran similar operations in the forests around Warsaw."

Later that evening, she joined Kaz and on the porch and stared at the Milky Way. A quarter moon hung just above the trees. It threw a soft light over the world around them. "We used to do this at the orphanage."

"A lot's happened since then."

"More than you know," she sighed. "My life has not turned out as I expected."

"How do you mean?"

"Oh, lots of things." She scraped at the floorboards with the heel of her shoe. "I wanted to go to the university. Read literature. Become a writer. I also expected to get married and have children."

"With Charlie." Kaz tried to hide the jealous tone in his voice. He didn't know if he succeeded.

She shook her head. "No, not really. Charlie was a brilliant comet in my life, I loved him, but he wasn't necessarily the man I expected to settle down with for life. He was too reckless." She paused as she considered her comment. "It's funny. I always thought of you as the daredevil, yet it was Charlie who ended up taking the most risks after the war started. It was his reckless behavior that finally got him caught."

A cloak of silence hung over them. Kaz didn't know what to say, and she seemed uneasy to reveal more. He'd never thought of Charlie as being too reckless. Charlie had always seemed to be reasonably cautious. Yet, he'd taken too much risk at the apartment, had been too determined to rescue everything, never mind the danger. Which was his undoing. Kaz knew that if they'd changed places, he would have climbed back through that transom a lot sooner.

"Is Charlie the reason you came here?" The Tatras were much closer to Auschwitz than the forests around Warsaw.

Silence returned. Deeper this time. Blacker. Kaz could feel a sudden tension blurring the stars. He waited.

"There's more," she finally said. "After Charlie was taken, I left my job and joined the fighters in the forest. I needed to *do* something. Somehow, I equated attacking Germans with rescuing Charlie. It was a crazy notion, but I was very emotional at the time, not thinking straight. I never regretted my decision, though. It was exciting. It made me feel alive."

She paused and rubbed her heel against the floor boards while she searched for the right words. "I took part in a raid that went bad. Someone tipped the Germans that we were coming. They ambushed us." The scraping heel made a squeaking noise. Kaz pictured a small mouse hidden beneath the porch.

"I was captured," she continued in a soft voice. "They took me to a camp where they tied me up and interrogated me." There was that horrible word again: interrogated. Kaz braced for more. "They beat me for awhile and burned my skin with cigarettes." A pause was followed by a long sigh. "Then, they took turns raping me. I finally got away when Simon the Black attacked the camp."

Kaz blinked and looked back up at the stars. Here was a new, ugly word, a word even more painful to hear than 'interrogated.' He thought about the beating he'd taken at the hands of that SS officer with the rubber hose. It had been horrible, but there was never the threat of rape. That was a form of violence only a woman had to endure. It was something that left no physical marks but could destroy the psyche. Kaz looked at Christina and saw tears glistening on her cheeks in the moonlight. He reached out blindly, found her hand and held it.

"I'm damaged goods, Kaz. Now, I'll never be a mother or a wife."

Kaz's tongue seemed to swell inside his mouth until his cheeks puffed out. He couldn't push any words past the barrier. He sat for an eternity just holding her hand. His mouth slowly returned to normal. He stood up, pulled her into his arms, and held her as tightly as their bodies would allow. Her face was moist with her tears. The skin on her neck pulsated in rhythm to her beating heart.

She pulled away and looked him square in the eye. "All I want to do now is kill Germans."

The next two weeks flew by in flurry of meetings with Tolek, calls on farmers and reports to Kaiser. Christina quickly learned her new assignment and eagerly participated in the black market schemes arranged by Tolek and Kaz. There was a hard edge to her, now. The softness Kaz had known in the orphanage was gone. Each time they reported to Kaiser, he had the feeling that she was just a breath or two away from taking a gun and shooting him. Kaz gave her some distance while she acclimated to her new world, but he couldn't help following her with his eyes. Something about her demeanor and her desire to 'kill Germans' attracted him to her like a magnet. She showed some of the same spirit that he'd found so appealing in Daneta, only Christina's charms were far more deadly. A fierce glint often shone in her eyes that told him she was not to be treated like some windup clock.

For her part, Christina followed his lead while she assumed her new responsibilities. Slowly, signs of her old self returned. She touched his hand and gave him quick smiles. The hard edge retreated when they relaxed together after a long day. The threat of violence slipped behind a curtain of repose, but he could see that it was still there. At no point did she betray the weakness of the woman who'd cried on the porch in the moonlight.

"It's time for you and Christina to take a run up the mountain to the cottage," Tolek informed Kaz on a morning when the sun beckoned to him to abandon his desk and embrace the outdoors. He couldn't wait to show Christina the idyllic setting of the cottage nestled above the deep canyon. They left the next morning.

Christina demonstrated an easy familiarity with horses as they rode the steep mountain trail into the heart of the Tatras. They entered a treelined mountain pass of firs that flowed forever over the rocky terrain. High valleys revealed sparkling lakes. Streams rushed past them as they plunged down the steep slopes toward the fields far below. Eagles and hawks circled in the sky. Tree limbs groaned in gusts of wind. By the time they reached the cottage, the landscape had captivated Christina, just as Kaz had hoped it would.

"The forests around Warsaw are lovely, but these mountains are enchanting," she enthused. The interior of the cottage and the view of the canyon and castle ruins mesmerized her even more. "It's like a fairy tale."

Kaz smiled. "I knew you'd like it."

For the next week, Kaz introduced Christina to the farmers, and they busied themselves after dinner with reports and other paperwork. Before the hour grew too late, they bundled up against the cool, night air and sat on the porch counting the stars. They shared stories about their exploits with the partisans. Kaz was amazed to learn that Christina had participated in half-a-dozen raids before the ill-fated one that resulted in her capture, and that she'd killed three Germans. She was just as impressed with his story about the raid on Montelupi Prison. She already knew about his involvement in the ambush of the rock quarry train by Simon the Red. He told her about Daneta and the clothing factory. How he caught Marek stealing goods from the warehouse and how he resented the accountant, Dominik, who spent so much time with his wife. He confessed his guilt at having spent so little time with Edwina. Their stories rambled on into the night.

Kaz watched the warmth return to Christina's cheeks and her smiles regain the upper hand over bitter memories. She became less brittle. Laughter surfaced in her eyes and on her lips. The mountain was healing her just as it had him. It was bringing them closer together. He could sense it in her shifting moods. One minute she was all business. The next, she was teasing him and brushing lint off the back of his shirt. It seemed inevitable that the time would come when they wouldn't want the night to end. They lingered, hesitantly, in the hallway between the bedrooms, their hands touching, their breaths dancing to a slow tempo of music playing inside their heads. Kaz silently pulled her into his arms and, for the first time in his life, he kissed her. It was a tender kiss, more exploratory than passionate. Not one filled with fire. They could have stopped and dismissed the moment. There was still time. But Kaz had waited his whole life for that kiss, and he wasn't about to let it go so easily. He pressed his mouth against hers and found it willing. A warmth began to build inside of him. It grew and spread with the ferocity of a wildfire. He could feel the heat rising in her, as well, in her skin and on her cheeks.

"Are you sure, Kaz?" She pulled back and searched his face. "Are you sure you want me now that I'm damaged goods?"

"Don't be foolish. The Germans are pigs. They could never make you damaged goods, least of all to me."

The serious lines of doubt on Christina's face broadened into one of her old, beckoning smiles. It melted Kaz's heart. He tried to think of something to say, but no words were needed. So, he took her hand and silently led her into his bedroom.

The next few days were spent in a kaleidoscopic mixture of mirth, hard work and ardent lovemaking. Kaz was astounded at the intensity of their sex. They reached crescendos, paused to recover their breaths, then reached new crescendos. The harsh world around them tumbled away into the deep canyon below them. It was an unrealistic world they created for themselves. He knew that, but it was addictive.

Their private world was cut short one morning by a polite knock on the door. They were just finishing breakfast, and the interruption was so unexpected, neither moved.

Christina looked at Kaz. "Are we expecting someone?"

"I think this may be an invitation." Kaz rose from the table and opened the door. Sure enough, there stood the same peasant who had called on him before. The man handed him another envelope with a handwritten request for Kaz and Christina to join Drochojewski that evening for dinner.

Christina was intrigued. "Has this happened before?"

"The last time I was here. I didn't know if he would invite us this time. He's a nobleman who lives by himself in the villa below us."

"Kaz, why didn't you mention him before?" She was brimming with questions, but Kaz refused to divulge any further information.

"Wait until this evening," he replied mysteriously. "All will be revealed."

They made a few calls that day, but hurried back to the cottage in time to clean up and get ready for dinner.

"I have no dress," Christina complained. "Only trousers. What will he think?"

Kaz laughed. "Not to worry. He knows we're here working. He'll understand."

As they saddled their horses and set off down the trail amid the granite peaks glistening in the late afternoon sunlight, Kaz wondered just how much information Drochojewski would share with Christina. He felt guilty that he hadn't revealed more to her about this strange intrigue, but he hadn't thought it was his place to do so. He knew that Drochojewski was a very private man, and he wanted to respect that. At the same time, it seemed like he was betraying Christina's trust by not telling her anything.

The same stableman waited to take their horses when they arrived. Christina marveled at the place as they approached the front door. "Imagine what an effort it was to build such a magnificent home way up here."

This time the door opened before Kaz could knock, and the housekeeper invited them in. Drochojewski was waiting for them in his study.

"Welcome to my abode, Christina." He took her hand and kissed the back of it. "I have been looking forward to meeting you."

"You know my name."

"As Kaz has learned, I know many things. You are staying in one of my cottages, by the way." Kaz noted how smoothly he shifted the conversation away from her name. The comment surprised him.

"I hadn't realized that," Kaz remarked. "I thought it belonged to the Germans."

"It does now. They confiscated it when they arrived."

"Oh, I'm sorry we're using it uninvited," Christina exclaimed.

"Don't be. It was not your doing, and it was a small price to pay for keeping my estate intact. I'm the only living descendant of my noble family, which reaches back for generations. The Germans seem to respect that for some odd reason, and they pretty much leave me alone."

Drochojewski followed the same pattern as last time: small talk over glasses of wine and general conversation during most of the dinner. They were nearly finished when he turned their talk to more important matters.

"Has Kaz said anything about me?"

"Not until your invitation arrived and then very little." She gave Kaz a mocking grin. "He's been very secretive."

"Good. That is what I expected of him. It confirms what I thought, the he can be trusted."

Kaz blushed but said nothing.

"What's going on here?" Christina admonished.

Drochojewski's expression grew serious. "I have researched your background, Christina, just as I did Kaz's, and I find you a woman to be trusted, perhaps, with my life. Let me explain."

Drochojewski briefly reviewed the information that he had discussed with Kaz at their last meeting. "Your work with the partisans, Christina, makes you ideally suited for this undertaking. I hope you will join us."

A look of angry determination crowded her brow. "I will do whatever it takes to throw the Germans out of my country. And when the time comes, I want to join Simon's men. I've fought the Germans before."

"I'm aware of that, and the time may, indeed, come, but for now, I need you and Kaz to spy for me.

He turned his attention to Kaz. "I have arranged for a vendor's table to sell my wines in front of the town hall during market days in Nowy Targ. The vendor is my agent. Please prepare a weekly, detailed report of everything relevant and pass it to him. He will deliver it to me the same day. If you have more urgent information that cannot wait until market day, bring it to me yourself. These are matters of life and death. My door will always be open to you."

Kaz and Christina rode back up the mountain trail in silence. It was only after they had stabled their horses and returned to the cottage that Christina spoke.

"I don't know whether to smack you or kiss you. You knew about this but kept it secret, as if you didn't trust me."

"Of course I trust you, but it wasn't my place to say anything. Drochojewski is a very important man in the Tatras. His life is on the line, as is ours. I had to let him decide when and how much to tell you. I didn't know what else to do."

Kaz looked at her imploringly. "Why don't you smack me, then kiss me? I probably deserve both."

Which was exactly what Christina did. But the smack was gentle and the kiss ardent. "No more secrets," she demanded.

"No more secrets."

Chapter Twenty-six

Winter announced its arrival with a series of light snow storms followed by a three-day blizzard. Temperatures plummeted and most farming activities ground to a halt. Not so, the German buildup of men and arms. A large military base was established on the outskirts of Nowy Targ. It was gradually filled with troops and armaments needed to support the Eastern front where the Germans were trying to stop the advance of Russian troops eager to revenge the brutal sieges of the previous year. There also seemed to be little doubt that some sort of push was still being planned in the Tatra Mountains against the partisans. This seemed evident from the number of horses being shipped to the military base. Horses would have little use against Russian canons, but they were ideal for an offensive into the partisans' stronghold in the spring after the snows had melted. Kaz did his best to keep an eye on the developments in the encampment without drawing attention and to send useful reports to Drochojewski via the wine merchant in the market place.

Winter did not discourage the partisans. Swift, mobile bands of white-clad skiers swept across the snow covered slopes at night, struck German units that strayed too far from home with the vengeance of an avalanche, and disappeared like ghosts into the rugged terrain. With each new attack, German frustration mounted, and the pressure built to mount an offensive. The general who commanded the base knew better than to attack in winter. In the meantime, more soldiers and equipment arrived at the base.

If the Germans couldn't control the partisans, they were determined to increase their influence over Nowy Targ. They appointed a town manager to run things. His name was Gorka, a local politician who had somehow survived even though he was despised by just about everyone. He was stocky, over weight and waddled like a well-fed pig. His eyes were narrow, and he had a penchant for sticking his nose into everyone's business. He reported directly to the general.

His brutal nature was put on full display when the partisans shot a Gestapo officer on a Nowy Targ street. Twelve suspected supporters of the separatists were rounded up and marched through town to the rail station. Kaz recognized two of the men, both known sympathizers, but had no knowledge of the others. Everyone assumed that the men had been picked by Gorka. Kaz was relieved not to see the wine merchant among them.

The prisoners were forced to stand in the open bed of a truck beneath a newly constructed gallows. Sacks were pulled over the men's heads and nooses hung around their necks. The truck was driven away without fanfare. The crowd that had formed to watch groaned as the the men's legs kicked in a losing battle against the ropes tightening around their throats. When the dance of death was finished, the corpses dangled in the cold, winter sunlight while a group of arriving German soldiers looked on from the windows of their train. It was a bleak scene, one that reminded Kaz of the harsh treatment that could be expected from the Germans for the slightest offense. A German officer announced that the bodies could not be cut down before nightfall. They were to remain there as reminders of German justice. People muttered among themselves as they departed. Kaz heard the name Gorka more than once.

In a twist of irony, however, the partisans figured out how to exact their revenge. More and more German soldiers were deserting as the war effort faltered. So, when one went missing, it was often assumed that he had fled in the night. That meant that reprisals against the partisans only took place if the Germans found the bodies of their dead. The fighters soon devised some ingenious ways of disposing of German corpses. Many of the slain were simply packed onto horses and carried over the back trails into Czechoslovakia, where they were buried in makeshift graves in Czech cemeteries.

Such operations didn't satisfy the locals' need for revenge against Gorka. They watched and waited for the right opportunity. It came when Gorka got drunk one night in a popular bar and got into a fight. Gorka took a beating and left the bar threatening to file a complaint with the German police. He returned with an officer a half-hour later, but it quickly became apparent that the officer had little interest in Gorka or the incident. He left without filing charges. That was all the information that the locals needed. It was obvious that Gorka had fallen out of favor with his protectors. One week later, Gorka disappeared. His body was discovered by a farmer days later standing waist deep in a frozen creek. Nobody bothered to chop the body out of the ice. It was finally found by a German patrol and removed for burial.

One partisan raid was so bizarre it was talked about for weeks. The partisans were having a difficult time getting sufficient weapons and

POLAND INTERRUPTED

ammunition to prepare for the anticipated German offensive in the spring. It was time for desperate measures. One night, they descended on the ammunition dump outside Nowy Targ and three of the men burst into the guards' quarters holding grenades with the pins pulled out of them and thumbs holding down the firing mechanisms. The moment a thumb was raised, the grenade would explode and kill everyone in the room. The guards were poorly trained, older men who'd been drafted for non-combat roles, such as guard duty, so that regular soldiers could be released to fight at the front. They had no idea what to do when accosted by the fighters and went white with fear when they saw the live grenades.

"What do you want?" one stammered.

"Pack up our horses with rifles and bullets, or we'll blow you and this whole dump sky high!" The speaker lifted his grenade above his head.

"Okay. Just don't lose control of those things."

The guards did as they were told, then the partisans bound and gagged them so they couldn't sound an alarm. They disappeared into the night with enough weapons to attack Hitler himself. Nobody revealed what happened to those grenades, but the locals were convinced that they were duds. The story quickly spread amid guffaws and slaps on the back.

As the sun warmed and the snow melted, wild flowers bloomed, bears awoke from hibernation, icicles melted and rumors abounded that the Americans were about to cross the English Channel for a final assault on Germany. More rumors spoke of German retreats and growing desertions on the Eastern front with Russia. There was a new sense of energy among those who supported or participated in the resistance, a sense that the wheels of justice were beginning to turn in their favor. There was a new resolve to keep the Germans at bay.

Kaz and Christina shared that resolve. They were in the midst of preparations for their first spring trip to the cottage when word came that a supply train had arrived. Kaz walked down to the station to see what he could learn. More horses were in the process of being unloaded, but Kaz's attention was drawn to several flatbed cars where tarps hid a mysterious cargo. Kaz was itching to find out what was being so carefully hidden, but he didn't dare get any closer.

He hung back and waited until one of the Poles who worked in the rail yard wandered past.

"More horses," Kaz commented in a friendly manner.

"Yeah. The Germans seem obsessed with them."

"What's under the tarps. Hay to feed them?"

The man stopped and hitched up his pants. "Naw. Those are motorcycles. Big ones. Must be a hundred of 'em. I was told the general ordered 'em. Nobody knows why."

"Well, none of us can figure out the Germans," Kaz replied with disinterest. He turned and walked away, but his mind was churning. What *would* they want with motorcycles in Nowy Targ? To police the town? That hardly seemed likely. And they wouldn't need so many. No, they had something more insidious in mind. There was only one possibility. They were to be part of the offensive in the Tatra Mountains. The Germans intended to use them to chase down the partisans in the forests! Kaz raced back to the office.

"I have to get to the villa at once," he declared to Tolek and Christina. He explained what he'd just discovered.

"I'll come with you," Christina offered.

"No, you'd better wait here. I think our plans are about to change."

Christina stopped what she was doing and faced him so that he couldn't pass. "Kaz, don't leave me out of the loop. Tell Drochojewski that I intend to be involved. Tell him and Simon that I'm an experienced fighter." Her eyes shone with fierce determination. The muscles around her mouth twitched. She placed her hands on hips like a boxer posing before entering the ring. The last time she'd expressed herself like that, she'd talked about killing Germans. She might have shone a softer side to him, but deep down, she hadn't changed. She still saw herself as damaged goods, and she still wanted to take her revenge on the Germans.

Kaz's first instinct was to protect Christina, to shield her from the storm of battle to come, but he could see that she wouldn't be denied. He'd just found her again, and he didn't want to lose her. Yet, how could he deny her? All he could do was release her into the winds of war and pray.

Kaz agreed to talk with Drochojewski and Simon. He gathered a few essential belongings and saddled his horse. He was gone within the hour.

"That is astounding news," Drochojewski agreed when Kaz arrived, tired and disheveled, from his journey up the mountain. "I must get word to Simon at once. Why don't you go up to the cottage, eat and get some rest? I'll send for you when Simon arrives."

Two hours later, Kaz answered a knock on his door and was told to go to the villa immediately. He'd left his horse saddled in anticipation of the request and was off at once. Simon and Drochojewski were waiting for him in the study.

"Did you see the motorcycles?" Simon wanted to know.

"No." He wished he could tell Simon more, but the machines had been very carefully hidden from view. "However, the yard worker I spoke to did say they were big ones. I expect they're pretty fast."

"Yes. It would seem so. If they get in among our horses, they could do real damage. It's a shrewd idea. Lucky for us that you learned about them. Thanks to you, they've lost the element of surprise, and we can plan some strategies of our own."

Simon explained that to a novice, the forest appeared to be an endless maze of trees, but to the partisans, they were home. The woods were filled with underbrush, bushes and secondary paths, many no bigger than deer trails. It would be difficult for motorcycles to follow them through such rugged terrain.

"And we know every inch of those mountains. Every valley. Every pathway. Our knowledge gives us an edge. With it, we can set some interesting traps for them."

"What do you want me to do?"

"Return to Nowy Targ and keep your eyes and ears open. As soon as you see them preparing to move out, get back to us. We'll be waiting for your report."

"There's one thing more. Christina. She's fought with Simon the Black's men. She wants to be part of the fight."

Simon rose and prepared to depart. "Can she ride a horse?"

"Better than I can," he admitted. "And she can shoot."

"Then, bring her with you. We have a number of women fighters. Christina is welcome to join us."

"We'll have to keep you behind the lines," Drochojewski interjected. "My villa will act as headquarters. I'll need you to receive and send messages to Simon and his commanders. There will be much confusion when the action starts. We'll need to know what's happening and where our men should go."

Three weeks passed before the assault began. Kaz spent as much time as he dared watching the Germans prepare. He and Christina clung to each other at night with the knowledge that their lives were about to change. This would be the biggest battle the partisans had faced, and Kaz knew the Germans were better trained for it. The partisans were most effective using hit-and-run tactics and making raids, not battling an army face-to-face. They would need all their guile to survive the coming confrontation.

Everyone in Nowy Targ knew what was about to happen. Voices whispered constantly. Conjecture was rampant. Rumors spread on every spring breeze. Tensions were so high they obliterated the sun. Clouds hung over the town and obscured the mountains. Little work was done. Kaiser rarely came to the office to check on things. The staff barely hid their malaise.

When the day finally arrived, Kaz knew it in an instant. There was no doubt in his mind. There was no declaration or sudden massing of soldiers. No new commanders appeared. Nothing seemed out of the ordinary, except for one thing. The Germans rolled out their motorcycles and lined them up in the square. It was the first time they'd been revealed. The brash display of steel and power brought gasps from the town people. Over one hundred machines of war gleamed in the dull sunlight peeking through the clouds.

Kaz and Christina saddled their horses, slipped out of town into a stand of trees that hid them from inquisitive eyes and raced toward the mountains. Christina reminded Kaz of a warrior in her gray parka and flowing trousers. They were the clothes she'd brought with her from the forests around Warsaw. The colors blended into the landscape. It would be hard to see her once the fighting began. Despite his concerns for her safety, Kaz thought she looked magnificent.

When they reached the villa with the news, Simon and his commanders quickly dispersed to their respective fighting groups, each of which had a specific role to play in the coming battle. Christina was assigned to a unit that would wait in ambush for the leading German troops.

The assault began two days later. The partisans needed no additional warning. They could hear the angry buzz of motorcycles plunging up the mountain trails toward them. A fighter would later describe the sound as 'wood being split asunder by a dozen saw mills.' Men on horseback sallied out to contest the advancing army but quickly fell back in disarray as the motorcycles roared into view. The partisans turned and raced up a broad valley which slowly narrowed. The motorcycles drew closer, and the banks of the valley grew steeper. The Germans seemed not to notice or care. They were focused on catching their prey. The partisans whipped their horses into a frenzy of hoofs intermingled with dust and raced around a wide bend in the trail. But instead of continuing to flee, they brought their mounts to an abrupt halt and scattered among boulders that had tumbled down the slopes centuries ago. Other fighters were already there, well hidden among the natural barriers, rifles at the ready.

The first hint of trouble for the Germans came when bullets rained down in a fusillade from the cliffs on either side of the narrowing valley. The ambush was joined by a withering fire from the rocks where the horsemen had dismounted and joined their comrades. The battle quickly turned into a rout as the Germans tried desperately to retreat. In less than five minutes, over thirty motorcyclists lay dead and the remainder were roaring back down the valley. The partisans quickly destroyed the fallen motorcycles with sticks of dynamite, then mounted their horses and disappeared into the mountains.

There was little celebration, however. Simon and his commanders knew that they had only bloodied the Germans' noses. It wouldn't be long before they returned to seek revenge. The sound of saw mills echoed through the mountain valleys the next morning as the invaders resumed their assault. This time, soldiers mounted on horses joined the cyclists, and the troops moved forward more carefully. The partisans waited in ambush and engaged the enemy in a series of hit-and-run skirmishes that always ended with them retreating further up the mountain. The cyclists assumed the lead position and pressed their advantage. The partisans retreated more quickly. Just when the Germans were about to put their boots on their opponents' necks, they discovered themselves penned in by downed trees that blocked the trails. The horses could jump the fallen timber but not the motorcycles. The ensuing battle was eerily similar to the one before. Ambushes on either side of the trails opened fire on the cyclists while the retreating horsemen slipped behind prepared fortifications made of logs and joined the melee. The German horsemen tried to attack, but the fire was too fierce. In the end, another hasty retreat was made down the mountain, and another three dozen motorcycles were abandoned.

Their noses were getting bloodier, but the Germans soon mounted a third offensive. And each offensive began further up the mountain. The Germans were gaining ground. This time, the partisans led their attackers into a dense section of forest that was so overgrown with bushes and dead brush that visibility fell to a few yards. No fallen trees blocked the route, but the trails soon disappeared into a tangle of limbs and foliage. The motorcycles were useless there. Even the horsemen had difficulty picking their way through the undergrowth. When they did engage the partisans, they fired blindly at positions where gunfire had been returned. It was impossible to know if they hit anyone. Foot soldiers were pressed forward, but their battle lines soon fell apart due to the terrain. The partisans struck and moved so smoothly, it was as if they were ghosts. Another retreat was sounded; another victory was chalked up to the resistance fighters.

"We're not going to win," Simon announced to his commanders at a hastily called meeting back at the villa. There were a dozen men in Drochojewski's study. They murmured their discontent. Kaz had spent the past two days charging back and forth between the villa and the commanders, sending messages from Simon and receiving messages in return. He'd hardly slept, and he dared not sit down now for fear he would nod off. Tired as he was, he could tell that the fighters were unhappy with Simon's assessment.

"We've defeated them in three battles," one of the men groused. "We can win more." Others agreed.

"What you say is true, but it doesn't change the fact that with every battle we lose more men and more ground. There are too many of them. I'd hoped we would undermine their resolve by this time, but we haven't." He paused and looked his men in the eye. "We face a choice. We continue what we're doing and are defeated ... captured ... imprisoned ... executed, or we do what we've always done. Disappear back into the mountains and fight another day on our terms, not theirs."

Silence flooded the room. Boots creaked. Throats cleared. Eyes stared at the floor. Kaz marveled at how Simon commanded the attention of these hardened veterans. It was clear that they looked to him for guidance, even as they disagreed with his analysis. They wanted to fight on, to bloody more noses, but Kaz could see their own resolve weakening. They knew in their hearts that Simon was right.

"I'm afraid I must agree," Drochojewski interjected. "You cannot protect this villa much longer. If you leave now, you'll be safe. The Germans will win a battle, but not our war with them." He got to his feet with a sigh and leaned on his cane. "I've come to my own decision. I won't let them have this place. We must burn it to the ground. And I must leave my beloved mountains. I'm too old to travel with you. I'll try to reach friends who can hide me." The wrinkles on his face seemed to grow deeper as he spoke. His eyes moistened. He was declaring an end to a way of life.

He turned to Kaz. "You must slip past the German lines while there is still time and return to Nowy Targ. Hopefully, you haven't been missed, and you can still do things for these men."

Kaz's tired mind snapped awake. He hadn't thought about his own future until now, and that raised a terrifying question.

"What about Christina? Where is she?"

Simon rubbed the beard on his face as if pondering some great thought. "We don't know where a number of our fighters are at the moment. We've become scattered by the continuous assaults. We're looking for her along with many others."

The words landed with the weight of rocks thrown into a pond. They sank quickly to the bottom of his ability to think. Sleep nearly overwhelmed him. He could barely comprehend what Simon had just said. Christina was missing! His worst fears were about to be realized. He pictured her body lying dead in the forest. It was more than he could bear. He let go a sob, then blushed at his sign of weakness.

Simon walked over and put a hand on his shoulder. "There's a lot we don't know. Don't lose hope." It felt like fatherly advice, something he'd never experienced in life. The hand warmed him. His emotions subsided back under control.

Decisions were made. They would find as many stragglers as they could and trust the rest to make their way back to the hideouts buried deep in the higher mountains. They would become ghosts and disappear before the Germans' eyes.

Kaz packed his few belongings and saddled his horse in a state of disbelief. The villa gone. Christina missing. The battles over. It seemed too much for him to bear, yet bear it he must. He had to get back to Nowy Targ before *he* was captured. Drochojewski packed his own horse while the men splashed cooking fuel over the villa and outlying buildings. He said that he would take another route down the backside of the mountain. He looked at his dear home one more time. Dusk was fast approaching. The remaining light framed his stoic expression. He was a proud man who had given everything for the resistance. Sacrificed everything. Maybe even his life.

When they were ready to leave, the men lighted matches and tossed them into the rooms. Kaz was already starting down a secondary trail when they did so. The cooking fuel accepted the tiny flames eagerly and roared to life. Multiple fires rose on a light wind to meet the sky. Kaz looked back and watched the magnificent blaze as it built into one great, orange glow. Black smoke rose above the firs. Even at his distance he could feel the heat and smell the burning wood. He looked away and started down the mountain. With luck, the trail he chose would get him past the Germans, and he would make it back to Nowy Targ before he fell asleep.

Chapter Twenty-seven

Everyone was asleep by the time Kaz staggered into town and unpacked his horse. He didn't bother to wake Tolek. He collapsed on his bed fully clothed and went to sleep instantly.

He dreamed that he was back in Montelupi Prison, seated in a cell. He tried to rise but discovered that he was tied to a chair. He tried to call for help, but he had no voice. All he could do was sit on the chair and shiver in the cold air. At last, the sound of boots broke the silence. They were SS boots, Kaz knew this, somehow, without seeing them. Sure enough, a SS officer stopped in front of his cell and waited for a guard to open the door. Kaz saw that the officer held a piece of rubber hose in his hand. He trembled at the sight of it. The man stepped inside the cell and spoke to him in German. Kaz shook his head to indicate he didn't understand, but the officer kept talking to him and laughing. Then, he raised the hose and smacked Kaz across his face. Blood poured from his nose, but instead of crying out in pain, he shook off his bonds and rose from the chair. When he did so, the officer shouted at him and hit him again. Kaz wanted to raise his arms to fend off the blows, but they remained frozen at his side. Still, he couldn't scream. The officer continued to hit him until he blacked out.

Twelve hours later, he awoke stiff and sore from his recent journey. Or was it from the dream? It was still fresh in his mind, and it bothered him. The last time he'd had such a dream, he'd lost Charlie. Was it possible the dream was an omen? He immediately thought of Christina and shuddered. She was safe, he told himself. It was only a dream.

Tolek greeted him when he wandered into the kitchen in search of coffee and something to eat. "The Gestapo came looking for you yesterday. I told them you were off working with farmers, but I'm not sure they believed me. Any reason for their interest?"

"None I know of. Maybe, they were just checking everybody in the village. I wasn't caught or identified. Anyway, I have other worries." He told Tolek about Christina.

Tolek gave him a comforting smile. "I'm sure she'll show up. She's a very resilient woman."

Kaz said nothing. He couldn't shake the dream from his head.

For the next few days, Kaz moved listlessly through his duties. Kaiser showed up every day to see that work was being done, but the Gestapo officer didn't return. All Kaz could think about was Christina. He looked for the wine merchant on market day to see if he had any word, but the merchant had disappeared. Now that Drochojewski's villa was gone and Simon had slipped into hiding, he no longer had a contact in the mountains. He had no way of finding Christina. His only hope was that she would show up or a partisan would appear with a message. Nothing happened for two more days. Then, his world turned upside down.

Five trucks arrived early one morning and unloaded troops, who began rounding up the townspeople, Tolek and Kaz included. They were herded into a semicircle in the main square and forced to stand facing the wall of the clock tower for over an hour. Kaz sensed that something dramatic was about to take place, and his heart raced in anticipation. He knew the Germans liked to put on a spectacle when they punished the Poles. Something unpleasant stirred the air. Odors from the nearby bakery wafted over the crowd. Somewhere down a side lane, two dogs barked ferociously, then whimpered when their owner shouted at them. Kaz wondered why the dog owner wasn't forced to stand in the square with everyone else. A fly buzzed his face. He impatiently swatted it away. He wished the Germans would get on with their farce so he could return to his misery.

The roar of a truck's engine broke the calm as it approached the square. The truck halted and half-a-dozen soldiers jumped down. An SS officer stepped out of the truck's cab and walked to the center of the square. He was tall, imposing. He stood erect and lifted his chin in an imperial manner. While he waited, the soldiers forced ten prisoners, whose hands were tied in front of them, to awkwardly descend to the pavement and to line up against the wall.

"These are bandits captured in the recent, successful action undertaken by Germany to rid these mountains of such vermin," the SS officer announced in a harsh voice. "They are not prisoners of war, but rats that live in the forests and prey on innocent civilians. They shall be dealt with according to German law."

As he spoke, a dozen soldiers lined up opposite the prisoners with submachine guns held at the ready. All the prisoners wore caps that partially obscured their faces. Tension gripped Kaz's back muscles as he stared at the prisoners. The dream he'd had played before him like a scratchy newsreel. Every nerve in his body flared with dread. One-by-one, he looked down the line. When he came to the second to last

POLAND INTERRUPTED

figure on the right, his eyes stopped moving, and his heart stopped beating. He was looking into the fierce, unrepentant face of Christina. Even with the cap pulled down, he couldn't mistake her flared nose.

Kaz recoiled in horror as the officer gave the command and the soldiers lifted their weapons. He heard a long, forlorn cry of 'noooooooo' rushing from his lips, but the cry was drowned in the shattering reverberation of bullets bursting across the square. The figures fell in a bloody heap at the base of the wall. Kaz blinked in disbelief. It was over in an instant. The wall before which Christina had been standing was suddenly chewed with bullet holes. Her body had disappeared, as if by magic. But it was no magician's trick. When he looked down, he spied her lifeless figure snuggled among the ones who'd stood beside her. Kaz's legs collapsed. His body slumped. He was aware of strong hands grasping him and holding him erect. They were Tolek's hands. He knew this without looking. He heard the voices of onlookers moaning and crying out in vain. The harsh scent of smoking guns permeated the air. He looked for Christina again, but she was now hidden by the seething mass of spectators shifting around him. Tolek dragged him away.

"The Gestapo are watching everybody in the square. We've got to get out of here." He pushed Kaz through the stunned villagers and down the cobbled street to their building. Kaz hardly saw where he was walking. He simply went where the pressure of Tolek's hands guided him. Once inside, he collapsed in a chair and sobbed uncontrollably.

"Get it out of your system." Tolek's voice sounded unforgiving, just like those screaming bullets in the square. Kaz wanted to shut him up, but he didn't have the strength to move. "My guess, Gestapo agents will be here shortly. We have to be calm and ready for them."

Something in the tone of Tolek's urgent voice connected with Kaz. The image of Christina's body tangled with the others at the base of the wall faded. The SS boots and uniform from his dream reared to life in its place. The Gestapo had already visited the center once. They would come again. His chair scraped the floor and tumbled over backwards when he stood up. He stepped around it and headed for the bathroom to wash his face.

"I'll be ready," he said in a monotone voice.

A SS officer and two soldiers with rifles and bayonets arrived within the hour. The officer's posture and raised chin reminded Kaz of the officer in the square. Rage churned inside him. It rose and fell as he breathed. Kaz gripped his hands. It took all his control to keep him from attacking the man. It would have been suicidal to do so, but he didn't care.

"We are looking for Kaz Swiba."

Despite his despair, he was relieved to hear that the Gestapo had not figured out who he was. Kaz Kowinsky remained buried in the archives of Krakow.

"That's me."

"Show me your papers."

"They're in my room."

"Get them, but first, turn around and stand with your hands against the wall."

He did as he was told. One of the soldiers quickly frisked him for weapons, then accompanied him to the bedroom to retrieve his I.D. papers. The officer reviewed them and stuck them in his pocket. Kaz knew that wasn't a good sign. His foggy brain was starting to come alive. He had to be very careful.

"Kaz is my employee," Tolek volunteered. "He manages the husbandry program."

The officer's lower lip trembled with anger. "Do not interrupt us again."

Tolek lowered his head.

"Do you know a man named Drochojewski?"

"I've met him. I was staying at a cottage on his property when I worked with the farmers in the area."

"Did you know the man plotted with the fugitives in the mountains?" It was a nonsensical question. If he admitted any such knowledge, he would be put against the same wall as Christina.

"I had little to do with him. The cottage was isolated."

The officer's eyes narrowed in a sign of distrust. Kaz was seated in the same chair that he'd tipped over. It forced him to look up at his interrogator, who hovered over him with an expression of irritation scrawled across his face.

"There was a woman with you."

It was an accusation, not a question. Kaz's pulse rate jumped. He could feel it throbbing in the veins of his neck. The sprawled image of Christina resurrected itself. Kaz nearly leaped out of his seat, but he gripped the sides of the chair with trembling hands and forced a breath deep into his lungs.

"She was my co-worker. I hadn't seen her for days, until you shot her." His voice nearly croaked, but he managed, somehow, to hold it steady.

The officer tapped the toe of one foot on the floor while he stared at Kaz. "You will come with us," he said finally, "for more questioning."

The two soldiers pulled him from his chair and led him away. They marched him down the street to a makeshift jail in an old brick building just off the square. From his cell on the second floor, he could see people come and go on the street below. He was relieved that he couldn't see the square.

The next week settled into a steady pattern of interrogations followed by long periods of isolation in his cell. Each time he was taken to a room to be questioned, he expected to be beaten or tortured, but all they did was grill him over and over about the 'bandits' in the mountains. There were no sleep deprivation tactics or freezing cells to disorient him. After a few days, the Gestapo officer disappeared. Kaz figured he had more important matters to attend. Nazi leaders were growing less concerned about occupation areas like Nowy Targ. They were concentrating all their efforts on shoring up their sagging front lines. Local officials were left to pursue their duties in a near vacuum. Kaz's interrogation was a good case in point. It was left in the hands of two soldiers with weathered faces and graying hair. The soldiers made a halfhearted effort to maintain the discipline of daily sessions, but they looked bored with the process. It was obvious that they were just going through the motions.

The time in prison gave Kaz a chance to heal a little from the pain that had dug so deeply into his soul. First, Daneta, then Christina. The losses had seemed too much to bear. As the days passed, his emotional turmoil ebbed, and he grew stronger. As another week slowly trudged by, Kaz began to get restless. He wondered if he would be stuck in his miserable cell for the rest of the war. To his surprise, it was Herr Krieslandwirt (Kaz still thought of him as Kaiser) who came to his rescue. More villagers were being arrested on vague charges, including Tolek, who was sent away to work in a labor camp. A minor official was put in charge of the animal husbandry and agricultural programs, but he had no idea what to do and was quickly overwhelmed.

Which led to a frantic call for help from Kaiser. Kaz was released and put to work sorting through the inventory and logistical nightmare that had developed in Tolek's and his absence. He was relieved to have something to do and attacked the paperwork with new found energy. He did not return to the cottage, however. There were too many memories of Christina waiting to haunt him there.

As things unraveled along the eastern front, the villagers and farmers of Nowy Targ felt less compunction about following German orders. Anger, resentment and hatred were stirred in equal parts into a cauldron of discontent. German officials dared not walk the streets alone at night. The black market flourished; goods were traded openly on market day. People drank more vodka, and supplies dwindled. Alcohol stills popped up in homes and on farms. Everything that could be fermented was used, including potato peels and spoiled fruit.

Herr Krieslandwirt became worried about his horses, six stallions which he kept stabled outside the town. He decided to move them away from the Czech border. Kaz and two other villagers were selected to transport the horses to another city. Kaiser didn't want to use German soldiers for fear they would be ambushed in the mountains. The three men rode the horses to a stud farm located halfway to Krakow, then arranged a small reward for themselves on the return trip when they hitched a ride in a military lorry laden with cases of food tins. When they neared Nowy Targ, they opened some of the cases and threw tins of fruits and meats into the tall grass that hugged the road. Once the truck dropped them off and left, they returned and gathered their booty in anticipation of some tasty meals and lucrative trading on the black market.

The next few months floated past in a flurry of smaller stories tucked inside of the main event: the gradual retreat of the German army. Kaz was caught up in a sweep of workers to dig defensive trenches for the German army. Villagers and peasants were rounded up each morning and marched to the trenching site outside of town. Each home was required to provide one laborer, man or woman, to wield a pick or a shovel for the day. At night, they were returned to their homes. That way, the Germans didn't have to feed or house them. After five trips to the trenches, Kaz decided that he'd had enough. He hid from the Germans the next morning and resumed his duties at the agricultural center. No one came for him again.

The farmers who kept horses were required to shear their manes and tails and to deliver a sack of horsehair to the agricultural center. Kaz had to see that the sacks were all accounted for and turned over to the German authorities. The hair was used for cross hairs in gun sights and for stuffing cushions and pillows. Polish horses were easily identified by their bobbed tails and manes.

The Poles had also been smuggling horses from Czechoslovakia for the partisans. These animals were often stolen from German farms. However, they were easy to identify by the German border guards because of their full, flowing manes. In the winter, the beautiful, black animals stood out in the snow. The border guards could spot them a mile away, which created a dilemma for the Polish thieves.The innovative Poles quickly found a solution to their problem. They whitewashed the horses, then donned white sheets and rode them undetected across the border at night.

The most satisfying event for Kaz took place when he spotted the arrogant face of the SS officer who had commanded the firing squad that killed Christina. Kaz's insides twisted into a giant knot when he saw him walking through the square. Kaz learned that his name was Mulhardt. He was now in charge of a Gestapo unit whose mission was to whip the villagers back in line and to restore order to the town of Nowy Targ. Partisans had been moving freely in the town for some time, and Kaz quickly contacted them with the news of his discovery. They were as eager as Kaz to revenge the slaughter of their comrades.

They quickly formed a plan to set a trap. Word was leaked to the Gestapo commander that an important meeting of partisan leaders was set two nights hence at a nearby ski cabin in the mountains. Simon the Red was planning to attend. Mulhardt jumped at the bait and commandeered a knowledgeable, local skier by the name of Pilat to lead them to the cabin. Pilat had been a heavy weight boxer many years ago and was popular with the locals. Mulhardt figured that he would make a good hostage in case of trouble. The SS officer took thirty of his men, and with Pilat leading them, headed for the cabin. The partisans had set the stage by leaving a dozen horses tied up out front. No guards were posted. Mulhardt smiled. He could already see the medals on his chest from a successful operation. He put Pilat in front to lead the way and began a cautious approach to the cabin. When they were about a quarter of a mile away, he raised a gloved hand to signal the assault, but before he could lower his arm, a gun barked from the woods above the cabin and a bullet punctured the hand. Mulhardt stared at the blood spurting out of the wound in disbelief.

"It's an ambush," he cried. His men already knew that and were starting to retreat toward cover behind nearby trees. Mulhardt grabbed Pilat and tried to pull him closer as a human shield, but the man was too big and strong. He pushed the German away and stepped back. Two more shots were fired. Both found their mark, and Mulhardt crumpled in the snow.

Pilat stared at the bloody figure with satisfaction before turning and making his way to the frightened troops. "Go back," he warned.

"These hills are crawling with partisans. It's obvious they don't want to kill us, or we'd be dead already. It was Mulhardt they were after." Pilat pushed his way through the soldiers and headed back down the mountain. The soldiers looked around frantically and hastened after him.

News of the ambush whipped through the town. Memories of the firing squad were still fresh. Smiles blossomed. The townspeople quietly thanked the partisans for taking their revenge. Kaz had never been a religious man, but he said a small prayer for Christina.

New contingents of troops were shuttled into the area, but these units were largely composed of nationals from other countries who had joined the German army to get out of prisons or labor camps. Only one in four was German. Their discipline was ragged, and they deserted at an alarming rate.

The defining moment for Kaz, the moment he knew that the war was over, happened one bright, blue morning when he saw his first Russian airplanes. They swooped low over the mountains to strafe German positions near the Czech border. Train traffic came to a stand still. German mechanized units pounded through the area in full retreat. When they ran out of fuel, the tank crews abandoned their vehicles and fled in all directions. They peeled off their uniforms and threw them away as they ran. Lost clothing and rifles were soon common place along the roads as soldiers 'mustered out' of the military and sought to hide among the civilians.

Suddenly, there were no Germans at all. It was as if a giant vacuum had sucked them into the clouds. One day they were there, the next they were gone. The only visible signs of law and order were a handful of Polish police who had worked for the Germans, and they were seen as traitors by the locals. Fights broke out. Pro-German officials were executed, some after kangaroo court trials set up by the partisans, others without any trappings of justice. The minor official that had been assigned to the agricultural center disappeared in the middle of the night. Kaz never learned whether he had fled or been shot. People who'd been without food formed mobs and stormed the German warehouses. Nobody got in their way. Anarchy reined, and no one seemed to care. In less than two days, Nowy Targ had become a jungle.

Kaz thought he knew why. Their brief respite from hardship and cruelty would be short lived, and the people sensed it. Freedom would be snuffed out again in a matter of days or weeks. Poland would be interrupted, once more.

The Russians were coming.

Part III

Poland Interrupted

The Russians

Chapter Twenty-eight

The invasion of Poland by Russia proceeded with all the precision of a giant fire storm sweeping across the plains. As the Germans retreated, they were set upon from the rear by partisans, Ukrainians and other ethnic groups, while the Russians kept up a relentless attack from the front. A gap of several miles often opened between the receding German lines and the advancing Russians. This was filled with all manner of strange bedfellows: stranded soldiers, trapped partisans, escaped prisoners, thieves, and refugees who did not know which way to run. As the Russian army swept into a town or city, special forces took control and quickly suppressed any remnants of opposition. Local officials were replaced by Russian administrators. Captured partisans were forced to join Soviet military units or were shot. Peasants and farmers handed over their remaining livestock to feed the advancing army. Potential trouble makers were deported or executed on the spot. The exiled Polish government in England was condemned and replaced by a Soviet administration.

One of the greatest casualties of the war's end was Warsaw. The German army had five divisions embedded in the city and were determined to make a heroic stand. The resistance movement tried to defeat the Germans before the Russians arrived, in what became known as the Warsaw Uprising. The partisans were no match for the disciplined German army, and the Russians made little effort to come to their rescue. The resulting battle destroyed the city and forced the surrender of the partisans. By the time the Russians entered the city, it had been evacuated and lay in rubble.

For two days, Nowy Targ suffered through the agonies of insurrection and rioting, but by the end of the second day fresh German troops miraculously appeared and restored some order. The town was to take center stage in a holding action to protect the exposed flanks of the retreating army. The center piece of the stand was an artillery unit who spent the early evening moving a howitzer into position beneath some willows that lined the creek running along the edge of the town. Kaz wandered down to the creek and watched the sweating and cursing, green-clad soldiers as they muscled the large gun into a spot well-hidden from the air and covered it with camouflage nets. A dozen men swarmed over the gun oiling it and making final adjustments.

The faint crackle of rifle fire echoed among the nearby hills, followed by the muffled boom of an artillery piece. The windows in the building above their heads reverberated.

The local dentist joined Kaz to watch the proceedings. "Sounds like the shelling has already started up the valley," he commented as he lit a cigarette.

"I'd say the Russians are close," Kaz replied. "It won't be too long before this gun is put to use."

"I hope they don't destroy the town."

"Hard to say. Maybe not. The Germans are moving pretty fast. I imagine they'll make their main stand farther north, probably around Krakow."

The dentist shivered and drew his coat more closely around him. "My offices are just up there." He pointed to two windows overlooking the creek. "You're welcome to join me for a shot or two of vodka while we watch the show."

"That's the best offer I've had in days."

Drink in hand, Kaz joined his host in a chair by the window. A small group of soldiers appeared in the willows to consult with the commander of the gun crew. They carried a disassembled machine gun. The officer in charge pointed down the creek, and the soldiers stumbled off through the willows. Intermittent bursts of rifle fire erupted somewhere near the city.

"That's getting damn close," the dentist remarked in a worried tone.

"We should probably get out of here."

"I don't want to leave the place to looters. I'm staying."

"I might as well, then. Be a shame to miss the fireworks."

No sooner had Kaz spoken than the gun hidden in the willows boomed and belched a sheet of orange flame into the fading light. The window rattled violently as the percussion wave hit it. The crew immediately set about reloading the gun. Shortly, it roared again. The target appeared to be in the nearby foothills where Kaz presumed the Russians were advancing. The shelling continued until a wave of Russian planes appeared in the darkening sky. Bombs whistled overhead, but they overshot the big gun and crashed into houses a block or two north of the main square. The whole building trembled.

A second wave of planes swooped to the attack. More bombs landed long. As soon as the planes were gone, the gun roared again. The deep shadows of night stretched across the landscape below the window, making it harder to see the target, but that didn't deter the Russians. More planes swept in and pressed their attack indiscriminately on the town. A fire siren sounded, indicating that some of the buildings caught in the bombings were ablaze. Between bombardments, the big gun continued its barrage on the foothills.

Kaz felt as though he were back in blood alley waiting for the coming train. The scene mesmerized him. He wanted to sit there sipping vodka and watching the entire world burn around him. The bombs were falling much closer. Each explosion showered the building with a wave of debris. Kaz moved away from the window just in time to avoid injury when a bomb blast shattered the window and sent glass and metal flying. The lights flickered and went out. Common sense got the best of him.

"Time to leave."

The dentist agreed.

"I have a cellar under my building," Kaz offered. "You're welcome to join me there."

"Thanks, but I have a daughter at home across town. I need to check on her."

They finished their drinks with a salute and left.

Kaz jogged down a side street toward the agricultural center. Smoke and dust spiraled from a wrecked house across the street. Between the bombs and shells, he could hear heavy rifle fire in the foothills. However, the howitzer had fallen silent. Kaz wondered whether the crew had run out of ammunition or one of the bombs had found its mark. If the latter, it was likely the dentist's building was no longer standing.

The center's door stood open. Kaz ducked through it, half expecting to surprise looters, but the place was quiet. If there had been looters, they were gone. He grabbed candles and matches and pulled open the heavy door to the cellar. It was pitch black inside, so he lit a candle before closing the door and descending the cellar's rickety, wooden stairs. The place smelled of damp walls, drying firewood and molding potatoes. Kaz pulled out a torn, horsehair mattress and laid it on the concrete floor to sit on. The thought of food wormed its way into his consciousness. With all the excitement, he hadn't thought about dinner. He pulled out his pocket knife and peeled several potatoes that were still edible. They crunched like apples in his mouth. It wasn't the best meal he'd had in a while, but it filled his stomach.

The noises of war grew steadily closer, yet their rhythm was somehow comforting. The sounds were constant and repetitive. They formed a rocking motion that soon put Kaz to sleep.

He awoke suddenly to the flickering light of his candle and the sputtering of a small machine gun in the street above his head. The first, gray streaks of morning light filtered through the cellar door. Russian voices could be heard shouting. He jumped up, tensed and ready to run, but where? Again, the machine gun sputtered, this time in tune with the crackle of rifles. The noise moved down the street and turned the corner. Kaz continued to listen. No more bombs were falling. Just the chirping of rifle fire moving farther away. He decided to poke his head out of the cellar to see what was happening. He pushed open the heavy door and stepped into the gray dawn. The air was thin and bitter cold. His breaths puffed in small clouds which rose toward the morning sunlight. The street was deserted, but boisterous voices echoed from the main square. The voices were punctuated by the short, staccato chatter of more machine guns. There was no return gunfire.

Kaz walked cautiously up the street and peered around the corner toward the square. A hundred feet away, two burly Russian privates tugged at the frozen corpse of a dead German officer sprawled on the pavement. They swayed and swore as they worked. One put a foot unsteadily on the corpse's chest while the other yanked at the dead man's boots. They were obviously drunk. The man with his foot on the body looked up and spotted Kaz, who froze for a moment before deciding it was smarter to engage the two than try to outrun their rifles.

"What are you doing?" he asked in Polish as he slowly walked toward them. One of the men stared at him blankly, but he smiled in recognition.

"We're getting some fresh boots," the man replied in Polish, "but this son of a bitch doesn't want to give them up."

"He's frozen stiff. You might have to chop off his legs." Kaz meant it as a joke, but the Russian looked at the corpse thoughtfully.

"No ax," he said finally. He returned to his tug of war.

Kaz shuffled past them into the square, where he discovered a dead German Lieutenant lying face up. His throat had been torn away by a large caliber bullet. Every drop of blood had drained from his cheeks.

He reminded Kaz of the wax figures he'd seen in the military museum in Wawel Castle.

Two blocks from the square, Kaz encountered a group of Russians chopping madly at a frozen fire hose that blocked the street. He greeted them, and they swarmed around him, slapping his back and shouting. Kaz could only understand the word 'vodka,' which was repeated many times. They were already teetering on the edge of incoherence, but all they could think about was finding more of the stuff.

He spotted a local fireman struggling with the fire hose at the hydrant connection. "What's going on?" he asked.

"We were trying to put out the fires from the bombings last night when a new wave of planes dropped more. We had to abandon our hoses and run for cover. By the time we got back, they were frozen solid."

Shattered glass, cinders, corpses, dead horses and other debris were intermingled with the hoses in a frozen mass of dirty ice. The fireman's job seemed hopeless, but the dilemma was quickly solved when a Russian tank turned a corner and bullied its way down the street. Everything was crushed as the tank rolled through the hoses and debris. A grinning commander waved from the open hatch and raised an empty wine bottle. He shouted a greeting as he threw it into the street.

"It's a wonder the whole town didn't burn," Kaz commented to the fireman.

"Half of it did." He pointed to the gutted buildings along the street.

Kaz continued to wander down the street inspecting the damage. The rising sun glowed red through a gaping hole in the second floor of a doctor's office. An artillery shell had passed right through the building without exploding. An iron balcony that had graced a small veranda on the front of the office dangled from a single screw bolted into the wall. Russian soldiers darted into the damaged buildings and emerged triumphantly with stolen prizes. Kaz's attention was drawn to a group of Russians, half of them women, who were were gathered on the sidewalk screaming and shouting with joy. The women were camp followers, Kaz realized, who traveled in the wake of the army and gave comfort to the soldiers. Kaz edged forward to see what held their interest. Two of the men were down on their knees playing with a wind-up toy truck that zipped around in crazy circles on the cold cement. Perhaps, Kaz mused, it was the first time they'd ever seen a mechanical toy. A little further along, he came across soldiers prying ice shoes off two dead horses lying amid the fallen bricks and rubble of a bombed out building. They wanted the ice shoes for their own horses.

A troop truck broke the calm when it burst around the corner and slammed on its brakes in front of a shoe shop that had ridden out the storm unscathed. Two bearded men jumped down with machine guns at the ready and charged into the building. They emerged moments later with a struggling, pale-faced Gestapo officer who'd been seen hiding in the building and reported to the Russians. One of the men snatched the officer's hat from his head, spat on it and tossed it into the air. He fired a short burst from his machine gun that made it dance briefly before tumbling back to earth. The other slammed the Gestapo officer to the ground face down and cut the prostrate body to pieces with his own weapon. Kaz imagined that the same, swift justice was being delivered all over Poland at that moment.

Kaz tried to stay clear of the drunk men, but one caught his lapels and spun him around. "Where Berlin?" he asked in broken Polish.

"One day," Kaz replied and pointed west over the roof tops. He realized that the soldier knew little about maps of the world and had probably never heard of Berlin before the war started.

"One day," the man repeated.

"Close," Kaz assured him.

"Close." The man pointed toward the rooftops.

To his surprise, Kaz came across the dentist from the night before rushing along the street. When he spotted Kaz he hurried over to him. "I don't know what to do. The Russians have invaded our house. They have taken over the second floor and won't leave. I sent my daughter to neighbors and came to find someone in charge, but everything is chaos."

"Did you ask them to leave?"

"I've been afraid to go up there. There's so much loud noise and drinking. They've taken all the vodka. They act like they belong there."

"They may feel they do. It's common for soldiers to move into the houses of the defeated. If you had been German, they would probably have killed you." He motioned down the street. "Let's go have a look."

He followed the little man for several blocks to a small, two-story house on the edge of town. When Kaz entered the place, he was struck by a foul odor that nearly stopped him in his tracks. Voices could be heard, but they sounded like women's. Kaz ventured up the stairway to the second floor landing. The first door on his right stood wide open. When he looked inside, he discovered three naked, Russian women standing in the middle of the room. They were taking turns enjoying a 'stand up bath' in a washtub filled with dirty water. When they saw Kaz's surprised face, they laughed and kept on washing.

More camp followers, he thought as he politely withdrew from the room. The stench he'd first noted downstairs grew stronger as he approached the second room. Smoked drifted toward him, and for a moment, Kaz feared the house was on fire. He quickly found the source of the smoke and was relieved to see that it was simply the remnants of a campfire comprised of bits of broken furniture that was burning merrily atop a layer of bricks laid on the floor. Four burly men with the narrow eyes of Mongolians squatted on their haunches around the fire tending a bubbling pot of strong tea. The kettle dangled from a make-shift crossbar over the fire. Two half-finished bottles of vodka rested on the floor nearby. The only furniture left in the room had been broken into pieces for more firewood and stacked in one corner. In another, piles of excrement and urine stains gave off a sour odor. They didn't seem to have any idea how to use the toilet across the hallway. Beds were useless to them, as well. Mattresses had been ripped apart and the straw spread along two walls for sleeping. The place looked and smelled like an outhouse.

One of the men motioned for Kaz to join them for tea. He smiled and declined with a brief shake of his head. He backed from the room and headed back down the stairs.

"There's not much you can do," he advised. "They appear to be Mongolian and have little understanding of western culture or hygiene. Just try to keep them upstairs. With any luck, they'll move on once the vodka is finished."

No sooner had he spoken than four new men stomped the slush from their shoes as they climbed the steps to the front porch and stormed into the house without so much as a nod of the head. They headed straight for the cellar and disappeared below.

"That's the other problem," the dentist wailed. "This is the third group that has come to raid our potato bins. Soon they'll strip us clean!"

Kaz glanced out the window in time to see an impeccably dressed Russian officer strutting past. Kaz turned to the dentist."Do you speak any Russian?"

"A little, My wife's parents came from Russia."

"Follow me. Maybe we can get some help."

Kaz hurried out the front door and down the steps to intercept the Russian officer. He motioned to the dentist to translate.

"Greetings," Kaz called.

"Hello," came the reply. "How are things with you, comrades?"

Kaz put a frown on his face. "Not bad, but we will soon be out of food."

The officer looked confused. "Why?" He tapped his fingers on his leather belt.

"There are four men and three women who have taken over the second floor of our house, and there are four more in the cellar right now stealing potatoes. What should we do?"

The officer's face flushed with anger. "The men are supposed to bivouac on the edge of town. Under no circumstances are they to steal food. Lead me to them." He picked up a piece of a broken wooden railing lying in the street and followed them into the house.

The dentist showed him through the kitchen to an open doorway leading down to the cellar. Voices and scrabbling sounds came from below.

"They're down there," the dentist said.

The officer leaned forward and shouted in a commanding voice. "Come out of there at once."

The voices stopped talking. After a moment's silence, whispers could be heard.

"I said come out of there, now!"

Muffled footsteps scraped on the wooden stairs, and the ruddy face of a Russian soldier appeared in the open doorway. When he saw the officer, he smiled. He carried several potatoes in his arms. Without warning, the officer whacked the private across the forehead. A second blow smacked his bare hands and sent the potatoes flying. The terrified private bolted out of the cellar and through the kitchen toward the front door. A second soldier appeared at the top of the stairs and gingerly pushed his head into view. The officer's stick caught him across the back of the neck. Howling with pain, he emerged from the cellar under more blows and raced for safety. The last two privates met similar fates as they emerged from the cellar and ran the gauntlet of heavy blows. By this time, potatoes were scattered everywhere.

The soldiers upstairs heard the commotion and peered over the second floor railing. When they saw what was happening, they didn't wait for an invitation to leave. The ran back to their room, grabbed the vodka bottles and their few belongings, and tumbled down the stairs and out the front door. The women were slower to react, and by the time they started down, the officer was waiting for them. He raised his wooden cudgel as the women ran past screaming in terror, but he didn't strike them. When they were gone, he tossed the piece of wood out the door.

"There," he said with satisfaction, "that's the way you handle those fellows. You have to show them who's boss. They are simple peasants from Siberia who lack the discipline of army regulars, but they make excellent fighters. We often use them in the front lines."

"Thank you for your help," the dentist said as he looked ruefully up the stairs at the disaster that awaited him.

"If they bother you again, come to my office in the square." He bowed stiffly from the waist, turned on his heels and departed.

Kaz chuckled. "I didn't know what to expect when we accosted that officer. Certainly not such quick action." He followed the dentist's gaze up the stairs. "You better make sure the fires are out and clean up the crap. Probably best that you stay downstairs for a few days while you air the place out. There's no furniture left up there anyway."

The dentist nodded sadly. Kaz didn't envy him. He left the man to his troubles and returned to the square, where he was pleased to see some order being restored. The drunk shock troops had been put to work piling debris out of the way so vehicles could pass. One shop owner was trying to board up his broken window with strips of wood that had survived the bombs. Others combed the the rubble of ruined stores in search of anything that might be salvaged.

Kaz hurried to the agricultural center and found things in disarray. Chairs were overturned and papers were scattered. Looters had made off with some of the food and vodka, but much was left untouched, suggesting that they'd been interrupted. The upstairs bedrooms were still intact. No fires had been set, and no feces had been left behind. Kaz thanked his lucky stars for that small favor, although he couldn't imagine what new adventures were in store.

The first month of the Russian occupation was often comical. The shock troops who had taken the town were largely a band of illiterate, unwashed bears. They seemed insensitive to pain or cold and took orders from the Russian officers like mindless animals. They laughed at everything, including themselves, and demonstrated a bottomless capacity for strong alcohol. They drank anything that was fermented and ate whatever they could find. The Poles quickly learned that it was best to stay out of their way. It was much easier to deal with them when they were drunk and well fed. The officers did try to keep them under control, but Kaz thought such a task was about as productive as herding sheep in a snow storm. Their attention was there one minute and gone the next.

When regular troops finally arrived, the change was instantly apparent. They were more efficient, shrewder, better trained and ready to carry out their duties. They were directed by a new authority called the NKVD, and they went about their work with the same ruthless thoroughness as their Nazi predecessors.

One of their first orders of business was to direct everybody associated with the underground to present themselves at the offices in the square to register. Kaz didn't like the idea, and when he checked with a few other partisan supporters, they felt the same. It sounded like the Russians wanted to control the organization or disband it. None of the partisans in the mountains complied, and only a handful of local sympathizers showed up at the Russian headquarters. That was all the Russians needed, however. They interrogated those who registered, and after enough pressure was applied, secured the names of other underground members. The web of names spread through the community, and the number of prisoners in the old, city jail quickly grew.

Strange faces began to appear in the town. There was no way of knowing if the newcomers were fugitives from Warsaw or Krakow, or simply agents planted by the Russians to spy on the populace. Kaz thought he recognized one of the men from Krakow and asked him who he knew there. The man mentioned a few names. None of them were familiar to Kaz. He'd hoped to hear about Agata, but no information was forthcoming. His suspicions grew.

A blanket of unease settled over Nowy Targ. A local militia was formed to help the Russians police the town. Its ranks were salted with Russian sympathizers. Even a few partisans joined up, feeling it was safer to blend in with the new order than to remain ensconced in the mountains. It became more difficult to distinguish friend from spy, and after awhile, the townspeople, weary from the war and confused by all that had transpired, didn't really care. The one dream everybody still shared was a Poland free from the yoke of suppression, a Poland no longer interrupted. It didn't seem likely that the Russians were going to let that happen. Depression mingled with the unease that overlay the town.

A handful of the hard core partisans gathered in an abandoned hostel in the mountains to discuss ways to keep the underground functioning against the new threat of Russian domination, but they had to scatter when word reached them that someone had betrayed them. Cut off from their sources in Warsaw and Krakow, the underground was left in a near vacuum. The remnants of the once-proud organization were no more effective than a snake with its head chopped off. It was impossible to function as they had in the past.

Kaz continued to work at the agricultural center, but he couldn't resume his black market activities. A new manager was brought in who knew how things worked. He poured over the books and quickly noticed past discrepancies. Kaz feigned ignorance, but it was clear that the game was up. A few weeks later, militia showed up at the office, and Kaz was taken to NKVD headquarters. Someone had turned him in.

Chapter Twenty-nine

The uniforms were different; the language was different; the faces were new. Aside from those disparities, Kaz could have just as easily been back in a Gestapo holding cell. The surroundings and the procedures were much the same.

"Empty your pockets," a NKVD officer demanded.

Kaz pulled a few coins, his ID card and a comb from his trousers and dumped them on the metal table in the middle of the room. Why were interrogation tables always metal, he wondered? Perhaps, to make the prisoner feel less comfortable. There was something warmer and friendlier about wood.

"Sit down." The officer pointed to a chair at the table. Kaz complied, but the officer remained standing. That was a new twist. "Why didn't you register as a member of the underground? Don't lie. We know all about you."

So it begins, Kaz thought. The same frightening pattern of questions, insinuations and threats. Soon, there would be beatings. The Russians operated much like the Nazis, only they moved into the charade a little quicker and with less finesse. Kaz braced himself for what must come.

For the next several days, Kaz played cat and mouse with his interrogators. It was evident that they were already aware of his activities against the Germans. So, he slowly confessed details about what they seemed to know and avoided any information that could compromise Simon the Red or other resistance fighters who might still be operating in the area. To his surprise, the Russians didn't beat him. Instead, they chose to torture him with repeated questions and threats, a cold cell and barely edible food. Kaz carefully agreed to their assertions about the black market run out of the agricultural center and his brief meetings with Drochojewski, but he never betrayed the names or locations of the partisans.

After a week, he was hauled into an office where he was greeted by the officer who'd chased the soldiers from the house belonging to the dentist.

"Greetings, again, comrade." He indicated the chair in front of his wood desk in a warm manner. "Please sit down."

Kaz was surprised to learn that the man spoke Polish. He responded with relief, then grew wary, certain that a trap was being set for him. The officer offered him a cigarette and sat down as well.

"Congratulations, Kaz Swiba."

Kaz smiled inwardly. His true identity was still buried in Krakow.

"You have passed your test."

"What test?" he asked suspiciously.

"The test of truth. We have quite a dossier on you, your black market activities, your contacts with the partisans, your involvement with Drochojewski. Your file was flagged, and you were seen as a potential trouble maker. So far, however, you have shown yourself willing to work with us. We believe you are someone we can trust. Do you agree?" He flashed a warm smile.

Kaz remained calm on the outside, but his insides were churning. Did they expect him to work for them? To be a spy? That would never happen, but he knew he had to play their little game for now, until he figured out what to do.

"I'm glad you think so," he replied cautiously. "I don't want to be any trouble."

"Good." The officer stood up and tapped his fingers on his belt, just as he had the day they met. "You're free to go back to work. We'll keep in touch."

Kaz felt eyes watching him as he departed the NKVD headquarters, eyes of the Russians intent on trapping him, and eyes of the locals wondering how much information he'd divulged. He was caught in the cross hairs of both sides. It was an unsettling feeling.

On a whim, he decided to drop by the dentist's house to see how he was faring. He noted as he approached the place that despite the chilled air, the upstairs windows were all flung open. He couldn't help chuckling to himself. It would not be easy to rid the house of those offensive odors.

The dentist answered his knock on the door and offered him some tea. "It's all I have left. Those darned soldiers cleaned me out."

Kaz shivered as he entered the cold house. "Where's your daughter?" He'd yet to meet her.

"She's visiting her aunt in a village nearby. She couldn't take the smell." He laughed and wrinkled his nose. "I'm doing the best I can to disinfect the place."

The odor was far less noticeable, but it was still there.

"I hear you had a run in with the NKVD." The dentist looked at Kaz curiously. Was it an innocent question? Kaz couldn't be sure. "It's good that they let you go. So many end up in their freshly painted jails."

Definitely suspicion, Kaz whispered to himself. The townspeople were concerned.

"I was surprised, also," he admitted. "I think they want me to spy for them. That's not going to happen." He stared at his cup of tea while he pondered his next words. A plan was forming in his head. "Maybe it's time to move on."

"Where did you come from?"

"Krakow. I've thought about going back there. Or making my way to Gdynia."

The more he thought about it, the more he realized that Krakow was the last place he wanted to go. There were memories waiting for him on every street corner in that city. But if he could get to Gdynia, he might be able to find work on ships. He might even be able to escape Russia's clutches altogether. Find a ship leaving Poland. Maybe find one going to America! The thought sent shivers through him. It was the first time such an idea had entered his head. He was tired of trying to outfox the authorities: first the Germans, now the Russians. He was tired of living under a repressive regime, and he knew that the Russians weren't leaving. Life was only going to get worse. It was just a matter of time before he ended up in jail. His life would always be interrupted, just like his country.

"My only problem is having the right travel documents." Kaz pulled out his ID. "This won't work. I need to use my real name. Kowinsky. The Russians know nothing about Kaz Kowinsky."

"I can help you with that." The dentist's quiet voice jarred him.

"What do you mean?

" I have a good friend who works at the militia headquarters. He should be able to take the photo from your ID and prepare fresh documents under any name you like. It just depends on how closely he's being watched."

"You would arrange that for me?"

He gestured around the house with his hand. "You helped me get my home back. The least I can do is help you."

Kaz gave him a broad smile. For the first time since the Germans had left, he felt he had a friend.

"Come back in two days. I'll know something by then."

When Kaz returned, he was greeted at the door by the dentist's daughter.

"I'm Stenia," she said with a quick smile that raised a matching dimple on either cheek. Her hair was shoulder length and blonde, her body plump. She looked to be in her early twenties. When her face grew serious, the dimples disappeared. "Father is expecting you."

She led him into the living room and went to fetch her father. Kaz was pleased to see that the windows were closed and the was room warm. The odor that had invaded the place was only a faint memory.

The dentist arrived with a tight smile that disappeared as quickly as his daughter's.

"Any trouble?" Kaz asked anxiously.

"It appears so. The Russians are preparing to register everybody in the town. They have a list of names of those who were associated with the partisans. You're on that list, of course."

"I already told them that I had some involvement. That's when that interrogation officer suggested I spy for him."

"Which is why you aren't already in jail."

"How do you know this?"

"My friend in the documents office. He knows some Russian and hears things. He said he'll be taking quite a risk if he forges new ID papers for you. Everyone is being watched closely. But he'll try."

Kaz felt his stomach tighten. "How long do I have?"

"Not long. The Russians are going to register all the men born between 1910 and 1927. Anyone who ignores the demand will be thrown in prison. You need to go before the registrations begin." The dentist stared at his feet. His face turned ruddy. He lifted his hand to his mouth and coughed. "I have a favor to ask."

Kaz could see the tension in the man's face. Something was wrong. "What is it?"

"I want you to take Stenia with you as far as Gdansk."

Kaz arched his eyebrows in surprise. "Whatever for? Traveling to Gdansk might be dangerous. There are still a lot of Germans roaming around the countryside."

The dentist sighed and looked at his feet once more. "My daughter is pregnant. She had an affair with a German officer. She's already an outcast in the town. God knows what would happen to her once people learn she's with child. There's a lot of anger right now."

Kaz tried to sort through this unexpected development. He wanted to help, but he was worried enough about his own safety. Taking a young, pregnant woman along would make things even more difficult.

"Why up north?" he asked.

"I have a married sister who has a farm near Gdansk. I have no way of contacting her, but I know she'll help. Stenia can say her husband was killed in the war and have the baby there. No one will ask questions." He looked at Kaz with pleading eyes. "I will give her money. She won't be a burden. Please, take her with you."

His instinct was to say no, but how could he? Kaz needed that new ID. It would be impolite to accept the dentist's help and not reciprocate. "How will it look, the two of us traveling together?"

"Everything is in chaos. No one will care. Least of all the Russians."

It was settled. Kaz would take Stenia with him. He only hoped she wouldn't slow him down.

Two days later, Kaz had his documents, printed in both Russian and Polish. It identified him as a Lieutenant in the Nowy Targ militia en route to Gdynia. It bore the NKVD stamp and the forged signature of the local commandant. The Russians only allowed the Poles to carry 500 zlotys, so Kaz hid the rest of his money in his shoe. He remembered the man who refused to hide his zlotys in his shoe, because he feared it was the first place the Germans would look. Kaz hoped the Russians were not as thorough. Then, he stuffed a knapsack with dry Polish sausages, a loaf of hard, dark bread and extra clothes. It was Saturday. The agricultural center had already closed for the weekend. He wouldn't be missed before Monday. Neither he nor Stenia dared to show their faces at the train station. They would have to hike and ski their way through the mountains until they were a safe distance from Nowy Targ. Only then could they consider trying public transportation.

When he was ready to go, he threw the knapsack over one shoulder and his snow skis over the other. Kaz couldn't keep Christina from his thoughts as he trudged through the town's familiar back streets to the dentist's house. He pictured her waiting for him at the cottage in the forest. He saw Drochojewski smiling from the villa down below. The memories gave him warmth, even as he reminded himself that the villa had been burned to the ground and the cottage taken over by Germans. Who lived there now, he wondered? Russian soldiers? It didn't matter. He wasn't going near the place.

Kaz stared straight ahead as he walked. Suddenly, the streets seemed unfamiliar. He was a wanderer lost in a strange land, a spec of cork floating in a cold, lonely sea. As he neared the edge of town, he saw a large, red Russian flag fluttering in the wind against a silky, blue sky. The flag reminded him of his mission, and he glanced around furtively to make certain that he wasn't being followed. How long would that flag stay there, he wondered? Days? Months? Years? It no longer mattered. He would be gone. Somehow, he would leave the Russians behind and be gone.

Stenia was waiting for him with her own backpack and skis. She gave him a look of gratitude. She might be short and a little plump, but he was pleased to see her lift her pack and skis onto her shoulders effortlessly. The young woman had hidden strength.

The dentist hugged and kissed his daughter goodbye.

"Keep her safe, Kaz."

"I'll do my best ... for both of us."

"Thank you, Kaz," Stenia added. "I won't be a burden to you."

They slipped out the back door into a tiny alley and headed for the mountains.

For the first two days, they stayed in the forests during the day and hiked as much as they skied. Kaz was pleased to see Stenia working her way through the snow with determined efficiency. He soon forgot about his concerns and discovered that he liked the company. It was better than traveling alone.

They spoke very little at first. Stenia was a bit shy, and Kaz was uncertain what to say.

"Your father told me what happened," he ventured when they stopped to rest.

"I know." She bowed her head and looked away. "I was so lonely at that time, and he was so handsome. I thought I was in love, but now I realize how foolish I was. I acted like a silly school girl."

Kaz thought about Daneta. "We all do foolish things one time or another."

As the sun set, they made his way down to the valleys. Some of the farmers there knew Kaz from his work at the agricultural center, and he was able to find food and a place to sleep. On the third day, they left the familiar territory behind. They would be at the mercy of strangers. Kaz thought it best to stay away from towns until they put more space between themselves and Nowy Targ, so they stayed in the forests during the day and spent the next two nights shivering in old barns. They huddled for warmth, and Kaz was chagrined to discover that he was aroused by the soft body pressed against his. On the fifth day, they'd traveled less than a dozen kilometers before the weather warmed, and it started to rain. Great sections of half-frozen earth were soon exposed, which made skiing impractical. They lashed their skis across their backs and proceeded on foot.

After another day of hiking, they agreed that it was time to find a ride. They hesitantly approached a rail station in a small town where a freight train steamed idly beneath a patched up water tower that had some how survived the war. Kaz was amazed to see hundreds of people milling around. Most held battered suitcases or large sacks filled with belongings. They were hoping to catch a train just like him. Two Russian soldiers were trying to push the crowd back. Another stood guard further down the tracks. No one seemed to be checking papers, so they hid their skis in some brush and walked across the tracks into the station. The platform was alive with buzzing voices. Kaz spotted a man stooped at the shoulders standing to one side and walked over to him. Stenia followed at a distance.

"What's happening?" Kaz asked in an offhand manner.

"Nothing," the man grunted. He gave Kaz an inquiring stare. "Where did you come from?"

"My girlfriend and I hiked through the mountains. We want to get to Gdynia. Are there any passenger trains scheduled?"

The man grunted again. "Supposed to be one this morning. As you can see, it never came." He pointed toward the ticket window. A closed sign hung from a hook. "Doesn't appear to be one coming anytime soon, either."

Kaz pondered the situation for a moment. He stared down the tracks at the Russian guard. "Got any vodka?"

The man's lips lifted into a half smile. "You need a drink?"

"Not for me," Kaz replied casually. "For that guard down there." He nodded down the tracks. "He looks awful thirsty."

"You think he'd take it?"

"Worth a try. Give me the your bottle and follow me as far as the water tower."

The man hesitated.

"I won't steal it," Kaz assured him, "although I sure could use a good swig about now!"

The man's mouth worked its way into a full smile. "I could as well." He pulled a bottle from his bag, opened it and took a long drink, then handed it to Kaz, who did the same.

"Okay, follow me." Kaz signaled to Stenia to join him, and they approached the guard. Kaz took another swallow from the bottle and handed it to the surprised soldier. "You speak Polish?"

The man looked at him blankly. Kaz pointed to Stenia and the stooped man standing near the water tower, then at the boxcar behind the guard. "Why don't you let us ride in there," he pointed at the boxcar again, "and keep the vodka?" He indicated the bottle in the soldier's hand.

The soldier looked up and down the tracks and nodded with a grin. "Da."

Kaz signaled to the stooped man while the guard slid the open bottle into a large pocket in his coat. Kaz handed him the top to the bottle, hopped up into the box car and pulled Stenia after him. The stooped man followed.

"Got to admit, I wouldn't of had the nerve to do that," he laughed.

"There wasn't much risk.'

"He might have kept the bottle and turned us away."

"He might have. In any case, I owe you some vodka." Both men laughed.

Kaz looked around. The car was empty except for a few pieces of farm equipment. Soon, the engine made a chugging sound, and the train lurched into motion.

"Any idea where this thing is going?" Kaz queried.

"None."

"As long as it's north, it doesn't matter."

The train made several stops during the night. More voices of anxious travelers could be heard on the platforms. It sounded as though half the country was on the move. No one bothered to check the cars. At one stop, they slipped outside to relieve themselves. Otherwise, they stayed out of sight.

A gray dawn was filtering through the door when the train halted a few miles from Auschwitz. Kaz recognized the station from his days when he drove trains there. The town was called Sosnowiec. Everybody decided to take a chance and stretch their legs. When they clambered down, they were greeted by a parade of ghostly images trudging along the road away from the concentration camp. The figures weren't much more than skeletons. Their tattered rags offered little protection from the morning chill, but they didn't seem to notice as they plodded along. Their ashen faces were pocked with dark hollows that cradled sullen, haunted eyes. Shriveled legs propelled them forward. Kaz had no idea where they were going. Someplace where they could get food and rest.

Kaz immediately thought about Charlie and realized that if he was in this group of forlorn souls, Kaz would never recognize him. Not that there was any chance of seeing him, again. He would have died long before now.

Kaz saw a yard worker throwing switches and realized that the freight train was to be shunted onto a siding. It wasn't going any farther, at least for now. Kaz and Stenia said goodbye to their travel companion and headed into what was left of the town. Most of the buildings had been partially or completely destroyed. Restaurants were shuttered; shops were boarded up. People wandered about in a daze looking for food and shelter. Kaz remembered that one of the train engineers he'd gotten to know on the runs from Krakow lived there. He suggested to Stenia that they look for him, but he found it difficult to recognize streets or landmarks as he picked his way through the rubble. He recalled an old Catholic church down the block from the house. He finally turned a corner and spotted a burned out shell where the church had stood. He might not have recognized it but for the cross it still displayed above the shattered doorway. He was pleased to see that the street beyond remained largely intact. His friend's house was still standing.

A short, balding man answered Kaz's knock. His face beamed with a smile. "Kaz. Kaz Kowinsky. As I live and breathe."

"Hello, Sigmund. I'm pleased to find you in good health."

"Health is about all I have left. But, at least my home is standing, so I can't complain so much. Who's your friend?"

"This is Stenia. I'm taking her to family in Gdansk."

Stenia smiled and shook his hand.

"Well, it's good to see you both. Come in."

When Kaz entered the living room, he saw a large crack in the plaster and noted a ten degree lean to the wall. It had survived the shelling and bombing, but just barely. "Where's your family?"

Staying with relatives in a nearby town. There's less damage there. I've remained to protect the place from looters and to fix things up a bit. Right now, I need a solid piece of wood to shore up this bearing wall." He patted the door frame that Kaz had noticed. "If it tilts any further, the whole building might collapse."

"I saw some pretty solid pieces of timber in the next block. They might do the trick."

"Yes, but I can't drag them back by myself, and everybody has their own problems." Sigmund rubbed his forehead in frustration.

"Why don't we tackle it together?" He turned to Stenia. "We've got some time, don't we?"

"For a friend, definitely," she responded.

Sigmund looked at Kaz with gratitude. "That would be a godsend."

They spent the next three hours retrieving beams of wood that had been splintered but not burned and nailing them together to form a buttress to brace the tilted wall.

"There," Sigmund declared with satisfaction when they were done. "It's not pretty, but it should support the wall until I can get some construction workers in here." He headed for the kitchen. "Come on. I've got some vodka stashed away and chicken left over from last night. With some potatoes, we can have ourselves a feast."

"What are your plans?" Sigmund asked after they were settled at the kitchen table. "If you stick around here, I can find you work on the trains. The Russians need engineers."

Kaz shook his head. "The Russians are looking for me by now, only under a different last name. I'm safe for the moment, but I need to get to Gdynia and Stenia has to get to Gdansk."

Sigmund frowned. "The war's only just ended up north. The train tracks are a mess. You might be able to get to Gdansk, but from what I've heard, you'd probably have to walk from there."

"If that's what it takes, we don't mind. The biggest problem seems to be finding a train. We hopped a freight to get this far."

"There should be a train heading that way sometime tomorrow. It's supposed to be a mixture of freight and passenger. Can't say exactly when, though. There's no set schedules at this point. But I should be able to get you both on it. My guess is you need a place to stay tonight. You can take the children's bedrooms. We'll go to the station tomorrow morning after breakfast."

Kaz grinned from one side of his face to the other. "Now you sound like a godsend."

The children's bedrooms were located down the hall from Sigmund's with a bathroom in between. Kaz lay in the dark trying not to think about the fetching woman sleeping in the next room. It'd been awhile since he'd slept with a woman, and he had to admit Stenia was very tempting. He didn't want to betray her father's trust, however, so he closed his eyes and tried to concentrate on the journey ahead of them. Kaz was about to doze off when he heard the door creak open and quickly close again. He went rigid in disbelief. At first he though it was just his imagination, but when he heard bare feet padding toward him he knew it was no dream.

His bed jiggled as Stenia sat down on the edge.

"Move over," she whispered.

Kaz hesitated. "What about your father?"

"What about him? I'm a grown woman who can do as she wants, and I can't get any more pregnant. Move over." Her voice was insistent.

Kaz let out the breath he'd been holding and complied. She slid in beside him and pressed her body against his. Her skin was deliciously warm and smooth. Kaz soon forgot about her father. Sometime during the night he slept. She was gone the next morning when he woke. When they gathered for breakfast, she smiled warmly but gave no indication that anything had transpired. Maybe, it had just been a dream, he thought.

The train station was teeming with people, all trying to escape the rubble that once had been a town. Sigmund bypassed the crowded platform and took Kaz and Stenia to the familiar yards where he'd run so many trains. No train was in sight, but the station master assured them that one was coming.

Five hours later, an old steam engine dragged a hodgepodge of box and passenger cars into the station. Kaz had positioned himself and Stenia near the edge of the platform and muscled his way through a wall of seething bodies to a car marked first class. He held the tickets that Sigmund had obtained for them, but nobody paid them any attention. Stenia followed close behind as he fought and clawed his was up the narrow steps into the car and quickly claimed two seats by the window in the front compartment. The remaining seats were instantly filled by other passengers. A large, drunken man tried to bully his way into Stenia's seat but stopped when she bared her fingernails at him. Kaz shoved him aside and both of them gave him a fierce look. The man scowled, then took a seat on the floor in the walkway outside the compartment.

The compartment was tiny, but it seemed reasonably comfortable, at least until the engine chugged to life in preparation to depart. The man seated next to Kaz promptly stood up and opened the window, allowing two of his friends to clamber head first into the train car. They immediately made themselves at home on the floor between the seats. Legs and feet had to move aside to accommodate them. Any prospect of comfort quickly vanished.

Kaz decided to address the unspoken tension that he felt between himself and Stenia. "About last night ... "

"Last night was wonderful," she interrupted. "I hope we have a chance to do that again before we reach Gdansk." She gave him a bright smile that lit up her blue eyes and dimples. "It helps me forget my unhappy prospects, at least for a little while."

Kaz retreated behind a foolish grin and said nothing more.

The train wheezed its way slowly along the tracks as if unsure of its footing on the weakened rails, and it stopped at every town to rest. At one stop, Kaz watched from his window as rail men discussed the safety of the next section of track. He recalled the early days of Germany's invasion when he'd ridden a similar train through volleys of bullets from Stukas. The tracks had been just as weak then. He was tempted to go talk with the men but knew if he did, someone would claim his seat over Stenia's protests. Most likely, he'd end up standing the rest of the way to Gdansk.

The men finished their discussions, and the train proceeded on its way. It crept along the tracks at a speed not much faster than a brisk walk until it reached Torun. What should have been a journey of two hours had taken nearly six. Night had arrived ahead of them, and to make matters worse, they were informed that the tracks needed further repairs before the train could proceed. They were stranded there until the next morning. A conductor walked through the cars telling everyone to disembark until then.

Although Torun was far from the coast, it had been a favorite stop for seamen heading home or returning to their ships. Kaz had spent a few hours at a seaman's house there on his way back to Krakow after learning about the birth of Edwina. He hurried to the inn with Stenia and was pleased to learn that a room had just become available.

"It looks like we'll have to share a bed again,' Stenia teased, "unless you want to sleep on the floor."

Kaz laughed despite himself. "The bed will be fine."

Dinner was followed by another passionate night under the covers. Despite the lack of a good night's rest, Kaz found himself surprisingly revived the next morning. They returned to the station in time to reclaim their seats before other passengers boarded. This time, a conductor was checking fares, and their first class tickets gave them priority. The conductor informed them that the train would be leaving within the hour. Four hours later, and bulging to the rooftops with passengers, the train departed.

The train reached Gdansk twelve hours later. As Sigmund had predicted, it was the end of the line. The tracks to Gdynia had been destroyed. Gdansk itself lay in ruins, a gutted city comprised of twisted metal, skeletal doorways, blackened walls, collapsed chimneys and roofs, bombed factories and cratered streets. A smoky pall lay over the ruins, accompanied by the strong odor of burnt wood and flesh. The devastation reached beyond the normal havoc of war. The city's art treasures had been smashed or stolen. Stately homes had been ripped apart: precious oriental rugs cut to pieces, silk drapes torn down and used for toilet paper, paintings and tapestries slashed, antique furniture split apart for firewood. In one home, soldiers had butchered a cow on a fine damask sofa and cooked it over an open fire in the middle of the living room. It looked like Nowy Targ all over again, only on a much larger scale.

Just as Kaz was about to lose all faith in humanity, he and Stenia stumbled upon an International Red Cross shelter blossoming amid the ruble in the center of the city. White tents sprouted like mushrooms across the desolate landscape. There were cots and blankets for the dispossessed, and hot coffee and chunks of fresh bread for everyone. People murmured 'bless you' as they waited in line.

"I'll escort you to your family's farm," Kaz offered after they'd eaten.

"I can make my way from here," Stenia declared. Her dimples flared on her cheeks. She handed him a piece of paper with the name Symanski written on it. "That's the name of my relatives. Their farm is west of here, in the next valley. If you find yourself traveling that way, look for us. You'll always be welcome."

With that, Stenia leaned forward and gave Kaz a farewell kiss.

He was amazed at her strength. In many ways, she reminded him of Daneta: strong-willed and independent. He regretted saying good-bye, but he knew better than to argue. "It's been a memorable adventure."

"Yes, memorable." She squeezed his hand. "Good luck." She turned and walked away without a backward glance.

Kaz felt a sudden sense of loss. Stenia had proved to be a charming interlude in his topsy-turvy world. He was going to miss her.

Refreshed by the Red Cross's food and coffee, Kaz set out on the twenty kilometer walk up the coast to Gdynia. Fresh scars of battle were evident everywhere along his route. Most of the bodies and weapons had been carted away, but broken artillery pieces and disabled tanks still littered the roads and fields.

Kaz reached Gdynia in the early afternoon and was immediately struck by two things. First, most of the harbor facilities had been destroyed. Fishing trawlers and war ships lay in ruin beside each other along the charred docks. Other boats had been sunk in the channels, blocking traffic. There were no freighters to be seen, and it seemed unlikely that any would come very soon.

Second, posters were plastered everywhere declaring that all able men born between 1910 and 1927 were to report to the conscription office immediately for duty in the military. The dentist's information had been correct. Kaz stared at one of the posters and considered his options. He could ignore the directive and look for temporary work until ship traffic returned, then try to find a seaman's job. But the city was half empty, and there were no crowds to provide him cover. If he ignored the conscription notices, it would only be a matter of time before he was picked up and thrown in jail. He could go into hiding and wait for an opportunity to stow away on a ship leaving Poland for Sweden or some other country beyond the reach of the Russians. He had no place to hide, however, and he knew it would take months to clear the harbor and to rebuild the docks. Normal ship traffic couldn't return until then. That left only one option: report to the authorities and bide his time.

The conscription office consisted of two Russian officers seated in a large tent behind an old, wooden table with paper stuffed under one leg to keep it steady. A senior officer wearing the black hat and golden embroidery of a naval admiral stood behind them with an expression of studied aloofness. A Polish veteran that Kaz recognized from the navy sat at the end of the table. They'd served on the old U2 submarine together. He was acting as a translator. Kaz fidgeted in line as he waited his turn. His one concern was his fictitious status as a member of the militia back in Nowy Targ. If they chose to verify that, he would be in trouble. It was a risk, but he didn't see any other choice. Before he knew it, he was waved to the table. The officer in charge reviewed the information Kaz had filled out on the registration papers and compared it with his ID card.

"Any real military experience?" he asked. Kaz had written militia under current employment.

"Two years in the navy."

He studied the ID card some more. "When."

Kaz gave him the approximate dates.

"What type of ships?"

"An old frigate and two submarines."

The officer reviewed the papers and ID card some more. "Good," he said at last. "You will be assigned to the navy. Go see the doctor across the room."

Kaz reached for his ID card, but the admiral said something in Russian, leaned across the table and took it. The interrogating officer handed Kaz a printed, official-looking card instead. Kaz studied it skeptically. Everything was in Russian except for some coded numbers in the upper right corner.

"That is all you will need at present. A new ID card will be processed."

Kaz hesitated but saw from the stern look on the admiral's face that there was no point in arguing. He felt vulnerable without his own, personal card, but there was little he could do about it. The interrogating officer motioned with his hand for Kaz to move along. He walked to the other side of the room where men in white coats waited.

"Any health problems?" one of the doctors asked.

Kaz was suddenly unsure about his prospects in a new Polish navy. He tried to think of something that might get him dismissed. "I have trouble with my eyes sometimes," he lied. "They get a little blurred."

The doctor held up his thumb. "What's this?"

"Your thumb."

"Excellent. There are Germans still hiding from us, and they are much bigger than my thumb. So you should have no trouble recognizing one and shooting him." The doctor stood up to indicate that Kaz was dismissed. "You are now in the Polish navy."

By that official decree, one sentence spoken without enthusiasm, Kaz realized that his life had come full circle. He was back in the service from which he'd been mustered out just a few years ago. Only this time, there would be no Polish officers. He was to serve under Russian command.

Kaz was assigned to a platoon under the command of a Russian lieutenant, but there were no boats to sail. They all lay at the bottom of the sea. So, instead of drills on seamanship, the newly assigned recruits were put to work helping the Russians repair the docks and raising sunken ships. Kaz soon learned that he was one of the few who had any real naval experience. Most had been picked for their muscles. Kaz didn't mind the work. Discipline was rather lax, and the men were free in the evenings to explore the carnage along Gdynia's waterfront or walk to Gdansk, where the rubble was being cleared and makeshift bars and restaurants were sprouting from the ashes.

One of the men assigned to his platoon was the Polish navy veteran who had served as translator during Kaz's interrogation. He joined Kaz in the barracks the first night.

"I'm Piotr Wozniak. We served on a sub together."

"I remember." He shook the man's hand. "Kaz Kowinsky."

Kaz remembered Piotr as a robust man who seemed too big to maneuver around the cramped quarters of a submarine. Now, he was rail thin, almost skeletal. His sunken cheeks made Kaz think of the refugees he'd seen the other day trudging down the road from Auschwitz.

"That happened to you?" Kaz inquired.

"Gdynia was overrun by the Germans right at the start of the war. I was captured before I had a chance to see any real action. Spent most of the war in prison camps."

Kaz shifted his weight on his bunk bed. "I did everything I could to get to Gdynia when the bombs started falling. I rode a train from Krakow, but we were turned back. It was too late."

"Lucky thing for you. You would've either ended up dead or imprisoned like me." He offered Kaz a cigarette and lit one for himself. "That admiral was suspicious of you, by the way. He was watching you in line. You looked a little nervous."

The hair on Kaz's arms pricked up. "Damn. I thought I acted okay."

Piotr shook his head. "That admiral seems to have built-in radar." He inhaled deeply on his cigarette. "Look, it's probably nothing. If you get called into the processing tent, I wouldn't worry. But if you're ever summoned to the headquarters building, I'd run. Not many men come out of that place once they go in."

Kaz spent the next three weeks in a state of heightened alert, but when nothing happened, he began to relax. At the end of the third week, he was called back to the tent where he'd been processed. Kaz's nerves twitched with uncertainty, but he remembered Piotr's advice and reported as ordered. There was no sign of the admiral, which he took as a good omen.

"You new ID card is ready," a low ranking officer informed him with obvious boredom.

Kaz looked at it with relief but wondered about his old ID card. When he asked the officer about it, all he got was a firm 'nyet' and a familiar wave of the hand to indicate that he was dismissed.

A few days later, everyone was called back to the tent to don new uniforms, which consisted of blue trousers, a fitted top shirt and a white seaman's hat. Kaz had to admit that they looked spiffy in their new clothes.

The days were spent repairing the docks and the nights looking for adventure. One inventive recruit suggested sneaking into the supply warehouse left behind by the Germans to look for items to supplement the bland food they were being served back at the naval facility, and for vodka. They discovered a treasure-trove of liquor and canned rations. Some were consumed and the rest used as barter for cigarettes, chocolates and other goods. On the third sortie, however, they were discovered by Russian guards and summarily kicked out with a severe warning never to return. To emphasize the point, the guards wrote down everybody's names from their ID cards.

"Well, that's the end of that," one of the men lamented, "but there's always fishing."

"And just what do you propose we use for hooks and bait?" another snorted.

"Grenades."

Everybody looked at him and burst out laughing. It was a splendid idea. There were plenty of German grenades stored at the naval facility. The workers were constantly discovering them while clearing the docks and surrounding countryside of war debris. It would be easy to filch a few. Then, it was a simple matter of walking to the end of a dock, pulling the pin on a grenade and tossing it into the water. Two men stood by with an old row boat ready to retrieve the catch. Unfortunately, one grenade had little effect. Hardly any fish floated to the surface. It was decided that things would work better if several grenades were tied together to generate a much larger explosion under the water. The bigger the explosion, it was assumed, the greater the catch of fish. Half-a-dozen grenades were attached to a wire, pins were pulled and the make shift bomb was flung into the water. The men raced for the shore as a great, black geyser of muddy water burst fifty feet into the air, engulfing the end of the pier in a putrid shower and roiling the water for a hundred yards around.

Once the water settled, the men spied plenty of dead fish, but they also smelled something indescribable. The explosion had ripped into the mud at the bottom of the bay where several sunken boats rested. The churning water had dislodged the rotting remains of several dead men who floated to the surface with the fish. The odor was so terrible, the men retreated without bothering to collect their bounty. Their fishing expedition was over.

The days slid by in orderly fashion. The docks would soon be ready to receive cargo ships, and the channels were nearly cleared of sunken vessels. It wouldn't be long before shipping returned. Kaz began thinking about his plans to stow away, but before he could do anything, a black cloud darkened his prospects. It arrived in the form of Piotr, who returned from his translation duties with a scowl on his face. He pulled Kaz aside and spoke to him in a hushed voice.

"The damned ruskies are starting a new round of interrogations at the headquarters building I warned you about. They have a short list of potential troublemakers. Your name is on it."

Kaz froze. A stream of questions raced through his mind. Had they checked his ID from Nowy Targ? Were they about to arrest him? Where could he hide? What should he do?

"You need to get out of here," Piotr continued in anticipation of his questions.

"How soon will they come for me?" Kaz could hear the shaky tone in his voice.

"Maybe tonight. Tomorrow for sure."

There was no time to plan his escape or to stow away. He had to run NOW. But where? He pulled the piece of paper Stenia had given him from his pocket and stared at the name written on it: Symanski. If he could find the farm where Stenia was staying, he might have a chance to hide and wait for his opportunity. He'd never expected to see Stenia again, but now she seemed like his only chance.

"Is there someplace you can go?" Piotr asked in a worried voice.

Kaz nodded. "Best I don't tell you."

Piotr agreed. "You better go now."

Kaz threw his few belongings into his knapsack and gave Piotr a grateful hug good-bye. He slipped away without a word to his other comrades. His seaman's uniform blended with many others as he began his walk back to Gdansk, but he knew that would change as he got farther away from Gdynia, so he found a thicket where he couldn't be seen from the road and changed into his civilian clothes. He reached Gdansk without incident and immediately started down the road Stenia had chosen when they parted. Dusk was settling into the fields around him. He wondered how he would ever find the Symanski farm, especially in the dark.

The sound of an approaching horse drawn cart behind him broke through his thoughts. He waved the driver to stop.

"I'm trying to find the Symanski farm. Do you know where it is?"

"Yep. I'm headed that way. Hop on board. I'll give you a lift." Kaz climbed onto the wooden seat next to the driver. "You must be related to the little pregnant gal who's staying there."

Kaz looked sharply at the man, surprised by the casual comment. A brisk retort rose to his lips, but he suppressed it. News obviously traveled quickly in farm country "I know her and her father, but I'm not related."

The man shot him a skeptical, sideways glance but said nothing more about it. He changed the subject.

"You must come from Nowy Targ, then."

Kaz nodded in the fading light.

"I understand you folks had quite a ruckus with the Germans around there. You part of that?"

"If you mean the fight in the mountains, yes."

"Too bad you lost."

Kaz bridled at the comment. The farmer had a sharp tongue. "We took out hundreds of them, but they kept coming. There were just too many." Kaz didn't much care to talk about it. For a brief moment his thoughts fled to Christina then darted away again.

"Must have been a hell of a fight. I tip my hat to you and your comrades. Wish we could bloody these ruskies that way." The driver gave the reins a slap to perk up the horse's pace.

"I'm trying to stay out of their way," Kaz admitted. "They don't seem to like partisans."

"If they have their way, they'll screw things even tighter than the Germans did. They see the partisans as trouble, and that don't fit their plans. They want to have total control of Poland."

The man's words reinforced Kaz's thoughts on the matter. He didn't have the stomach to watch what the Russians would do to his country. He knew if he stayed, there would be consequences. Prison most likely. Or, maybe put against a wall like Christina.

It was dark by the time Kaz was dropped off at a fork in the rutted road.

"Down that road 'bout a quarter mile. First farm on your right."

Kaz thanked the man and set off on foot. Soon, the yellow-orange glow of lights filled the windows of a farmhouse set back from the road. Kaz walked up to the door and knocked. A chair scuffed against a wood floor. Footsteps crossed the room, and the door was flung open, causing light to escape into the cool, night air.

"Can I help you?" The man's large frame nearly filled the doorway. Kaz surmised by his crinkled face that he was well along in years, but his muscular build showed he was still fit and not afraid of hard work. He stood a full head taller than Kaz.

"Is this the Symanski farm? I'm looking for Stenia."

The man studied him for a moment. "You must be Kaz, the fellow who brought her here."

"Yes sir."

"Well, come on in. We appreciate you looking after her."

"She did a pretty good job of looking after herself."

The man laughed. "She can be a handful, that's certain." He turned and called out Stenia's name. "You got company."

When Stenia entered the room, Kaz almost didn't recognize her. The slightly plump young woman he remembered had been replaced by a soon-to-be mother with a stomach so big it looked like she'd swallowed a balloon that had inflated inside of her.

"I never thought to see you again," she declared as she raced forward and hugged him. Her dimples spread in their familiar pattern.

A tall, gray-haired woman with a stocky build followed behind Stenia.

"This is my uncle and aunt, Nikolai and Janny," Stenia enthused with a wave of her hand.

After greetings had been made, Stenia studied Kaz with a steady gaze. "I thought you would be on a ship by now."

"The harbors are not completely cleared, so no shipping yet. I was biding my time until I learned I was on a short list of men the Russians planned to interrogate and, most likely, throw in jail." He glanced nervously at the Symanskis. "I had to run, and I didn't know where else to go. I don't want to get you in any trouble."

Nikolai grunted. "The Russians aren't very popular around here. You'll be safe for awhile. You're planning to stow away on a ship, I take it. I imagine the ruskies will be keeping a pretty close eye out for that sort of thing."

"I used to be a seaman, so I know ships. Anyway, I've got to take the chance. There's no future for me here."

The farmhouse was sizable with extra bedrooms. "Used to be a full house before our children grew up," Nikolai commented. The heavy creases in his face deepened. "The Germans suspected our two boys of helping the resistance and put them in a labor camp. We haven't heard from them since the ruskies got here. Don't know where they are."

Kaz was shown to a back bedroom where a hunting rifle hung on one wall above a chest of drawers, and a bed with a dusty cover nested against the other. A small window grudgingly filtered light into the room. Several wood whittling projects in various stages of completion sat on top of the drawers, most in the shapes of birds. The room was a sea of contrasts: a bed that looked as if it hadn't been touched in ages, and unfinished wood carvings that suggested somebody would be back tomorrow. Kaz shook the bed cover, which instantly set fine particles of dust to dancing in the pale light while he put his few belongings in the top two drawers.

Dinner was a simple affair. The uncle said grace, and everyone directed their attention to their plates of beef, beans and cornbread. Conversation began with talk about the Russian occupation but soon drifted to farm matters. One of the cows was not giving much milk; a section of fence needed new posts; the vegetable garden was sprouting more weeds than carrots. Kaz offered to help with the fence and other chores. He wanted to keep busy, to pay for his keep. Nikolai accepted his offer with thanks. Kaz suspected that without the boys, maintaining the farm had been a difficult task. The dinner gave him a glimpse of a very different sort of life than he'd known. The term 'down to earth' came to mind. It spoke of hard, physical labor and simple satisfactions.

Later, after everyone had retired for the night, Stenia crept into Kaz's bedroom and slipped into his bed.

"The doctor says no more sex until the baby's born," she announced in a heavy whisper, "but that doesn't mean there aren't other ways to pleasure ourselves."

Kaz was no longer surprised by Stenia's forthrightness, and even in her pregnant state, she was hard to resist. Her no-nonsense approach to life was unsettling and stimulating at the same time. He caressed her smooth, cool skin, and felt himself come alive.

When they were done, Stenia nestled in Kaz's arms. "I have to tell you something."

Kaz looked at her expectantly.

She held him tighter, but avoided his gaze. After a pause, she began a monologue about herself. She had always struggled with her weight, which made her feel unattractive to boys and, later, to men. To compensate, she'd let boys touch her in special places, and she'd learned how to give pleasure without 'doing it.' Her reputation slithered down the slippery slope of gossip and whispers. She was described as a loose girl, someone with whom boys could have their way. That wasn't entirely true, of course, but the young men who dated her wouldn't admit that. They embellished their stories to prove their manhood. After she left school, she found a young man who seemed to truly love her, and they became engaged. Stenia grew more confident in herself. She felt that she belonged to someone, that she belonged in society. But it was a mirage. Her beau's eyes wandered to one of the young women who used to torment her in school.

The girl was pretty and thin! Willowy was the term people used to describe her. Before Stenia knew what had happened, the engagement was off, and her beau was involved with that 'other woman.' Stenia was so devastated, she retreated into her shell and hardly spoke to anyone. That was when she met the German officer. He showed a real interest in her, found her attractive. She soaked up his kindness and melted in his arms. It wasn't long before he wooed her into his bed. Stenia knew she was sleeping with the enemy, but she didn't care. She had someone who wanted her, needed her, and she curled up in that knowledge like a baby ensconced in a womb. Then, the Germans retreated from Nowy Targ, the Russians arrived, and everything went to hell. Her German officer left, and the townspeople treated her like trash. She was back to square one, only this time she was pregnant, a reality that terrified her. What would the townspeople do when they found out? People had been tarred and feathered for less.

"But now I'm safe, thanks to my uncle and aunt, and thanks to you." She gave him a playful tug on his arm. "There's even a farmer and his wife a few miles west of here that would like to adopt my baby. My father and uncle are arranging things. They told the farmer I was made pregnant by a Polish resistance fighter who died."

She shifted onto her back and put her hand on her bulging stomach.

"The thing is, though, I'm not so sure I can give it up. I feel it moving and kicking, and I know there's real life in there. A tiny person, one who belongs to me. How do I just give that up?"

"What would you do?" Kaz asked with concern. "You couldn't go back to Nowy Targ, could you?"

"I don't know what I would do, but Nowy Targ is out of the question. I might go to Warsaw or Krakow. Find a job and raise the baby. Eventually, find a husband."

Silence hung in the air. Kaz didn't know what to say. "I'm going to talk to the priest tomorrow." She looked up at him. "Will you come with me?"

Kaz's first instinct was to say no. He had little use for churches or priests. They had never answered *his* prayers. It didn't seem right to let Stenia down, though, and he knew the church was important to her. The more he thought about it, the more he felt the need to support her. He was drawn to Stenia's vulnerability. He wanted to help, to offer his friendship. The situation reminded him of Daneta. She'd been strong yet fragile at the same time. She'd become pregnant and needed his support.

Stenia noticed his hesitation. "If that makes you uncomfortable, I understand."

"No, it's okay. I'd be glad to go with you." Kaz pulled her closer and shoved thoughts of Daneta from his mind.

The Catholic church seemed too elaborate for such a small community. A large, stone courtyard was surrounded by a wall filled with archways and carvings of saints. The church's heavy, wood doors cast a spell of invincibility, much like the doors to Wawel Castle. Kaz opened the doors with some effort, and they quietly slipped inside. A priest emerged from a confessional as a young woman with head bowed hurried past them and out the door. Christ gazed down on them from his cross behind the altar.

Stenia walked to the front of the pews and knelt before the priest. She looked up at him, then down at her abdomen. "As you can see, father, I've committed a sin. I'm unmarried and the father is gone."

The priest was gray-haired with a wrinkled but kind face. His left eye twitched ever so slightly. His moist lips compressed into a look of concern. "How can I help you, my child?"

"I've thought about giving the baby away for adoption, but part of me wants to keep it. If I did, would I commit the baby to damnation?" Tears reddened Stenia's eyes. She lowered her head just like the young woman who left the church. "What should I do?"

The priest motioned for her to stand and to sit in the front row of the pews. "Your question is one that has echoed through the ages." He sat down beside her. "There are no easy answers, but there are choices that will allow the baby to be baptized and saved.

"The first is to wed. If you cannot find the father, or he is unwilling, another upright man can stand in his stead. Such a joining of two souls will allow you to enter the good graces of the church, once more, and to legitimize your child. You can then have it baptized.

"The second choice is to bring the newborn child to the convent in Gdynia. The convent was destroyed in the war, of course, but it still functions in temporary quarters. The nuns would raise it according to the precepts of the church, and the baby's soul would be saved.

"Finally, you can give it up for adoption with the understanding that the new parents will bring the baby into the church's family." The priest paused long enough to adjust his position on the hard bench. The wood creaked in protest under his weight. "Regardless of your decision, you must seek confession and make reparation for your sins."

Kaz and Stenia both flinched at this last comment. He'd never thought of her as a sinner, just a bright, vibrant woman who was trying to find her way in life, but in the eyes of the church, he supposed she was.

Stenia quickly stood up and smoothed her tight dress across her stomach, making an effort not to tear the seams which appeared as though they might rend at any moment. It was getting too small, Kaz thought absently. She needed new clothes.

"Thank you, father," she said in a whispering voice. "I will think on your advice and decide what to do."

Her body shook as they left the church. Kaz put his arm around her shoulders to comfort her.

"That's it, then. If I keep my baby, it will be damned."

"Unless you get married."

Stenia looked at her extended belly. "Not much chance of that."

They walked back to the farm in silence.

That night, Stenia didn't come to Kaz's bed. He lay on his back in the darkness and thought about what the priest had told them. He'd told her to marry. There was time. All she needed was a man to stand up for her. His mind tumbled in a turmoil of confusion as he considered this. As badly as he wanted to escape the Russians and to start a new life, he found himself wondering what it would be like to marry Stenia. He knew it wouldn't be for love. Christina was the only woman he'd ever loved, perhaps the only one he ever would. But marrying Stenia would save her and the baby from a life of hell. Not to mention the afterlife, if one believed in that sort of thing. *Marry!* Was it possible? It would be a good thing to do, and it might give his own life more purpose. Marrying Stenia wouldn't be so bad. She was pretty and lively, fun to be around. He could do worse.

He thought about his own child, Edwina. What had happened to *her*? Had she and her new family survived the war? Was she playing somewhere safe? He would never know. She was gone forever. If he married Stenia, he could start that part of his life over again. He could still be a father to a newborn child.

There were practical matters to consider, his status with the Russians, for one. Now that he'd fled into hiding, his name would be at the top of their list. He was a fugitive. If he stayed, he would have to get his hands on new ID documents and find work that didn't draw attention to himself. On the farm, perhaps. The Symanskis could use the help. Kaz tossed in his bed. The word "marry" played again and again in his head. It pressed down on him, weighed on him.

One voice in his head told him that it would be a mistake. He needed to flee Poland, not settle down there. He wanted freedom, a new country beyond the reach of the Russians. Like America! But another voice asked him if he could abandon Stenia. It didn't seem right.

Marry! It was too big a decision to digest right then. He would have to sleep on it. Take his time. Not do anything hasty. He finally fell asleep with the word hanging over his head. *Marry.*

Stenia returned to the church by herself the next morning to take confession. She came back with a heavy step that told Kaz she didn't feel absolved of her sins. Kaz kept busy replacing fence posts. He wasn't ready to share his thoughts with her yet. He went to bed that night exhausted but hoping Stenia would appear. She didn't visit him, however, and the next morning he returned to his fence posts with less certainty. Stow away on a ship, perhaps all the way to America, or stay where he was and marry Stenia. The two ideas battled each other in his head.

Another day passed, and Kaz could wait no longer. He had to decide what to do. If he didn't, he felt as though his brain would dissolve in a pool of quicksand. Ironically, it was Stenia who came to his rescue. She resolved his dilemma by walking up unannounced and throwing her arms around him. It was a simple gesture, the first sign of affection since they'd talked to the priest, but the warmth of her body pressed against his was all the assurance he needed. He would go to her room that night and discuss his proposal with her. He would offer to marry her. If she said yes, his life would be settled. If she said no, he would leave. Relief swept over him. The weight of his doubts and fears lifted. His spirits rose. His future was in Stenia's hands. He eagerly waited for nightfall.

Night did not come gently, however. Night came with screams of pain and muffled voices and cries of anguish. A frantic call was made for the doctor. Kaz tried to enter Stenia's room, but Nikolai asked him to wait outside. One brief glimpse through the partially opened doorway revealed bloody sheets and night clothes. He stood in the hallway, shaken by what he'd seen. Bile rose in his throat as he tried to control his fears. It was too soon for the baby to come. Something was terribly wrong. God was punishing Stenia for her sins. The confession hadn't been enough. The doctor arrived, at last, and hurried into the room. The door remained open. Kaz could see the bloody, limp form of Stenia in her bed. She lay still, her eyes fixed on the ceiling. There were no more cries. Not from Stenia; not from the baby. The house grew silent. The doctor shook his head.

Kaz stumbled outside into the chilled, night air. Stenia dead! The baby stillborn! How were such things possible? She'd reached out to God. Why had he forsaken her? Kaz had been reaching out to Stenia, but in the blink of an eye, she had gone, never to know what he proposed. Never to see her baby or her father again. He smiled and thought about the irony of life. He'd put his fate in Stenia's hands, and she'd answered. There was no more reason to stay on the farm. His future now lay at sea.

Once again, his life had been interrupted, just like Poland's. Once again, he'd lost someone he cared about. Once again, his world had been turned upside down. Now, it was time to sail far away, perhaps to America.

Chapter Thirty

It was late at night, and the pier stood eerily silent after the hectic activity of the past two days. Kaz stood in the shadows and surveyed the scene. One lone guard was patrolling the docks in a circuitous route that left different sections of the pier unguarded for long periods of time. A light fog hugged the harbor, which helped to reduce visibility. Water lapped against the hull of a freighter shifting restlessly at its moorings at the end of the pier. A single, yellow light below the ship's bridge beamed its lonely beacon into the mists. The ship was called the Falcon, and Kaz had been watching it while the crew unloaded its cargo and hauled coal into the holds for its return journey. Once finished, the men were given shore leave, with the result that on this night, only a single sentry aboard the ship stood guard against interlopers.

Kaz had worn his navy uniform for the last two days so that he would blend in better with other sailors walking around the docks, but he was careful to avoid the Russians. If they stopped him and asked questions, he would be in trouble. Now that the workers were gone, the pier was empty except for the guard patrolling the waterfront and the sentry. Even in the dim light, the gangplank to the ship was clearly visible. He would have to use stealth to get on board. He waited patiently until the guard on the docks was out of sight and the sentry on the ship had his back turned, then hurried up the gangway. At the top, he froze and watched for any movement from the bridge. There was none. The sentry was now at the stern of the ship. Kaz calculated that he had less than three minutes to reach his objective and to hide, but that should give him enough time. He crouched low and crept along the rail until he reached the forepeak, where he scrambled into the anchor chain compartment and pulled the hatch closed behind him.

He was engulfed in darkness, and the compartment stank from dried sea water and fish. A feeling of claustrophobia swept over him. He had to fight an urge to open the hatch and escape. He thought about Stenia, and for some reason that settled his nerves. It was too late to change his mind. There was no going back. He was officially a stowaway, and he knew that if the Russians found him, he would be imprisoned and most likely shot. He'd made his decision. His greatest concern was not knowing exactly where the ship was going. He'd heard snippets of conversation, enough to know there were no Russians on board. He thought the language was Swedish, but he couldn't be certain. It was a country other than Russia or Poland. That was all that mattered. The compartment reminded him of a prison. He would be trapped there for at least two days, maybe more, with a few containers of water and some bread and cheese. If he became desperate, he could always show himself once they were at sea and rely on the mercy of the ship's captain. The captain would most likely throw him in the brig and turn him over to authorities at his first port of call. That was not an alternative that he wanted to consider. He had to endure his self-imposed confinement and stay out of sight.

Kaz made himself as comfortable as he could on the massive coils of chain and closed his eyes. He was tired from his ordeal and relieved to have his destiny in his own hands. He breathed easier. Soon, he was asleep.

He woke to the sounds of feet pounding along the deck and voices shouting from the bridge and on the pier. A rumbling noise throbbed through the hull; the ship was about to get underway. Kaz smiled and congratulated himself on his plan. It was only a matter of hours until he would be beyond Russia's grasp. The ship began to slide forward. He could feel it in his body, feel the way the engine tugged at the heavy vessel and slowly propelled it away from the dock. Then, the whole ship trembled as the engines were thrown into reverse, and the ship's motion stopped. What just happened, he wondered? Did they forget someone or fail to release a mooring line? A faint noise interrupted his thoughts, the put-put-put of a small boat. He suddenly knew the answer to his questions. The noise told him why the ship had stopped. The sound grew louder as it came alongside the Falcon. Russian voices called out to the bridge, followed by the thump of two mooring lines being thrown onto the dock. The ship was secured for boarding.

Kaz had not seen any patrol boats in the harbor, but there was clearly one now, and it threatened to shred his plans into tiny pieces. The gangplank was lowered onto the dock with a thud, and heavy feet announced the arrival of at least three harbor officials ready to inspect the ship. Kaz tensed. If they were only concerned about verifying the cargo, they would check the manifest against what they found in the hold and leave. As long as all was in order, that would be the end of it. But, if they were looking for stowaways like Kaz, they would comb the ship from bow to stern, and that could put him in the lion's mouth. If they opened the hatch cover where he was hiding, all would be lost. Another thought struck him. What if they demanded that the anchor chain be dropped? It would happen without warning, and if he remained seated on top of it, he would be churned into ground beef. He grabbed his backpack, scrambled off the chain and moved further back into the compartment. When he did so, he bumped his head on a wooden partition that stuck out part way into his cubbyhole. He felt around with his hands and discovered a space just large enough for him to slip behind it. If they opened the hatch cover and merely looked inside, he should be safe from view. If they decided to climb into the compartment, however, his fate would no longer rest in his own hands.

He huddled in his tiny space with his knees pushed up, his chin resting on his chest, and waited. Footsteps marched about above his head. He could hear voices, some in Russian and some in what he now assumed to be Swedish. It was impossible to know what they were saying, but the voices were calm. He found that reassuring. If the inspectors were agitated, the voices would have been more strident. So far, all seemed to be in order. Then, somebody fumbled with the hatch cover and the chain compartment suddenly filled with light. Kaz froze. He gripped his knees and prayed. A shadow against the far wall told him that someone's head was poking around in the brilliant light, but the inspector seemed hesitant to climb all the way in. A voice nearby said something and the inspector hastily withdrew his head. The voice laughed. Kaz realized that the man was talking about rats. Kaz cringed at the idea of rats crawling around him, but he was thankful for the man's humor. The hatch cover slammed shut and darkness returned. The voices moved toward the stern.

Kaz's aching muscles slumped in relief as he crawled out of his hiding place. It'd been a close call. Time passed. He listened intently for any further signs of trouble. There were none. Finally, the boots thumped down the gangplank, and it was dragged back on board the ship. Engines roared to life; the ship began to move, once more. Kaz heaved a deep sigh. His gamble had paid off. He was about to leave Poland and ride the ocean waves out to sea. His destination was unknown, but that didn't prevent a sense of pure joy from washing over him.

Kaz was thankful that the Falcon hadn't needed to use its anchor in Gdynia, since it meant that the chain compartment was dry. It was about the only comfort he could take from his voyage. There was little space beyond the anchor chain. Sitting on it was uncomfortable and after awhile, it became downright painful as the metal links pressed deeper and deeper into muscle and bone. The absence of light pressed down on him until he wanted to scream. To make matters worse, the ship's primary cargo was coal. A fine powder of coal dust soon found its way into the compartment and settled into everything, including his clothes, hair and lungs. Sleeping was difficult, because the ship kept lurching in the heavy seas and banging Kaz against the anchor chain. Footsteps thumped overhead at regular intervals, forcing Kaz to coil his body in anticipation of a frantic retreat to his hiding place should the hatch open. No one bothered him, but it was nerve-racking, nonetheless. Several times, he heard someone rattling around in the adjacent compartment and banging things against the bulkhead. At those times, he had to sit perfectly still so that he wouldn't make a noise that might alert the crewman. It was a trying, uncomfortable journey, and after twenty-four hours, he began to question his sanity. The only good news was that the ship was making steady progress to somewhere, and he had sufficient food and water to nourish his spirits.

His familiarity with life aboard ship helped. He had a pretty good idea what the crew was doing from the pattern of sounds overhead. When things grew quiet, he knew it was dinner time, and he decided to risk a little fresh air. The compartment had become so stuffy and full of floating coal dust that he thought he would gag. He also needed to go to the bathroom! He slid the hatch cover partway open and gulped in the fresh, night air like a parched man plunging his head into a watering hole at an oasis. The sky was filled with so many stars he thought he was floating in space. He looked around furtively but saw no immediate danger. Quickly, he slipped behind some equipment that hid him from the bridge and relieved himself over the rail.

Kaz scanned the skyline for signs of shore lights. He saw nothing but stars. They were still well out to sea, although he estimated they should be approaching land soon, another day at most. He pondered what he should do when he reached port. If they were unloading the coal, the ship would most likely dock at a pier. If not, they might drop anchor. Kaz didn't want to risk staying in the compartment if that happened. Even behind his partition, he risked being struck by a piece of chain whipping about as it was unwinding. Once the ship slowed to harbor speed, he would have to risk opening the hatch in anticipation of abandoning his lair.

Kaz left the hatch cover partly open until morning light seeped through the haze. There were no workers in his immediate area, so he peeked out to see what was going on. He was greeted by the blissful sight of rolling, green hills and rocky cliffs passing the ship's bow. Land! Moisture filled Kaz's eyes at the sight of it.

It wasn't long before he felt a change in the rhythm of the ship's engines. The captain was cutting power. The Falcon gave a tell-tale shudder as the engines were reversed. Kaz knew he might be spotted, but he had to keep the hatch open so that he could exit the compartment if they started to lower the anchor. Then, he saw a crane and several workman unloading another freighter secured to a wharf and knew that he was safe. The Falcon was coming slowly into the docks. The ship lurched as the engines shifted forward and backward while the captain maneuvered his craft closer to a pier. On a signal from the bridge, crew members scurried into position and tossed mooring lines to men standing on the dock below.

Kaz ducked back into the compartment and closed the hatch nearly all the way. He left just enough of an opening to get some light and to hear more clearly what was happening. The dockworkers and crewmen were calling back and forth. The ship's engines were cut and the gangplank lowered. For the next hour, the crewmen busied themselves securing the ship. When they were done, most of them went ashore. It didn't appear that the coal was going to be unloaded immediately, so the captain was permitting shore leave.

Kaz had to make a decision. There was only a skeletal crew remaining on the ship, but it was broad daylight. If he tried to sneak off now, he would be spotted from the bridge. If he waited until dark, the crew might return, and there would be many more sets of eyes to spot him. Equipment partially blocked the bridge's view of the anchor compartment, so he could slip onto the deck unnoticed from above. He only had to worry about crew members on deck. However, once he moved toward the gangplank, he would be visible to nearby crewmen and the bridge. His only other option was to make a run for it and hope that he could get off the ship and disappear into the warehouses along the waterfront before he was caught.

Kaz decided on the last option and carefully lifted himself out of the compartment. He held his knapsack in his hand and looked around. It was at least a hundred meters to the gangplank, but as long as no crewmen were in sight, he figured he could make it before the bridge sounded the alarm. Then, he looked to his left and saw a seaman's jacket draped over a metal storage bin. Someone had taken it off while working and left it there. It was only ten feet away, and it gave him an idea. Why run if he could walk? Instincts took over. Before he had time to change his mind, he stepped away from his cover and walked purposefully over to the jacket. He set down his backpack and slipped his arms into the jacket, retrieved his belongings and strolled toward the gangplank. He knew someone had to be watching him from the bridge, but no one raised the alarm. That couldn't prevent his heart from hammering in his chest. The gangplank was tantalizingly close, but at any moment he expected to hear voices shouting and boots pounding after him. Nothing of the sort happened. He found his feet walking down the gangplank, and he left the ship without a backward glance.

The docks were buzzing with activity. Voices shouted and trucks ground their gears. Workers stacked crates so they could be hoisted into open holds. Ropes were being coiled. Crewmen heaved provisions aboard ships. A sharp odor of sweating bodies and fouled seawater floated on the morning breeze. Sunshine beat down on him. All the sights and sounds were familiar, and he soaked them into his consciousness. They were the sounds and smells of freedom. A great sense of joy rose in his chest. He wanted to shout and dance along the dock's rough, wooden planks. There were no angry Russian voices to be heard, no grim German faces to be seen.

Kaz tried to walk along the waterfront with a casual air, but quizzical stares followed him. He realized he must look like a coal miner emerging from the mouth of a tunnel. He could see coal dust on his clothes and taste it on his lips. He spied a bucket of water where no one was working at the moment and plunged his face into it. The water was bracing on his skin. It quickly turned murky from all the coal dust. He wiped his face clean with his hands. The seaman's jacket he'd taken from the ship helped hide his navy uniform, but it was uncomfortably warm. He wondered what to do with it. He'd only meant to use it as a disguise, not to steal it. He considered dumping it and walking on, but that didn't sit too well with him. Seamen didn't take and abandon each other's gear. Somehow, he needed to return it.

As he mulled over his options, a burly man with a weathered face and a thick, brown beard walked up to him and asked him something in Swedish. Kaz looked at him in confusion. The man didn't dress or look like an official. What did he want? Perhaps, he was just curious about his dirty clothes. After a moment, Kaz realized that the man was looking at the jacket, and he recognized him. He was one of the seamen he'd seen loading the ship in Gdynia. Kaz shook his head in response to the man's question and asked him if he spoke Polish.

"Some," was the reply. The man's eyes never left the jacket.

Kaz took off the jacket and handed it to him. "I was just borrowing it," he explained.

The man's eyes narrowed as he studied Kaz's uniform. Kaz knew that at any moment the confrontation could turn ugly. If it did, he could easily find himself locked up in a Swedish prison while waiting to be deported back to Poland. In desperation, he threw himself on the man's mercy.

"I left Gdynia to escape the Russians. If they find me, they'll kill me. I was in the resistance during the war."

He wasn't sure how much the man understood. He shifted his weight from foot-to-foot in anticipation of a frantic sprint down the docks.

A broad smile broke out on the man's weathered features. "Ruskies." The man spat as he said the word.

Kaz nodded with relief. "Ruskies."

"You are stowaway, from Poland." He laughed and produced a handful of coupons from his pocket. He handed one to Kaz, along with a Swedish coin. When Kaz looked at him with a questioning frown, the man pantomimed smoking a cigarette. The man was giving him a ration coupon for smokes! Kaz's own face broadened into a grin. He thanked the man, who patted him on the shoulder and walked away in the direction of the Falcon. It had been a strange encounter, but it gave Kaz hope. It was obvious the Swedes didn't like the *ruskies* any better than the Poles.

Kaz stopped at the first tobacco shop he could find and handed over the coupon and coin. He was given a pack of Swedish cigarettes and a tiny box of matches. With a lighted cigarette in hand, he left the waterfront and wandered into the surrounding streets. The contrast to what he'd left behind in Poland overwhelmed him. Gone were the rubble-strewn boulevards, the twisted ruins of buildings, the rotting corpses of horses and people. No planes roared overhead. No cannons boomed. No tanks rumbled down the avenues. No skeletal men or women staggered past in search of food and shelter. In their place stood tidy shops with displays of fine linens, confections, jewelry and housewares. Small grocery stores revealed boxes of fresh vegetables and fruits. Well-dressed businessmen strode past in crisp, white shirts and neatly pressed trousers. Women bustled along the sidewalks in bright dresses and hats. It was as if Kaz had stepped into a fairy tale world where wars were not permitted and no one was poor.

He walked in a daze, his head spinning with images. Several times, he stopped someone to ask if they spoke Polish. None did. He was adrift in a sea of unfamiliar words and voices. At last, a couple overheard him and approached. The man was outfitted in a wool suit with a vest. The woman wore a full skirt and blouse that fluttered in the breeze.

"We are from Poland," the man announced. "Although we emigrated to Sweden many years ago. How can we help you?"

Kaz explained his plight. "I need to find the Polish consulate, to see if I can remain here or go to another country that is not controlled by the Russians."

The man rubbed his closely trimmed beard. "I believe Mr. Wintermark can help you. He's not a consulate as such, but he handles consulate functions for the Polish government. It's a bit confusing because the Polish government has operated in exile for the past few years in London. Now, there's a new government being formed under the Russians. We're not sure what is going to happen, but if anybody can help you, he can."

The man hailed a streetcar and gave the conductor instructions. He paid the fare and told Kaz to get on board. "He will let you off in front of Mr. Wintermark's offices."

Ten minutes later, Kaz stood in front of a receptionist in an office defined by two clattering typewriters and the staccato beat of busy feet on hardwood floors. The young receptionist seated behind her desk gave him an uncertain smile as she appraised his disheveled appearance and unusual clothes. When he tried to explain his purpose for being there, he was pleased to see that she understood him. She hurried into an adjoining office.

The attire and beard of the man who appeared in the doorway were nearly identical to the man with whom Kaz had spoken on the street, except this man's hair showed streaks of grey.

"I'm Mr. Wintermark," he said in a deep voice. He looked at Kaz's uniform with considerable curiosity. "Please, come into my office."

When they were settled, Kaz got right to the point. "I stowed away on a ship from Gdynia. I'm looking for a new home."

Mr. Wintermark pursed his lips and drummed the fingers of his right hand on the arm of his chair. He sat upright, seemingly lost in thought. Kaz sensed that the news wasn't encouraging.

"You are wearing a navy uniform, yes?"

Kaz nodded.

"Your situation is complicated. Technically, you're neither a refugee nor a displaced person. You're a deserter from the armed forces of another country. By international agreement, your disposition must be handled by the Swedish government. They will want to intern you until they decide on a course of action."

Intern. Kaz knew that was a fancy word for another prison. The muscles in his jaw tightened. "There's no other choice? Couldn't I just board another ship, one going to England, perhaps? Or America?"

Mr. Wintermark shook his head emphatically. "That would only make matters worse and put me in a difficult situation. By law, I'm supposed to turn you over to the authorities, and my own position is precarious. I'm representing a Polish government that no longer exists. I have no idea what the Russians will do. Most likely, I'll soon lose my position.

"Look, even if I don't turn you in, you're not likely to get far. It's one thing to board a ship in your homeland when you are in uniform. It's quite another to do so in a foreign country where you stand out. More to the point, if you go with me now, you'll be looked upon much more favorably. If you run and are apprehended, your case will be quite straight forward. You'll go before a judge and be deported back to Poland."

Mr. Wintermark gave Kaz an encouraging smile. "The news isn't all bad. You arrived in uniform, which is good. Otherwise, you might be considered a spy. Go with me now, and they'll consider your case. Given your circumstances, I would say there's a good chance you'll be allowed to stay."

Kaz tried to absorb what he was being told. His instincts told him to run, but the risks were considerable. His instincts also told him that Mr. Wintermark was a good man, and he believed that he was being given sound advice. He felt as though he was standing before an abyss, and he needed to quickly decide whether to jump into the chasm and run, or to put his faith in this man.

"There must be similar cases," he responded hopefully. "What happened to them?"

"As a matter of fact, you are the first Pole to arrive here in uniform since the Russians took control of your country. There's no precedent. Yours will most likely be a test case."

The answer wasn't helpful. He was going to have to make his decision without knowing what to expect. "Alright," he said at last. "I'll trust your judgement." With those words, Kaz knew that he was sliding into the heavy jaws of justice. He just prayed that the jaws wouldn't be Russian.

"Good." Mr. Wintermark eyed his uniform, once more. "You want to leave that on until you've been processed and interviewed by the Swedes. However, you could do with a change of clothes. Follow me."

Mr. Wintermark led Kaz up a flight of stairs. "We have spare clothes up here which have been given to us by international relief agencies for the refugees pouring out of Europe. They're used but clean. You can pick out some things and wash up a bit in the bathroom sink. Stay in your uniform for now, however. It's important that you're wearing it when you're interned. You can change later."

By the time Kaz stepped into the street, a brisk wind had taken hold of the fine day and shaken it. Dark clouds rolled overhead. The sun had already fled behind them. Kaz felt the moisture in the air and began to wish he'd held onto the seaman's jacket.

"It's only two blocks," Mr. Wintermark assured him. "We should make it."

They did, barely. Mr.Wintermark led Kaz up the stone steps of an impressive, granite building and into the dark halls of government just as the first rain drops fell. Mr. Wintermark spoke to a clerk who left and returned a few minutes later with a middle-aged man in a brown suit. He and Mr. Wintermark exchanged greetings like old friends.

"Mr. Johansson will help us," Mr. Wintermark informed Kaz.

Kaz shook his hand and followed the two men down the hallway to a spacious office with tall windows overlooking the street. After a brief exchange between the two men, Mr. Johansson turned to Kaz. To his surprise, Mr. Johansson addressed him in reasonable Polish.

"I worked in the Swedish embassy in Poland before the war," he informed Kaz. "As I understand it, if you return to Poland, you fear for your life. Is that correct?"

"Most definitely. The Russians were looking for me when I left."

"Because of your status as a resistance fighter during the war. Not because you committed a crime."

"Exactly. They've been rounding up all the partisans. They seem to think we may cause trouble. At best, we were to be arrested. At worst, shot. I didn't want to learn which."

Mr. Johansson smiled at his comment. "Well, it's an interesting case. Technically, you're a deserter from the Polish navy, but as I understand it, there is no Polish navy at this point, just as there is no longer a Polish government in exile. Everything is being handled by the Russians."

"Handled is a very polite word for it."

Mr. Johansson looked at him over his reading glasses. "Yes, I agree. Well," he stood up suddenly. "There is a process that must be followed. It will take a few days. You can stay here for the night. There is a room down the hall with a bed and shower. It's a comfortable holding cell, actually, but your door will not be locked. You can come and go as you wish, but I would advise against it. If you wander outside and are picked up by the police, it would only complicate matters. Food will be brought to you."

Kaz was led down a tiled corridor to a small room with a bed and recessed lighting that made the place pleasant despite the bars on the door. As promised, the door was left ajar so that Kaz could come and go to the bathroom without disturbing anyone. If he wished, he could go out and explore the city, but after Mr. Johansson's brief lecture, he decided to stay put.

The next morning, he was transferred to facilities with more traditional prison cells. It was a small complex, one that appeared to be used for holding people in flux, such as Kaz, rather than criminals. The place was more Spartan but still comfortable. He was given his own cell with a cot, fresh sheets and a towel. The cell was locked at night but left open during the day, so he could exercise in the yard if he wished. There were guards, however, that prevented him from exploring the surrounding streets.

Kaz was bored and lonely by the third day when Mr. Wintermark finally returned.

"You are to be interviewed this morning by a government official. I will come along to translate."

They were transferred back to the government building where Kaz had presented himself three days earlier and taken to a small interviewing room. Kaz nearly smiled when he saw the metal table and chairs.

Mr. Wintermark sat next to him across from a young man whose skinny build made him appear too thin for his suit. It hung on his frame much like a drapery over a window. The man had neatly lined up two pencils next to a blank notepad. He picked up one of the pencils and held it poised over the yellow, lined notepaper. Kaz felt a heightened sense of tension that chilled him to the bone. He was facing a man who looked to be no more than thirty, who didn't know how to dress, yet was obsessed with neatness, a low level bureaucrat who would write down Kaz's fate with his pencils and notepad. The enormity of the situation made him light headed.

The interviewer began without introduction.

"I understand that you stowed away on a ship from Poland. Do you have any interest in returning there?"

"None." Kaz repeated the explanation he'd given three days ago. "If I go back, I'll be shot."

The interviewer took notes. "Why did you choose Sweden?"

"I didn't. I had no idea where the Falcon was going. Anywhere was fine as long as it was away from the Russians."

"Do you want to stay in Sweden?"

Kaz paused while he considered this. "I'm not certain. I hadn't thought about it. I'm looking for a new country to call home. Someplace where I can work. Maybe marry again. Raise a family."

The interviewer was taking furious notes. "You said marry again. Are you divorced?"

A flash of anger rose in Kaz's throat. He forced it down. "My wife died in a German prison."

The pencil paused. "Oh, I see."

Kaz felt a momentary advantage. He plunged ahead. "If Sweden doesn't want me, I was thinking about America."

The interviewer ignored this last remark. "You mentioned work. What can you do?"

"Well, let's see. I'm a train engineer. I've driven trains all over Poland. I'm a machinist. I've managed a distribution and warehouse center for a clothing manufacturer. I've worked on fishing and passenger boats. And I've sailed on submarines in the Polish navy."

The interviewer looked at Kaz with surprise. "That's quite a lot."

"My circumstances kept changing. I had to adapt."

The pencil was scribbling again. "You said you were in the resistance. What did you do?"

"Participated in a train ambush. Helped a famous scientist escape from Montelupi, a German prison in Krakow. Passed along secret documents and plans for field operations. Transported food and weapons for partisans hiding in the mountains. Took part in the battle near Nowy Targ."

The questions continued: about family, about friends, about plans for the future. Kaz answered as best he could. He pointed out that he'd been on his own since he was sixteen, that his friends were all dead, and that it had been impossible to plan for the future when life could only be planned day-to-day. He suggested America, once more. The pencil wrote furiously.

When they were finished, the interviewer left without any word about what to expect next. Mr. Wintermark gave him some idea of the process on the way back to the prison cells.

"A panel will review your information. Normally, they would try to verify your story, but that's not possible in your case. So, it will depend somewhat on how credible you are, and I would say you get high marks in that department." He gave Kaz another of his encouraging smiles. "If your information is accepted at face value, we will return to Mr. Johansson for a final ruling. If there are any doubts about your story, you may be called before a judge. That would be more difficult. A judge might deport you."

Kaz's throat constricted at the news. If he was called before a judge, he might have to find some way to escape his guards and stow away on another ship. Anything would be better than facing the Russians back in Poland.

A day and night crept past. He had no clock, but the sunlight moving across the high window in his cell told him when morning turned into afternoon, then evening. It was like waiting for glue to dry. He grew restless and hesitant at the same time. He vacillated between the desire to learn his fate and fear of what that fate might be.

Mr. Wintermark returned the next morning. "We are to see Mr. Johansson not the judge. I believe that is good news. I doubt that you will be deported."

Kaz's spirits rose. There was hope.

Mr. Johansson greeted them warmly. "Your story was compelling, Mr. Kowinsky. The panel saw no merit in sending you back to Poland."

They were seated less formally around a small conference table this time. It made Kaz think of the meetings he'd attended at the little restaurant back in Krakow. His hand reached instinctively for a glass of vodka but found only water.

"The panel has decided to give you a six month visa that will allow you time to find work and a place to live. With your work background, it shouldn't be too difficult. There's a small Polish community here that can help you, and the government will give you a stipend until you're settled. Then, if you wish to move on, say to America, the emigration office will help you with the paperwork."

"In the meantime," Mr. Wintermark interjected, "I know someone who can teach you a little Swedish and some English, if you like. There's a fee, of course, but she's reasonable."

Kaz's head was spinning. It was almost too much to hope for. At any moment, he expected someone to enter the room and inform him that the decision had been rescinded. He caught himself looking over his shoulder for a piece of rubber hose.

"You will report to me each month on a designated date," Mr. Johansson concluded. "At the end of six months we can decide what you want to do."

Kaz stepped into the sunshine a free man. It was the first time that he'd felt that way since childhood. The world was scrubbed clean of disappointment and fear and death. He could breathe, really breathe, the mint fresh air of unabridged liberty. He sat down on the steps in front of the government building and soaked in the exalted feeling. Today was the first day of the rest of his life. Christina had said that once when they were sharing a private moment together back at the orphanage. He hadn't understood its meaning then. He did now.

His thoughts drifted back to Christina, and Daneta, and Charlie, and Edwina and Stenia, and all the people with whom he'd worked in the resistance. Their images flooded over him. Where was Agata? And Simon the Red? Unhappy images surfaced: an uncle who had become lost in despair; a mother who had no place in her heart for a child; a father whom he'd met briefly but never known. All the images swarmed together into a life filled with pain and uncertainty. Now, he was headed for a new life filled with just as much uncertainty, but also hope.

He would work hard and report to Mr. Johansson on his progress. He would learn Swedish and English. But he already knew what he wanted to do. At the end of six months, he was going to America.